ROGUES AND VAGABONDS

A NOVEL

MARILYN LIGHTSTONE

Stoddart

Published in 2001 by
Stoddart Publishing Co. Limited
895 Don Mills Road, 400-2 Park Centre, Toronto, Canada M3C 1W3
PMB 128, 4500 Witmer Estates, Niagara Falls, New York 14305-1386

www.stoddartpub.com

To order Stoddart books please contact General Distribution Services
In Canada Tel. (416) 213-1919   Fax (416) 213-1917
Email cservice@genpub.com
In the United States Toll-free tel. 1-800-805-1083 Toll-free fax 1-800-481-6207
Email gdsinc@genpub.com

10 9 8 7 6 5 4 3 2 1

National Library of Canada Cataloguing in Publication Data
Lightstone, Marilyn
Rogues and vagabonds
1st ed.
ISBN 0-7737-3320-5
1. Theatre — Fiction. I. Title.
PS8573.I4262R64 2001   C813'.6   C2001-901929-7
PR9199.3.L4441R64 2001

Publisher Cataloging-in-Publication Data (U.S.)
Lightstone, Marilyn.
Rogues and vagabonds / Marilyn Lightstone. –1st ed.
[304] p. ; cm.
Summary: An epic story of the lives and careers of those involved in the theater.
ISBN 0-7737-3320-5
1. Actors and actresses — Canada — Fiction.
2. Theater — Canada — Toronto — Fiction. I. Title.
813.54 21   CIP   PR6062.I44 2001

Jacket Design: Eric Graham
Jacket Art: Heather Cooper
Text Design: Tannice Goddard

THE CANADA COUNCIL | LE CONSEIL DES ARTS
FOR THE ARTS | DU CANADA
SINCE 1957 | DEPUIS 1957

*We acknowledge for their financial support of our
publishing program the Canada Council, the Ontario Arts
Council, and the Government of Canada through the
Book Publishing Industry Development Program (BPIDP).*

Printed and bound in Canada

For Moses

Curtain Raiser

1943

ARABELLA AND THEO

The rain fell as it had for days, saturating the lawns and gardens of Little Church Stretton, aping the bombs that descended nightly on London, far away to the southeast. Strong winds whipped great sheets of it into the teeth of the long-suffering villagers, grating on nerves worn raw by a war that had already gone on far longer than anyone had thought it would.

The ancient walls of the church afforded some measure of protection, but mildew and rot were everywhere and its creature comforts were meagre. As in many English buildings of its time (the cornerstone marked its construction in 1629) the church's great age precluded the installation of proper heating — even if the costs hadn't been prohibitive, there was the distinct possibility that, tampered with, the whole structure would simply crumble and collapse about their ears.

Dame Arabella, however, was undaunted, in spite of her terrible, crippling arthritis. A leading actress for fifty years — thirty as head of her own company — Dame Arabella Thamesford had long run her world exactly to her liking. In spite of never being a conventionally beautiful woman, Arabella had been tall and striking in her prime. Even now, gaunt and grizzled, she had something that many of her rivals had not — magic. Her free hand fussed with the brace of vintage sables at her breast, arranging them with the same flair as on their first appearance in her dressing room, forty years earlier, the gift of a titled admirer. Unlike the furs, the suitor had *not* passed the test of time. "A gift of sable," Arabella had said to Kathleen, her maid and personal dresser at the time, "and the soul of a table."

"George," she said to the vicar, "that boy has something special."

"My dear Bella," the vicar replied, "he's done nothing but scrap with the others since his arrival!" The task of getting the evacuees settled was formidable enough without troublemakers. "It pains me to say it," he sighed, "but this lot's the rowdiest yet." Sometimes, of late, he found himself wondering if his prayers went unheard as well as unheeded; looming large among his wartime concerns was the terrible fear he might fall into despair. "Did none of their parents teach them right from wrong?"

Arabella gripped the knob of her stick and lifted herself from the nest of fraying horsehair that passed for the vicar's best chair.

"Some have lost all they had in the world, George. The O'Hara boy — the one always in need of a handkerchief — lost both parents last Wednesday in the raid on the foundry . . ."

They made their way to the vestry door at a snail's pace, bowed as much by the weight of their shared knowledge as their venerable age.

"Of course you're right, Arabella . . . dreadful! Perhaps I forget these terrible things deliberately?" He gave her a minuscule smile. A man who all his life had tried to think well of his fellow creatures, he was finding the task increasingly difficult. "Or it may be I'm becoming senile."

Arabella thwacked his hand with her gloves. They were of kid leather and butter soft, but each sported eight hard little buttons. Arabella did not lightly suffer contemporaries who were determined, as she put it, "to hasten the process of decay." She consulted her diamond lapel watch, which had been her favourite gift until the arrival of the sables, two suitors later. Her chauffeur, Ellis, had been instructed to come for her at five-twenty and it was exactly that now.

"I'll see you at Lilacs tomorrow at four, George. Tell the boy."

"But, that's when . . ."

"Of *course* it is!" snapped Arabella. "Which is *precisely* why I ask you to say not one word!"

"Bella, my dear!" countered the vicar.

Arabella cocked one eyebrow, a sight at which generations of leading men and ingenues had quailed, but this once the vicar wouldn't be quelled.

"It would be remiss of me not to tell you this has me most worried! This boy, Theo Malloy, threatened to punch young Jerry Biddle in the chops for borrowing his mathematics book without leave!" It was all a waste of breath, he knew. Arabella, challenged, became more adamant still.

"And you think I can't manage? Piffle!"

To that, Father George had no ready reply. When he and Ellis finally settled her in the antique Rolls-Royce he breathed a sigh of relief. He dared not dwell on the agony even that small manoeuvre must cost her, but Arabella refused to countenance even the mention of an invalid's chair.

"I'm as tough as old boots," she declared, as if aware of his thoughts. "Everyone says so behind my back." She batted the nape of her chauffeur's bull neck with the butt end of her navy suede handbag. "Don't they, Ellis?"

Ellis, decades in her service, knew enough to keep his counsel.

ૐ

Arabella rose from the circle of children like a thundercloud over a garden. "What do you *mean*, he won't come in?"

Lily flushed pink. This conversation should not be in front of the children. "If you please, Ma'am, could we step into the hall, Ma'am?"

"Oh, very well, Lily!"

Left on their own, the children buzzed with excitement. Perhaps putting on a play would be more fun than they had first thought. Many of them were evacuees from London, separated from family and all that was familiar. They took their fun where they could find it.

Out in the corridor, Arabella turned to Lily, the comely young woman who had been in service at Lilacs since she was little more than a child. Though she herself had missed out on beauty, Arabella appreciated it in others, and enjoyed having it about.

"What is this nonsense, Lily?"

"I'm sorry, Ma'am. The vicar's brought the lad, but he can barely keep him from running off, never mind coming through."

Arabella took a deep breath, an actor's breath that filled the lungs. Lily marvelled her mistress could breathe at all, given the whalebone corset encircling her torso. The garment should give no quarter, as Lily, who dressed her, should know. Equally impressive was her mistress's progress to the door, as Arabella dismissed her cane and — straight as an arrow — greeted the vicar and his charge.

The boy at the door was not impressed.

"Don't care!" he muttered, tossing his coal-black hair. "Not gonna be in any bleedin' play!" His blue eyes snapped fire.

"Theo!" The vicar was aghast — had he but known that the regal Dame Arabella had been accustomed to far worse language than anything this brash stripling could muster.

"It's quite all right, vicar," said Arabella in a voice like old velvet. Then, much to Theo's surprise, she took the boy's upper arm in a grip like steel. Arabella's methods (tempered by actors as self-indulgent as children) were anything but spiritual. The grip eased not a whit as the steamboat jockeyed the clippership through the Great Hall.

The vicar took his leave, not the least reassured. Theo, who had lived most of his fourteen years on the streets of East London, gave ample evidence of being a tough little brute. Both his parents were fishmongers: his dad, a dour man quick with his fists, was fighting with the third infantry in Egypt; when not tending their stall, his mum took full advantage of her man's absence to kick up her heels. The boy had balked at being sent to "the bleedin' country," and had given the gentle souls in charge of his transport a literal run for their money when he had — more than once — tried to escape. Theo was tall and long-legged for his fourteen years. He had once gotten half-way across a farmer's field before they even noticed that he was gone, and sent someone to run him down and put him back on the train.

The boy who sat in Arabella's entrance hall, though strong enough to break free, did not. There was something about this old lady that made him want to hear her out. She wasn't like the others, all goody-goody. Instincts honed by survival told him that, somehow, in this most unlikely of places, he had come up against someone as tough and bloody-minded as he was.

"Not gonna be in no soddin' play," he mumbled.

Arabella allowed the iron grip to soften a degree. "Then what *do* you intend to do here?" Using his arm as a rudder, she turned him to face her. "Thrash people? 'Punch 'em in the chops,' as you threatened to do to Jerry Biddle?"

"Not gonna stay 'ere!"

Ahh! thought Arabella. *More than a touch of Irish in that voice. What was his name now? Malloy . . .*

"And where do you think you're going, Theo Malloy?" Arabella's highly developed concentration focussed on the boy, noted the belligerent chin shadowed by the first fuzz of manhood. *A strong chin,* thought Arabella, *or was that just to keep it from trembling?*

She relaxed her grip a bit more.

"Goin' t'join the army!"

Much to Theo's surprise, the old lady released him. For an instant they glared at one another, teetering in a state of hard-won balance; he free to bolt, she knowing he wouldn't.

"I see." The pain in her joints was agony now, but she knew that one sign of weakness and it would be game over with this young

Malloy, who had been trained in a school as tough as her own. He would take every advantage, as would she. She sat down on one of the several antique settees that bordered the room, careful to disguise her relief at being off her feet.

"Want to fight for your country, do you?" she asked mildly.

Swagger gave way to grin. Was this a sympathetic ear?

"Yeah. Wants t'kill me some Nazis!"

Arabella felt her heart's bitterness twist her lips into a grimace. This vile war had children wishing themselves killers — and who could blame them?

"Well then, I've a proposal I'd like to put to you." She patted the ancient upholstery of the settee in invitation. Once a vibrant cherry red, it had darkened and sobered, and now made her think of blood-stains, of young men fallen in battle.

The boy's blue eyes narrowed. Things were falling into the familiar pattern. By hook or by crook they conned you into doing what *they* wanted! Still, she wasn't talking down to him, as if he were some kid in nappies.

"Yeah? What kind?"

Got him! thought Arabella, and felt the old thrill of conquest — poised to sign a fat contract, or stealing the season's most exciting new playwrights from under the noses of the competition. But caution was still the watchword. In spite of his pugnaciousness, she could sense that the boy was really quite shy.

"Look here," she began, reason itself. "You're underage and you look it; you know you do." When he bridled, she pretended not to notice. "*If* you manage to run off, there's precious little chance any of the services would have you. England's not yet that desperate, praise be to God! Surely, that must have occurred to you."

It had, but he had decided to cross that bridge when he came to it. "Might 'ave," he admitted, "but what's it got to do with you?"

"I know all sorts of people in the Army!" said Arabella casually. "And the RAF. His Majesty's Navy, too."

The boy looked at her with increased respect. Now she was talking! Except for once down the tube during a raid, when his gran had spotted Leslie Howard, Arabella was the first person he had ever seen with access to the great. His equally casual reply might have succeeded but for Arabella's knowledge of voice, her lifelong experience with tone and timbre.

"Yeah?"

"Yes, lots of my old chums. Several bigwigs among them. If you're determined to leave, I might be able to get them to make some use of you." Arabella's long and illustrious career had given her entree into many corridors of power. If it came to it, she could live up to her side of the bargain. "Though it might not be killing Nazis at first."

No Nazis. "That'd mean no gun then?"

Dame Arabella nodded. "But," she added, "if the war goes on — which I pray God it doesn't! — you'll be old enough to be given a gun before you know it."

The young-old eyes narrowed again.

"What's in it for you then, eh? Why'd you do this f'me?"

"I'd do it — if you still wanted me to — after you'd done something for me."

"Ha!" hooted Theo.

Dame Arabella lifted her famous brows. "I didn't say I was going to grant you a favour. I said 'proposal' most distinctly. Your memory isn't so short-lived, surely?"

The boy thought for a moment, and had the grace to say "No, Ma'am" with no more than a trace of chagrin. Nothing for nothing, he should know that.

"You see, we're going to have this play at the parish hall . . ."

It was all she could do to grip his arm fast enough.

"Told you! I'm not goin' t'be in any . . ."

"Bleedin' play! So you did." Arabella's tone bore just the slightest smudge of rebuke. "But you still owe me a courteous hearing."

Theo, a touch self-conscious, resumed his seat.

"Thank you. And now I have something to confess. I've been watching you do your turn from the little window on the landing that overlooks the schoolyard."

The young face reddened.

"Doing my *what*?"

"I've been watching you make the other boys laugh. When you weren't too busy knocking blocks off, that is."

Theo didn't like the notion of being observed unawares one bit; on the street you have to watch your back as well as your flank. His face hardened, but Arabella pressed on.

"Yes," she said. "I saw your bit as the vicar giving his Sunday sermon."

At last, Theo knew exactly where he stood. It was comforting. Any second now and all this fine talk would add up to an accusation or a reproach. Fine, he knew how to handle those.

"Weren't doin' nobody no 'arm."

"Indeed!" Arabella concurred, taking him quite by surprise. "You were making them laugh. I've also seen your Mrs. Waverly, dishing out at lunch."

Theo's short-lived composure smashed into a thousand smithereens. It was one thing to be seen mimicking the antique vicar with his *harrumphs*, and his way of pulling at his nose with his thumb and forefinger while pretending to find the phrase written clear as day on the notes right under his nose. But Mrs. Waverly was a woman! A mincy-prancy one at that, whose fluttering lashes and provocative sashay showed far more confidence in her powers of attraction than the rest of the village thought warranted. A widow of a certain age, Mrs. Waverly had set her sights on young Mr. Hadley, an RAF pilot shot down over France, who was filling the final days of his convalescence by coaching the boys at football.

So slyly that she had never once noticed, Theo had been observing Mrs. Waverly. He had noted carefully just how she placed the thumb and first two fingers of her left hand on her hip, the other two sticking out at an angle she thought was enticing; the way she leaned her upper torso over Mr. Hadley's table as she served him his portion, ensuring that her deep bosom would be just at his eye level as she said, "For you, dear Mr. Hadley. And you must promise to eat everything in front of you." She would resume her duties, still smiling coquettishly at poor Mr. Hadley, who would be doing his best to hide his scarlet face in a dish of cold pudding.

Every time Theo mimicked the sway of Mrs. Waverly's well-padded bottom as she wended her way back to the great baking dishes of shepherd's pie, the boys almost killed themselves laughing. Yup, he'd got that one down a treat!

"See you, I did," said Arabella. "And enjoyed it immensely!"

What was this? When he'd done his mum ticking his dad off after an all-night booze-up, all he'd got for his pains was the back of a hard hand. He just wanted to make 'em laugh. Sometimes they would, in spite of themselves, and things'd go easier for a bit.

Arabella raised a cautionary finger.

"You mustn't tell anyone I said so. She's got a kind heart, has Mrs. Waverly; it'd be wicked to shame her for having a soft spot in it for Mr. Hadley."

Hypocrite! she thought. Her true opinion was that mutton trying to pass for lamb must be prepared for the consequences, but life had taught the boy enough cynicism without further help from her.

"Let's get back to the play, shall we? The truth is," Arabella sighed, a figure of abject woe, "we're in desperate need of someone who can make people laugh."

Theo harrumphed.

"Thought you was doin' somethin' by that Shakespeare bloke."

"We are. It's called *A Midsummer Night's Dream*."

"Then watcha need someone t'make people laugh? S'all funny talk nobody understands anyways."

"Oh, that's not quite so . . ." Arabella played out her line. "I promise you, it's a very funny play."

Only then did the obvious arise. *What an idiot I am!* she thought.

"Have you ever seen a play by William Shakespeare, Theo?" Had he ever seen a play at all?

Theo felt himself losing ground. He could lie of course, and say yes, but what if she asked him *what* he'd seen? And he wasn't sure he wanted to lie to this ramrod figure with the thinning white halo of hair. He had his code. She was being straight, that obliged him to be straight in return.

"Mmm, no," he admitted. "Can't say as I 'ave."

"There's a very funny part I think's right up your street — Bottom. He and his chums head off to the wood to rehearse a play they hope to perform at the wedding feast of a Duke, and they get caught in the crossfire between two rival fairy bands. There's a whole lot of silly confusion in the midst of which Puck — a sort of general dogsbody to Oberon, the king of the fairies — turns Bottom into a donkey. The head part, at any rate."

Theo guffawed in a way he hoped would convey his disdain for such childish muck. "Sounds stupid, if y'ask me!"

But Arabella was undaunted. Now, the lure.

"But the *real* reason Bottom gets himself into such a mess is because he's such a smug creature, always strutting about, absolutely full of himself." She dropped her voice and inclined her head to the boy's. "A good deal like . . ."

"The mayor! Mr. Rush—"

"Shhh." Arabella raised her finger to her lips. "A good actor keeps mum about his sources of inspiration. Otherwise you take away the magic, and no audience will thank you for that."

Disgraceful! Libelling Mr. Rusholme in such a fashion, thought Arabella. But could she help it if he was born with that ridiculous bray of a laugh, or that he stuck his plump little chest out like a strutting pouter pigeon? He had addressed the evacuees on arrival, which made him the perfect target, or who else might she have had to malign?

Theo found himself on unfamiliar and shifting ground. Nothing had ever prepared him to be asked to do the very thing that, until now, had only earned him blows from parents and admonishments from teachers.

"Not sayin' I would, mind, but if I *was* to, I could do this Bottom bloke sort o' like . . . well, you know . . ."

"Yes!" replied Arabella, barely able to contain her elation. He had taken the bait. "Or anyone else you might choose. Or you can use your imagination and make someone up, as long as the person you've made up fits in with the story. Or a little bit of both. That way's the best fun of all."

Now, to set the hook.

"Of course, I could be wrong. You mightn't like it a bit, and then I'd have to live up to my part of the bargain."

It was time to be silent. If she couldn't win by the force of her argument and personality, she didn't deserve to, no matter how much she yearned to nurture his grace, his powers of observation, the accuracy of his ear, his wit — all the gifts so apparent from the window on the landing. Her x-ray eyes had seen inside the grubby chrysalis of cheap, battered boots and shabby trousers, and she had been overcome by the urge to turn him into a butterfly.

The only sound in the Great Hall was the duet of their breathing. Arabella, a study in indifference, idly scanned the portraits of her late husband's family, resplendent in farthingale, armour, and ruff, Theo remained entirely innocent of the fact that inside him raged a fierce debate over the first major step away from a life where brute force was the order of the day. He turned to face her.

"Right then. I'll give it a try."

"Splendid!" said Arabella. "I know you'll find it much more amusing than knocking people down."

Casting

1954-1961

JEANNE

The front lobby of Toronto's Imperial Theatre was atwitter as with a thousand birds — this time penguins. Except for the stiff white collar and cuffs, regulation dress for the girls of St. Mike's was unrelievedly black.

Though many of Bernadette Donahue's classmates wore ducktails in homage to Elvis, her own long chestnut hair was dressed as simply as ever, the tortoiseshell barrette more to keep the hair out of her blue-grey eyes than out of any concern for fashion. Bernadette was as oblivious to the shrieks and giggles of girls bridling at the idea of being herded about by Sister Anne (yet determined to draw attention to themselves) as she had been to the primping and preening on the streetcar. But if she seemed an island of calm in the surrounding melee it was only because no one but she could hear the blood-borne timpani of her heart. How fast could a heart beat? How much louder before it combusted, or shattered to bits?

It seemed an eternity before a young man appeared wearing an ill-fitting maroon uniform, fitted out with enough loops and fringes of tarnished gold braid to satisfy the most vainglorious dictator. With a great show of strength, he released the bolts that secured the doors dividing the outer lobby from the inner, and was carried away by a sea of white-crested black.

For two and a half hours, the playing time of one Wednesday matinee, the iron grip of St. Michael's was softened, and Bernadette Donahue, fifteen years old and on tenterhooks for weeks (Yes, she could go. No, she couldn't!), was about to see her very first professional theatrical production.

St. Michael's serviced a community where, aside from bingo, the idea of money to spare for pleasure outings would have raised a bitter laugh. The girls of St. Mike's owed their presence at The Imperial to an enlightened management that preferred to do a good turn rather than let their actors play to a half-empty house. In particular, it was the work of Sister Anne, a doe-eyed novice who looked no older than her charges. One of Sister Anne's several brothers was a chartered accountant, and it was his firm who oversaw the theatre's accounts.

As far as Bernadette was concerned, the tickets came straight from God.

She gazed, wide-eyed, at the ceiling. Catholics all, the girls of St. Mike's were no strangers to the baroque style, but the subject matter they were familiar with was usually yet another saint enduring horrific torment for the greater glory of God. Here, every surface was riotous with the story of Troy, and buttocks and bosoms were everywhere.

The sounds of the orchestra in the pit striking up "God Save the Queen," and "O Canada," as all present rose, were followed moments later by a great rumble as everyone resumed their seats. The houselights melted away to almost nothing, which made Bernadette feel as if she were being wrapped in black velvet. Then, with a swish and a swing, the great rose-velvet curtains parted and — slower than she would have ever thought possible — the lights rose onstage. A hush fell over even the rowdiest girls.

A young woman stood there, small, but proud and unafraid:

St. Joan, the very same saint of whom the nuns spoke. But theirs was a pale, anemic thing compared to this luminous creature. To Jean Anouilh, the creator of this St. Joan, she was the Lark. But Bernadette heard in *Jeanne D'Arc*, her real name, a clarion ring around which troops could not help but gather.

⳹

The ride home on the streetcar was much as things always were when the girls of St. Mike's were on their own. They monopolized the seats and hanging straps, shrieking and shouting from one end of the car to the other.

Bernadette clung to her strap and thought of the bells that had summoned the Maid, the cows in the bier, the mists that had arisen in the morning in the blue-grey hills of Domremy.

"What's with you, bozo?" Fiona O'Brien always had to know everything. "Y'been moonin' around like a dummy since the end of the show."

"She's been like that all day," Mary Margaret called from the other end of the car. "Maybe she's in love!" Everyone laughed, not knowing Mary Margaret had unknowingly spoken the truth.

Fiona's next comment — "Yeah, or maybe she's got the curse!" — was met with shamed silence. Public mention of menstruation was taboo. They were still St. Mike's girls, and Reverend Mother could think of some tough penances when she put her mind to it.

Bernadette walked the three blocks from the streetcar stop to the house at a snail's pace, though she knew her mother's blood pressure would be rising by the second. Ethel Donahue had agreed to the afternoon's expedition only after tearful entreaty by her daughter, and enough pressure from Sister Anne to make her thoroughly cross. If not for the Sister, Ethel's middle daughter would have been home and doing chores long since.

Before going in, Bernadette sucked in the last mouthfuls of the cold night air, and with them the last pleasures of the day. If only she could go directly to the room she shared with her sisters — but it was unthinkable to her mother not to be waiting with at least one thing that urgently needed doing.

Ethel Donahue, gaunt and grey, had the runnelled complexion of the lifelong smoker. She spoke little, and when she did her face was largely immobile, all movement confined to her thin lower lip. She didn't look at her daughter, just tossed a vegetable peeler onto the table: "If I'da known you'd be so late . . ."

Bernadette reached for the apron hanging from a hook at the back of the stove and slipped it over her head. The way she steeled herself not to respond was so automatic she was unaware of it. She bent over the chipped enamel basin of unpeeled spuds.

"Sorry, Ma."

Ethel shot her a hard-eyed glance. Her own world view was unrelievedly sour, and she considered her daughter's inability to share it a betrayal, a perverse determination not to please. Often she asked herself how this unlikely creature had come to be born to herself and Tommy. That someone like Bernadette was a member of her family was almost enough to make her believe in the stories about babies being accidentally switched in the hospital. Mrs. Krakowski from next door had told her about how the gypsies in her native Poland would steal a healthy child and leave a sick or crippled one in its place. Bernadette, though always a physically sound child, had been a mystery to her mother since she was a baby. She never fussed or ran through the house like the other kids, and was as unlike the rest of them as chalk was to cheese. She was crazy about paper dolls, and spent hours making their clothes, having them act out stories she made up in her head. Ethel watched her move them from one cardboard shoebox to another, smiling and talking to herself, but when she would ask Bernadette what she was doing, all the girl would ever say was, "Just playing, Ma."

It was Bernadette's deep love of reading that truly mystified Ethel and made her most suspicious. If she happened to spot Bernadette with her nose in a book she would say, "Won't be much time for readin' when you start punchin' in at the plant." Ethel believed that as long as she prepared herself for the worst, nothing could catch her by surprise. Bernadette was an unknown, and the unknown had the power to frighten.

And the girl was so nervy! Ethel had known others like that, but those girls usually got themselves pregnant by the time they were seventeen, or entered convents and became nuns. If Ethel had had her way, Bernadette would have been the nuns' problem by now but, to her chagrin, even that solace had been denied her. Each time she raised the subject, Bernadette wailed like a banshee. But the thing that had most made Ethel want to give Bernadette the back of her hand was the letter she had received from the Reverend Mother at St. Michael's, asking her if she would "be so kind as to find a few moments for a chat with myself and Sister Anne." Ethel had put it off as long as she could, but there was only so long she could ignore a summons from so lofty a figure as the Reverend Mother. She'd had to stand there and keep silent while Sister Anne urged her not to "pressure Bernadette to take the veil, Mrs. Donahue. If she had a true vocation, I'm certain she'd be eager to embrace it."

"And the little chit had the gall to take my hand while she was saying it," said Ethel, who had recounted her story to Bernadette the minute her daughter had gotten home. Bernadette, who knew just how Sister Anne would have looked and sounded while she was saying it, did her best not to smile, which made Ethel even more cross.

There were many devoted Sisters teaching at St. Mike's, but a number of them had gotten old and tired in the service of their order, and Sister Anne had entered their midst like a bolt from the blue — stimulating, challenging. She had re-established the moribund gym program at the school and though she was wearing a habit, the first thing she did was to teach her students how to climb up a rope. She had them read aloud to one another in class, convinced that it would help both their speech and their confidence. She brought art books to the classroom so they could look at beautiful paintings, and laughed a lot, showing the dimple in her right cheek and pretty white teeth. Sister Anne had transformed St. Mike's for Bernadette.

Bernadette plopped a peeled potato into the basin and began on another. She was accustomed to her mother's corrosive glare, and she was fortified by a radiant new armour. She had prayed for a sign and it had been granted; she was absolutely sure from the instant the lights rose on that first scene. All the way home on the streetcar, her brain had been in a whirl. The first thing would be to change her name to Jeanne — pronounced the French way, with that lovely soft *zzhhh* sound at the beginning. To say it filled her with pleasure; the free, open sound of *ahhhh* an endearment, sweet on the tongue and the ear.

In bed that night, she told her sisters that from now on she wished to be known as Jeanne, but the request only aroused a snort of derision from her older sister, Mary Elizabeth, and frightened and bewildered ten-year-old Colleen. Did this mean Bernadette wasn't going to be her sister anymore? She burst into tears and ran barefoot across the icy linoleum to their parents' room on the other side of the hall.

Ethel Donahue's disposition was never improved by being waked out of a sound sleep. She sprang to a sitting position, her whole being pursed in disapproval. "*Now* d'you see what I'm sayin'!" she hissed at her husband.

Tommy flipped the worn sateen quilt back with enough fury to raise a draft that made Ethel shiver in her peach nylon nightie. He snatched up the trousers he had dropped at the foot of the bed and drew the belt from its loops. He stomped across the hall in his boxer shorts, Colleen at his heel, and threw open the door to the girls' room with such force that the knob smashed into the plaster wall. He stood over Bernadette's bed and brandished the belt in his great ham of a hand. "You're gonna stop that kinda talk, y' hear me?"

Tommy Junior cheered him on from the sagging hide-a-bed in the front parlour. Two years Bernadette's senior, his idea of fun was to fill frogs with water and drop them from a height. That, and grabbing Bernadette's breasts when he thought he could get away with it.

"You're gonna stop it *right now!* Or I'll give you what's comin' to you!"

For the moment, Bernadette remained Bernadette, sustained by the certainty that one day everything would be quite, quite different.

MILO

E ven Milo's enormous love for his grandmother Roseanna couldn't keep him out of trouble. He was a scrapper and, being little, he usually got the short end of it. Roseanna prayed daily for guidance, lighting endless candles to whichever saint was thought to be most influential in the current situation, arriving at last at St. Jude, patron saint of hopeless causes. When no help was forthcoming from that quarter, she turned to her confessor, Father Andre. What did he think? Should she send the boy to her brother's farm in Ste. Sophie?

Father Andre, who had known Milo since the day he baptized him, couldn't see the boy living a life of feeding the chickens and early-to-bed. The child was definitely of the genus *Urbanus*. He liked movies and hanging out at the corner store, and was much more familiar with walking the steamy pavement eating hot dogs and greasy frites from a horse-drawn wagon than shovelling manure in a barn. But it was Roseanna's well-being that was Father Andre's primary concern and, aside from prayer and fortitude, he had nothing to offer.

The priest was right, there was no love in Milo's young heart for the pastoral. Milo Tessier had plans. He wasn't going to stick around

Montreal for the rest of his life. He was going to New York, Chicago, Miami. . . . Milo had never been fond of study for its own sake, but his mind was quick, and he had an ear for languages. Even before starting school, he had picked up enough English to make himself understood. Why shouldn't he? It was the language of his runaway American mother. His country cousins took pains never to speak English if they could help it, and cold-shouldered him when he did. Well, they were hicks! If MeMere sent him to live with them he'd run away, just like his mother did right after he was born.

If having a runaway mother and a father who had been killed wasn't enough, there was his height. Or lack of it. Every runt dreams of taking on the bully who kicks sand in his face, and for years Milo prayed for a miraculous surge of growth. At sixteen he had an energy you couldn't help but notice, nice brown eyes and a thick head of curly brown hair. Not bad on that score. Even his acne scars weren't too bad. But what was the use? At five-foot-six he'd never make it with the really sharp chicks, or be the captain of the team, the leader of the pack.

A succession of pricey presents began to appear at the flat: a fruit bowl of hand-cut Bohemian crystal, a Raleigh racing bike, a Telefunken short wave radio. For someone whose official source of income was after-school delivery for the corner drugstore, Milo always seemed to have a lot of spare cash. He spread it around, a soft touch for friends, standing treat to frites and Pepsis for members of the various neighbourhood gangs. An only child, he was drawn to their camaraderie, but in his heart he was a loner, no matter how often he picked up the tab. How could the English guys think of him as one of them, with him half French on his dad's side? Did his French buddies resent him for speaking such good English?

The high living lasted a couple of months, giving him quite the Little Caesar image in the quartier, until Roseanna received a house call from Father Joseph. The high-school principal was concerned about Milo's prolonged absence. Was there perhaps some problem at home?

A confession was forthcoming, but even then the boy didn't come clean. Instead, he selected the most innocuous of the available scenarios, and owned up to spending time at Blue Bonnets, Montreal's popular racetrack. "Yeah, MeMere, I got real lucky with the Exacta. That's how come I could buy all this stuff!"

Roseanna bought none of it, and each day her fear grew that he would wind up at The Boys Farm, the facility for delinquent boys in the Laurentian Mountains north of Montreal. She had threatened her own sons, including Milo's father, with such an end when they misbehaved, though it had never occurred to her that someday she might have to do it in earnest.

She decided to call Roger.

⚬⚮

Roger Blais, Marco Spinelli, and Guy Masson had been Marcel Tessier's closest pals before his accidental death on the dance floor of the Chez Paree. The fact that he had been shot to death made it no less accidental, given that Mayor Houde's Montreal was a wide open town in those days, and Marcel had just happened to be in the wrong place at the wrong time.

All three men worked as chauffeurs in the driving pool down at City Hall, so they had *some* leverage in the Mayor's Office, but only for small stuff — fixing a ticket or breaking a lease. They were working stiffs, small potatoes, not bigshots sitting behind a desk. Word was, Marcel's boy was skirting the edge of things harder for certain people to overlook. He could reflect badly on them.

"Shit," said Guy. "I screwed up plenty when I was his age, till my ol' man took his belt to me."

Marco nodded. "She's too easy on him, sa grand'mere." He plucked a fresh Player's from the pale-blue pack in his shirt pocket and lit it with the butt of the previous cigarette. "He can wind her around his little finger."

They sat there, wrapped in gloom. A beery angel passed overhead.

It could have been any one of them splashed all over the dance floor at the Chez Paree.

"So?" Roger asked. It was he whom Roseanna had telephoned asking for help, and he who had arranged this meeting. He looked at Marco.

Guy followed suit. "So?"

It took a few seconds for Marco to realize that the buck had been passed and was sitting right in his lap. "Hey! Why you lookin' at me?"

"It's *gotta* be you," argued Roger. "You're single. Thérèse already gives me shit for not spending enough time with the kids. If she hears I'm playin' Daddy to Marcel's boy, she'll kill me."

"Anyway, you speak the best English," said Guy. "Milo loves speaking English!"

"Yeah," said Roger, grasping his buddy's drinking arm. "Take him to a hockey game! Saturday night; the Habs and the Bruins. I know where I can put my mitts on two beauties right on the centre line!"

Jeez, thought Marco. *There are lotsa things I'd rather do than babysit Marcel's kid, but why all this fuss about reining in one little pipsqueak?*

"Okay, okay." He raised a hand in capitulation. "Relax. I'll talk to the kid."

✒

Montreal boasted a number of good delis, but the smoked-meat sandwiches at Schwartz's were part of the city's legend. A varied clientele from all over town lined up to eat there. Garment workers rubbed elbows with millionaires. Punks and policemen dropped in to sample the great fries and the char-broiled steaks. Politicians dropped by to chew the political fat and satisfy a craving for kishka and karnatzelach.

Marco's table was at the back, giving him time to give the kid a good once-over before Milo spotted him. The ugly duckling was never going to become a handsome swan, but the kid wasn't half bad looking in a pint-sized, rough-and-ready kind of way. The face still bore the scars of an adolescent battle with acne, but the war was over.

He even managed to carry off the silver-studded black leather motor-cycle jacket. Marco wondered if there was a matching bike and, if so, where the hell it had come from.

Milo threaded his way through the wooden tables. He knew he was in for some heat, but he was still glad to see Marco, who had been one of his father's younger friends and more like an older brother in Milo's eyes than a contemporary of his dad's.

He high-fived him. "Hey, man!"

Benny shuffled over. Benny had worked at Schwartz's for so many years, even he couldn't remember how many. He bunged a couple of glasses of water on the placemats, printed up to do double duty as menus.

"Benny! How'zit go?" asked Milo.

Marco lifted two fingers. "Twice, Benny, medium fat. And a couple Pepsis."

Benny shuffled off.

Milo gave Marco a bemused look. "So?"

Marco knew the look for the camouflage it was. "Have a pickle." He pushed forward a bowl of briny kosher dills and green tomatoes. "Coleslaw?"

Before the fat, steaming sandwiches arrived, they were down to it; by the time they had finished cheesecake and coffee and started on their toothpicks, they had covered most of the ground.

Milo denied everything.

"Marco, lighten up! I had a few good days at the track. What's everybody getting so excited about? Listen . . ."

Marco listened, his right hand fiddling with a few stray graham-cracker crumbs from the cherry cheesecake. First he rolled them into a ball, then into a cylinder, which he flattened. Soon there were several of them, arranged in a neat little row.

Like coffins, thought Marco. "Before you tell me any more big ones . . ." he said. Marco was immune to Milo's breezy charm, and he had also done his homework. The file he was carrying had been neatly typed and placed in a brown legal-sized envelope, folded in four to fit the inside pocket of his jacket. When you needed a little help from the cops, it paid to work for City Hall. Marco, with great deliberation, unfolded the envelope, removed its contents, and passed them across the table to Milo.

Milo blanched. Even his lips went white. He knew he was gonna catch it for *something* when Marco had asked to see him, but he thought it would be for the times he'd stayed out all night. Not only were all his misdemeanours known, but someone had taken the trouble to catalogue them! By the time Marco came to the part about kicking the shit out of him if he didn't "settle down — understand what I'm saying?" Milo knew his life was about to take a major turn.

First things first, thought Marco.

"You're gonna stay in school until you get your certificate, if we hafta chain you to your desk!"

He leaned back in his chair and plucked a fresh fag from his pocket. So far so good. The second thing was keeping the kid so damn busy, there would be no time to poke his pecker where he shouldn't. Marco lit his cigarette and took a long drag. Milo reached for Marco's still smouldering butt and lit one of his own. Privately, he thought smoking made his mouth taste like garbage, but it was part of the uniform.

"And something to do after school," Marco said. "Boxing, maybe. That way you can let off steam and build yourself up at the same time."

Boxing! thought Milo. Maybe he wasn't doomed to be a ninety-pound weakling after all! He pictured himself in red satin trunks, pummelling away at some guy in blue. The guy's good, mind you. But he's outclassed and he knows it. Milo can see it in his eyes — fear, naked fear. And then — it's over! Milo stands there, arms raised. The victor, fierce, defiant. The golden belt about his middle dazzles like the sun. Yeah! A succession of faces — everyone who's ever crossed him or MeMere — appears in front of his eyes, out cold on the canvas.

⁓

It's hard to maintain a heroic self image when you're knocked repeatedly to the mat. It was so bloody unfair! Milo's footwork and rhythm were better than that of anyone else in the club, even the instructor said so. But he was *still* too small, even in his weight class.

Bad enough that life was a struggle, as MeMere always said; worse that it was not of your choosing. *Not fair! Not fair!* raced through his brain each time someone ten pounds heavier tried to quickly dispatch him. In his frustration he forgot all about form and threw punches wildly, getting himself even more thoroughly trounced.

It was impossible to quit the ring outright without losing face, so at first Milo left the gym on the pretext of having a pee, and took his own sweet time getting back. When his ever-longer absences drew no comment, he decided to take a look at the rest of the place.

The "Y" was a hotbed of activity. The chess club met in the front lobby, while somewhere at the back boys hammered away at sheets of copper destined to become bookends; boys sawing, nailing, and varnishing; boys turning bits of wood into tie racks and pipe stands. All the sports stuff was in the gym, of course, and the drama club met in the auditorium, which also functioned as the theatre. It was on the opposite side of the building from the gym, so it took Milo a while to get round to it. When he finally did, a rehearsal was in progress.

"Hey, you at the door! Would you shut it, please? We're trying to rehearse in here."

"Sure, buddy, sure," said Milo. He shut the door and slipped into a seat at the back of the auditorium. A bunch of kids were onstage, dressed in old-fashioned nighties, and somebody seemed to be trying to pass himself off as a dog. It all rang a bell, somehow, but he wasn't sure why until *he* arrived through the window — and he was flying. *Peter Pan! Yeah, that's what the play was. Peter takes Wendy and the kids up to Never Land, or something.*

Milo moved closer to the stage. He told himself it was in order to get a closer look at the harness they were using for flying, but the truth was that he was caught up in the tale of Peter and the Lost Boys. Dammit, *he* could be up there saying that stuff, and mean it, too! Milo had had vivid dreams about flying since he was a baby. Sure, the guy was hooked up to a wire and stuff, but he was still moving through the air — flying.

Everyone onstage seemed to be having such a good time. Even when they had to stop because someone screwed up a line, they joked around with each other. Just like Maurice Richard and the guys in Les Canadiens would joke around when they played hockey. And look at Peter, strutting his stuff! *He's the fuckin' lead in this thing*, thought Milo, *and he's just as short as me.*

∽

Milo called Marco and requested a meeting. Boxing wasn't for him after all, he said on the phone, but Marco wasn't to get himself in a sweat. Milo had another idea.

So, they're beating the crap out of him, Marco mused, as he hung up. Okay, no more boxing. He couldn't force the kid to be pounded to a jelly twice a week. But what was this other idea? Why did Milo sound so hesitant? The kid he knew tried to come across so tough. For once, he sounded very young. As if he didn't think he had all the answers.

Milo, covered in powdered sugar and looking about ten years old, was half-way through his second jelly donut by the time Marco arrived. Milo licked his sticky fingers. "What I said about dropping boxing — you think it's 'cause I'm yellow?"

What was eating the kid? Was he turning queer? "Don't be a jerk." Marco signalled the waitress for a coffee and a refill for Milo, and ordered a couple of crullers. "Do I care if people in boxing gloves knock each other down? You wanted to build yourself up a little, we wanted to keep you outta trouble. No big deal."

"Well, I got another way."

"Hockey? Water polo? Now *there's* a sport to keep you in shape!"

31

Milo took a slug of coffee. He had to find a way of saying this without coming across as some kind of major wimp. Marco had been one of his dad's best buddies. Whatever impression he took away would be passed on to Guy and Roger. "Uh, no. It's kinda not so athletic, like." He flushed and took another slug, taking refuge behind the big ceramic mug. "It might sound kinda . . ." Milo sighed, exasperated with himself. He was never at a loss for words!

Look at that, marvelled Marco. *He's blushing!*

Milo avoided eye contact. It came out in one great blurt. "I've joined the drama group at the 'Y,' and we're practising this play for Christmas called . . . well, *A Christmas Carol*. And I'm playing the Scrooge part." He paused for breath, then continued, "It's the biggest part. I'm in almost every scene of the play." Then he waited for lightning to strike.

It didn't. Not that Marco could understand the attraction of being onstage. He had been forced into being an altarboy as a kid, and had hated it. But what the hell, as long as it wasn't something *really* jerky. Like handicrafts! The important thing was keeping the kid out of trouble. Marco could go back to the boys with a clear conscience.

"Great! Make sure you get me and the guys tickets." He pointed to the trays of fist-sized donuts, arrayed in powdery splendour under glass. "Wanna take some home for your gran?"

CHAS

———

"Everyone has two countries," Chas's father Saul always said. "The first is where you happened to be born." In his case, it was Ukraine. "The other, boychik, you choose with your heart."

As a boy, Saul Mandelbaum never tired of hearing tales of cowboys and Indians, of wagon trains and the Royal Canadian Mounted Police. Montreal, for all its cosmopolitan allure, was never intended as more than a pause in a longer journey. He did not cross the cruel Atlantic to live cheek by jowl in the crowded city. When he had put by enough dimes and quarters as a Montreal furrier to add up to a stake, he and his wife Clara headed west to Whistler Creek, Alberta. There, in the foothills of the Rockies, Mandelbaum — Yiddish for almond tree — became Almond, and the ranch that they bought was named Treetops.

Their eldest, Chaim Itzhak, known as Chas, shared his father's love of the land. The young man looked with pleasure around the well-kept barn, and gave Cyclone, his stallion, a pat. He shifted his gaze to the panorama outside. After the whipping they took in today's storm, the trees were at peace now, and you could see the hills in the near distance.

Les and Danny, his younger brothers, were sure the show would be cancelled and he'd have driven thirty tough miles for nothing, but they hadn't got to know the Bristol Touring Players as he had. Chas had reminded the boys that this was their last chance to see the troupe perform before it moved on, but Sid Caesar was on TV that night, and that was no contest as far as Les and Danny were concerned.

It was lucky that everyone in the company was staying at the hotel in town. The Windsor Arms was Whistler Creek's *only* hotel. It was just around the corner from the Town Hall where the performance was to take place, so the actors could get there even if the snow-ploughs hadn't cleared all the roads by curtain time. The same thing couldn't be said of their audience. It could take days to dig out the back roads after a big storm, and that would mean lots of empty seats. Miranda, the Bristol's leading lady, had told Chas what it was like to play to an almost empty theatre.

"The few who *do* turn up feel such guilt on behalf of those who don't, they bend over backwards to be appreciative. It can be embarrassing sometimes. After all, Quentin's no Ralph Richardson, or Larry Olivier. But there are other times when it's absolutely super; as if you'd been summoned to court for a command performance."

Quentin, the company's artistic director and leading man, had explained their rule of thumb regarding cancellation: "Only if there are fewer bums on the seats than onstage, dear boy. Otherwise, it's business as usual."

The Bristol Touring Players had been stranded in Vancouver by a management as inept as it was unscrupulous, and they needed every scrap of revenue for their passage back to England. If tonight's performance was cancelled, there would be no chance to make it up. After nine days in and around Whistler Creek, the company was moving on.

Chas gave a final pat to Cyclone's flank, and quit the horse-fragrant warmth of the stable for the cold and wet of the storm's aftermath. After a day of black and sodden skies, visibility had returned to normal, but the late afternoon light was fading fast and Chas knew better than to linger. It was a good stretch to the gravel service road, portions of which were unreliable in bad weather, and further still to the reassurance of blacktop. He leaped into the cab of his battered red pickup, keen to get on the road. But he still had to deal with his mother.

∿

Pianists, monologists, musicians classical and jazzical. Dancers of ballet, tap and modern. Even the rare Borscht Belt comic who unwittingly strayed farther afield than expected. If they were performing within fifty miles of Treetops, the Almonds would be in attendance. Country folk they might be, but their children would have every advantage.

But tonight is different, thought Clara. The roads would be pitch-black and unpredictable after the storm, and Charles would probably be driving back even later than last night. She was his mother; it was her job to worry.

"*Why* must you go? If they're your friends, they wouldn't want you driving on such a night." She reached for his glass. "Anyway, you've seen those plays so many times by now, I'd think you'd be sick of them."

But Chas knew his mother better. He had been very small and young when she told him how, as a girl in Bucharest, she had gone on short rations for a month to buy third-balcony seats for the opera.

"We'd sit up in the gods," she said, pointing at the ceiling. "It took us ten minutes to get to our seats, and when we got there all we could see were the tops of the singers' heads. We didn't care. For Mozart, we'd have climbed ten hours!"

Chas sat at the long kitchen table and spooned cabbage soup into his mouth. There was ample room for twenty people on the long wooden benches, and you could squeeze in thirty for a big job like haying. The "Two Sophies" drove up each day to clean and cook, but the cabbage soup had his mother's unmistakable touch. A great kettle of it simmered at the back of the big black stove. The flavours of cabbage, onions, beef, lemon, sugar, and tomato would alchemize over the next couple of days, approaching perfection even as the supply dwindled. Chas wiped his bowl clean with a chunk of dark pumpernickel and held it out for more. He knew how much pleasure it gave his mother to see him eat.

"It's their last night, Ma. They're expecting me." He followed the arc of his mother's arm as she ladled soup from the pot to the bowl. It was a full round arm, no longer young, but firm and shapely from physical work. "Quentin's gonna show me how to put on a wig if there's time."

Clara almost dropped the ladle.

"A wig! But you have such beautiful hair!" Her free hand caressed her son's blond curls, thick and shining, with one wayward lock that fell over his green eyes.

"That's not the point, Ma," said Chas. "You see, your hair has to match the part you're playing, just like your costume. For instance, if I had to act the part of a guy a lot older than me; someone who was bald, maybe. Or had long hair, like in the olden days."

Clara's face puckered in mock distaste. "Old? Bald? Feh! Go already!" She dismissed him with a wave. "Just be sure you drive slow."

♪

The Bristol Touring Players would never rank among the great practitioners of their art, but they were nonetheless saturated in a tradition that came upon Chas, at seventeen, like a vision of the Messiah. He had followed them to every church basement in and around Whistler Creek — every Legion, Mason and Town Hall. But not until the Wednesday matinee of *King Lear* did Chas summon the courage to go backstage, where the company gravitated to his enthusiasm and fresh young beauty as moths to a flame. Chas Almond, genuinely unaware of his charms, was amazed to find himself welcomed with open arms.

Over beer and pretzels, they fell all over each other regaling him with tales of the theatre. It did not go unnoticed that Miranda emerged the favourite.

It piqued her that the men in the company were as eager for his attention as the women.

"Let the so-called men in this company make do with one another, darlings," she said to the other occupants of the ladies' dressing room, "as they usually do."

Chas drank in the stories, and gratified them by laughing long and hard in all the right places. He was a different breed from the usual civilian who crossed their path, a person just as likely to ask, "How do you remember all those lines?"

"As if that was acting!" snorted Miranda. "Regurgitating one's poetry assignment for the rest of the kiddies in the third form!"

Chas wanted to know much more than that.

"How," he asked Edward Hart, *Twelfth Night*'s Sir Toby Belch, "do you make a false nose? And once you've made it, how do you keep it from falling off?"

Edward was thrilled to demonstrate his nose skills with putty, latex, and spirit gum, though he was disappointed that his double entendres about sharing the rest of his repertoire with Chas fell on uncomprehending ears. The roll of Chas's narrow cowboy hips inspired lust in them all, but his innocence was equally a part of his appeal. He was unquestionably a virgin. Edward was considering a pool on how long that state of affairs would last, but Miranda got wind of it and threatened to report him to Actors' Equity.

"So just watch it, my darling." She waggled her finger at him. "Or I just might put something nasty in your cold cream."

In the days that followed, Chas peppered Quentin with questions on how to make up to look older onstage, and Miranda with an equal number about how to look younger. The actress found the question amusing, falling as it did from such rosy young lips. She tugged at the lock of blond hair that curled over his forehead, then ran a slow index finger along his jawline, her face very close. She could swim in those gorgeous green seas that were his eyes. "Not much call for that just yet, love."

"What do you do," he asked them, "if you can't remember your lines during a performance? How do you get a whisper to carry to the back of the hall?" Did any of them still get stage fright?

I want to know everything, Chas thought. How to tumble without hurting yourself, like Jeremy, who played Feste in *Twelfth Night*. And when Jeremy played the Fool to Quentin's Lear, how did he manage to look so expert with the lute, when Chas knew he couldn't play a note? How long did it take to learn to fence? Was it hard to juggle?

Not nearly as hard, Chas knew, as telling Saul and Clara about his plans, though he knew they would back him once they got over the initial shock. Not like his poor friend Cully Binnie. When Cully told his folks he wanted to study clarinet in Calgary instead of breeding cattle with his dad, old man Binnie had gone off his head.

The pickup Chas was driving was his own, paid for out of his rodeo winnings, but it trailed a fine but steady sprinkle of rust as it bumped along. He had done a lot of work on the engine, but it was still ten years old and had seen lots of hard service. Despite the bravado for his mother's benefit, Chas was relieved to see the first lights pierce the darkness as open country gave way to town. If he had run into a problem on the highway, there would have been no telling how long he would have had to sit there.

He stopped to buy donuts for the strike after the show. Some of the actors doubled as crew and didn't have time to eat before the performance, while many preferred to eat after the show when they could relax. The Windsor Arms was officially a NO COOKING PERMITTED IN THE ROOMS establishment, but a cornucopia of cheese and bread, sausage and fruit lined the windowsills. Some of the more ambitious guests had discovered that extraordinary North American artifact, the electric frypan, and after a good fryup of liver, bacon, and onions, many a window was opened wide, though the air temperature outside might be twenty below.

"Our work may seem airy-fairy to some," said Quentin, "but if you're playing a major role, it can be as physically demanding as digging ditches."

Well, they would go all out tonight. This was cattle country, and a stack of filets in brown butcher's paper were waiting the strike out in the Ladies Auxiliary kitchen. The mention of a strike had confused Chas, until someone told him that "striking the set" simply meant packing everything up and loading it on the bus.

When they asked if he would lend a hand, it felt like a rite of passage.

♪

It was just minutes before curtain when Chas took his seat in the Town Hall assembly room, and the house lights were just being extinguished. He was disappointed to see how few people had managed to make it to the performance, and it was small consolation that he had his virtual pick of seats. To leave the area with a whimper would be a big let-down for the company. Besides, even front row centre wasn't close enough for him. He would sit on the stage itself if he could, as Quentin told him the English nobility used to. Cully, who had accompanied Chas to a performance of *As You Like It* some days earlier, didn't agree.

"You can get a crick in your neck from sitting this close, for crying out loud! And I can live without my personal view of the actors' nose hairs, thank you very much!" He had insisted on moving back a few rows, which seemed madness to Chas.

Things were different tonight. The stagelight spilled into the front row. The actors could see him almost as well as he saw them, and Miranda — as Helena in *A Midsummer Night's Dream* — winked at him after she finished her soliloquy. Everyone in the sparse little audience saw it. It even got a laugh.

39

"And didn't old eagle-eye Quentin spot it from the wings, and give me a note," Miranda said after the show. "He can be unbelievably stodgy when anyone breaches the fourth wall!"

It made sense to Chas that Quentin didn't want the actors crossing the imaginary barrier between the real life of the audience and the imaginary one of the play, but nothing could have induced him to say so to Miranda.

"It's our last show here," she went on, "and we've been on short rations for weeks; at least let's have a bit of fun! Anyway, it was *my* soliloquy. I'd never do it during one of *his* scenes! That would be unprofessional."

The strike was as dirty and as tiring as predicted, but Charles couldn't have cared less. He packed props into boxes, and carried racks of costumes and assorted furniture out to the van with a full heart, enjoying the easy banter and camaraderie. It reminded him of how they worked at Treetops, with mutual trust and cooperation.

Miranda's pretext of needing him to see her safe to her room, transparent to anyone else, was accepted without question by Chas, fresh to the etiquette of the boudoir.

Atmosphere, thought Miranda. That was the first problem. No one understands the need for good lighting better than an actress, so the overhead fixture was out of the question. Ditto the little plastic number by the bed. Candlelight was always best, but a bit contrived in the circumstances. Miranda opted for the light in the bathroom, the door left slightly ajar. Looking for a copy of their itinerary to give to Chas, she leaned forward over the dresser, so that the tops of two small but shapely breasts hung like luminous moons from the deep scoop-neck of her black wool sweater, everything beautifully reflected in the dresser mirror. While the lady racked her brains on how to get him into bed — it wouldn't do to shock him by just how bold she could be — Chas was in the grip of contradictory forces: the return of his shyness and an overwhelming rush of desire.

It was not difficult for Miranda — who was actually thirty-four but could pass for twenty-eight in a good light — to find the young cow-boy attractive. Her nightly adieu after a drink or two at the Spur and Saddle, to "retire to my virginal couch," was in fact a reality. Nothing the least bit interesting had come her way since that Harry fellow in Seattle, and it was a lot longer since anyone had truly tickled her fancy as much as this sweet boy. And therein lay the problem. Chas *was* a boy. Self-indulgent she might be, but never to the point of bad taste. But . . .

Oh, what the hell! The flesh is weak, and specimens like him were hard to come by in Britain. Surely she was due *something* for enduring this fly-by-night tour, with nary a bean put by if they ever did get home. And weren't rules made to be broken?

And *God*, he was lovely!

🙤

It was five a.m. after the strike, and black as pitch outside. The engines of the company's two beat-up buses had been idling for the last half hour, the vapour from the exhaust steaming up the icy air. The next booking was a long way off and the roads were still uncertain. They had their job cut out to open *Twelfth Night* in Harris Pass that night.

Chas lifted Miranda's luggage above the snow as the company boarded, bleary from lack of sleep, dragging their battered gear like convicts en route to some distant gulag. His presence was tantamount to admitting he had spent the night with Miranda, and he hoped the others would attribute his scarlet cheeks to the bitter morning air, but everyone was too busy nursing hangovers to notice or care, while the lady in question seemed unconcerned.

Quentin was the last to board, but before he did he placed his arm around Chas and spoke directly into his ear, in order to be heard above the noise of the exhaust.

"It can be much better. A great *deal* better. Sometimes — though you may find it hard to believe — it can be a great deal worse! But if it's what you truly want, don't let anyone stop you!" He leaped on the

41

bus. It had just started to pull out the drive when a window opened and Quentin stuck his head out. "And you must read!" he shouted. "You must read, read, read!"

♪

Saul and Clara had to admit, if only to one another, that they were afraid for their son. Their idea of the artist was from another time, another place, where one's gifts ripened under the protective scrutiny of a caring master. How would he live? If he had lost his heart to the violin or the piano, they would have known what to do. But *acting!*

It was equally shocking to Les and Danny. They had never thought their easy-going brother would take all this acting stuff so far. Like Saul and Clara, they assumed it would be the three of them at Tree-tops, with Chas next to Saul in the chain of command. Still, a movie star in the family!

When Chas explained that he intended to work on the stage, not in the movies, and that he had no intention of going anywhere near Hollywood, his brothers lost much of their enthusiasm. And there was the delicate matter they took pains not to discuss in front of their mother and father.

"I've heard all the guys in the theatre are fairies, Chas," said Danny, "'specially the ones who do that Shakespeare stuff."

"Yeah, Chas," added Les, "what'll you do if one of 'em grabs your ass?"

♪

Once a carefree youth in love with his horse and half the pretty girls in town, Chas now spent every spare moment with his head in a volume of Shakespeare, or a translation of Stanislavsky's Russian classic *An Actor Prepares*. When he wasn't reading, he made his way to a ramshackle barn in a distant field, where he practised the art of greasepaint with the aid of an old shaving mirror and an instruction book he bought mail-order from Calgary.

He competed in every rodeo he could, and stashed away every purse he won. The balance in the blue deposit-book in the centre drawer of his maple schoolboy's desk grew steadily. When it was big enough he would go to New York and study with the best teachers he could find, see every play there was to see. He would eat, sleep, and drink plays.

Until then, he read every one in the local library. There were not that many, and none of any recent vintage, but among the mimeographed binders of toothless farces geared to community theatricals, and instructions on how to mount historical pageants for feast days, there were exciting discoveries like Eugene O'Neill's *Mourning Becomes Electra*. He roared at Chekhov's *Comic One Acts*, and was intrigued by the "new" ideas of Bernard Shaw. For the moment, it was enough to read, and reflect on all that had happened in only a few short days.

ↄↄ

"Observe people," Miranda had said as they lay together under the hotel's old Hudson's Bay blankets. Chas was on his back, his arms pillowing his head, Miranda close at his side. "Listen to what they say. Watch what they do."

The ghost of a frown had crossed Chas's brow then. It all sounded so serious and psychological. A great desire for sleep sucked at his loins and his brain, but there wasn't much time left before the morning bus call and Miranda was feeling invigorated rather than fatigued.

"Nothing to worry about, silly. It's how you learn about human nature."

She licked her index finger and moistened his left nipple, small and delicately pink, which broke out in goosebumps.

"You probably do it now, without even knowing. All actors do!"

With a feather touch she rotated the excited nipple, blew on it softly. The silky hairs that circled the pink corolla were not alone in standing to attention.

"Not that what you see and hear is necessarily the truth. It's often just a cover for the truth. You lot aren't as bad as we English, but we both put lots of effort into concealing our real thoughts and feelings."

"*I* don't!" protested Chas.

"Yes, you do, my darling. We all do. It's the supposedly civilized way of dealing with our humanity. For some reason, we think it makes us less vulnerable." Oh, the smell of young skin, sweeter than flowers. She tongued the hard nipple and sucked it into the heat of her mouth. "We hide our feelings even from ourselves." Miranda raised herself on her right elbow. "Watch and see how often there's a discrepancy between what people say . . ." Her free hand trailed lightly over the firm pectorals, the diaphragm. ". . . and what they're really feeling, the subtext that underlies the text. When in doubt, watch the body." Her hand moved over the flat stomach. "Its message will be true, even when the words are false." Knowing fingers encountered a patch of silky hair. "Body language is much more difficult to control." Miranda giggled. "A dead giveaway to anyone who knows how to read it." She licked his armpit.

"And the . . . words?" gasped Chas.

"The interior life." Lick. "That's what the actor . . ." lick, ". . . must concentrate on. Not words, or line readings." She licked once more, then made a sinuous adjustment of her body so that her long hair raked the length of him, her mouth poised above his navel. She lowered her head. "Put yourself into the character's state of mind and everything falls into place . . ."

ↀ

"Don't spend it all in one place!"

The bank teller's round schoolgirlish figures winked up at him from his bank book. Seeing the total made it official. Chas's outward calm belied his inner excitement. Now he could get on with things. If only he didn't have to break it to Mom and Dad. He tucked the passbook into the inside pocket of his sheepskin jacket and crossed the square to the donut shop, where he had arranged to meet Clara.

He was relieved to find her in the back booth. Mrs. Yevshenko, the owner, sometimes had difficulty with the concept of privacy. Ordinarily Chas didn't mind, but today was different; even Mrs. Yevshenko could see that. Once she had brought the coffee and Boston cream pie, and rehitched her girdle, she returned to the counter and busied herself with her knitting.

I'll tell her when I finish my pie, thought Chas.

But Boston cream pie gave way to chocolate eclair, and the words so long on the tip of his tongue remained there.

When they went to the cash to pay, Clara beat him to the check, a bittersweet echo of when he was still a child, living by her rules, not strong enough to wrest himself from her embrace. She stuffed the change Mrs. Yevshenko gave her into her purse and smiled at the woman's remarks, though she hadn't registered a word. All she could think of was how much she and Saul would miss Chas.

"You'd better say goodbye to Mrs. Yevshenko now, Chas. You might not get the chance to come in again."

Mrs. Yevshenko looked from one to the other, her face a fierce mixture of disapproval and concern. Clara was being far too cheerful; it was a show for her sake, she was sure of it.

"Where you go, Chas?" she demanded.

"You know how interested Chas is in the theatre, Krystina."

Krystina Yevshenko liked the Almonds. So, though it gave her no pleasure, she acknowledged the fact.

Clara's behaviour always had an old-fashioned, European formality, even with her family. Nonetheless, she put both her arms around her son and kissed him soundly.

"He's going away to become an actor."

MARIE

———

Marie was introduced to Theo by Kristy and Amanda, two hard-up dolly-birds from London who lived in the same theatrical rooming house on 48th Street as she did. She didn't hear their first few knocks because she was shampooing her hair while listening to Callas sing *Tosca* at the Met. The radio was turned up to full volume to override the sound of running water.

The pint-sized Southern belle who opened the door to them wore faded blue jeans and an oversized man's white shirt. A scrubbed, heart-shaped face peered out from beneath a blue-and-white striped towel wrapped turban style around her head, and she smelt of lily-of-the-valley and Breck shampoo.

Theo would have been considered tall by women much taller than Marie. The first she saw of him was a pale blue shirt tucked into a pair of well-cut, cavalry twill trousers. A strong but graceful neck sported, she was pleased to see, a small gold St. Christopher's medal. She had to tilt her head back for the rest of him, and encountered a curving mouth, chiselled nose, cool — heart-stoppingly cool — blue eyes, and a thick head of blue-black hair.

They became lovers that same day.

The place they took together a few months later was called a railway flat by New Yorkers, because it had rooms lined up directly behind each other, like railway cars in a train. The rent was reasonable, but except for the veranda at back it was undistinguished in every way, a state of affairs that never failed to inspire Marie. Some trashbin treasures, a fabric remnant or two from the Lower East Side, and — voila! — the stuffy three-room flat was Shangri-La. "Like a conjurer pulling a rabbit out of a hat," Theo would say.

Theo, whose work as teacher and director was deemed more demanding than Marie's, got the use of the front room, while Marie set up shop in the kitchen at the back, producing a steady stream of crafts for which the shops in the area never ceased to clamour. Three years of *The New York Times* Literary Supplements left behind by the previous tenant made a lot of papier mâché candlesticks, and it's amazing what her skilled hands did with a glass cutter and a few cases of empty Jack Daniels bottles.

For two years the apartment was their refuge from the dirt and din of Manhattan, Marie's first real home since coming north from Baton Rouge. Before then she had taken furnished rooms to stretch her cash, all the while yearning for a kitchen of her own and dreaming vivid dreams of the one back home — Lou, the family cook, standing over the big stove as shiny and black as her own ample self, pouring biscuit batter from the salt-glaze mixing bowls handed down from her great-grandmother. It was Lou who had handed her skill on to Marie. Marie's mother believed that a lady never entered the kitchen except in case of emergency.

Marie had picked up an old hotplate and a cast-iron skillet from a local thrift shop. They were somewhat the worse for wear, but nothing that a few hours of elbow grease and a box of steel wool couldn't put right. Armed with these primary tools and a shoebox full of recipes that had been in her family since before the Reconstruction, she regaled her lover with bread pudding and filé gumbo to rival the best of New Orleans, where folk don't take such things lightly.

All through the winter, when not taking a dance class or running to auditions, she bent over her worktable, comforted by the play of sun and shadow from the great chestnut tree outside her kitchen window, whose bare branches almost touched the veranda. Five years removed from her native bayous, Marie still found the Yankee winter a sore trial. Theo, inured by England's lack of creature-comforts, was enthralled by the central heating. During hot weather the situation was reversed. Marie was in her element while Theo was too hot to sleep, even with an electric fan whirring nonstop at each end of the apartment.

Fearing a third fan would play havoc with the ancient fuse box, Marie set to work. With nothing more than her flying fingers and endless yards of diaphanous cheesecloth, she transformed the pedestrian veranda into an airy sleeping place worthy of the *Arabian Nights*. When the candles were lit and the air was still, their bodies cast shadows like Indonesian puppets at play. When blessed by a breeze, the light-as-air draperies would rise and fall, caressing their linens, their lips, their legs. In early June, the chestnut's torch-like blossoms perfumed their sleep; by midsummer its leaves were broad-spanned, whispering sibilant counterpoint to the lovers' murmurs. It was democratic, too, not confining its gifts to humankind, but watching over the sleepy rustle of many another creature forced to endure the trials of a New York summer.

They slept there until the frost.

Theo's body, satin to the touch, had an intoxicating natural scent that clung to Marie even after showering, so heady she feared it would give pause to passersby. All the next day, still liquid, she would move to his rhythm.

Until Sy's call from the coast.

It all happened so quickly, like a flash flood. "Screen test!"

"There's no guarantee," Marie told Theo, "but Sy's heard that a lot of musicals are go—"

"D'you want your tits spread all over the pages of some trashy film rag?" Theo's laugh held no humour. "'Marie Verity with her latest blah, blah, blah . . .' I thought you were *serious* about the theatre; that you wanted to be a *real* actress!"

She lost her way, as she always did, in the hypnotizing cadence of his voice.

"Have I misunderstood?" asked Theo.

"I do want to be a real actress, but . . ."

"But what?"

"But it's so hard!"

"Of course it's hard!"

"But . . ."

"Marie, for heaven's sake, please don't keep on saying *but*!" Theo raked his fingers through his thick hair, something he did only when particularly irritated. "You must know by now how it pisses me off!"

"I don't have the voice, Theo! You know I don't!"

"What sort of crazy . . . ? Who's been at you? You're a bloody singer!"

"And I can hold my own in the chorus!" She did her best to keep back the tears; Theo hated scenes. "My speaking voice doesn't carry, Theo. No one can ever hear me at the back of the house!" The effort it took not to weep made her throat ache. "I'm small. My voice is small." He must know that everything she said was absolutely true. He must listen. "That doesn't matter in the movies; the microphones pick up everything y'all say. That means . . ."

"That you don't need to work at your craft. That you can forget about our plans. *That's* what it bloody *means*!"

Theo, Oxford graduate in classics and philosophy, had little use for Hollywood movies (television was totally beyond the pale). "Escapist, lowbrow and dehumanizing" were some of his kindlier epithets. Actors who capitulated to the lure of the screen did it for the money. "Bloody sellouts," he called them, "not worthy of kissing Dame Arabella's little toe!"

One minute they were at dinner, the next it was three hours later and she was alone, staring at two congealed bowls of cream of mushroom soup. The sight and smell of them nauseated her, but she had no will to remove them. Theo would never lay a finger on her in anger; still, the whole of her felt as if she'd been set upon by thugs in an alley.

Every bone in her ached for bed, but Marie was determined to wait up for Theo. She strained for the sound of his step on the landing, the turn of his key in the lock, willing everything to be right again, for him to say, "Of course you're right, love. I don't know why I made such a fuss. You'd be smashing in films! Why don't I go out there with you?"

He returned hours later, saying nothing of the sort. He just wished her goodnight in an expressionless voice and took himself off to bed. When she followed soon after, she found him at the edge of the mattress with his back turned, pretending to be asleep — usually they nested in the centre, like spoons; her knees behind his, her lips against his satin skin. Sleep eluded her for hours, the echo of his judgements ricocheting from one corner of her weary brain to the other. Could there be some truth in what he said? Perhaps she *was* lazy and not committed to excellence.

But no, it wasn't so! The Veritys, while a century removed from their antebellum glories, were people of character and culture. It puzzled them that their only child should feel the need to turn her God-given talents (so advantageous in winning a husband, even in these degraded times) into a profession, but they had been open-handed with her training. Unfortunately, no matter how trained in elocution Marie had been by Baton Rouge's finest, however many the New York voice coaches or the number of vocal exercises Theo taught her, nothing succeeded in enlarging the sound that came out of her tiny frame, or made her any more believable in serious dramatic roles.

The fact was that, although no one was likely to cast Marie as Medea or Hedda Gabler, she would be perfect for the movies. She was as American as apple pie, and at least as good a dancer as Jane Powell. These were sellable commodities. People all over the world flocked to Hollywood movies. They made them feel good; made them laugh and cry. Movies filled a void in their lives, just like live theatre. Why was one a sacred brotherhood and not the other?

She *would* go to California!

♪

Now, after a train journey that seemed to take weeks instead of days, she was back. Travelling coach on a long trip is bearable if you can commandeer a couple of adjoining seats and stretch out, but Marie had had no such luck. Each car had been fully booked, and the aisles were jammed with people on their way to the bar, or to have a pee. By the time the train pulled into Grand Central Station, Marie was grey with fatigue, her eyes like lead in their sockets.

The heat in mid-September New York could fry your brains. The bus was stifling and Marie was pressed up against a lot of other sweaty bodies. The windows were open in hope of a breeze, but all that came in was more hot air and the cacophony of yet another road crew tearing up the streets. She would have given a lot to be whizzed home in an air-conditioned taxi, but there were only forty-two cents left in her pocketbook, a miracle away from cab fare between Grand Central and Sixty-Fourth and First, even without a tip.

Food had been cheap in L.A. compared to New York, and bunking in with an old sorority sister had saved her a bundle. Even so, her hard-won savings had melted away like snow in the California sunshine. The only way she had been able to get back East without having to wire Theo for money was by downgrading her ticket from sleeper to coach.

For Marie, the overhead strap on the bus was an impossible stretch. She braced herself for the jerking and swaying as best she could, but there was often nothing for it but to grab onto the other passengers, which forced a certain sweaty camaraderie. With each lurch of the bus the suitcase at her feet banged against her shins. Even so, Marie was in no haste to arrive at her destination. She was returning victorious, but the closer she got to the flat, the heavier her heart became. Homecoming meant having to deal with Theo and, as hard as she tried to convince herself otherwise, she still wasn't ready. Theo, at thirty, was an accomplished actor–director who could spit out words at enormous speed, still make sense, and sound piss-elegant all the while. She was a musical entertainer, trained to let her body do the talking. It was not an even match.

She started to climb the four flights to the flat. Ordinarily, she would fetch Theo and he would bring up her bags, but under the circumstances she was reluctant to ask. Sy wanted her back in L.A. right away, but he had been very sweet, trying not to rush her. "Two weeks should be enough to get yourself organized, right?"

The young agent was ecstatic. He had managed to get Marie a screen test with Universal Studios, and they had offered her a seven-year contract. Now, wasn't she glad he had moved the agency out to the coast? Why bust your buns in New York for peanuts?

What the contract meant, in fact, was that the studio got to pay her very little money to work exclusively for them, placing her in any role they chose no matter what she thought of the part. If she delivered the goods they would give her increasingly large roles. If she didn't, they wouldn't; although, being under contract, she couldn't work for any-one else. Nonetheless, this one-sided state of affairs was the heart's dream of every American would-be starlet.

Marie paused on the third landing, her chest tight with anxiety. The contract in her purse felt like a bomb. For a few panicky seconds she thought she could hear it — tick, tick . . . Any minute now it would explode, and tiny fragments — the bloody, lifeless remnants of her happiness — would splatter the stairs.

Even so. If she could catch Theo at just the right moment every-thing might still be as it once was. There were people who cared about the legitimate theatre in Hollywood, and they were crying out for people just like him to teach and direct, just as they did in New York. Her contract would give the two of them financial security. He could open his theatre school sooner, instead of God-knows-when.

Strengthened in her resolve, Marie reached the door of 4D, but no sooner did she place the key in the lock than the door swung open wide, as if someone had signalled a silent "Open sesame." Before she could draw breath, a strong arm had encircled her waist and lifted her over the threshold, tossing her bags aside like so many pieces of tissue. Strong teeth gripped first one strap of her heat-limp sundress and pulled it from her shoulder, then the other.

"Ohhhhhhh, Theo . . ."

Clever hands slid the straps still further, grazing the pale pink tips of her breasts, then unzipped her. Her knees began to buckle, but Theo's hands grasped her hips, his weight pinning her to the wall.

Determined to drown her in pleasure, he tugged at her panties with a slow hand until they were down by her ankles and probed her most private places with soft, licking kisses. When she sank, quivering, to the floor, he lifted her small foot, the tip of his tongue exploring the inner curve of her dancer's arch; and all the while his fingers drew in and out of the places he knew so well, composing internal sonnets. A shudder shook her small frame. Then again and again, until she was awash in salt tears and sweet sweat, and the heady tidewaters of her own primal sea.

Oh, Theo. You miserable bastard, Marie thought, drowning.

There would be no Hollywood. There would be no contract with Universal.

There would only be Theo.

ADAM

—

"What do you *mean* you're not coming on tour?"

Adam knew every colour and inflection of his mother's voice, and never had he heard it more calculated to inspire terror. Still, his bank account was in his name, and in five days he would be twenty-one. He preferred Cleone not be unhappy, but this once he was not going to oblige her for the sake of the family.

"Has this anything to do with that miserable viper, Richard?"

Richard had been their double-bass player for years, until she happened upon him bare-assed naked in Adam's hotel room during their last tour. Cleone was very liberal about matters sexual, as long as it didn't involve *her* family, thank-you-very-much!

To see Cleone's ample bosom quivering under the silver brocade muumuu made Adam sigh. The process was going to be as painful as he had feared.

"No, Mother. It's nothing to do with Richard."

He and Dickie were no longer a thing, and Adam hadn't seen him for ages, but experience had taught him that the less he told his mother the better. She had a way of turning the most innocent information against you when it suited her purposes, and her purposes were many.

"It makes no difference to you that we're booked until the year after next? Right up to New Year's, 1963?"

Oh, Mother, thought Adam. It would be so much easier on everyone, especially Spencer, his father, if she would knock it off! Sometime soon in this discussion Adam would have to make eye contact with his dad and he already knew what he would see. Hurt. Not just because Adam considered his individual interests as separate from the family's, but because he had not taken his father into his confidence.

"I've enrolled at NAADA," he mumbled.

"Where?" Regan, at twelve, was the middle child of the five Willison offspring.

"The North American Academy of Dramatic Art," said Doreen. Doreen was more than just Adam's sister, she was his twin. So alike were they that before they developed secondary sexual characteristics, their own parents confused them, a state of affairs that lasted until Adam shot up to six feet, two inches — four inches more than Doreen. Other than that the resemblance was uncanny: the same high cheekbones, dark hair, and grey eyes; the same Kirk Douglas cleft in the chin, the same bemused smile. The twins were as close to one another emotionally as they were physically. Doreen was the only one in the whole family who knew that Adam had written to NAADA requesting an audition.

The air itself seemed to chill at his mother's displeasure. Silver-blue lids flickered over eyes of the very same shade.

"And what is that, when it's at home, pray?"

Adam hesitated for a second, but Doreen could step in where angels feared to tread — or even tip-toe.

"It's a new acting school in Toronto, Mummy," said Doreen. First-born by twenty-six seconds, she had always claimed the responsibilities of the elder. "Adam auditioned for it when we played The Imperial last spring."

Adam could feel the heat that radiated from his mother's corpulent form. Her impossibly red ringlets trembled. Not only treason, but conspiracy! He wasn't worried about Doreen, whose unflappable nature was a good match for their mother's. But one lift of Cleone's artfully plucked brows, and all the rest of them were cowed into submission.

His mother, bristling in her chair at the head of the table, was renowned for her rich contralto. It had made her — and all the Willisons — a household name for a half decade during the days of black and white TV, and it now enjoyed the acclaim of the world's concert halls. Her speaking voice was equally impressive. It resonated around the ornate oval dining room of the Greenwich Village town-house. The family had played many a similar scene for the camera, although on those occasions his mother would relinquish the role of authority figure to his father.

"You knew about this, Doreen, and you didn't tell the family?"

Doreen nodded, making no attempt to justify herself and refusing to be reduced to jelly. The only sound was Regan, pushing scrambled eggs long-gone-cold from one side of his gold-rimmed plate to the other.

In the early fifties, the Willisons had starred in *The Shaughnessy Family Minstrels*, a hit TV variety show that was set in the heyday of the great Mississippi paddlewheelers, though unencumbered by over-fastidious fidelity to historical detail. For once, the network had been clever enough to cast a real family as a family, and it had paid off. The entire family, all seven of them, hosted a selection of musical guests in the context of a very slight plotline, and everyone sang, danced, and fiddled.

By the time it was all over, the family had accumulated a few choice bundles of real estate in L.A., New York, and Nashville, and Spencer Willison had acquired an impressive stock portfolio. He derived enormous pleasure in reading the *Wall Street Journal* from cover to cover, and there were long telephone conversations with his broker. Cleone wasn't interested in the market, which, Adam felt, in some way accounted for the strength of his father's passion.

After five years in primetime on Saturday, the Willisons had a ready-made international concert market, and travelling the world enabled Cleone to indulge *her* great passion — gemstones. It was a special point of honour for her never to declare the treasures she spirited away from India and Thailand, and from behind the Iron Curtain; she derived as much pleasure from the act of smuggling as from the stones themselves.

Pilar, the Willisons' housekeeper, felt the charge in the atmosphere the moment she entered the room. She should have known. It had been too quiet; in this household that never boded well. Now was definitely *not* the moment to clear the table. China and flatware, however precious, had been known to be used as missiles.

"I want to be an actor," Adam said.

His mother half laughed, half snorted. "And what do you think you are now?"

Out of the corner of his eye, Adam saw Pilar make her break for the kitchen.

This was it then, nitty-gritty time. His mother's musical accomplishments were impressive by anyone's standard, but she couldn't accept that her performance as Nora Shaughnessy, wife to Captain Mike and mother to the brood that entertained the passengers of the *Aurora Belle*, failed to rank her with the great Bernhardt, or even the likes of Gertrude Lawrence and Jeanette MacDonald.

"Well . . . not an actor, Mother," said Adam. "A *performer*, yes; but that's not the same thing."

Hoping to act as peacemaker, Spencer had stayed out of the fray until now; but this was too much, even for him. He drew himself up to his full height of five foot nine.

"How dare you say that to your mother?" he cried in a strangled voice. "And what is so shameful about being a *performer*?"

"Nothing, Dad; of course not! It's just that . . ."

"Your grandfather — in case you've forgotten — was a *performer*, as you say with such contempt. You, yourself, have had an exciting and privileged life because you come from a . . . a family of . . . of . . . *performers!*"

Adam had vowed not to rise to the bait, not even to challenge *that* statement. Had his father or mother — or anyone, for that matter — ever asked him if he wanted to spend his childhood in television studios and hotel rooms? Had he ever been asked if he wanted to study with a tutor, instead of in a regular classroom with other kids? No, he had never been asked. None of them had.

". . . And don't think you can waltz right back when you don't become the next Sir Lawrence Olivier," said his father. He drummed the table with his index finger to show the extent of his resolve, but he wasn't wearing his glasses and his finger wound up in someone's French toast. "Force us to replace you and replaced you'll stay!"

Adam kept his eyes fixed firmly on the tablecloth. He watched the flower pattern of the Battenberg lace cloth split into a hundred abstract components and, in the blink of an eye, become flowers again.

"Yes, Dad."

His mother, an empress disdaining to suffer the imperial court, rose from her chair and sailed from the room.

The North American Academy of Dramatic Art

1961

ACT ONE

Marie moved among the students in a state of high excitement, introducing herself and presenting each one with a long-stemmed red rose.

The last months had *seemed* real enough while she and Theo were living through them, and Lord knows they had set themselves a formidable task. They had had to find a suitable and affordable home for both the school and themselves, and — even more importantly — gather an exemplary staff that could do justice to Theo's ideas. But all that had been only a shadow life, she discovered, now that the students were actually here. She looked about the room, dazzled by the energy and the potential. It was she who had helped Theo bring these beautiful young people together, she who had helped him realize his dream. In the process, it had become her dream, too.

She watched him circulate through the crowd, chatting briefly to distinguished members of the profession who had come to offer their congratulations, but reserving most of his time for his charges, every one of them eager to begin their new adventure. To see him so radiant made her heart turn over. He blew her a kiss across the crowded room in a gesture so small that nobody but she would have caught it.

Jeanne, who was feeling very shy, stood at the side of the room and watched Marie distribute her roses.

As if we were devotees embarking on a distant pilgrimage, she wrote later to Sister Anne, who was away on a lengthy retreat. It would have pleased Jeanne to know that she had made her friend smile.

"Happy to be here, Jeanne?"

She could as much sense as see Theo approach. The man moved in an energy field one couldn't ignore. "Ecstatic" was the word she herself would have chosen. There was so much she wanted to say, but all she could do was wag her head up and down and blush. She wondered if he remembered the Juliet and Jeannette she had done for her audition. Had he spoken on her behalf when they were making up their Yes list? He must have, surely; he was the head of the school. And she was here, wasn't she?

"'Gallop apace, you fiery-footed steeds,'" declaimed Theo. It was the first line of Jeanne's audition speech. "Everyone on the audition panel thought your Juliet was absolutely refreshing."

He *did* remember her. Imagine, among the hundreds of auditions and the undoubtedly numerous Juliets! Jeanne walked beside Theo with seeming aplomb, but inside she felt dazed and the words wouldn't come. She finally mustered a breathy, "Thank you, Mr. Thamesford," and thought, *What an idiot he must think me!*

"Please call me Theo. 'Mr. Thamesford' might be a touch formal when we're down on all fours pretending to be fishes and roots of trees."

"F-fishes?" Was he making fun of her?

I do believe the young lady hasn't a clue what I'm talking about, Theo thought.

"Just a bad joke about acting school clichés, love."

This too fell wide of the mark, leaving Jeanne even more at a loss than before. "I beg your pardon?"

"Not to worry," he smiled. "All will become clear." Jeanne, to Theo's surprise and delight, seemed to be as close to a tabula rasa, theatrically speaking, as he'd ever come across. *Where has she been all her life?* he wondered. *In a convent, sequestered by nuns?* Yes, he reminded himself, as a matter of fact she had been. Well, it was better preparation than most for a life in the theatre. She had done the Juliet balcony scene, and then that Jean Anouilh piece in an appalling translation. Something else about her audition had struck him at the time. What was it now? Oh, yes.

"Don't worry, love. Anyone who could give us as funny a Juliet as yours has no cause for alarm."

He went off, leaving her in the company of the singing teacher. Professor Brillante was a charming man, but Jeanne found it hard to fix on what he was saying. She couldn't stop thinking of what Mr. Thamesford — Theo — had said.

By now he was on the other side of the room, chatting with a most striking young woman. Her tawny-port eyes were limned in sooty black, and her dead-white complexion was topped by a great mass of hennaed curls. Even Jeanne, who knew nothing of couture, could tell that the simple black garment the young woman wore so cunningly draped over her slim-waisted voluptuous body had not been purchased in the kind of shop that Jeanne frequented on the rare occasion that she bought herself new clothes. She could never picture herself in the sort of thing this titian-haired beauty was wearing; she whose hand was — ever so lightly — touching Theo's chest, while her forehead — ever so briefly — came to rest in the curve of his neck. *A woman who knows how to flirt*, thought Jeanne.

Up until this point in her life, Jeanne had never given much thought to her appearance. Still, she did wish her own outfit, three times marked down at Eaton's Junior Budget Department, hadn't been chosen with her job at Sano so much in mind. She was glad she could stay on there part-time, but the company sold industrial cleaning supplies and the girls in the office dressed in a very workaday manner. She could imagine how her grey pleated skirt and pink shirt must look to the black-T-shirted young men, the girls in their black leather cossack boots.

Like Eve in the Garden, she had become aware.

And she was puzzled.

"*As funny a Juliet . . .*" Funny? *Funny?*

ॐ

"You want to be a star," said Theo, "that's fine!"

He ran a hand through his still-thick black hair, though the white ones were beginning to come. The task of getting the school up and running had been a formidable one, but it was still a mesmerizing Theo the students met on NAADA's second day.

"Maybe you *will* be one of those who hit it big — and good luck to you. But if that's the main thrust of your motivation, there's little we can offer you here."

You could hear a pin drop. Not one of them would have willingly forgone the attentions of this trim, twill-trousered figure in his customary open-neck, wash-blue shirt. Not one didn't know his reputation for the work he had done at the Old Vic and didn't yearn to follow in his footsteps. Blond Chas Almond, lean and lanky in cowboy boots and jeans, had done scene-study classes with him in New York. Grey-eyed Adam Willison, the tall dark-haired American, had flown to London just to see his Hamlet.

"If you want to become an *actor*," he continued, "that's something else again. That we can help you with. The difference between the two can be summed up by a little something we call 'craft.'"

A tall girl with long straight blonde hair asked, "Is that the same thing as technique?" Michelle Needham was from rural Manitoba, raised by parents who had been part of a left-wing, back-to-the-land commune. At sixteen, Michelle was actually under NAADA's minimum age for its students, but her forthright gamine quality had so charmed the audition team they had decided to make an exception.

Theo had been asked this question many times before, but anyone listening would have thought the answer had just sprung from his brain, new-minted.

"Good question, Michelle." Theo knew the names of his students from the beginning of the first class. It flattered the hell out of them, and put him immediately in control. "Some people call it technique," he said. "But I think the work we'll be doing over the next three years will convince you that technique's but a poor second cousin to craft. Anyway, 'technique' isn't a word you'll hear much at NAADA. It smacks too much of the mechanical, the bloodless, the technical — as the word itself implies — rather than the true building blocks of our trade."

He looked around the room and felt the onus of the work that lay ahead. These fifteen young men and women were a gifted bunch, hand-picked from hundreds. He had felt the heat of their spark during the auditions. Still, it was by no means obvious that any of them had a clue as to what the true building blocks of their trade might be. This is what attracted him to teaching, the chance to create something where before there was nothing.

"They are — to name a few — the emotions, the intellect, and the human spirit; all of which you'll put to use as members of the ensemble." The coercive force of Theo's intelligence swept them along. "I expect that word — ensemble — to be burnt into your brains before long, you'll be hearing it so much." He laughed. "Tattoo it on your bum, if you have to.

"Working as an ensemble, we're going to find a way that will enable us to, not depend on, but tap into the wellsprings of inspiration in a reliable and healthy way — in other words, a way to work. And it's going to mean a lot of very hard drill."

A hand shot up. It was Milo Tessier, his chair tilted against the back wall. He had the look of a young Brando: short, but well-muscled. All that was missing was a toothpick at the corner of his mouth and a pack of smokes tucked up the short sleeve of his black T-shirt. His right bicep proclaimed him to be HELL ON WHEELS in shades of blue, black, and red.

"Whaddya mean, drill?" he asked, raking his hand through his curly brown hair. "This isn't the army."

Not everyone bought Milo's style, but what he said struck a chord. There was a ripple of nervous laughter that further emboldened him.

"We're here to learn how to be *actors*, man! Self-expression. Free-dom. Alla *that* shit. Can't see where no *drill* fits into the picture."

From the first words of his audition piece — "Now is the winter of our discontent" — Theo and his staff had pegged Milo as a diamond in the rough. When his Stanley from *Streetcar* proved equally out-standing, they had nudged shoulders and gleefully footsied each other under the table. They didn't worry about the swagger; that would self-regulate in the next three years. Even so, they had their work cut out for them. As did Mr. Milo Tessier.

"I see," said Theo, with mock gravitas, after which he broke into a smile. "Well, even if you can't at the moment, don't worry. All will yet be well, I promise you."

Everyone, including Milo, joined in the laughter, melting away any hint of confrontation.

"All I know is that you must learn to work together as closely as — well, not to make too big a thing of it — as closely as seaman on an unstable ship in unknown and treacherous seas. As closely as trapeze artists in the circus."

Yes, he thought, *if you work well, and the chemistry is right. If you are trusting, and large of soul, and capable of great leaps of faith. AND if you're lucky; you'll have the satisfaction of undergoing some of the most stressful, painful — as well as most joyous — experiences known to woman or man.*

"The profession of making people laugh and cry is a delicate one. Tricky. Like keeping bubbles afloat in the air. You'd better have lots of friends around to help you blow.

"Just remember, you've all been chosen," Theo permitted himself a pause. "Like gladiators for the arena."

❧

Milo and Chas had enjoyed quite an afternoon.

Their first session after lunch had been with Professor Lantos, the head of NAADA's weapons program, rehearsing the duel he had devised for them as Romeo and Tybalt in *Romeo and Juliet*. Theo had cast them against type, with Milo as Romeo and Chas as Juliet's hot-headed cousin. The distinguished Professor Lantos would ultimately instruct them in a great many ways to maim and kill in service of the muse, and with a variety of weapons: from the lightweight foil of the Musketeers, as on this occasion, to the heavy broadsword of Caesar's day, as well as endless combinations of short sword, javelin, dagger, staff, mace, pike, lance, and ball and chain.

The last class of the day had been to integrate the fight choreography worked out so meticulously with Professor Lantos into the larger scene, directed by Theo. To feel the text and action meld together and come alive as the scene played itself out had been gratifying beyond measure. Milo's body was covered in perspiration. The teachers had not hesitated to put the two younger men through their paces.

Milo was still huffing and puffing when he bumped into Marie in the hall.

"Honey lamb, don't you *ever* check the call-board?" She removed a note from the board and handed it to him. "I left this for you hours ago!"

Milo accepted the note at arm's length. He was in such a sweat, he was afraid to offend Marie, whom he already adored. There wasn't much that didn't involve Marie in the running of this place, including getting her hands very dirty if need be. She was, for example, the only one able to coax any action from the ancient wall-mounted heater–air conditioner thing that lived at the back of the theatre.

"Oh, shit!" said Milo.

Marie had taken the call and written out the message.

"Too bad about that, love."

Chas joined them in the hall.

"Problem?" asked Chas. "Anything I can do?"

Milo passed him Marie's note.

Gino can't make it tonight. Do you know anyone who could fill in? There's an extra ten in it for you.

Chas passed the note back to Milo.

"Gino the guy you work with?"

"Yeah," said Milo. He wiped his face with the towel he had slung over his shoulder. "I don't think I can handle twelve floors by myself, but if I don't it'll look like shit and I'll be blamed anyway."

"I'll give you a hand."

"You?" To Milo, Chas was a member of the upper crust. The idea of him swabbing floors didn't fit. "Don't you have this bartender job?"

"Yeah, but not tonight. Come on, Milo, I grew up on a ranch! If I can muck horseshit out of a stable, surely you can trust me to swing a mop." He clapped Milo on the shoulder. "C'mon. Let's do it."

"Well, all right," said Milo. "You twisted my arm." He grinned. "As long as you don't expect me to help out with the roping and branding."

The door to Eleanor Brewer's classroom door opened just wide enough to frame the white Greek mask of a face. Miss Brewer was engaged at NAADA to coach the students in vocal technique and text interpretation.

"Mr. Tessier! Mr. Willison!" Her voice was low but commanding. "Is it possible that even gifted players like yourselves could still lack consideration for your fellows?" Miss Brewer would never be so vulgar as to *demand* their silence. "We are trying to work, gentlemen, but find ourselves continually interrupted with talk of 'horse manure' and 'roping and branding' out in the corridor."

Chas and Milo stood there like shamefaced ten year olds. "Sorry, Miss Brewer," they declaimed, more or less in unison, which made

Miss Brewer smile, disclosing an unexpected dimple. She melted back into the classroom and closed the door.

⚓

There was a lot of ground to cover, but goddamn, he and Chas had fun! All Milo had asked for was a favour, and instead he had found a friend. Come to think of it, he hadn't even had to ask; Chas had offered freely. For someone like Milo, abandoned by his mother at birth, orphaned soon after, and raised as an only child by an elderly grandparent, each new friend made up a little for the brother or sister he never had, for all the times he never heard "You behave your-selves, the two of you!"

"Hey, Chas! Watch this!"

The corridors were broad and long enough for cartwheels and backflips, at both of which Milo was adept. But the young men moved to the open space around the elevators for a repeat of that afternoon's duel, this time with mops, the sodden heads tucked under their arms. They squared off beside their respective pails-on-wheels.

"Now, Tybalt," Milo began, the change in him instantaneous. One minute he had been kibitzing and showing off, the next he was a young man whose honour had been impugned, and who would defend it whatever the cost.

take the 'villain' back again
That late thou gav'st me, for Mercutio's soul
Is but a little way above our heads,
Staying for thine to keep him company.
Either thou, or I, or both, must go with him.

The muse that had sparked Milo had infused Chas as well.

"'Thou, wretched boy,'" he said as Tybalt, the Capulet champion, testosterone incarnate.

. . . that didst consort him here,
Shalt with him hence.

They launched into the routine Professor Lantos had devised for them — not a difficult one at this early stage. They thrust and they parried, lunging, attacking, defending. Each move had a number that they called out before they launched into it.

"One!"

The thrusts and slashes had to look convincing.

"Two!"

They fenced their way along the corridors. Past Shmelminski and Sons, Attorneys-at-Law; past Burridge and Burridge, customs brokers; and The Evelyn Hannon Foundation. They returned to the open space around the elevators for the big finale, and circled their buckets. Just when Milo was about to close in for the coup de grâce, he tripped on his mophead and fell, looking like something out of a Laurel and Hardy film.

"Professor Lantos was right," said Milo. He picked himself up from the floor and launched into a dead-on imitation of the elegant, erudite refugee, a man of principle who had been forced to flee Hungary when the Soviet tanks rolled into Budapest but a few short years before. "To be carried away emotionally during swordplay — or any kind of stage fighting — is not acceptable behaviour in an office building, gentlemen. The blades or, as in this case, mop handles, though blunted, can still do serious damage. Every move; every cut and thrust, feint, lunge and parry; every slip on a mop must be as meticulously choreographed as a pas de deux in the ballet."

Milo had twisted his knee a bit when he fell. Thank God it was the last floor. All they had to do was take the equipment down to the basement and sign out.

Knees can be a bitch, Milo thought. By the time they were out on the street, it hurt bad.

Chas noticed Milo's limp. "Maybe we should get you over to

Emergency at the General."

"Forget it. I hate hospitals." Milo clapped his friend on the back. "Let's have a drink instead."

⌘

Finding a drink at that hour in Toronto wasn't easy, even in 1961, but Milo remembered an illegal boozecan someone had once told him about. It was close by, so he didn't have far to walk with his bad knee.

Whoever operated the place was playing the outlaw role to the hilt. There were blackout curtains on the windows, and the light level was about as low as it could be and still be called light. By some bat-like radar, however, the waiters seemed to know you were there. Drinks got served. Bills got paid. The buzz of voices was loud enough to know that there were others sharing the darkness, but faces and features were lost in the murk.

Chas drank Molson's while Milo preferred Labatt's.

"So why're *you* at NAADA?" asked Chas.

"I dunno," Milo shrugged, grinning. "An easy way for a shy boy to make friends and show off at the same time, maybe?"

They both heard the voice at the same time. It came from the booth behind Milo.

"It's Adam!" said Milo. "Let's ask him to join us."

Milo started to rise, but Chas's hand on his shoulder restrained him.

"Maybe he'd rather not be disturbed. Somehow, I don't see Adam as a solitary drinker, do you?"

No, Milo saw Adam as someone who had loaned him twenty-five bucks the week before so he could get his bike out of hock.

"Lemme take a look. I'll be so fast, they'll never be sure they saw me."

Milo got to his knees and sneaked a look over the partition. He swivelled back almost immediately. "Ouch!" His knee was killing him. "He's got company."

"See, what'd I tell you?"

"They're both sitting on one side of the table."

"So?"

"I think they're kissing. Either that or they're sharing a very short French fry."

There was little prurience in Chas's nature, but he couldn't help but wonder who Adam's fellow French fry fan might be.

"Anyone we know?"

Milo came right to the point.

"It's a guy, Chas! It's a goddamn *guy*!"

The two didn't talk much as they finished their beers and left.

"Shit!" said Milo, once they were out on the street. "What should we do? The cops could throw Adam in the clinker for what he was doing in there!"

Chas found that hard to believe. "You've gotta be kidding!"

"Jesus, Chas! Sometimes I think you and I must have been born on two different planets. Being queer's against the law, buddy! Guys who screw other guys can get hauled up on charges of depravity if they're caught. They put your name in the papers!"

Chas was shaken. He thought for a moment.

"Does anyone else at NAADA know Adam's queer?" he asked Milo.

"I dunno. *We* didn't a couple of hours ago. Why should they? It'd mean a lotta trouble for Adam if anyone did."

"But, why?" asked Chas, truly perplexed. "There are lots of queer actors. It's no secret."

"Chas, where you been these last coupla months? Walking around with your head in a bag? It's never been spelled out in black and white, but Theo's made it quite clear he wants NAADA straight. As in sexually."

"Milo, can I ask you something?"

"Ask away."

"Has Adam ever done anything to offend you? I know he's a pain when he uses up all the toilet paper in the john and doesn't put in a new roll. But has he ever pinched your butt? Made a pass?"

That Chas could even think such a thing! Adam was a respected colleague. And the guy who had bailed out his bike.

"Of *course* not! But *I* always thought he was straight. Didn't you?"

"Yeah. And no one else's said anything, either."

"Then why don't we leave it like that?" said Milo. "Whaddya say?"

IN THE WINGS

———

Jeanne, still known to her family as Bernadette, awoke that morning in the same iron bed she had slept in since she was a child, in the room that she shared with Colleen. The Donahues had their usual breakfast of fried everything in the kitchen, after which everyone went about their business, which in her case was washing the dishes. Tommy Junior waited until his father was in the shower and his mother making her bed to sneak up on his sister as she wiped out the bacon and egg pan. He shoved his hand up her skirt, putting it where he always put it when he came for her. Jeanne tried never to be left alone with him, but that couldn't always be managed. She had told her father about it years ago, when Tommy Junior had first started in. But her brother was never chastised, and Ethel had washed her mouth out with soap "for telling such *filthy* lies!" Jeanne tried to break free but Tommy Junior, no lightweight, was pressing her up against the sink so hard she thought her ribs would be crushed. There was no way she could speak, never mind cry out. Instead, she summoned up all her strength and let him have it with the cast-iron frypan. With a cry, Tommy dropped to the kitchen floor.

Jesus, Mary, and Joseph! Jeanne's thoughts raced. *Have I killed him? Hurt him?* He was her brother. She had struck him. She would go to hell . . . Lurking under the terror was something even more frightening. She was glad she had done it.

Everyone came running, including her father, a towel hurriedly draped around his flat butt and big belly. They began by glaring at Jeanne, then saw Tommy on the floor, nursing his head.

"She tried to kill me! The bitch tried to kill me!"

"Sweet Jesus, there's blood!" Ethel ran to the sink for the dishcloth and rinsed it out at the tap. "Colleen, get the Band-Aids."

Colleen stood, transfixed, in the kitchen doorway and prayed a child's prayer. What was going to happen now? Oh, *please*, God. Let it not be something horrible.

"Go on, girl!"

"Anything you have to say, Miss Bernhardt?" said Tommy Senior.

"He . . ." said Jeanne.

"Yes?"

"He tried to . . ."

"It'll be Christmas before she gets out a sentence!" He thrust his face into Jeanne's. "Spit it out! I thought you were an actress. Now's your chance to act!"

"He put his hands where they didn't belong."

She'd said it!

Tommy Senior looked fiercely at his son. He was cowering on the floor, uncertain which way the wind would blow.

"Is this true?" He turned back to Jeanne. "You're supposed to be a good Catholic girl! Do you know what happens to a family that gets a name for that sorta thing?"

"She's lying!" Tommy turned on his sister. "You think you're too good for this family, dontcha?"

"It's true!" said Jeanne.

Tommy Senior looked from one to the other, though there was no question he would throw his lot in with his son. "Well, Miss High-

and-Mighty, maybe it's time you find out what it's like, not having a family around to take care of you."

Ethel said nothing; just continued to fuss over Tommy, dabbing at his head with the dishcloth.

"Maybe one of your artsy-fartsy friends will give you a bed." Tommy Senior helped his wife get Tommy to his feet.

"Take your pick," he said to Jeanne, as they guided their son's exaggeratedly limp form back to his bed. "You can pack your things now and get out, or we'll put 'em out on the doorstep."

Bernadette looked from one parent to the other, waiting for one to rescind on behalf of them both, for one of them to realize they had gone too far.

"We'll expect your cheque on Fridays," said Tommy Senior, "same as usual."

☙

Bobby Hayden, whose clothes and flirtatious manner had so fascinated Jeanne that first day, had the full-hipped-and-breasted body of an Indian temple carving. Her dance and exercise clothes were equally special, with a different outfit almost every day. Today she wore a copper-coloured leotard with matching tights, echoing the shade of her blazing hair, and reflecting their warm tones on her very white skin. A silver bracelet circled her upper left arm.

Bobby had come to the Ladies for a pee and had decided to stay on for a much-needed smoke. She loved Miss Brewer's text class above everything, but Miss Brewer was so intense and Bobby wanted so much to please her that sometimes Bobby's hands would begin to tremble, and she would stumble over text that she knew as well as she knew her own name. Or she became nauseous.

Only one of the ten cubicles was occupied. When the sound of the flushing finally subsided, Bobby could hear other sounds — a few sobs and sniffles, an occasional hiccup. A couple of cardboard boxes sat on the bathroom floor, three Eaton's shopping bags on the window ledge. The doors of the bathroom stalls ended a foot above the floor, so Bobby leaned over to check out the occupant's feet. Navy wedgies — it could only be Jeanne.

Bobby tapped on the door. "Are you all right, Jeanne, love?"

Thanks to Theo and Mitch, there was lots of everyone calling everyone "love" at NAADA. British actors loved to play at being working class.

"Yes, Bobby," said Jeanne, but her voice, thick with tears, belied her.

"Come on out of there, baby, I want to see you." Bobby did her best to keep her tone light. "That's the only way I'm going to believe you're all right."

Jeanne emerged and crossed to the washbasin, head bowed.

"I thought I'd get a room at the 'Y,' but they're full up."

Bobby handed her a paper towel from the dispenser and tilted her head at the boxes and bags.

"What'll you do with those?" she said.

"I thought maybe Marie'd keep them in the office till I find myself a room. Do you know of anything?"

"I think I do, as a matter of fact," said Bobby. "But look, I've got to get back to class. I'll show you the place at lunch. If you don't like it, you can bunk in with me."

Bobby's classmates knew she was rich. What they didn't know was just *how* rich, and Bobby was determined that it stay that way. Her philanthropy had already benefited both Milo and Chas, who unbeknownst lived in her building at a greatly reduced rent because it, and a great many others, belonged to Bobby's father.

With the house money Jeanne paid to her parents as well as rent, she didn't think she would be able to manage more than a furnished room, and was overwhelmed when she saw the apartment. It had its own bathroom and kitchen and everything. The miracle was that she could afford the rent. Bobby herself was only one flight up, and Milo and Chas lived in the building, too. Jeanne walked around the studio apartment. It was old and shabby, and Bobby told her that the electricity was inclined to blow, and the toilets to flood. She loved it.

She was terrified. She was sad. She was ecstatic. Was this how it felt to be free?

↩

Adam wasn't the least bit alarmed when he was asked to stop by Theo's office at the end of the day, but he didn't know that his secret life had been discovered.

"If I have to twitch one more shoulder to the sound of that god-damned drum, Theo . . ."

"You're not enjoying Paul John's class?" Theo was surprised. He thought the dance teacher from Trinidad had won over everyone at the school.

"Oh, I enjoy it when we actually get to *dance*, Theo. I love all that African stuff. It's the stupid muscle isolation exercise."

"So," said Theo, "it's not just that you don't *like* it; you think it's stupid."

"Well, uh . . . Yes! I do think it's stupid. Not for everyone of course . . ."

"You think that the rest of the class will profit from taking this class, but that you won't?"

"Theo, I've been doing routines like this since I was seven. I know all about muscle isolation."

"And that's what Paul John's exercise with the drum is?"

"Well, isn't it?"

Not all actors "got rhythm." Some, when asked to move their ribs side to side, will move their hips instead, and vice versa. Some can't rotate the right shoulder while holding the left one still. Paul John's solution was a peppy little routine based on the timbre and rhythm of his drums, a mixture of jazz-modern, some calypso, and the barest sprinkling of precision military drill.

"I'm told it was designed," said Theo, "to ensure that not a single move would be beyond the reach of anyone in class."

"My point exactly!"

"Well, I've watched the company go through it several times, Adam, and correct me if I'm wrong but when everyone managed to get through it without missing a beat the other day, you were all absolutely exhilarated. Miss Brewer said she could hear you cheering at the other end of the building."

"I'm sorry, Theo. I just think I could be making better use of my time."

"Possibly. But think about this for a moment. What if the main point of Paul John's routine is not the exercise itself, but the feeling of success when *everyone* does it right."

"I . . ." Adam lowered his eyes. "I must admit I hadn't thought of it that way."

"Your status as an individual is safe here, Adam. But you must see that your *role* here is as a member of the ensemble."

"I do, Theo."

"I'm not so sure about that, Adam. Not entirely." There was a change in Theo's tone. "When someone studies law, say, or medicine, there's an assumption that you can either put out or withold the *private* you as much or as little as you care to. All things considered, it seems to work pretty well for these professions."

Theo put his hands together and brought them to his lips in a kind of mute entreaty. It was also a prayer for guidance. The soul of young Adam was like fine crystal, and he would not shatter it for the world.

"Our work is different. Our only tools of the trade are ourselves. You and Bobby, Jeanne — all of you. It's the sum of *all* of you that gets put on the stage, and you've been holding out on them."

"I beg your pardon!?"

"Adam, let's not insult us both — you by pretending that you're not a homosexual, and me by pretending that I don't know about it."

Adam had lived in terrified apprehension of just such a moment since arriving at the school. Strangely, now that it had happened, he felt more relief than anything. Leading a double life had proved even more taxing here than it had been with his family.

"Where would civilization be without homosexuals, after all?" said Theo. "Just think of it: no Socrates, no Beethoven, no da Vinci, no Michelangelo. No Liberace! My God! Civilization, as we know it, would be impossible!"

They had a laugh at that, but Theo sobered quickly.

"It's dangerous, Adam. Being queer will put you in legal and emotional jeopardy for the rest of your life. And your family, too! Is it worth it? Can't you imagine a life in which you were *not* homosexual? If you can manage that, everything will be *so* much easier! Why are you looking at me like that?"

Adam sighed. "I'm just sorry you've turned out to be such a bigot, Theo. I wouldn't have thought it of you."

"Well, you can bloody well *stop* thinking it because you know it's not true. I've worked in the British theatre, at the Old Vic, for God's sake! I know more brilliant titled queers than you've had hot dinners. And yes, some of them are my closest friends. But we have an opportunity to create a different kind of theatre here."

"A more macho one?" asked Adam.

"Yes!" Theo rapped his desk with his fist. "A chance to create a new image for classical theatre; one that doesn't immediately make you think of a bunch of queens poncing about in tights. The more homosexuals there are in a company, the more the group chemistry shifts toward them. Among other things, it can be hard on the women."

"Women *adore* queer men, Theo."

"Of course they do. Queer men know how to have fun. The ones out of the closet do, at any rate. I imagine things must be trying for those that aren't . . . but we won't get into that. Back to the women!"

He lifted his eyes to the portrait that hung above his desk. "You've heard me speak of Dame Arabella?"

Who hadn't? Theo's stories about Arabella were already NAADA folklore. Adam's favourite was about the time she was seated at a piano on a raked stage, the angle of ascent so steep that the piano slowly but inexorably kept sliding toward her as she played. Or the time she performed Medea in Rio de Janeiro, with the entire audience following her in translation, all two thousand turning the page at exactly the same time, with a sound like a clap of thunder.

"Arabella, in her twenties at the time, was doing a season with a small rep company in Manchester. She'd worked with lots of queer actors, but there'd always been enough fellows who preferred girls to restore the balance. There might have been a little hanky-panky, but it was a lot of joking and teasing mostly, Arabella said. She thought it was good for the girls.

"The Manchester company, on the other hand, was chock-a-block with homosexual men. There were no kisses and cuddles for the ladies; no sexy teasing or games. As a consequence, they became dispirited and blue. Bitchery and frustration abounded, Arabella said, and all for the want of a pat on the tush. Her theory was that women look to men for a reflection of themselves. How are they doing? Are they attractive?

"The girls in Manchester faded away. They lost the spring in their step. 'You know, the female can't be forever putting her scent about,' Arabella said, 'when there's no one waiting to sniff it.'"

Theo, his voice low, leaned toward Adam. "Think of it, Adam. Jail and humiliation."

৵৹

The brick pile that was home to NAADA dated back to the late nineteenth century and sported a coat of vintage grime, inside and out. It had once housed a corset manufacturer, and sometimes Milo could feel the presence of row upon row of shadowy women bent over pedal-powered sewing machines, could catch a bit of their spicy verbal ratatouille.

The rooms were small, with only the theatre able to hold more than thirty people. The walls sweated damp, and five generations of feet had stripped the finish off the hardwood floors, leaving it a porous grey, saturated with the kind of dirt that lasts for eternity. The stage lighting was an eclectic jumble of grids and wires scrounged from church basements and defunct little theatre groups. It had received a clean bill of health from the inspectors, but Theo was never fully dissuaded from his concern that it would someday combust and incinerate everyone in the building.

It was Theo who introduced the idea that NAADA's humble modus operandi was a matter of choice, not necessity. "A beautiful woman knows full well the power of her jewels and designer gowns, but it's when she's naked that she's truly magnificent."

Wow, thought Milo.

They were in a circle on the floor, having completed an exercise that involved tossing a ball around the circle in a strict rhythm that was subject to sudden change. Theo was telling them how an actor in a theatre company was like an athlete on a team.

Milo, a big sports fan, jumped at the concept. "Sure. I can see it. The level of your performance has gotta be influenced by the others guys in the game."

He, Chas, and Adam had been dubbed The Three Musketeers. Hardly an original conceit, but if there was ever a place to play it out, NAADA was it.

"Like on the tennis court!" Bobby chimed in.

It gave Theo particular pleasure when Bobby, usually so reticent, put herself forward. *My, but that girl is breathtaking!* he thought. All she had to do to make her name was stand absolutely still on the stage and let the audience admire.

"Exactly!" said Theo. "Even the most mediocre talent — which of course excludes anyone in this room . . ."

There was a ripple of pleased laughter from the assembly, but there wasn't one of them who didn't believe it.

". . . can exceed all expectations when matched with someone just that much better. All too often, you'll have to deal with the opposite scenario, where you hope for someone to pace you during a race, but you've got to wait for a guy with a torn hamstring instead. Too much of that can cripple an actor-in-training." Theo was determined that NAADA not become the sort of place where people came to exercise, or exorcise, their psyches. "Be as neurotic as you like, so long as you're productive."

"But isn't being neurotic unhealthy?" asked Jeanne. *Hamlet* had been the last class project. There had been much discussion of neurotics and neuroses.

"By and large, yes," said Theo, "but neurotic emotions are still emotions, and all emotions are charged with energy. They're the engine that drives your character. The actor's job is to take that negative energy and turn it into something positive.

"You all know how rarely I use the word *art*. That's because it's a tricky word that's led many astray. Practise your craft and the art will take care of itself. Yes?"

There was a chorus of yesses. Theo expected each student to stand up and be counted.

"Our intent is always to *make* art. Just don't go and fixate on the word, like some effete salon slime, or you'll have me to answer to!" The most important thing Theo gave to his students couldn't be put into words except to say that he was one hundred percent an actor — through and through. It comprised his core, his essence, the very way he fit inside his skin. "However much it astonishes the public that actors can remember hundreds of lines and regurgitate them at the drop of a hat . . ."

He looked at Milo, who, unless shouted down, could quote endlessly. His favourite venue for declamation was the urinal, which caused Adam to say that he now knew the true meaning of piss-awful.

". . . you all know how low rote-learning ranks in an actor's training. Acting is ingesting. Through the eyes, nose, and ears. Through every muscle."

He turned his gaze on Chas.

"Text."

On Bobby, radiant in purple angora.

"Makeup. Dance. Movement. Voice. These are all tools. How they are used is what it's all about."

His gaze widened to include all of them.

"When it's a novice cook wielding the knife and cleaver, all the diner can reasonably expect is some kind of nourishing but primitive stew. The same tools in the hands of a master . . ."

He did a few karate movements to set the scene. He knew only a few, but they sufficed.

"Peking duck!"

It never failed to get a laugh.

"Go ahead and laugh. But cooking's one of the best analogies for what we do: throw all sorts of things in a pot, light the fire, and hope we come up with a dish at least somewhat resembling the picture in the cookbook. Alchemy's not a bad analogy either.

"The reason I'm going on so is that the secret of acting is . . . secret. I couldn't tell you even if I wanted to. Secrets lose their power in the telling. What I *will* do is push, praise, and goad each one of you until you discover it for yourself!"

There are *some* secrets, however, Theo thought later, that are nothing more than lies and deception, cunningly perpetrated by bastards against the very ones who love them the most. Secrets it would crush Marie to know, yet which would rob her of her pride if she were left unaware; contradictions that had hushed his mouth for many weeks, though the fact that he frequently didn't come home at night called for — indeed demanded — an explanation. He would have liked to think that there was some vestige of nobility in his actions, that he was unable to put her through the pain of knowing, but the fact was that he was a fucking coward. As usual, it was up to Marie to do the dirty work.

She stuck her head into his office.

"Theo, do you think you could spare me a few minutes later in the day?"

"Sure, but why not now?" Theo wanted what was going to happen to happen in the school offices. Perhaps the semi-public nature of the place would mitigate what was to follow. "I just happen to have a few moments right now. Or we could go up to the coffee shop."

"Mm, it's kinda private, Theo. D'you think you could come by the house?" She tried to give him one of her flirty little smiles, but all she could manage was a sad imitation. "I'll make you dinner."

One part of him longed to put her off, but that would only compound his sins. "Jambalaya?" he asked, playing the game.

"Sure," said Marie. "Why not?"

♫

When Theo and Marie had first started living together, he would always ring the bell when he came home, and Marie would come to the door. Of course both of them knew he could have let himself in with his own key, but that wouldn't have given her the chance to welcome him home, to usher him once more into their common space. Theo hadn't rung the bell for some time now. Should he do it tonight? Would that make it easier for Marie, or harder? He opted for using his key, but called out his presence as soon as he was over the threshold so that Marie could meet him in the hallway if she wished. She did and — after a kiss that was decidedly neutral on both sides — he followed her into the dining room. The table was set with a white cloth and a centrepiece of autumn leaves and grasses. It was beautiful, as were all Marie's creations, but melancholy. *The leaves may be red and yellow*, thought Theo, *but they're still dead.*

They sat at the table, and Marie dished out her heavenly jambalaya while Theo poured the white wine. He lifted a laden fork to his mouth, but changed his mind halfway and lowered it back to the plate, sighing deeply. "I'm sorry, love."

Marie tried to speak but found she couldn't. She bowed her head until she could find her voice. "Why? I thought you loved me. I thought you were my man."

"I *do* love you," said Theo.

Marie waited. "But . . . ?"

"What do you mean, 'but'?"

"I notice you didn't say you're my man."

Theo couldn't help seeing the humour in the situation. The woman knew what he was thinking every step of the way. He spoke softly, knowing he was about to cause pain.

"If I'm *your* man, it means I can never be anyone else's man. Not without cheating."

"I think I could live with it, Theo." If the choice was between that and never seeing him again, she knew she could.

"But I don't think I could." Theo rose from the table and went into the living room, followed closely by Marie.

"Don't ask me to explain my behaviour, Marie. I can't. All I know is that it's 1962 and there's a new feeling out there. Something young and exciting is in the air and I want to be part of it."

"Can't I be part of it with you?"

There was nothing for it now but to push on. "No, you can't. It doesn't work like that. This is a solo thing."

"Solo?"

"That's right. Though I do still care for you."

Marie looked at her hands, inert in her lap. "That may be so, Theo, but I don't think I can stay on at NAADA if we split up."

Theo turned to her, caught totally by surprise. Somehow, the thought of Marie leaving because they were no longer sleeping together had never occurred to him. "What?"

"Theo, honey; you're a shit par excellence, but that doesn't mean I can stop loving you. I just don't know if I can hang around, if we're . . . if we're . . ."

Theo finished her statement.

"Not lovers?" He took Marie's hand. "We've made something very special together, you and I." He turned her palm right-side up and brought it to his lips. "NAADA. Besides," he reached out and scooped Marie into his lap. "Who says that we're no longer lovers?"

SUPPORTING CAST

M itch Blakely's decision to join the faculty at NAADA had proven to be a big drawing card for other teachers of stature. At sixty, Mitch's energy was as undiminished as his shock of white hair and his golden transatlantic reputation. As Assistant Artistic Director, he would be directing several of the student productions, as well as teaching students how to interpret text. But what made him absolutely indispensable was his expertise with makeup. It was said that Mitch Blakely could teach the handsomest *jeune premier* to transform himself into the Hunchback of Notre Dame, and vice versa.

"I know it may be disappointing to some of you that we're not starting out with some of the flashier stuff." Mitch's words were aimed particularly at Milo, who had already been lobbying to make up as Caliban or Othello. "But actors spend far more time onstage looking much as they do in real life, than made up as Quasimodo. That's why a good, clean, straight makeup is so important."

The students sat at their makeup tables, looking into the mirrors, their makeup boxes open before them. There was no such thing as a professional makeup box, loaded and ready to go — those were for amateurs. It was usually hardware store stuff that found favour with the pros: the metal boxes the home handyman uses for tools, the fisherman for tackle.

"The urge to paint and ornament oneself is universal. You have the Hottentot and the native of Borneo, yes, but also examples closer to home." Mitch was pleased at the sight of so many young attentive faces. "Think of the dandies of the French and English courts with their coiffed and powdered wigs, little moleskin hearts or stars glued to cheeks caked with powder and rouge."

Under Mitch's direction, they covered their faces with a thin coat of flesh-coloured greasepaint. The makeup for the men was somewhat darker than the women's, but in both cases it made everything but the eyes lose definition.

"Now that you've put on a good base coat, your face is like a blank canvas, ready for the brush. Our task, as far as possible, is to fool the eye into *not* seeing whatever's inappropriate for the role in which we've been cast, and to highlight whatever is. Not by hacking off the offending bits and pieces in order to fit the glass slipper," he laughed, "like Cinderella's wicked stepsisters did, but with highlight and shadow. It's quite simple, really. *Darker* colours make things look smaller and thinner, and can even make them seem to disappear. *Lighter* ones make features bigger and fatter. But first, you must know your face."

The mirrors reflected back the laughter. Surely, they knew their own faces!

"Oh, you think you know how you look when you see yourself in the mirror while shaving, do you? Or putting on lipstick?"

The juxtaposition was too much for Milo, who proceeded to mime someone trying to shave and put on lipstick at the same time. *The little sod is good*, thought Mitch.

"What about the bones underneath the skin? How many of you are familiar with your own personal projections and hollows? Well, you're going to be. By the time I've finished with you, you will know each of your features intimately — your eyes, your nose, your chin. And not just by looking at them in the mirror. You will touch them, feel them, so that your fingertips know them by heart. Don't assume that just because you've been looking in the mirror for the last twenty years, you've actually *seen* what you've been looking at! Let me give you an exercise. Close your eyes and picture yourself as you look at this moment. I'll give you a minute, a full sixty seconds. That's not too difficult, is it?"

Half the class thought it would be a very easy exercise. The other half knew Mitch wouldn't have introduced it if it was. At the end of the sixty seconds there was no question.

"Not so easy, is it? Would you have done better if you'd had more time? Did any of you manage it to your satisfaction?"

No one.

"If you're playing someone your own age and type, why do you need makeup at all?" asked Michelle. Because of her tender years, Michelle had become the school's mascot. She was a pretty girl of medium height, with a long blonde braid that stopped just short of her waist. Her bright brown eyes showed an eagerness to learn that the *laissez-faire* home schooling she had received from her counter-culture mother had never quite managed to quell.

"Why do we need makeup?" repeated Mitch. "Because of the lights, my angel. They're there to highlight the action onstage, and that includes you. If you don't give them something vivid to capture, they'll turn your features into pudding."

Everyone seemed to enjoy the process of applying the straight makeup. *It's a kind of a Zen experience*, thought Milo — he had been reading the Beats: Kerouac, Ferlinghetti. Painstakingly, he set about applying a thin layer of pancake; then eyeliner, mascara, and rouge. Next, he outlined and darkened his lips, after which he gave the whole thing a liberal dusting of powder to take away the shine and fix the makeup in place.

Enlarging the eyes was a big part of the process, and Mitch was gratified to see how well Jeanne was handling it, first putting a little white on the wide end of a toothpick and running it along the inside of her lower lashes to make the eye look wider. She extended the outer corners with eyeliner and filled that in with white as well, to make the eye look longer. *Well and neatly done!* thought Mitch. He noted Chas in the act of applying a red dot near the inner corners of his eyes, balancing out all that white, and preventing himself from looking cross-eyed.

Mitch scrutinized the group's efforts. Except for Jeanne and Milo, there were adjustments to be made. Some (like Chas) had come at it with too heavy a hand, and some (like Adam) had tried to be too subtle. But not too bad, all in all.

"Mitch, when are we going to—"

"May I complete your sentence, Milo?" Mitch didn't wait for permission. "When are we going to tackle something a little more challenging? Next week," he laughed, "when I think you'll find the word 'challenging' is open to interpretation."

"Sorry?" Milo had so far prided himself on being on Mitch's wavelength.

"Well," said Mitch, "there is the odd case of a performer who adopted a character early in his career, and never played anything else for the rest of his life."

"Eugene O'Neill's father!" *I'm back on track*, thought Milo.

"The model for William Tyrone in *Long Day's Journey Into Night*. Yes, indeed!" said Mitch. "An actor–manager, who made a lifetime career out of playing the title role in *The Count of Monte Cristo*."

Milo was going to say that he liked the idea of never being out of work, but Mitch got in first. "But the problem, Milo, was that it turned him into a one-character actor, a hack. Which I'm sure you would never settle for, my friend. Actors like Mr. O'Neill are still around, but now they star in television series."

Everyone in class felt enormously superior. They couldn't know that one or two of them would eventually accede to being fabulously well paid for plying their trade on TV. At this moment, they felt they would live and die in the theatre.

"The point is, he played the character so long that, whereas at first he had to do an elaborate makeup to play the old Cristo, the older he got, the longer it took to do the young one."

As the class wound down, Theo arrived carrying two battered metal boxes, one of which he handed to Mitch.

"*Your* makeup boxes!" cried Bobby. Unlike the new featureless boxes the students had, Mitch's and Theo's had a layered patina, a character that had been years in the making.

Theo had had his grey toolbox since Oxford; Mitch's box, a beat-up old red thing that had once held fishing tackle, was even older. Both were held together by masking tape and thick elastic bands, the dents and scratches a living résumé, a litmus of their lives.

Mitch withdrew a small hank of carrot-red hair from his case. "I was doing Malvolio at The Royal Court, and I decided to play him bald as a billiard ball except for one very large kiss-curl in the middle of his forehead." He became misty-eyed, and then gave an embarrassed little cough. "Umm. Sorry about that."

Theo stepped in to the rescue. "And what about this rouge in my box?" He held up a round container of gilded cardboard. "Mitch gave me this rouge. The first time this box saw use, I was twenty years old and passionately in love with a woman twenty years older named Olga."

"Is the rouge still good?" asked Jeanne.

"Yup! Greasepaint goes rancid in time," said Theo, "but rouge is forever."

Like the memories, thought Mitch. The fun and the sadness, the camaraderie.

Each compartment was rife with associations — with reviews good and bad, memories of cities where the audiences were cold but the parties were hot, and vice versa.

"But this," said Theo, "is the *pièce de résistance*." He took a tiny box from the bottom of his kit and put it on Adam's makeup table. "This box of patches was given to me by Sir Lawrence Olivier on the opening night of *School for Scandal*."

"God! Did you ever use them?" asked Milo. If they had been his, he would have been tempted.

"I've wanted to every time I've done a Restoration piece, but I never could in the end."

Of course not, thought Milo. They were holy relics, to be forever carried about in Theo's makeup box, as if in a shrine.

⚘

Eleanor Brewer seemed to have few pleasures other than seeing the light of understanding dawn in a student's eyes. In fact she was so closemouthed about anything of a personal nature, she could have been leading a double life as a dominatrix and no one would have been the wiser. In truth, she had no such exciting clandestine agenda. What she had was a mother who was old and ill, and whose care had fallen to her only daughter. That was why she was here in Toronto working with Milo and Jeanne, instead of in London acting with the Royal Shakespeare Company as she had done for a decade.

She was wearing one of her signature shirtwaist dresses, each with a white Peter Pan collar that reflected light onto her face, like a Hollywood spot in the days of black and white when, as someone once said, there still were faces. Her large grey-green eyes had been rimmed with dark grey pencil, and her wide but thin mouth was a vivid blue-red slash. Her hair, black shot with grey and centre-parted, was cut in the bob you see on small boys in English romantic paintings. For those granted the good fortune to have been at the Old Vic on the nights when Eleanor Brewer had assumed the mantle of the mother of the doomed Oedipus, it was forever the face of Jocasta.

Milo and Jeanne knew very well what the scene was about. Richard, the humpback, meets Lady Anne by design on the road. She is part of a funeral procession transporting the corpse of her father-in-law, for whose death she blames Richard. Yet, cunningly, Richard manages to alchemize her hatred and contempt into desire in as little time as it would have taken her to slip out of her panties, had women worn them back then.

"Look how *my* ring encompasseth *thy* finger . . ." said Milo. It was his second attempt at the phrase, but he was immediately stopped by Miss Brewer.

"Mr. Tessier, the emphasis is neither on *my* nor on *thy*." Miss Brewer spoke to everyone with the same grave courtesy. "The ownership of the ring, or the finger, isn't in question. Nor is it a question of the ring being on Lady Anne's finger as distinct from anyone else's finger. Richard is doing his best to *seduce* the lady. Surely, the emphasis would be on 'encompasseth.' 'Look how my ring *encompasseth* thy finger.' Iambic pentameter, remember?"

"Oh, shit, Miss Brewer!" said Milo. "Isn't that what I *said*?"

"My dear Mr. Tessier. It would be so helpful if you were to try not to swear quite so freely."

"But it's so *hard*, Miss Brewer!"

Miss Brewer's face dimpled ever so slightly. "Did anyone ever say it was going to be easy?" She patted his hand. "I'll give you your cue: 'To take is not to give'."

Sometimes, having begun by drawing a student's attention to an error in accent or understanding, Miss Brewer would get carried away and act out whole scenes, playing all the parts, and causing her students to marvel as she let fall her habitual mantle of diffidence and humility, and shed forty years in the space of a breath. Chas swore that her chalk-white cheeks had sprung roses the day she performed the balcony scene as both Romeo *and* Juliet. When they would gawp at her in amazement, she would raise the text aloft and sing out in her steel-velvet voice, "The text, ladies and gentlemen! It's all in the text."

DIRECTOR'S NOTES

Anything can be part of a *tableau vivant*. A whole story is in even the most commonplace objects, like a piece of luggage — be it the lone bag bought for a few bucks from an unlicensed street hustler; or part of a snappy set of four, custom-made by Louis Vuitton and ticketed non-stop to Rio; or the army surplus duffle, bought new from that neat place on Queen Street, with the owner's name stencilled on it in big black laundry-proof letters. Then there are the bags that are hastily packed: armfuls of stuff tossed into whatever's at hand — gym bags, garbage bags, plastic bags from the supermarket — anything to make a fast getaway.

Books are also telling; not the trashy thrillers you take on vacation, but the fine books that you pack when you're not coming back. Adam ran his finger along the spine of the maroon leather-bound copy of *The Concise Oxford Dictionary* Doreen had given him on the occasion of their mutual eighteenth birthday; *The Complete Works of Shakespeare*, another gift from Doreen the day he was accepted at NAADA; the already dog-eared *An Actor Prepares* Sean had given him just last

Christmas. There was an inscription, which Sean had instructed him to sing to the tune of "Loch Lomond":

You take the classical,
And I'll take the musical,
And I'll be on Broadway
    Afore ye . . .

Adam's hand trembled as it brushed the cover. He gentled the book alongside the others in a Carnation Milk carton, unaware of Sean in the doorway, his thin face white under the close-cropped blond curls.

"Where the fuck do you think you're going?"

Adam removed the last of his possessions from the brick and plankboard shelves. When he had assembled them eight months ago, Sean had said, "Not bad for a spoiled show-biz brat!" and he had felt like Frank Lloyd Wright. Adam gripped the tackle box that served as his makeup kit, counting on the heft of it to strengthen his resolve. He wished it was a magic box, so that it could open wide and swallow him whole. *Why couldn't Sean have finished rehearsal at the usual time?* thought Adam. He'd have been long gone.

"Marie's going to put me up for a while."

Sean brushed past him, his voice as taut as his body. "Do me a favour, will you? Stop talking like you're going somewhere. You're not going anywhere."

He yanked aside the plastic shower curtain that screened the sink and the hotplate. It had blue herons on it, standing in limpid pools among green rushes.

"And put your dumb stuff back." He reached for the kettle, mumbling under his breath, "So fuckin' melodramatic . . ."

Adam's eyes followed Sean as he performed the ritual of making tea — kettle, water, gas. Not a word was said, except for the voice that thundered inside Adam's head: *Go! Go!* Dammit, why couldn't he move?

Except for the water stirring in the kettle, there was a deafening silence. It held until the water boiled, held while Sean snatched the kettle from the hotplate and emptied it into the huge brown earthenware pot.

If Sean insisted on a battle of nerves, Adam would give in gracefully. "I was trying to make it easier," he said. The room seemed airless, it was difficult to breathe. "How come you're so early?"

Sean placed two heavy mugs on the tiny table and sat. "Tina's on the rag. She got cramps. We kept having to stop all over the place, so we decided to call it a day."

"Couldn't you have stayed away just one more hour? *Tried* to make this a little easier?"

Sean's veneer of calm finally cracked. "Why in hell should I?" Hurt and bitterness struck out like a fist. "So you can give in to this power trip your goddamn *guru* is on!? I can't believe you've fallen for his stupid party line! Homosexuality is not a psychological disease, no matter what the doctors say. *We are not sick, man!* If they can't accept this, then *they're* sick! Fuck 'em!" Sean had done jail time for having sex with men. His sisters wouldn't let him see his nieces and nephews, and his father had died without saying goodbye because he couldn't accept the idea of a son who was queer. He gripped Adam's shoulders with fingers hard as steel. "Who the fuck does he think he is?"

"Theo is my teacher, Sean." Adam wrenched himself from Sean's grip and breathed deep, determined not to raise his voice. The last thing in the world that he wanted was a shouting match with Sean. "He's a great teacher. If you ever sat in on one of his classes you'd see that. If he's got a theory about fag actors, can't you at least admit there might be something in it?"

Sean didn't much care for Adam's low-key approach to the scenario that was unfolding. It was lucky for Adam that, with his own things packed away, the flat was monastically bare. Sean was capable of throwing whatever came to hand. He grasped Adam's collar instead, and propelled him into a chair as if he were weightless.

"Theory about . . . ? You turd! Your precious Theo Thamesford's stealing you away from me, the fucking sexual fascist!" He thrust his face into Adam's, his breath hot with anger. "Who stays and who goes depends on who they screw? That's like fucking little Hitler with his fucking science of eugenics, you stupid little fucker! Hitler had no use for pansies either!" He turned from Adam in disgust. "Officially, that is. And, speaking about closet queers, what about your precious, fucking British theatre that you're so goddamned in love with? Guys've been poking guys there since there *was* a British theatre!"

An opening. "You've hit the nail on the head. North American audiences don't buy it. They don't want to think every man on the stage is really some limp-wristed queen."

Sean stared at Adam, unbelieving. Surely, his pain must be audible, smellable. This was the same Adam who had sobbed in his arms two months ago, when Doreen had called to tell him that the family dog had died. The lover who had covered him with kisses, who swore he had never been so happy.

"I'd rather be an honest old queen than some ersatz, hetero stud!"

Adam reached for the other man's hand. "Please, Sean. Don't. I love —"

"Like shit you love me." Sean's voice, low now, was even more menacing. "Get out of here. Get out, or I swear I'll vomit right in your pseudo-hetero face, and kick you right in your pseudo-hetero balls. I can't stand the sight of you." Sean's lower lip began to tremble. He looked away. He'd be damned if he would let Adam see that.

Adam wanted desperately to go. That had already been decided — hadn't it? — but his feet were leaden. Maybe he didn't want to go. He loved Sean and Sean loved him; how could he go?

"Choose," Theo had said. He wanted his students straight. "There's absolutely nothing wrong with faigele show biz," Theo had said, "but not in *this* school!"

Choose.

Willing himself to put one foot in front of the other, Adam left the flat, closing the door softly behind him. At the bottom of the stairs he heard it open. He feared to look back lest, like Lot's wife, he be turned to salt, but he looked anyway.

Sean was leaning over the balustrade.

"Don't think anyone else's ever gonna love you the way I did! And you'll never love them the way you loved me! I'm putting a curse on you and your precious Theo, Adam Willison. Think about *that* when you're trying to get it on with some cutesy dolly-bird, you stupid little asshole!"

♪

Marie wanted to rip her hair out by the roots. Only something as punishing as that could convey her anguish over what she had done. She had made love to Theo, realizing too late how it bonded her to him more than ever. And if the school was a somewhat better compensation than the Biblical mess of pottage, it still hurt to think that she had been passed over for Theo's determination to screw all the women he could, in order not to have any regrets when he lay on his deathbed.

She was in a sorry state when Adam arrived at her door, but his was sorrier still. He stood there in the doorway, surrounded by his things, utterly forlorn. Marie ached for him.

"Lamby pie, you come in here right this minute."

Adam had always cut a proud figure, his back always straight and his head held high. Tonight, he looked as if he were melting, as if he were hurting in the utterly complete way a child hurts, and needed the comfort of being rocked in someone's arms. Marie reached up and put her arms around his neck, but it was a difficult position to hold, with him so tall and her so small. She drew him down to the floor. Or was it he who led her there?

Heartbreak can mutate into desire, especially heartbreak times two. Marie kissed his forehead in a gesture intended to comfort the kisser as much as the kissed. Perhaps if they had adjourned immediately into the kitchen to drink hot chocolate, the impulse would have passed as quickly as it had arisen, but they never made it to the kitchen. The act of kissing, Marie discovered, increased the appetite for kissing. She moved from forehead to eyes, nose to lips, lips to chest, unfastening buttons as she went, and all the while Adam was undressing her. They never made it to the bedroom or even to the sofa; they just dropped to the floor in the hallway.

Marie couldn't remember being that vocal in her lovemaking before, and the sounds of love can be much like the sounds of pain. Marie hoped her next-door neighbour, Mrs. Clemente, wouldn't take it into her head that someone was knocking Marie around and call the police, or bring over her two swarthy sons to effect a rescue.

Marie tried for a day or so to be conscience-stricken about making love to Adam, but it just didn't take. They were too happy, splashing and playing in the tub like children, eating ice cream in bed, watching old movies in the wee small hours of the morning. And making love, of course, making lots and lots of wonderful love. She might have been Adam's first woman, but he knew an awful lot about a kind of love that she hadn't yet got round to, and he made it his task to instruct her. When all the humid joy of life had been drained from her, leaving her a dry and empty husk ready to be crushed or blown away by the wind, Adam had appeared at her door and replenished her.

INTERMISSION

The end of August 1963 brought NAADA safely to the end of its second year and the beginning of the annual two month break. It was a timetable designed to give its students a chance of gainful employment without having to compete with every other student in town. By the first week of September, everyone but Theo and Marie had slipped away. Mitch had begged Theo to go back to England with him, if only for a couple of weeks. "Burn yourself out and you'll be no good for anything. *Especially* the school!"

But Theo was not so much tired as he was restless. If Arabella were still alive, he wouldn't need urging to go back. He looked up at her likeness overlooking his desk, her strange ugly beauty compellingly captured.

You don't think I should leave the country now, anyway, do you? he asked her. Not a day passed that he didn't inquire at least once what she would do in his place, and she always gave good advice, although sometimes she was rather sibylline, her advice often requiring extensive interpretation. Unlike the clear request in her will that Theo scatter her ashes over the Atlantic half-way between Britain and

North America. "I never felt more free," she used to say, "than when crossing the ocean."

And now, she was free forever.

~

Marie found Theo in the theatre, pacing excitedly.

"Arabella was right, Marie!" said Theo. The old witch had done it again. Given him the answer to a question he hadn't even known he wanted to ask. He lifted Marie up and swung her around like a child.

Marie was very glad to see the change in Theo from that morning, when he had galumphed about the halls in a state of what could only be described as post-partum depression. Without the sweet camouflage of youth, the place was appalling, the paint coming away in strips, the springs of the sofa in the green room popping out all over the place. It was an incessant aggravation to Theo.

"It makes me want to spit," he had said to Marie. "And will you look at those fucking windows!"

He put Marie down, and continued.

"Her slogan was, 'Never be dependent on the buggers,'" he said, "and she was right."

Marie, who had expected to be greeted with scowls and laments, was somewhat disarmed by the suddenness of his transformation.

"A summer Shakespeare festival," said Theo. "*That's* the answer!"

"To what, love?"

"To where this first lot will work when they graduate next year!" He opened his arms wide. "Look at this place. For two years we've worked here in conditions just above squalor, but we're doing what we set out to do — producing a cadre of professional actors the like of which this country has never seen before. That gives me confidence." He took her hand and led her to the stage, where they both sat. "*You* know the kind of crap young actors have to wade through before they get a crack at the good stuff!"

"But Theo . . ." *Should I even say this?* she wondered. She had danced this dance with Theo often enough to know that he was one visionary who would prefer to do without the evocation of potential pitfalls. To envision disaster was to empower it.

"Isn't it a rather . . . *large* project so soon after getting the school up and running?" *And how*, she thought, *will you be able to do it without me? Yet, I must get away*, she thought. *I must!* That was what they should be talking about, but instead she said, "And what about the Shakespearean festival in Stratford?"

"What about it? This is a big country, Marie." He took a pack of cigarettes out of his shirt pocket and lit up. He actually twinkled at her. "We can do it."

Marie felt as if someone had just kicked the chair from beneath her. "Theo . . ."

Theo's brow clouded. "Yes?"

Marie turned away, unable to hold his gaze. He was too strong. She was too weak. "I need a sabbatical year, Theo. I'm . . . tired. I'd like to get away for a while. Maybe go see Mama and Lou."

"Get away?" said Theo, genuinely astounded. He grasped her shoulders. "Marie, listen to me. In five years we'll have the finest classical company in the country — no, the continent — full of actors we've trained right here at the school. You know I can't do it without you." His smile was dazzling. "What do you say?"

"Theo," she began, hoping that the right words would come. But they did not.

"You see," grinned Theo. "You can't resist a challenge; just like me. You'll see. We'll find a place. Somewhere beautiful, down by the water."

ൟ

How to start? thought Theo. Arabella had never been one to sit around and wait for something she wanted, though her first tactic was to get someone else to get it for her. People liked doing things for Arabella.

It was a hot Indian summer day. Theo walked to the window and opened it wide; he lit a cigarette. Across the street, Johnny Vatsis's young son Jimmy was taking off on his bike on a delivery. Johnny was sprinkling the stairs that led down to his coffee shop with water before sweeping. It helped keep the dust down. Johnny's wife and all five of their kids worked at the restaurant. Theo always felt more optimistic about the human race after tucking into a bowl of Helena's split pea soup or a plate of Johnny's moussaka. He ate there frequently after he and Marie had split, though she still dropped off the occasional care package.

Johnny looked up from his sweeping and spotted Theo at the window. He waved a beefy arm. "Mr. Theo! How are you?"

"Fine, Johnny. Where've *you* been?"

Johnny Vatsis beamed. "I go visit friend's dairy farm in the Caledon Hills."

"Splendid, Johnny. You know how to live."

"Why you no go vacation, Mr. Theo? You work hard. Like me!"

"I can't, Johnny. I'm not a rich man like you."

"You don't need money to go on the vacation! Drive in the country. Look at the nature."

"Ah, Johnny," shrugged Theo. "I've got no car."

Johnny shrugged back. "Then you rent one, Mr. Theo."

"Good advice, Johnny; maybe I will. Where d'you think I should go?"

Johnny gave the question serious consideration. He and Mr. Theo, it seemed, were doing more than just passing the time of day.

"Hmmm . . . Hard to say, Mr. Theo. There are many good places, but I always go my friend's farm." His handsome brow furrowed a moment, then smoothed. "I know," he said. "Why you no look at the map?"

"A map?"

"Yes, Mr. Theo, look at the map. It will tell you where to go."

A map. What a splendid idea!

"Yes, Johnny, I will. Thank you."

They left the building together, and once again Marie wanted to tell him her secret. She longed to be comforted by him, but she never knew how Theo might take news like this. If it made him recoil from her in horror, it would devastate her.

"Everything under control in the office?" asked Theo.

"Almost."

"Then it's off to the Louisiana bayous!"

Marie was to spend the autumn break at home in Baton Rouge, but there would be little time spent in even one bayou. Crackerjack gynecologist-obstetrician Dr. Sheila Cohen had gone on alert as soon as Marie mentioned that her periods, "usually spot on, if you'll pardon the pun," had become most erratic. Tests run at Toronto General had resulted in surgery being scheduled for two days into the break, by which time Theo would think her safe at home in Louisiana.

She had told no one, not even Adam. The fewer in on the secret, the more likely it would remain one.

SUBPLOT

Marie returned from Louisiana in the middle of October, two weeks before the beginning of the fall term. She was still tired from the flight, but after six weeks away the cupboard was bare and she was determined to get in some groceries. *Stupid too*, she thought. Why else would someone barely five feet tall, who tipped the scales at ninety-nine pounds soaking wet, carry home six bags of groceries just weeks after surgery? Instead of making a proper shopping list, she had run up and down the aisles, loading up her cart like some panicked hoarder. She had outdone herself in aisle three, overwhelmed by a sudden impulse to stock up on both rice and potatoes. Was it the bite in the mid-October air, a foretaste of winter's onslaught, that had prompted her primitive drive to lay in provisions? Not in her wildest childhood dreams had she thought she would wind up in this cold country, so far away from the scented cotillions of her youth.

It was a wonder she hadn't stocked up on everything in the market while she was at it. Perhaps there would be a freak blizzard, and she would be the only one with enough food in the larder to see the whole neighbourhood through. A metaphor for her life writ large in fruits, vegetables, and tins of tuna.

The market was on a busy stretch of Bloor Street near the university. There were always cabs, but she dismissed the idea of flagging one. Marie Constance Verity was not one to hail a taxi for a mere three blocks. *Might as well put a match to your cash, darlin'*.

The modesty of her NAADA salary ensured a frugal way of life that was second nature to her. The theatre was one of the few professions where mere survival is considered success. The ridiculous truth was that if theatre people were given the choice of working for free or not at all, the show would still go on. Marie was just one of the legions who toiled in the arts and thought themselves lucky to collect any salary at all.

How nice it would be, she thought, *to have someone help shoulder the load, however briefly*. Her sweet fling with Adam was over, but Marie had known all along it would be short-lived, as beautiful things often were. Anyway, real love doesn't leave; it just changes. Look at her and Theo. Maybe — for once in her life — she should take up with a civilian. One with a guaranteed-for-life job, perhaps, like a nice tenured professor. . . . But, no. No sugar daddy, pedagogical or otherwise, loomed on Marie's horizon, keen to sweeten her dotage. Surgery makes you think — perhaps it's the anaesthetic — and it was beginning to sink in that she might have to go it alone in this life. It was a hard thing to contemplate, though much of the time she gave such thoughts the Scarlett O'Hara treatment, vowing to think about them tomorrow.

Bent-legged and carrying a third of her weight in yellow plastic bags, Marie scuttled along Bloor and down Robert, parcelling the distance still to go into smaller and smaller increments. Her fingers aflame, she upped her pace a notch. The faster she got home, the faster she could drop these ridiculous bags. Just a little farther, Marie. Until that telephone pole . . . Yes. Now as far as the house with the gingerbread trim . . . That's it! Now, the one with the sagging veranda

. . . By the time her own porch hove into view she was at a many-small-steps-going-as-fast-as-she-could kind of run, stiff-torsoed so the bags wouldn't swing from side to side and cut even deeper.

Home! With a great groan of relief, Marie dropped the bags and arched her back. She ran an exploratory hand over her still tender belly. Were the stitches to rupture she would have to take time off work — maybe go back into hospital — and that would be difficult to arrange with Theo away so much. After two years her workload was the heaviest yet. The responsibility for the physical and emotional well-being of fifty-four gifted young people, most from out of town, did not sit lightly on Marie's shoulders.

She rummaged for the key in her battered kid handbag, crammed as usual with half-eaten Mars bars, used tissues, and other purse debris. A good thing Theo wasn't looking over her shoulder. He couldn't bear for her to be untidy. The damp autumn weather made the door swell and stick in the jamb. It took a forceful heave before it gave, and she was again reminded of her incision.

Marie's two Siamese cats, Troilus and Cressida, usually deigned to make an appearance when they heard her key in the lock, but their noses were still out of joint from her trip home to Baton Rouge. They felt betrayed, and the onus was on Marie to win them back. It mattered not a whit that they had been tenderly cared for by Adam and Michelle, who dropped by every day to feed and water the cats and the plants, and make sure that everything was secure. The two students had fallen in love with each other midsummer and were now inseparable.

Bent almost double, Marie dragged the bags, two at a time, over the threshold and into the hallway, waving en route at Mrs. Clemente.

"Good thing I'm so short, Mrs. Clemente. That way, I don't have so far to go when I bend over!"

Mrs. Clemente didn't reply, but the look that she gave Marie before going into her own house spoke volumes.

Panting with exertion, Marie dragged the last of the bags to the kitchen and hoisted them onto the counter. Restocking the pantry was not easy, as she had to clamber up on a stool to reach the upper shelves. Her body ached, but if she didn't put everything away now it would still be sitting there the next day, the chicken defrosted, the perishables sour and nasty.

Apples and bananas, orange juice and rice, cauliflower, cheddar cheese, icing sugar, boxes of pasta . . . What had possessed her to buy so much food? For a woman with no husband to feed, ravenous after a day's toil, or children to fill up with cookies and milk after school, it was senseless. There was a market three blocks away in any direction, yet she had toted home more stuff than she could consume in a month. It was obscene to stockpile food. It pointed to a lack of confidence in one's future, in one's God. Perhaps it covered a deeper truth. Now she would never have a family of her own to cook for. Her brain had absorbed the fact readily enough, but the rest of her had yet to follow suit, though the time for it was surely coming. There were more and more moments when she felt the grief rise within her and prayed to be alone when it finally spilled over.

When she was convalescing in her childhood home, her mother had told her of losing an infant boy to meningitis the year before Marie was born. "It was, by far, the hardest thing I'd ever had to endure," Mama had said.

How then to mourn for all one's unborn children? *Enough!* thought Marie. She'd think about that one tomorrow, too.

Once Troilus and Cressida were watered and fed, Marie kicked off her shoes and flopped full-length on the living room sofa, a brown plush forties model she had picked up for a song and a little southern charm at Kensington market. Her first intention had been to slipcover it, but the brown plush was good at not showing the dirt. Decorating wasn't quite as much fun with only herself to impress.

The doctor had cautioned her against any but the lightest house-work, but Marie was not the most fastidious of housekeepers at the best of times. She sometimes paid Michelle to come in and give the place a once over, but that option wasn't open unless she wanted word to leak out about how she had really spent her autumn vacation. Words like "cancer" and "hysterectomy" were irresistible to drama students.

She tucked an old pillow under her knees and ran her hand over her stomach and groin, still swollen and tender but with stitches intact, thank God. If there were complications, Theo would be bound to find out about the hysterectomy. The school break had been fortuitous; otherwise, he would have wormed the information out of her somehow, and got into a flap. He needed her at his beck and call, which could be twenty times a day or hardly at all. Theo discussed things with Mitch, too, but Mitch was for planning strategy. Only to Marie could he admit his doubts, exorcise his ghosts. She knew exactly what would follow should Theo discover her secret. His genuine concern, at first. He would bring her at least three cups of tea at staggered intervals, a great many for someone who generally brought her none at all; indeed, it was usually the other way around. Then he would ask her every ten minutes how she was feeling. This solicitous state would last a day or so, to be inevitably followed by a growing impatience with her for not healing more quickly, as if it were simply a matter of will. Theo didn't like the people in his life to be ill, both out of compassion and because it stole time and energy from his mission. She was to get better, immediately! Only when she was better could he stop feeling guilty for his impatience.

And what would "better" be in this instance? What was done was done. She had called him "long distance" from her hospital bed to maintain the illusion that she was in Louisiana, and thanked the Good Lord for giving her a month and a half to heal and grow strong in the care of Mama and Lou. There had been aid and comfort aplenty in Baton Rouge, and the patient was needy and willing. Clemmy and Sarah Mae, maiden aunts on Daddy's side, moved in to help Mama with the nursing, but it was Lou who bore the brunt.

At NAADA Marie was the nurturer, the willing ear, the compassionate eye. Her anticipation and fulfillment of everyone's needs had come to be expected, her desire to serve taken as a given. But back in the house of her mother — and her mother before her — Marie basked in the tenderness of those who had loved her longest and perhaps best, and enjoyed an idyllic convalescence between cool, lavender-scented sheets. Tall frosted glasses of mint-garnished iced tea arrived unbidden at her bedside on a silver tray. The voices of southern gentlewomen drifted in from the veranda, a sweet susurration.

She awoke in Toronto at midnight, stiff and chilled and acutely in need of the painkiller Dr. Cohen had prescribed "just in case." She had only herself to blame, she had been warned not to overdo! Troilus and Cressida had chosen to forgive her and were showing it by walking on her face, which is what had awakened her. They wanted to play and Marie, happy to be released from Coventry, indulged them, rubbing their silken abdomens and scratching behind their velvety ears.

Half-way upstairs to run a bath, Marie remembered the Stephane Grappelli album and went down again. It had been a gift from Adam, to play, he had said, whenever she was tired, lonely, or blue, and tonight she was all three. She switched on the turntable and the needle dropped — the perfect accompaniment to a long soak in a hot tub. She raised the volume as much as she dared, given the reality of Mrs. Clemente only a thin wall away, and headed back upstairs. She peeled off the blue sweater she had been wearing since seven that morning and stepped out of the short black skirt. As long as her wound was still dressed, Marie had been reluctant to look at her naked reflection in a full-length mirror. But the last bandage had come off this morning, shortly after her arrival, and the temptation to look was overpowering.

She looked, and was immediately sorry. Not because of the still livid scar — she had been massaging herself with Lou's special salve to speed the healing, and knew that if she applied it faithfully twice a day the scar would disappear as if it had never been. It was the indirect result of her ordeal that was so unappealing. Her muscles had lost their tone, her skin its lustre. Everything drooped a little more than she remembered. Too many cigarettes and not enough exercise, that's what Lou, Mama, and the aunts would say. They had been shocked that she would even think of smoking while convalescing, so she hadn't, but old habits had reasserted themselves quickly since her arrival that morning. *A smoke is such a treat when you're on your own. It gives intent and purpose, a shape, to the day.*

Had Theo noticed the changes in her — he whom, as a rule, nothing escaped? There had been little occasion for him to notice. He was so busy running back and forth to Arden on the shores of Lake Erie, the proposed site of the new Arden Shakespearean Festival. *What is he doing now?* she wondered. It was late, but he had gone to a big fundraiser for wealthy potential patrons, and those things tended to go on. A lot of his current work was done in black tie. At Marie's insistence he had bought a new tuxedo. The sentimental relic of his Oxford days still fit him, but it was battered and blistered by many an undergraduate bacchanal, and had turned brown and brittle with age. Mitch was with Theo, which meant tonight's do was important. Mitch had been heard to joke that Theo was exploiting Mitch's white hairs, which Theo admitted was true. "I have to convince them *someone* at the soon-to-be Arden Festival is mature enough to know what he's doing."

Marie lit a cigarette. She knew she was pulling some of Theo's load as well as her own. They all were — a dedicated staff who didn't need the boss looking over their shoulders. But how thin did Theo think he could slice himself? He was scheduled to direct the new second-year class in *Billy Liar* after Christmas, and the third year in *The Relapse* after Easter. And what about the first year and Lorca's *Blood Wedding*? And his off-the-cuff, end-of-week theatrical history chats? Where would he find time for all that if he was forever running off?

When the water was within an inch of the overflow Marie turned off the taps. Steam rose from the tub. She gave the bath-water the big-toe temperature test. Perfect!

Listening to good music while soaking in a tub is one of life's great pleasures. Not one of those mingy affairs in tacky apartments and cheap motels, sharp-angled and hostile, but a huge claw-legged enamelled cast-iron tub like Marie's, the back of which sloped at the most blissful angle.

She was just about to step in when she remembered the bottle Lou had pressed on her the day they said their goodbyes, a commonplace blue milk-of-magnesia bottle, stoppered with a cork and sealed with wax. Lou had made quite a thing about it, not letting up until Marie had promised to add thirteen drops of it to her bath water each day for a month. The pungent amber oil had been blended by priestess healers still doing their thing in the remote world of the bayous, using herbs, cobwebs, fungi, and Lord knows what else. Lou had placed the bottle in Marie's hands, cupping them in her bony fingers. "This'll help you heal, baby," were the words she had said, but her eyes said much more. "It'll help you recover from the loss of that which has been so cruelly wrenched from you," they said, "a bulwark against the sickness of the soul."

With an eyedropper, Marie released the thirteen magical drops into the steaming water and swished it about with her fingers. Holding fast to the tub's sides, she lowered herself in. After weeks of sponge baths to keep her bandage dry, it was bliss.

The music of Stephane Grappelli floated up from below. *One day,* thought Marie, *when the world is far more advanced than it is now, everyone will realize the true power of music: the beautiful, harmonious sounds that could heal, and the discords with the power to shake and destroy. One day, instead of going to medical doctors and psychiatrists and taking pills and potions, people will go to their music therapists to have their aura tuned.*

Her eyelids were drooping. Given the size of the tub, she could slip under and drown, like an unattended infant. A little movement perhaps? Her body swayed in the still steaming water. It was her dance partner, enveloping her, the slightest move of her hips moving her this way and that. Legs akimbo, she gently tapped her upper thighs with the flat of her hands, displacing the water around her. The human body being mostly water, the water within her responded to the water without in an invisible sensuous wave, as soft over her sex as the tremor of a breeze, a sonar as subtle and as potent as the one that allows one whale to call another across the seas. It was sex, with no movement but the breath and the mind, until the water began to cool and she had to run more hot from the faraway faucet.

DIVAS AND DYNASTIES:
THIRD YEAR

———

Unlike civilian kids, who eat their Fruit Loops and trip off to school, professional kids in a family act never get a break from Mum and Dad. It's an intense relationship that can drive you nuts, but it bestows strengths denied you if you're only one against the world. Adam continued to receive news of his mother via Doreen, as he knew she did of him. His new relationship with the fresh-as-flowers Michelle had empowered him, building on the strength and confidence he had acquired from the time he had spent with Marie. Perhaps this would be a good time to rethink his situation with Cleone.

The Willisons were coming to the O'Keefe Centre. Even if Doreen hadn't kept him abreast of their schedule, the Toronto papers had been full of their ads for weeks; a full quarter-page in the arts section of Saturday's *Globe and Mail*. He was looking forward to a reunion with Doreen, his dad, and the kids, but when his twin asked if she should try to set something up with "the Duchess" he had decided against it. Whatever was going to happen, he would let Cleone select the game and the turf. Then, if things didn't work out, the blame wouldn't rest solely with him. Life with Cleone, even in her more benevolent moods, was relentlessly political. The Willisons were scheduled to perform in Toronto on Thursday and Friday. By Thursday morning he still hadn't been contacted. Cleone was sticking to her guns. Should he have taken the initiative? Was it too late for him to get in touch with her? Would that be the right thing to do?

Noon found Adam in text class, failing miserably to concentrate, a dangerous state of affairs when it was Miss Brewer who was in charge of the class. Her antennae were everywhere. If anyone was less than one-hundred-percent present, in spirit as well as in body, she knew in a flash.

"Are we keeping you from something pressing, Mr. Willison?" Everyone in Miss Brewer's class was always formally addressed.

"Um . . . No. Sorry, Miss Brewer, I'm . . . a little distracted." He smiled to reassure her. "Family stuff."

Miss Brewer, an intensely shy and private person, was known to reach out with great kindness when there was need, and the school was already abuzz with the news that Adam's family was in town. She touched his upper arm with strong white fingers, letting them linger a moment, then picked up the text which had slipped to the floor in the course of his reverie and presented it to him with a slight bow. The blue-red lipsticked mouth twitched, a movement so brief and tiny only the initiate would know it for a smile. "Perhaps a little Orestes is in order."

The day passed in a haze of distraction for Adam.

The rehearsal for *She Stoops to Conquer* was the last class of the day, after which Adam was going to go home to shave, shower, and put on his nattiest suit. He would see the show, and worry about what to say backstage when he got there. Cleone was less likely to throw a fit when there were other people around, and there was bound to be a crowd.

Perhaps he should bring Michelle, a proven charmer of parents. He had watched her with Chas's old dears, and that barracuda father of Bobby's. Mr. Hayden had taken them all out for dinner, and Michelle had had the man eating out of her hand by the time the waiter at the steakhouse put the coleslaw on the table. On second thought, maybe bringing Michelle wasn't such a good idea. He knew exactly how his mother's mind worked, just as she did his; that's why they were always at each other. Overjoyed though his mother would be by any confirmation that he was straight, she would also be fiercely competitive with any love interest.

The rehearsal for *Stoops* didn't go well, which added chagrin to Adam's anxiety. He had prayed for the role of Tony Lumpkin, Goldsmith's loveable country hick. For someone like Adam the role was full of major challenges. To appear rural and gauche when you are, by nature, urbane and full of grace takes real skill. It was a role that required a good grasp of physical comedy and timing, things Adam had in abundance. A skilled actor could do a real star turn in the role if he kept his wits about him; a state of affairs which did not pertain to Adam's efforts that day.

The scene in which Jeanne — as Mrs. Hardcastle — and Adam — as Tony, her son — were performing had the two characters behaving totally at cross-purposes. While Mrs. Hardcastle seems extremely distressed that her jewellery has been stolen, her son Tony treats it as a great joke. There was an awkward pause as Jeanne waited for a laugh from Adam that never came, after which Adam looked at her blankly, as if it had been she who was in error.

"Are you going to laugh there or not, Adam?" asked Jeanne. "You're supposed to laugh twice here; once after you say 'is that all?' and then at the end. The second laugh's my cue, remember?"

The guilty party lifted his gaze from the floor and was about to apologize for an absolutely abject performance, when he heard the sound of clapping.

Guests frequently observed NAADA's classes, anyone from board members eager to see what was being done with their dollars to members of the press. If it was like working in a fishbowl at times, everyone was trained to ignore it. But the faces of his friends told Adam something further was afoot, and that it had to do directly with him.

He turned and watched them approach, awestruck at the cavalcade. Cleone in the lead, still portly, but gleaming like the Taj Mahal in a silver-grey shantung silk suit, aglitter with sapphires. In her wake walked Doreen and Spencer, with Marie bringing up the rear, looking anxious and guilty. When Mrs. Willison's personal assistant had called to arrange a visit to the school, Marie assumed there had already been a reconciliation. Her pleasure turned to trepidation when she learned on their arrival that the visit was to be a surprise.

Cleone was having just the best time. How wonderful it was to be gracious and forgiving when the place was such an obvious dump. What's more, her poor darling Adam was terrible! Surely, there couldn't be too much more of this before he was back where he belonged.

Adam stood there, slack-jawed. She had come to him; he couldn't believe it. The rest of the company was dazzled by Cleone, who was even more of a diva than Adam had led them to believe and was playing the part to the hilt.

"My son," she called out from halfway up the aisle, "aren't you going to come down from that stage and say hello to your mother?"

Adam leaped from the stage to embrace her. But once at her side, he felt shy, and kissed her on the check instead. There were introductions all round, and promises of comps for that night's show for anyone who requested them. One by one, the rest of the class drifted off, so the family could have some time on their own. The instant the door closed on the last of them, mother and son threw themselves into each other's arms. There were more hugs with his father and Doreen and the rest of the kids, and lots of laughing and crying.

Once the hullabaloo died down, Cleone didn't waste a second.

"But my darling son! What was all *that* about?"

"All what about, mother?" replied Adam, trying to bluff it out.

"Is that the *usual* level of performance at your beloved NAADA?" Cleone couldn't contain herself any longer. "You were *terrible!*"

"Mother . . ." Adam was at a loss for words. It was mortifying, but she was right; he had been terrible. But she had to realize there were extenuating circumstances. Knowing that she was in town, he hadn't been able to think about anything but her all day long. "I know you're not going to believe me, but you can't go by what you just saw."

"Oh, really? And what, pray, shall I go by, as you so gracefully put it."

The gauge on Doreen's Cleone-a-meter began to rise. She flashed her twin their signal for caution.

"Oh, no . . ." said Adam, "You're absolutely right, I was terrible! And if anyone else was terrible it was because of me as well. I was just so afraid that you'd leave town and I wouldn't have got to see you. I've been in a state all week."

Cleone had no choice but to believe his excuse for his miserable showing at rehearsal, though it had given her such an edge. She was also relieved. She wanted him home, but that any Willison should be that bad onstage was unacceptable.

"But why Toronto, my darling?" she asked. "Why not New York? The American Academy? Neighborhood Playhouse? Juilliard? Or you could study privately with Uta Hagen; I know someone who knows her. I'm sure she'd be thrilled to have you as a student!"

Adam was impressed. His mother, who had never before evinced the slightest interest in any kind of theatre that didn't feature music, had done her homework.

"You could have your own apartment. Come and go as you please." She looked at Spencer for confirmation, but he had dozed off in a corner.

Major concessions, thought Adam. But not enough to soften his resolve. For Cleone to come this close to his way of thinking was unprecedented, but she must be made to understand that what she proposed was impossible.

"I can't, Mother. I'd do anything to please you, and I think you know it. Anything but what you're asking." He sneaked a look at her, and was relieved to see she wasn't wearing her pre-Vesuvial demeanour. She was actually behaving very well, for her. "I got an enormous amount out of working with the family and I'm grateful, really. But I want to be a classical actor."

Cleone sniffed. "And there are no 'classical actors' in the United States of America?" Received at the White House by three different presidents, she was nothing if not a patriot.

"Of course, Mother, but . . ."

"But what, my darling son? Spit it out, for heaven's sake!" Her bosom was beginning to quiver.

It was Doreen, as usual, who saved the day. "I think what Adam's trying to say, Mother, is that the United States has made many contributions to the world stage . . ."

May God shower blessings on you, dearest twin! thought Adam. "Jerome Kern, Oscar Hammerstein . . ." he added, naming some of his mother's favourite composers.

"But, on the whole, Mummy," continued Doreen, "you can hardly say that the classics are an American forte. Not even Shakespeare. That's not what we're about."

Cleone was undaunted. "Why not London? The Royal Academy, or the London Academy of Music and Dramatic Art? You can't say they don't know their Shakespeare!"

"Of course they do, Mother," said Adam, "but I'm part of the new world, not the old. That's why a Canadian school's so perfect. It's so much like the States that sometimes I forget I've crossed the border. But there also are ties with England."

Cleone had never played favourites with her children, but in her secret heart there was a special place for Doreen and Adam. Aside from being first-born and twins, they had always been such interesting children! In truth, although she demanded obedience, she was appalled by docility. She herself had always been a scrapper, and she couldn't help but admire anyone who put up a good fight. Here was an argument that neither could win, but a truce had been sealed.

⁂

After combing the shores of Lake Erie, Theo had decided on Arden, Ontario, population 28,000. It had been one of the first towns he had visited, and he would have said "Yes" on the spot if he had thought that his committee would go for it. Some of his reasons had to do with marketing, but it was a pretty little town, and the name was the clincher. It even had a river with swans.

The gnashing of teeth could be heard in the other little towns up and down Lake Erie. People who attended theatre festivals needed food and lodging, so Arden's hotel and restaurant trades were sure to benefit. They bought books and music, T-shirts for grand-children, impulse buys they would never consider for a second at home in Winnipeg or Pittsburgh. The Arden City Council and Chamber of Commerce were ecstatic.

"It'll be good for everyone," Theo said, and it became the official slogan.

The Arden Shakespearean Festival
Good for Everyone!

NAADA's students were thrilled with the idea, though Theo knew they wouldn't be quite so thrilled when the roles were assigned. Their contracts would designate "as cast," which meant they would have no say in which roles they were assigned. Nor would the minor roles, in which they would most likely be cast, consist of much beyond saying "Yes, my lord," a lot for the boys, and curtseying when your betters came and went for the girls. And they would have the dubious satis-faction of being word-perfect in several hefty understudy roles they would likely never get to play. After three years of exultant Rosalinds, Hamlets, and Othellos, it was bound to be a let down, but Theo needed seasoned performers to open the festival, and the students were prepared to forgive, though it was hard to be so suddenly out of the spotlight.

COMPANY SOLIDARITY

There had been mighty changes amongst the NAADA fraternity in two and a half years. Michelle was now more likely to be seen with a volume of Yeats under her beautiful arm than the poetry book she had first brought from Winnipeg, full of homilies and doggerel verse. She still had that vulnerable quality which made people want to be protective of her, but there was also an emotional resilience. She had been a girl at the beginning of her relationship with Adam, and now she was a woman.

Milo was transformed. When Theo had cast him as Romeo back in first year, it was to draw out the lyrical side of his nature that usually got pushed aside in favour of physical business and bluff comedy. Now he knew that he could do both. Milo credited his progress to Miss Brewer, but the truth was that he had worked his butt off and it was paying dividends in confidence and skill.

Chas went home to work the ranch each Christmas, Easter, and autumn break with real pleasure, yet each time it was easier to leave. He had less of that "oh, shucks, ma'am" quality about him now, but he had not lost any of his sweet country-boy charm. In return, Chas, blessed by the good fairy, was loved by all.

As was Clara's mandelbroit. It was another of her son's favourites, and she and Saul came to visit bearing tins of the stuff; a half dozen for Chas and one for each of his instructors. They drew confidence from the very European demeanour of Professors Lantos and Brillante, and were suitably impressed by the British accents of Mitch Blakely and Theo. But their son's performance of a scene as Willy Loman in *Death of a Salesman* gave his work a reality they had been unable to picture. That a son of theirs could move people so! It was lucky that Clara had a packet of tissues in her purse so that she could pass her handkerchief to Saul.

Jeanne carried less flesh now, which made her high slanted cheek-bones more prominent, and her long, brown hair was drawn back into a sleek chignon; she looked like a flamenco dancer or a ballerina, a figure of growing strength and dignity. She rarely thought of home except for missing Colleen, who was forbidden to visit her, either at her digs or at the school. When she thought about family these days, she thought only of Colleen, Sister Anne, and the gang at school. They were her family now, though she was never entirely sure about Theo. "After two and a half years," she said to the Sister, "the jury is still out." Jeanne had been overjoyed to hear her friend's voice on the telephone. Sister Anne had spent the last year in Africa. Though she had sent Jeanne at least a letter a month, it wasn't the same as seeing each other daily, as they had at St. Mike's.

Bobby, another motherless chick, had also flourished, the school providing warmth and structure without too many of her own family's neurotic attachments. She was able to spend less and less of her energy trying to be loved for her performance, and more on the work for its own sake. It gratified Theo to see her make good on her original promise.

❦

It was early December, and soon the Christmas winds would scatter the company far and wide. They were chatting in the hallway after a voice class with Eleanor Brewer, where one of the texts they had addressed had been the banquet scene from The Scottish Play, and everyone was being very careful not to mention *Macbeth* by name, to quote from it, or in any other way to refer to it. That the play was bad luck was one of the most deeply rooted superstitions in the theatre world.

"Can you believe it? For one crazy minute I actually considered doing the you-know-what scene for my audition." Milo was referring to the soliloquy where Macbeth, on being told of the death of his lady, expresses his state of utter desolation.

"A good thing you didn't," said Adam. "I know a guy in New York who didn't get into the school for doing just that. He said Mitch gave him a look during the interview that could have frozen his testicles." Adam laughed. "I told the guy it's the price he paid for being an American. Lots of actors in the States have never heard of the curse."

To change the subject, they began to talk about Christmas.

"We *have* to have a party," cried Michelle. "It'd just be too cruel, otherwise."

Michelle hated the fact that this was her last year, but the three-year program couldn't end soon enough for some. They were fed up with taking classes, fed up with never having any money. In some cases, they were fed up with each other. If day-in, day-out proximity brought them close, it sometimes made them crazy.

"Just think," said Milo. "This is probably —"

"— the last time we'll ever celebrate Christmas together!" The others completed the sentence along with him.

A sort of liturgy had set in at the beginning of the school year, with "This is the last time we'll ever . . ." being its leitmotif and refrain. "This is the last time we'll ever welcome the new students together," gave way to, "This is the last Hallowe'en," and the last Thanksgiving, with a couple of last birthday celebrations thrown in for good measure. It became a running gag, with Milo most often the instigator, as well as the butt.

"Hey, Milo!" said Adam. They were having a fast coffee before changing into their warm-up clothes. "This is the last time we'll ever have coffee in the snackbar while Paul John ties his shoelace second table over, and you're wearing a green T-shirt!"

Occasionally, Milo would come back with some wise-ass riposte just to show he was in trim, but he was pleased to have his devotion acknowledged. He had been naked and needy when he arrived at NAADA, where he was given sanctuary, succour, and sustenance. The seed that was Milo, slightly stunted, had battered its way through hard stony soil to arrive here, and public thanksgiving embarrassed him not a whit.

✍

They were at Johnny's coffee shop discussing the party at the end of the day. With Michelle at the helm it didn't take long to figure out who was bringing what. Professional caterers were unknown in rural Manitoba — potluck country — and she could organize a picnic for a hundred without breaking a sweat. Mitch wandered in just in time to hear Milo say, "Hey! Why don't we invite Eleanor to the party?"

The idea was popular, but in the end they decided not to. Eleanor never accepted personal invitations, though a day or two after she declined, some lavish gift would arrive — expensive chocolates, or an enormous tin of imported biscuits — which her students knew she could ill afford.

Mitch held this little group in high regard, but they were still drama students and, almost by definition, self-absorbed little sods, inclined to believe that their study of a fascinating subject had somehow made them fascinating. Miss Brewer knew this. Perhaps that's why she stayed away.

As always, money was in short supply. Not for Bobby and Adam but, precisely because of their affluence, the others forbade them to do more than their share. The two made it a point to surpass the living standards of their friends only rarely, and to choose that moment with care — a good bottle of wine on someone's birthday; discreetly making sure there was enough tip on the table when they left a restaurant so that they would be welcome the next time; paying for a cab when it was pouring rain because they would be taking one anyway; and the implicit understanding that should anything dire ever befall, with the only recourse being to throw money at it, Bobby and Adam would be there. It was a fairly good method, but fraught with danger. A friend could be in need of a loan, but determining who will take money and under what circumstances was complex. Would it be insulting to offer? Should they wait to be asked? What if you misjudged, and mistook one kind of friend for another?

◈

Jeanne had taken to thinking and talking of her parents by their Christian names; it helped make their emotional distance more acceptable. Jeanne knew in her heart that Ethel and Tommy would really prefer her to mail them a cheque for the house money, but each week she pocketed her pride and dropped it off in person, afraid that if she didn't bring the money herself, she would never get to see Colleen.

The Donahue family fortunes had taken an upward turn, and they had moved from Seaton Street to St. Clair West, not far from a park. The house had three bedrooms, so Tommy Junior and Colleen could each have a room of their own, and the toilet had a ceramic tile floor. In the living room, an immense artificial white tree dripped with ornaments, cheek by jowl with a brand-new tufted turquoise three-piece and a brown tweed recliner. Jeanne had been happy to see it. Her parents had never shaken free of childhoods stained dark by the Depression. The seasonal arrival of the Eaton's catalogue might delight Ethel, a woman not swift to delight, but she was ever slow to make a purchase.

Tommy, heavier in the gut but still hard as a rock, had worked at the Keele Street stockyards for so long, they would have to think twice about getting rid of him. He was a big man with the union, so if anyone gave him a hard time he could give them some grief, though he still didn't have the clout to get his son a job there.

Whatever it was that got Tommy Junior off his butt and out of the poolhall, it had been given a kick in the right direction by the fear that one day his dad might succeed in getting him work, and Junior would spend the rest of his days under the watchful eye of his old man hosing down jumpy porkers bound for slaughter. After one false start clerking in a hardware store where he had been canned for having sticky fingers, and another training to do sheet metalwork, he had landed a job as a trucker with Allied Van Lines.

The perfect job for Tommy, thought Jeanne. *He can push furniture around, instead of people*.

Tommy Junior paid house money, too — much less than Jeanne, though he made considerably more. How much more she would never have known if he hadn't bragged to Colleen, eager to show his little sister how clever he was to make so much money, though he had never finished grade ten.

Jeanne denied herself many pleasures to come up with her portion. Except for the occasional hamburger at Johnny's, she rarely ate out, and seldom went for a beer. When the others ordered donuts and coffee from the snackbar, she stuck to a thermos she brought from home. If it weren't for the theatre tickets given to the school, she would never get to see a play, and a movie but rarely.

Jeanne breathed deeply, summoning up her courage. There seemed no gradual way of leading into the subject, and it might be an eternity before a sympathetic moment ever arose between herself and Ethel.

"Mom?"

Jeanne sipped her tea. She often came at teatime. Ethel couldn't refuse her own daughter a cup of tea, if she asked, even if Jeanne had to make it herself. In the end, she could usually prevail on her mother to join her. Conversation was easier over "the cup that cheers." Or so they say.

"Is it true that Tommy pays less into the house than I do?"

Ethel's cup rapped sharply against its saucer, and milky tea slopped onto the table. Her look held Jeanne personally responsible for the spill.

"And if it is? A man's gotta have somethin' in his pocket if he's ever gonna start lookin' around to get married!" she snapped. "Not like you girls, who get taken everywhere and never have to shell out a dime."

Could Ethel possibly be talking about her? Between classes and working at Sano, Jeanne had barely enough time to do laundry, go food shopping. Who was this fortunate creature escorted about in such style? Did her mother think she spent her time sipping cocktails and discussing Noel Coward? Not that Ethel would know who Noel Coward was, or approve of him if she did. Her mother's life had been no bed of roses. She must see how exhausting it was to do five full days of classes and still put in so much time at Sano! But, to her mother, she was alien corn. Always had been, always would be.

⁂

"The party won't be the same without Jeanne," said Michelle, "but I guess you can't turn down a Christmas invitation from a nun."

"*Ex*-nun," said Adam. "But I can understand why Jeanne feels she has to go. She's known this woman since she was a kid."

It was only a few short blocks from their place to the party venue at Chas and Milo's, but the large, foil-wrapped roasting pan Adam was carrying seemed to become heavier at every step. It was Johnny Vatsis's pan, and had been loaned on the proviso that Adam have it back first thing in the morning. "I make moussaka in that pan for twenty years," Johnny had said. "If it's not back first thing in the morning, there will be Adam's balls for the lunch tomorrow."

The cooking vessel in question was heaped with Michelle's sour cream and sweet potato purée with toasted marshmallow topping. To

Adam it sounded absolutely revolting, but when he and Michelle moved in together he had made a decision never to criticize anything she prepared, particularly when it was made according to an old family recipe. Whatever it took to preserve the precious calm they had achieved after months of turbulent adjustment, Adam was willing to do.

The next day, they would be off to New York.

When Michelle accepted Cleone's invitation to spend Christmas with the Willisons, Adam's first reaction had not been unalloyed joy. His mother was bound to be competitive. She would do her best to throw Michelle off-balance, and if she detected anything less than complete harmony between them, she would rip their relationship to shreds. Life as a couple didn't seem to get any easier, whatever the sexual perms and coms.

Jeanne had contributed two bottles of home-made wine to the feast, an annual gift from a colleague at Sano. When it had breathed to Adam's satisfaction, they poured it out and Milo made the toast.

"To Jeanne, our absent friend!"

"At least she's getting a taste of the high life," said Adam. He pursed his lips and put on a snooty accent. "The party's in Rosedale, dontcha know." Rosedale was one of Toronto's wealthiest neighbour-hoods, home to highly paid surgeons, university presidents, and investment bankers.

"When are we going to open our presents?" asked Bobby.

The past two Christmases they had done Secret Santa, a sensible face-saving device when there are lots of gifts to buy and cash is in short supply. But when Michelle had suggested that they do it again, Milo had balked. He wanted a free-for-all. "I know that means cash, so we make it a rule that no gift costs more than a couple of bucks."

There was quite a buzz as everyone contrived to make the most of their two dollars. There were points to be scored, with wit counting high on the list. Anything hand-done, particularly by the giver, scored well too.

Chas's childhood Monopoly set, a present all could enjoy, had been a great hit, as were Michelle's "handy-dandy" binders. Using contact paper in a heady array of Day-Glo colours, Michelle had decorated and personalized a standard three-ring binder for each of them. Jeanne's had a seahorse on its cover, Adam's an elephant. Inside each cover she had glued envelopes big enough for a small notepad and any script published by Samuel French. Adam intended to carry his scripts in binders by Cartier, but he made all the right appreciative sounds and Michelle seemed to buy it. The problem was that he would have to use the damn thing. He could arrange to "lose" some luggage during the New York trip, but he knew Michelle would just make him another one, even more eye-catching than this.

Milo scored high and came in under budget by giving everyone exactly the same gift, a carved wooden backscratcher from Chinatown, which cost a dollar twenty-nine. "So you can scratch my back, ladies and gentlemen . . ." he mock-leered, sketching Groucho in rough with his mobile brows, a finger under his nose to suggest the moustache, ". . . while I scratch yours." He had personalized each handle by burning the recipient's initials into the wood using some kind of craft that he'd learned at the "Y." Milo could still surprise.

The digs he and Chas shared was a small studio where living room became bedroom with the flip of a Murphy bed, though for the party it served as a couch. They were in close enough quarters that by this time someone should have noticed that Bobby had been gone far longer than it takes anyone to fetch a few bottles of wine, even with a trip to the loo thrown in for good measure. They were somewhat inured to Bobby in the role of drama queen, a blend of Alice in Wonderland and Gloria Swanson in *Sunset Boulevard*, and it would take something outsize to get their attention.

By the time she returned, everyone was glued to the Monopoly board. Adam, doling out the money he owed for landing on Milo's hotels, noticed Bobby's hands, hanging limp and empty on either side of her perfect thighs. "No vino, Bobs?"

Then he noticed it — The Look. Chas and Milo lifted their eyes from their struggle over Boardwalk and Park Place.

"Sonofabitch, Bobby!" said Milo. "What's wrong?"

She looked shell-shocked, or as if she'd been mugged.

"My father doesn't want me with him for Christmas."

◈

Jeanne checked her watch. It was already six-thirty and Sister . . . Oh, *why* did she keep calling her Sister Anne, when she had been Jacqueline Kingsmark — Jacquie — for weeks now!

Jacquie's party was called for seven and Jeanne still hadn't finished the filing. Then she had to freshen up and hope she could get a cab, which was not so easy during the holidays. She had two taxi-driving uncles who both feared and loved Christmas and New Year's, hating the drunks who threw up in their cabs, but making the best money they made all year.

Jeanne surveyed her clean but ordinary workplace. Nothing much new in all the five years she had worked there; worked every holiday, every Saturday, every Tuesday and Thursday evening, though she had yearned to partake of the small pleasures that were so much a part of the drama student's life — to sit in bars and cafés discussing life, love, and the theatre.

Each year, the president of the NAADA Board held a big sugaring-off party at his farm near Barrie, but she had never been able to go because she was always working. She never mentioned her chagrin, not even to Jacquie. That she was at NAADA at all was a miracle. Which led her to what was really upsetting her: Theo and the ever-so-slightly patronizing evaluation session they had just had. How could he treat her like some little housewife-to-be! Why did he, who was supposed to be her principal guide, not believe in her?

Jeanne inserted two carbons into the last invoice, something she had done a thousand times, but her distress about Theo and her anxiety about being late made her clumsy, and she got carbon ink all over her hands. If she didn't go to the ladies' and wash it off immediately, she would get it all over everything.

After washing her hands with Sano soap from a Sano dispenser, Jeanne dried her hands at the Sano electrical dryer. She looked at herself in the mirror over the sink, reaffirming her entitlement to her own life. She believed in herself, but she needed Theo to believe, too. All young artists need believers. But Theo didn't think of her as an artist. She valued ideas at least as much as emotions, and she had the habit of asking questions at times when he preferred people to take things on faith. Furthermore, she didn't live *la vie bohème*. She had a job as a filing clerk; not so colourful as Milo and his floor-washing job, or Michelle, who served drinks in a hotel wrapped in a sarong, with plastic hibiscus flowers in her hair. Physical beauty combined with a certain playful seductiveness held a great attraction for Theo, as it did for many men, and Jeanne didn't conform to his ideal there, either. She was tall and big-boned instead of petite, serious instead of delightful. Those were not bad things to be. Why couldn't he accept her as she was, appreciate her for the gifts she *did* have, instead of relegating her to the second rank? To give him his due, he went through all the right motions. Jeanne had no doubt that Theo thought his behaviour to her was exactly what it would have been had he been truly engaged, and that she wasn't a bit the wiser.

dþ

For some reason, Jeanne had assumed the Kingsmarks would live in one of the more modest residences in the elite enclave of Rosedale, but the houses that the taxi was passing were becoming grander by the second. She had known since childhood that this was where the rich lived, because whenever she needed an extra dime or quarter for something at school, one of her parents would always be sure to say, "The kid thinks she lives in Rosedale." How Jeanne had envied the children of Rosedale. She was sure that when they had to chip in a dime for Reverend Mother's sixty-fifth, they would get the money without having to grovel.

The driver pulled into the curb and pointed up the slope. "That's it."

Jeanne checked the numbers against the address she had written on a piece of Sano letterhead, paid the driver, and stepped out into the cold, taking care that her coat didn't brush against the car. The snow was still falling, but on the roads it had already turned to muck, and the cars were splattered with it.

The sound of the taxi melted away in the frosty night air.

The Kingsmark house was set on a steep rise at the end of a cul-de-sac backing onto a ravine, a luminous grey stone and glass beauty that overlooked a many-terraced Japanese garden, presently covered in tiny blue lights. Jeanne had never spent much time pondering the whys and wherefores of wealth, apart from how handy it was in keeping you from stress and want. The rich might or might not be the bastards her father claimed, but she had begun to understand their role in the creation of beauty. There, under the star-studded December sky, haloed by her own breath, Jeanne experienced a moment of pure grace, the way she used to feel after confession when she was little, twice welcome after the disappointments of the past few days. That one could be moved to tears by a pile of brick and stone . . . Jeanne had little knowledge of architecture, but this house was a poem, and Jeanne understood poetry.

A man in a white jacket greeted her in the entrance foyer, empty except for a many-limbed bronze dancer on a granite pedestal. He took away her coat and boots, and gave her a numbered ticket in return.

The decorative idiom of the house was elegant and idiosyncratic — a museum-quality Quebec armoire, a Calder mobile, an art deco piece, a carved cinnabar Manchu wedding chair in a mirrored wall recess. Well-dressed bejewelled people milled about, and Jeanne was ashamed to find herself covetous, but not of their triple strands of heirloom South Sea pearls or the vacation house in Bermuda. It was the feeling of safe harbour they carried with them, a place where it was never a struggle to pay the milkman or the insurance premium, where there was time and energy for beauty and pleasure.

"Jeanne!"

It was the first time Jeanne had seen her friend without her habit. The Jacquie that moved toward her through the crush was resplendent in a burgundy velvet cocktail gown. Although Jacquie had cautioned Jeanne that she would be in "civilian dress," Jeanne had to look twice before she was sure it was her. The colour of the dress became her, and the skirt was cropped just short enough to permit the flash of a well-turned ankle. When she turned her head, a shock of coal-black hair swung at an angle against her cheek, showing small well-shaped ears.

Jeanne was somewhat in shock, so it was Jacquie who reached out and embraced her former pupil. They helped themselves to drinks and hors d'oeuvres from a couple of passing waiters, and tunnelled their way through the crowd to a perch on a window ledge. Only now, on seeing her friend again, did Jeanne realize how very much she had missed her.

Jacquie had been offered a teaching post in the public school system, but one of the things she had discovered during her six-month retreat was that she no longer wanted to teach. She had taken a job with a publishing house.

"The salary's ridiculous, of course," she laughed. "I'm surprised they haven't asked me to pay them." Jacquie popped a bacon-wrapped water chestnut into her mouth and munched it with gusto. "But the writers are wonderful, and I'm learning a lot."

It was only a trainee position, but the competition for it had been fierce. There had been applicants far more qualified than she, including a number with Doctors of Letters from illustrious universities after their names.

"No doubt, my being an ex-nun had something to do with my getting the job."

"Why do you think that?" asked Jeanne.

"Well, believe it or not," replied Jacquie, "there are people who find that sort of thing titillating, and I'm not above using it to my advantage." She neglected to mention that she was also a hard worker and a quick study. Whatever qualifications she might at first lack, she would make them up fast. "I think I may be a natural at this, Jeanne," she said. "In a way that I never quite was in the Church."

"You were too."

"No," Jacqueline shook her head. "I think, after all, that my instinct is for the beautiful, not the holy." She laughed. "I've just been getting them confused all my life."

The scent of cinnamon and Burberry mingled with the pungent smell of fresh-cut pine and burning sugar, as someone in the kitchen put the final touches to a croque en bouche. Staircases and mantels dripped with pine boughs, ribboned with blue and silver. In the largest sitting room, a fourteen-foot tree brushed the plaster-medallioned ceiling, garlanded with cranberries hand-strung by the grandchildren that morning and hung with heirloom ornaments.

There were pâtés and smoked salmon, and a great earthen casserole filled with plump oysters in a white wine and cream sauce perfumed with garlic. Dessert was tarte tatin with home-made vanilla ice cream, and there were presents for everyone.

One little girl was over the moon with her new Barbie, which made Jeanne think of Colleen. She was too old for one now, but Colleen had once yearned for a Barbie doll and was never quite able to hide her disappointment when it didn't materialize on Christmas Day. Jeanne had wanted to get her one the year she started at Sano, but when Ethel and Tommy found out how she planned to spend her Christmas bonus they had hit the roof.

"If we'd wanted her to have one, we'd 'a got it for her," said Tommy.

"Why wouldn't you want her to have one?" asked Jeanne.

"Too expensive, if it's any of your business!" Ethel piped in.

"But I have the money!" cried Jeanne, pulling Mr. Morrow's cheque out of her coat pocket, as if the showing of it would convince.

"Yeah," said Tommy, "buy her the damn doll and she'll be whinin' all year for the rest of the stuff!"

Jeanne had lost thread of the argument.

"The wigs and the hairdryers. Alla that crap!"

જી

"Isn't that the most beautiful Christmas wrap!" exclaimed Nana Louise. While Jeanne's mind had been drifting they arrived at her gift, which occasioned the presentation of theirs to her, a long-sleeved black leotard of excellent quality. Jacquie must have told them what to get. Jeanne had mentioned in her last-but-one letter that her old leotard was falling to bits, in spite of all her heroic efforts with needle and thread.

It's a tricky thing, buying a suitable present for a wealthy family, even when price is no object, which didn't pertain here. It had been Colleen who had saved the day. The girl had an irrepressible urge to draw and paint. The nuns claimed they were hard-pressed to keep her in paper, but were even more grateful that she had found something she liked better than bikers. The Riverdale Zoo was her current inspiration: bison and camels, lambs, peacocks and monkeys. If it skittered or flew, pecked, chattered, or slid, Colleen could draw it with precision and personality. Jeanne's gift to the Kingsmarks was a coloured pencil drawing of a petting zoo togged out as carollers. Mother pig wore a green sweater with customized teat-holes so the piglets could nurse. A trio of chipmunks wore toques with a red maple leaf on a white ground, and the racoon had a purple and white polka-dot beret and matching gloves. A buffalo with soulful eyes lifted a top hat. The look in their eyes suggested they might be singing one of the more reverent pieces in the Christmas canon, "Silent Night" perhaps.

One can never overestimate the effect of familial love on one who's never known it, the surprise that "tidings of comfort and joy" are more than just words in a Christmas hymn. Jeanne's eye roamed the candlelit room, noting the affectionate deference paid to Nana Louise, the ease with which the youngest children dozed off in whatever lap was available. For the second time that night, Jeanne's eyes pricked with tears.

When she began to make her farewells, the family pressed her to stay the night. The snow was falling even more heavily now, and cabs were bound to be in short supply. There was plenty of room, she must stay!

There wasn't much left of the night by the time Jacquie led Jeanne through to her private apartment, a granny flat built over the garage for Nana Rose who had died last year. To have both privacy and family close by was balm to Jacquie's still-quivering soul. "Bride of Christ" had not been a frivolous term to her, and becoming one had not been a frivolous act. She had given it her best, as women will do to preserve a failing marriage, and when the urge to leave became pressing she had spent months in silent retreat, praying that her sense of vocation be reborn.

"This is my — what do you call it? Oh, yes, my pad!"

When Jeanne first heard of Jacquie's new quarters, she had imagined a sort of finished-basement decor, dominated by castoffs from the rest of the house. And so it was. But the castoffs, in this case, were sterling. There was a generous dining/sitting room to the left of the entrance, and Jeanne was assured that the handsome blue sofa converted into a surprisingly comfortable bed. At the right, a spacious bedroom with sliding glass doors gave onto a terrace that received the morning sun. The pretty adjoining bathroom was done in teakwood and flowered porcelain, and smelt of eucalyptus and spruce.

Jacquie remembered the schoolgirl who had once told her how much she enjoyed a wood fire. She knelt on the Delft-tiled hearth and, when the newspaper and kindling were arranged, struck a match and passed it to Jeanne.

"Here," she said, "you do it."

Jeanne dropped to the hearth beside her, touched the match to one crumpled piece of newspaper and waited till it lit, then to another. She was on her way to a third when . . .

"Ouch!" Jeanne let the match drop and sucked her burnt fingers.

"Do you want to run your hand under cold water?"

Jeanne was embarrassed. "No, it's all right. Really."

Jacquie took the afflicted finger and blew on it. "Better?"

It was. The smarting was less, somehow. "That's one of the explanations for the old superstition about three on a match!"

After hot cocoa by the fire, Jacquie set about finding nightclothes for Jeanne. She went into her walk-in closet and emerged with a full-length garment bag.

"I bet this'll fit."

It was a granny gown of fine white linen, with a small touch of lace at the neck and wrists, and a wider band of it along the hem. Paired with its matching peignoir, it was an outfit for Merle Oberon as Catherine in *Wuthering Heights*. Jeanne had never seen anything so beautiful close up.

"It looks like it belongs in your trousseau."

Jacqueline nodded. "My godmother sent it for my sixteenth birthday."

"Jacquie, you're not suggesting that I sleep in this?"

"Of course I am."

"But, it's . . . it's intended for your wedding night!"

"Take a good look at it," Jacquie laughed. "It's size twelve. You could fit three of me in there. My godmother hasn't seen me since I was two. I don't think she knows what size I am. She just assumes I'm the same big strapping sort she is. I wish I were!"

Jeanne, looking as if she had stepped down from some Gainsborough portrait, emerged in her finery as Jacquie rummaged through a hall cupboard for linens. Jacquie's nightdress was white satin splashed with oversized poppies. She handed Jeanne a new toothbrush, still in its case.

"My, how elegant!" she said.

The outfit became Jeanne so well, she stopped being self-conscious, and began to realize that she was having a wonderful time. Sleepovers had not been allowed at the Donahues. They made up Jeanne's bed together, weaving in and out, up and down, in a timeless woman's dance as they smoothed the sheets over the mattress cover, stuffed pillows into the pillowslips. The dance segued into the bathroom. There was a pause as, with the solemnity of surgeons, they squeezed toothpaste onto their brushes. It resumed when they began to brush their teeth, their two heads bobbing up and down, sometimes in counterpoint, sometimes in unison.

Jacquie lifted her head from the sink into which she had just spit. "Like two hens pecking at the gravel."

They laughed then, and looked at each other, their mouths rimmed with pale green foam.

A signal passed between them, but they never would know who the sender had been and who had received. It was like a confluence of rivers, inevitable.

"No!" Jacquie ran from the bathroom.

Jeanne's face fell into rags. "Don't, Jacquie. Oh, *please* don't . . ." *It's all right*, she wanted to say. *It's always been all right.*

The bedroom door clicked shut and there was the sound of terrible weeping. Jeanne, who could do so effortlessly on cue when required, was too bereft even to weep. She lay, curled into a ball, on the bathroom tiles.

Time passed, how much she didn't know, but she finally slept and awoke feeling chilled, her muscles stiff from lying on the cold tile floor. She rose and stretched, heard early-morning bird sounds. Barefoot, she padded across the Persian rugs to the sitting room, where a few valiant embers still fought the good fight on the hearth. With the tentativeness of the beginner, Jeanne built up the fire, then crawled between the sheets.

When she awoke two hours later, Jacquie lay at her side, one slim arm draped across her hip. Jeanne turned to face her, which wakened Jacquie and, eyes wide, they looked at one another.

"My love . . ." said Jeanne.

Jacquie touched the back of one small hand to Jeanne's cheek. "Yes," she said.

SCENE CHANGE

If anyone had told Chas a week before that he would have Bobby Hayden in tow as the train pulled into Whistler Creek, he would have sworn they had had one eggnog too many. Not that it was unusual for the Almonds to have guests; Treetops was known for its hospitality. As long as there was a bunk available, Saul and Clara would put out the welcome mat no matter how short the notice. As for Les and Danny, they would stick close as flies to the honeypot as soon as they caught sight of Bobby. Chas's brothers may have graduated from magazine pinups to real live girls but, dime to a dollar, they would never have seen the likes of Bobby, all topaz eyes and titian hair and a figure like Sophia Loren — Bobby, whose shimmering fey quality clung to her like perfume.

Chas, who took his own good looks completely for granted, was discovering that there were many for whom beauty had an irresistible allure. It pulled people toward it with little or no effort, to the chagrin of many plainer folk who couldn't help but feel hard done by, though they would go to great lengths to deny it. What he found strangest of all was that many of the plain people assumed that the pretty people, given the option, would rather surround themselves with other pretty people, and so edit themselves out of the picture. All of NAADA had expected him and Bobby to pair up, and such was the power of peers that they had had something going back in first year. Chas hadn't been above enjoying the envious looks that came his way, but he knew they weren't a good match. He was a happy person by nature, with the confidence and good sense to know it, while Bobby all too often seemed determined to snatch defeat from the jaws of victory. He still cared for her as a friend, but his groin no longer tingled and sprang to attention when he caught sight of her.

Bobby wasn't a responsibility to take on lightly, but he had no choice. It would have been heartless to cut her adrift for two weeks while the rest of them dwelt in the bosom of family. One of the others at the party might have extended an invitation if Chas hadn't been so quick to leap in, but he hadn't been able to bear that stricken look on Bobby's face another second. What's more, his friends all knew how easily the Treetops sprawling ranch house could handle a last minute guest because he had said as much many times. Adam's place looked to be jammed to the rafters, and Milo's grandmother Roseanna still wasn't comfortable with speaking English. Left on her own, Bobby might have fallen into a depression even worse than her last one at the end of second year. How would Chas feel if she chose this Christmas to finally succeed in her sporadic attempts to do away with herself? Thanks to Marie and a lot of extracurricular acting that would have greatly impressed their teachers, they had managed to keep the last suicide attempt from Theo, but no one wanted to go through that again. To prove that art and neurosis were not necessarily co-dependent was high on Theo's list of life missions. "Any of you who thinks they can indulge in self-destructive behaviour without it affecting their work," he would say to every incoming group, "go right ahead. But there'll be hell to pay if I catch wind!"

One more go and they would kick her out for sure, no matter how beautiful, how gifted.

Chas pointed out Saul and Danny waiting on the platform, and warned Bobby to expect a noisy, busy time. It was one of those years when Chanukah dovetailed neatly with Christmas. The Fourniers — Will, Rosie, and the kids — would share their holiday bird with the Almonds, who would reciprocate with an afternoon of potato pancakes, applesauce and sour cream, and playing dreidel with the kids for hazelnuts and "gold" coins that turned out to be chocolate wrapped in gold foil.

Bobby was to have spent Christmas with her father at his villa in the Caymans, having Boca-Ratonned with her mother, Gillian, last year. It was an old pattern established by the courts during the custody battle her parents had fought over her when she was four: private schools during term time, and alternate doses of Mummy and Daddy at holidays. Sterling Hayden, however, had chosen this Christmas to make an honest woman of his latest companion, and they were honeymooning in St. Moritz, while Gillian was off in Caracas with her latest amour.

Her schoolmates knew that Bobby was rich and that was fine with them. Had they known just how much their unstable, kooky, loveable Bobby was worth, it might have destroyed their friendship, which is why she took care that they never found out. The fact that she subsidized their rent was a deep dark secret. It would be a pittance for her to assume all their financial obligations — the amounts involved would be no more than lunch money to her — but she had played out that scenario more than once and lived to regret it. The advice of Polonius to Hamlet, to "neither a borrower nor a lender be" was sound, "for loan oft loses both itself and friend." Bobby had pulled more than one person out of hock, only to have them cross the street to avoid her when they couldn't pay her back. Even that was better than the sycophancy money engendered in others. That's why she gave her money away in secret, why she chose to share the hardships of her friends.

Everything conspired to make the holidays Hallmark perfect. Treetops was at its most beautiful under a fresh dusting of snow, and there were many fine riding days, a treat for an accomplished horse-woman like Bobby. She had a calm, sure hand with animals and they responded in kind.

On the days when it blustered and roared, Chas and Bobby would lay in front of the big boulder fireplace on overstuffed leather couches, singing and playing the guitar. They sounded pretty good together, whipping up some pretty good harmonies — Pete Seeger stuff mostly, but also a little Ian and Sylvia, and Peter, Paul and Mary. Gradually, the big room would fill up with people drawn by the music. The Fournier kids would trail in hot on the heels of Saul and Will. Even shy Little Sophie would pop out of the kitchen between tasks, sometimes to request a particular favourite, sometimes to add something of her own to the mix. Little Sophie was of mixed blood, and knew lots of songs Bobby had never heard before, including some in Cree.

The tricky thing was getting people to understand that he and Bobby weren't romantically involved. Even Clara, usually far more subtle, kept darting little glances their way, checking that this was really the case, something Chas thought unnecessary after their heart-to-heart the day he arrived.

"I'm waiting for Les and Danny to marry and have kids," he had said jokingly. "That'll take the heat off me."

The truth was his brothers were better set up for it. They were assured of running a successful ranch that would guarantee them a good livelihood. That was more than he could count on for years as an actor, if ever.

Mrs. Yevshenko at the donut shop was particularly pressing. She had been doing her research since Chas first deserted his father's hon-est calling to become a "gypsy player," and was greatly relieved to find Chas still interested in women. Her judgement was that, though no one had the right to be quite so beautiful, the girl had the good sense to give herself no airs and graces. And though Mrs. Yevshenko hadn't the eye to assess the deceptively simple clothes Bobby wore so well, she knew her gold. *Yes*, she thought, *it would be nice for Saul and Clara for their Chas to marry a rich one.*

As for Clara, she couldn't have anyone under her roof without making them part of the family, particularly a young woman who could, in spite of Chas's protests, be the daughter she had never had.

Bobby sucked it up into her very marrow, the zenith of her happiness being the day Clara taught her how to make taiglach, an old country confection that was one of Chas's personal favourites. It was made by knotting a strip of dough around an almond and a raisin or two, then boiling it in honey until it was hard enough to pose a severe threat to the teeth — half cookie, half candy, and all jawbreaker. Chas returned home after a visit with Cully to find Bobby, aproned and heat-flushed, in the kitchen with his mother and one of the Sophies, sticky and dusted head to foot with flour. She would stay forever if she could, he was sure of it, even if it meant never setting foot on the stage again. Could the answer to Bobby's demons really be that simple? The wellspring of her theatrical ambitions was her need for family, a place to belong. If she had nothing more than that, her cup would still be full.

༄

Chas would only confess to being slightly tipsy when he made his final round of good-nights and Happy-New-Years, but the Legion's annual New Year's Barbecue Dinner and Dance was a draw for the whole township, and it seemed that everyone wanted to shake his hand and buy him a drink.

They had given Bobby the festive season of her life. Perhaps, he even dared to hope, she had a capacity for happiness after all — though not partnered with him. Of that he was crystal clear, no matter how much booze he had consumed. Her dance card had filled up quickly, and the sight of her, hair flowing, as she two-stepped with

Saul or do-si-doed in a square dance, was something few there would forget. All the eligible men had come flocking, like bees to nectar. And even some of the not so eligible.

Chas sat on the edge of his bunk and removed his string tie. Yup, there'd be lots of explaining going on in the townships area right about now. The poor critters couldn't be held entirely to blame. Bobby, at her best, was a lethal weapon, giving no quarter to the likes of matronly Mrs. Gronchev who worked part-time at the co-op, or even to the Kellys' pretty daughter Sally, home for the holidays from her job in Calgary with her new fiancé in tow. Sally had spent half the evening looking for her Rusty, the other half waiting for him to finish yet another dance with Bobby. Would that relationship survive the night? Bobby, high on warmth, wine, and well-wishers, had no idea of the havoc she had wrought. Can the moon be chastised for eclipsing the sun?

Chas dropped his jeans and kicked them into a corner; beneficent sleep beckoned like sweet water to a desert traveller. With an enormous yawn, he crawled into his boyhood bunk.

He was never quite sure how far into the night it was when its nature underwent a definite change. Instead of the roiling of his gastric juices trying to right the ravages of all that barbecue and beer, he experienced a delicious sensation of well-being. The sweaty smell of dancers allemanding left and right across his brain was replaced by an elusive perfume. Arpège — wasn't that what it was called? Bobby had a huge flagon of the stuff.

"Bobby!"

"Hush, you silly thing."

She straddled him, but somehow he managed to pull himself up on his elbows. Even in the dark he could see the ivory gleam of her body. She hadn't a stitch on. Chas was wide awake now. Had she had the presence of mind to wear a robe, or had she made her way through the halls like this? If anyone spotted her it would make a mockery of all his denials.

"Bobby, what're you playing at? You know you should —"

Even if he couldn't see it, he could sense the little moue she made with her mouth, a look few men could withstand; but he was made of sterner stuff!

Then, she was kissing him as he remembered her kissing him two years ago, and even through the haze in his brain, he knew it was because of the booze. Bobby had an amazing capacity for alcohol and she had not stinted that night any more than he had. He tried not kissing her back, which was difficult when she was holding her end up so effectively. He had to wait until she paused for breath before he could register his next protest. "For crying out loud, Bobby!" He tried to be stern and brotherly, but she had a way of stroking the inside of his thighs.

A jumble of thoughts thrashed about his bleary brain. He didn't want to hurt her feelings, but this was wrong. If he kicked her out of bed she would be humiliated. Ditto if he picked himself up and spent the night on the floor.

She hushed him with a fingertip. "All right." She dismounted and lay alongside him. "It's just that it's our last night at Treetops and I didn't want to be alone." Her head nestled into his neck. "I'll be good, I promise."

Chas was mollified. She was listening to reason. At the back of the blur that claimed to be his brain he knew that this was a good thing; but his brain wasn't the organ slated for victory tonight. He lay beside her, silently entreating sleep to come, but it was fruitless. However much the rest of him had turned to mush as a result of the night's activities, his penis was growing harder and harder. He turned to her with a groan and pulled her close. "You're insane."

"I know," said Bobby.

ENTRANCES AND EXITS

Christmas and New Year's in New York had surpassed everyone's hopes, with Cleone on her best behaviour. She had found herself quite drawn to Michelle's unspoiled charm. Michelle, cautioned over and over again that the lioness might suddenly strike out with a hefty cuff of the paw or a nip of her strong sharp teeth, had instead been adopted into the litter, and in fact ran the risk of being licked rather more than she cared to be. In return, the monarch had been given due time and attention. Michelle had a kind disposition, and a sixth sense for when to deliver a timely compliment. She could deflect Cleone's bad mood with a joke or some other bit of nonsense when no one in the family would have dared. The final seal of approval was to be asked into Cleone's boudoir for a look at her "modest little gem collection," which by this time comprised a number of substantial stones. Many a dignitary had slept between the Willison sheets and dined at the Willison table, but Cleone's little boxes and bags of diamonds, sapphires, emeralds, and rubies were only for those who frequented the inner sanctum.

Cleone's manners, where her family's privacy was concerned, had gone from appalling to exemplary. If the door to a bedroom was shut, she actually deigned to knock before entering, something her children had requested with little success from day one. Cleone had waited far too long for Adam to bring a girl home to do anything to jeopardize the situation. She allowed Michelle to choose from the menu when dining out, instead of saying, as she usually did, "I've been coming here for so many years, darlings. Why don't I just order a whole bunch of things and we can share?"

Cleone insisted that their plans needn't always include her, and actually seemed to mean it. "You're not obliged to do everything en famille, darlings. Get out on your own!"

That's fortunate, thought Adam. *The Maids*, which he, Doreen, and Michelle went to see in the Village, would not have been to Cleone's taste, which ran more to Franz Lehár than Jean Genet.

Michelle and Adam shared a bed in Toronto, but Cleone was having none of that under her roof — officially, at any rate. In practice, she gave her son a wink and a nudge. However, their rooms were at opposite ends of the floor with Cleone's in between, and the old hardwood floors creaked so dreadfully he and Michelle were far too self-conscious to go padding about on nocturnal visitations.

The truth — not that he'd acknowledge it to his lady love — was that Adam was enjoying the first privacy he had known since moving in with Michelle five months before. He could wake up in silence, and shave in a pristine bathroom, innocent of drying pantyhose and long blonde hairs in the sink. He would meet her at breakfast, both of them scrubbed, rested, and eager to meet New York.

It was fun showing New York to Michelle. She loved her own parents dearly, but for them a family holiday was more apt to be living cheap in some communal villa on a Greek island than taking in a Broadway show, or haunting the Village for signs of Ginsberg, Dylan, and Lenny Bruce. Adam took Michelle to all his favourite places: the dinosaur exhibit and dioramas at the Museum of Natural

History; the Egyptian Department at the Met. He even let himself be talked into the corniest of New York tourist attractions, a carriage ride through Central Park. He and Michelle flew about the town — the Museum of Modern Art, the Circle in the Square, the Statue of Liberty. Today, it had been shopping at Bloomingdale's, where Michelle had taken advantage of the post-Christmas sales. By the time they arrived home they were exhausted and looking forward to a quiet evening.

"Nonsense!" said Cleone. "You and Michelle can be as domestic as you like in dreary Toronto. Tonight, we're going skating!"

Adam lowered his pilsener glass. "Skating?" He used the most neutral of tones, hesitant to do anything to upset the status quo. He and Michelle had had a delightful holiday, thanks to Cleone, and they were grateful, given that she could just as easily have made their lives an absolute hell.

"Yes, my dearest son, skating." She relieved him of his glass and pulled him to his feet. "Michelle's just told me you haven't taken her to see the tree at Rockefeller Center."

Adam and Michelle had planned an early lunch there the next day before catching their flight to Toronto. Cleone's plan had arisen from her uncharacteristic bonhomie, rather than any complaint of Michelle's, but Adam discerned from her body language that Michelle thought it best to say yes. She was never one to give up a hard-won advantage.

JP

The sky over Rockefeller Center was a deep royal blue; the air was cold enough to tell you it was winter, but not cold enough to be an enemy. The place was packed with a holiday crowd enjoying the pleasures of the season, the hard-won liberation from routine and familiarity, the excitement of being in one of the world's great cities. Adam's first reward for complying with his mother's wishes was Michelle's face when she caught sight of the giant tree in the plaza.

The second was the sheer pleasure of gliding along a frozen surface over good ice, a feeling akin to flying. His younger siblings, who usually bickered constantly, were helping each other do figure eights, while Cleone seemed perfectly happy to sip dry Manhattans and wave encouragement from the restaurant. Spencer had chosen to remain at home, but Cleone was already deep in conversation with people at the next table who, from the awestruck look on their faces, obviously recognized her. This didn't happen nearly as often once the old series was part of television history, and Cleone's fans were getting on in years. Except for the odd vintage-TV buff, few young people had ever heard of *The Shaughnessy Family Minstrels*.

By the time Adam caught his second wind he wondered why he had been such a Grinch in the first place. The *hiss-swish* of skaters' steel caressed his ears. The music over the loudspeakers — "Tales from the Vienna Woods," "The Skaters' Waltz," and "The Blue Danube" — was the same as when he had come here as a child. There were a number of skilled skaters on the ice, even a dancing couple or two. But most of the skaters, like Michelle and himself, simply circled the rink, exhilarated by the exercise and fresh air.

There was something about someone just ahead that caught Adam's attention. It was the man's body English; a way that he moved that reminded him of . . . Sean! *Jesus Christ Sonofabitch! It is Sean*, thought Adam. He seemed unaware of the couple and skated expertly on ahead, passing quite close to them on his first go-round, unaware of the emotional havoc he was leaving in his wake. He even turned in their direction as he passed, and waved to someone in the restaurant.

Adam felt hot, then icy cold. He went weak at the knees and, though he wasn't exactly sure what a coronary was supposed to feel like, one minute it felt as if his heart would explode, the next that it would cease to beat entirely. He wondered if he looked as ill as he felt. Only sheer force of will enabled him to conceal his distress from Michelle. They continued their roundabout, with Adam trying to stay as far away from Sean as he could. Their life together had ended badly. What point was there in an encounter that was bound to be painful and awkward? And Sean could never be counted on not to make a scene. He had a quick temper that reared up like brushfire, exactly the kind of queer behaviour that Adam deplored. What would he tell Michelle if Sean spotted them? More importantly, what would Sean say to her? Michelle knew Adam had had a serious relationship with a male lover, in fact everyone knew. But that was all they knew; he had kept the details of his relationship with Sean to himself. His secrecy was fine with his buddies. It made it easier to pretend that there never had been such a relationship — to the point where Milo deliberately told fag jokes just to prove that everything was A-OK and that Adam was one of the boys.

Michelle's cheeks were fresh-air pink. "Don't you just love this?"

Again, the slim black-trousered figure in the turquoise windbreaker streaked up from behind. He passed Adam on the left and this time, in the space of a heartbeat, turned back and looked him full in the face. It was a wonder that Adam's legs didn't buckle. In a flash, Sean had left the ice. But not before — in another flicker of a second — he had inclined his head toward the restaurant.

Michelle, in love with the night, finally noticed Adam's pallor. "What's wrong, love?" Her pretty forehead was puckered in concern. "Aren't you feeling well?"

Adam had a ready explanation. Cleone had insisted they go to Luchow's for dinner — not, perhaps, the most sensible choice, given their after-dinner plans. He manufactured a smile.

"This'll teach me to go easy on the sauerbraten in future."

"Do you want to sit down, love?"

Adam felt a right bastard. To deceive someone who cared for you was bad enough, without causing her needless worry pretending to be ill. His mind was racing as fast as his heart. What should he do? If he didn't follow Sean into the restaurant, it would compound the bitterness of their parting, a bitterness he had never ceased to regret. If he did follow him, what could possibly ensue that wouldn't be painful, facile, or meaningless? And how could he connect with Sean while avoiding Cleone?

"I'll be fine. Why don't you join the kids while I visit the gents'?"

How easily the lies roll off my tongue, he thought. Small wonder actors were considered such shady characters for so much of their history. "It looks like they could use a little help with their figure eights."

Michelle allowed herself to be reassured, and Adam left the ice breathing thanks to Apollo, god of poetry and, by extension, the creative cover story. He slipped into the restaurant riding a wave of boisterous teenagers, verified that Cleone was still at the window enjoying her celebrity status, and moved swiftly to the back. There was a crush at the bar, and it took a bit of looking to locate Sean. The snug black turtleneck and slim black trousers accentuated his whippet body, and Adam could see that he was thinner — too thin, his muscles ropy, the way he always looked after a period of too much drinking and smoking. Sean was sitting beside an attractive older man with silver hair, who gave Adam one long appraising glance and slipped away.

Is there protocol for a situation like this? Adam wondered. Who speaks first, for instance? He had to fight an almost overwhelming urge to hug Sean, because Sean certainly looked as if he could use a hug. But the impulse shrivelled. Just because someone could use a hug didn't necessarily mean that they would welcome one. To simply offer his hand was out of the question. Whatever he did, there was always the possibility Sean might slug him; it wouldn't be the first time. Adam wouldn't blame him. In his place, he might do the same.

But Sean neither hugged him nor slugged him. He rose from his seat and walked to the cash register at the far end of the bar, passing Adam en route, as silent and unacknowledging as he had been on the rink. He waited for change, never once looking back. Adam was totally nonplussed. He watched, equally mute, as Sean returned to leave a tip, passing him once again. Cool and unhurried, Sean took his turquoise windbreaker from the back of the chair and put it on, again passing within inches of Adam.

By this time, Adam's fear and trepidation were on the wane, his ego and temper rising. The bastard! He responded in good faith to Sean's ridiculous cloak-and-dagger invitation, only to be rebuffed and humiliated! He scowled and jammed his fists into the pockets of his jacket, and his fingers touched the note Sean had deposited there during all that to-ing and fro-ing. Adam couldn't help but grin. Sean was a master choreographer of special effects for large industrial shows, where cars driven by nubile young women were suspended from the ceiling, and appeared and disappeared in a whiff of white smoke. At parties he would be called upon to do his parlour trick, pulling a linen tablecloth out from under a fully laid table without upsetting the cutlery or overturning a single glass of water. Producers paid extra for special business, and dancers — always at the bottom of the pay scale — could use all the extra money they could get. He was also good at sleight-of-hand and sometimes, after sex, had pulled a quarter out of Adam's ear.

The message was written on a piece of cardboard torn from one of the folded cards on the bar that pitched the virtues of the Skater's Cocktail, a bilious-sounding concoction of blue curaçao, lime juice, honey, sweet vermouth, and cream. It was, the card said, presented in a special gimlet glass with a coloured decal of the Rockefeller Plaza Christmas tree and a mini-sprig of plastic holly. Sean still used a green ballpoint pen.

87 Hissop Street, Apt. 6,
Queens.

There was no telephone number.

The fear of encountering Sean in a crowded public place was nothing to the thought of seeing him alone. Adam still didn't know if he wanted to see Sean at all, or whether he could spend even one second with Sean without consequences. Above all, Adam wanted no consequences. He had decided how he wanted to live his life since he had last seen Sean: no more secrets; no hidden corners; no stigma to fight, to be ever on the alert for, suffer from, jailed for, as Sean had once been; no fear of seeing his name in the newspaper, his family humiliated. There were whole days now where he didn't *once* ask himself whether he had done the right thing. His teachers all commented about how much more open, more accessible he was in class. At his pre-Christmas evaluation, Theo had been particularly effusive, even embraced him.

Tonight's encounter was sheer fluke. It wouldn't have happened at all if Cleone hadn't insisted on going to Rockefeller Center. Adam had made a happy life for himself, a life without Sean. To force further choices on him was unfair. *Right,* he thought, *when next I meet those responsible for meting out life's choices, I'll be sure to give them a thorough dressing down.*

Why not just pretend tonight never happened? If Adam didn't turn up at 87 Hissop, chances were he would never see Sean again. He felt the hard twist of his conscience. There had been true love between him and Sean, and yet Adam had found it in him to turn his back — Adam, not Sean.

Adam knew that if he didn't get back to the rink pronto Michelle was sure to come looking for him, concerned that he had taken a turn for the worse. He put a bright look on his face and headed back to the rink. Let him at least not compound his sins by ruining one of the nicest holidays the family had ever had. The rest of the party had had their fill of figure eights by this time and wanted to go home, which was fine with Adam. Only when everyone was asleep would he have time to decide what to do.

But once they were home, out came the songbooks, and in no time Cleone had them singing three-part harmony. Adam put his voice on automatic pilot, belting out the baritone for "Amazing Grace" while he pondered his next move and hoped his mother would soon tire. However, when the golden voice had had enough of an airing, Cleone hauled out the old Shaughnessy Family Minstrels scrapbooks, any-thing to prolong the evening. By this time tomorrow her precious Adam and darling Michelle would be gone.

Adam decided to take the initiative. "Think I'll say good-night all."

"Oh, *don't* go to bed, darling!" said Cleone. "I thought we could look at some of our old home movies."

Beneath its glass dome in the next room, the gilded eighteenth-century French mantel clock struck, a sound-effect from the wings.

"It's already one, Mummy," said Doreen, whose eyes had been shut-ting involuntarily for the last ten minutes, the Shaughnessy Minstrels scrapbook for 1952 falling from her lap. She, too, had no desire to break their mother's unprecedented good mood. Adam and Michelle would be gone in a day, and she would remain. If there were a price to pay for all this bonhomie, chances were she would be the one to pay it. "And Michelle and Adam have a big day tomorrow."

So mellow was Cleone, she allowed her expressed wishes to be countermanded, and packed them all off to bed as if it had been her idea in the first place. Michelle was crushed repeatedly to her consid-erable bosom and told that Cleone could "never repay the debt of gratitude" she owed her.

Adam couldn't envision his mother giving Sean that kind of accept-ance. With Sean she would have been snotty and cold, and not because he was queer. Innumerable chorus boys had been strewn in Cleone's path during her years in variety, and she had worked, gossiped, laughed, and cried with some of the limpest wrists and biggest queens in the business. But Sean didn't fit the mould. Sean didn't gossip, shed never a tear, and was foul-mouthed and tough. There would be no sharing of recipes and makeup tips with Sean. Ultimately though, it wouldn't have made any difference if he were the nicest Nelly in town. A biological imperative as strong as maternity or menopause drove Cleone these days. She wanted grandchildren, and, since the younger Willison children were too young, and Doreen seemed determined to turn away any man who had the temerity to approach, her only candidate was Adam. There was no place in Cleone's happy family scenario for Sean.

∽

It was two o'clock before Adam thought it safe to peek from his bedroom into the corridor. There was a hush that spoke of sleeping bodies behind the doors, but he would take no chances. He tiptoed from his room in his stocking-feet, shoes in one hand, while he closed his bedroom door as gently as he could with the other, feeling like some cartoon from *The New Yorker* in search of a caption. He passed his mother's room and was gratified to hear a light snore, though Cleone insisted that she never snored. There was no sound from Michelle's room, so he looked through the keyhole to make sure she had really gone to bed. She often stayed up reading long after Adam was asleep, working her way through the world's One Hundred Greatest Books; her current read was *Bleak House*, a Christmas gift from Doreen. Darkness. He pressed his ear to Doreen's door; all quiet there, too. The other kids were in an adjacent wing, and Pilar had her own quarters off the kitchen.

He would have been on his way with no one the wiser but, as he was tying his shoelaces in the dark front vestibule, he heard the squeak of hardwood floor. A stealthy white figure was approaching from the direction of the kitchen, brandishing a weapon that looked strangely like a meat tenderizer.

The two of them looked at each other, equally startled. "It's all right, Pilar," Adam said. "It's only me."

∽

Adam kept hoping the neighbourhood would take a turn for the better, but trust Sean to indulge his taste for the downbeat. Eighty-seven Hissop turned out to be a dilapidated apartment building in an area of mixed zoning, though by the look of the detritus in the adjacent lot and the smell in the air the industrial component was fast taking over. The street lamp only half-functioned and the whole neighbourhood was in an advanced state of decay.

That was another good reason for him and Sean to have parted company — Adam had been listing them as the taxi made its way over the 59th Street Bridge. Given Sean's taste for the underbelly of life, it would be easy for Adam to slip back into the dark side of his nature. Adam was attracted to those who lived life on the edge, who risked burning themselves out, people like Sean, and Theo, and Cleone. It was odd to think of them together, but it suddenly came to Adam how alike they all were. Not one of them would let you off the hook, not ever! *High drama is all very well*, thought Adam, *but what about a little comic relief?* That's why Michelle was so refreshing. So downright restful.

Adam found himself off the beaten track. If he chickened out, he would have to hoof it some to find a cab. But surely he wasn't going to back off because he was afraid of Sean? There had been true love between them.

Get a grip on yourself fella, he thought. If he was really going to press the door buzzer he had better be in control. The dimness of the stairwell couldn't mask the sad paint and the peeling walls, and with each floor Adam's trepidation grew.

Sean was waiting for him on the sixth floor landing. As mute as before, he ushered him into one of the apartments.

The pristine interior caught Adam totally by surprise. A bamboo light fixture with a rice paper shade cast graceful shadows on white walls and sweet-smelling tatami mats. The few windows were also covered in rice paper, rendering the wretched neighbourhood outside irrelevant. There were kendo masks and bamboo swords on the white walls, and black lacquer zeisu (legless Japanese chairs) on the floor. It could have been the home of a poet, or a philosopher, or a priest. Sean could have undergone many transformations during the past year; Adam certainly had. But this was a place of peace. The skater

Adam had seen earlier, the man who had slipped him the note in the bar, had hungers the person who lived in this place had long abjured.

A barefoot Sean indicated to Adam that he was expected to remove his shoes, so for the second time that night Adam found himself fussing with his footwear. He vowed to stick to boots in future. Sean lowered himself into one of the zeisu and gestured to Adam to follow suit. The straight backs of the chairs required an erect posture, which lent the scene a kind of ritual formality. Adam felt like a character in a Kurosawa film. He was no longer unnerved.

Sean finally spoke. "I suppose you're wondering why I called this meeting."

It took a few seconds for Adam to twig to the joke. And then the ice broke — into tiny . . . little . . . pieces.

⌘

"Is she a good fuck?"

"For God's sake, Sean!"

"No, it's a fair question! Is she a good fuck?" Sean's mellow post-coital mood had hotted up a bit.

"Yes! All things considered."

"Better than me? Given that you're a natural bottom . . ."

The conversation was making Adam uncomfortable. "Sean, we haven't seen each other for over a year. Have we nothing else to talk about?"

"No, tell me. Does she go down on you? Diddle you in the ass with her thumb?"

"Sean, Michelle's barely nineteen. She's . . ."

"She's what, Adam?"

They were lying on a futon spread on the tatami. Sean propped himself up on his elbow. "*What* is she? More to the point, what is she to *you*?" His eyes were daggers. "Do you love her more than you love me?"

This brought Adam up on his elbow. They faced one another.

"Because you do still love me. You *know* that," stated Sean.

"What about all that silent business?" asked Adam.

"What do you mean?"

"Not saying anything when you spotted me on the rink. When I followed you into the bar . . ."

"If I'd bumped into you on the ice and said, 'Why, hello, Adam!' what would you have done?"

"Said hello back."

"Isn't that nice. And introduced me to your lady love, no doubt. Of course, your face would've gone white, the way it always does when you're upset."

"My face doesn't —"

"And she'd have said, 'I'm really pleased to meet you. Really!' She'd have meant it, too." He turned away for a pull at his cigarette. "While all I'd wanna do is cut her heart out, the little bitch."

"Sean!"

Sean exhaled. "Don't worry. I'm not *that* nuts."

"Glad to hear it!" *Please God*, Adam thought, *don't let this conversation take any kind of weird turn*. Sean was putting Michelle in a grossly unfair light. Adam felt guilty even discussing her with Sean — guilty and disloyal. She deserved better.

"Anyway," said Sean, "we'd have said hello, done the intros, and that would've been the end of it."

"Not necessarily."

Sean laughed. "Oh? You'd have invited me home with you? You and Michelle and Mum and the kids? Cleone'd have a shit fit!" said Sean. "No way. We'd have exchanged all the appropriate platitudes and gone our separate ways."

He's probably right, thought Adam. In life, circumstance forces you into action with its own inexorable logic, just as it does in a play.

"What about the silent treatment in the bar? Slipping your address into my pocket?"

"You're here, aren't you?"

"Yes . . ."

"Do you think you'd have come if I'd invited you in the bar?"

"Sure. Why not?"

"Like shit, you would've. You'd have had *some* excuse: late night, leaving tomorrow, can't leave Michelle and the family. With everyone waiting, you wouldn't even have had time for a drink. Besides, I know you. A little drama, that's what you need to get you interested. Something that makes you feel you're being pulled along by the finger of fate."

All the while, Sean's hand had been snaking along Adam's thigh. The finger of fate and his four buddies reached over and clasped his dick, now in an advanced state of arousal, exerting a mounting pressure that made Adam think he would die of pleasure.

SUSPENSION OF DISBELIEF

A routine monthly staff meeting took an unexpected and pleasurable twist when Marie suggested they end with dinner at her place. Marie's reputation for Creole cooking was stellar and, after an intense and profitable session, the staff needed a chance to kick back, enjoy a Jack Daniels (Marie's favourite tipple), and, naturally, talk about their students. They would soon be letting their charges loose in the world, and no one knew better than their teachers what awaited them, and how the way was fraught with peril.

Mitch Blakely was sanguine. Everything would become clear as soon as the Arden Festival was up and running. "If Theo's report's to be trusted," he said, "we're just one big donor away." There was always a risk of cognitive dissonance when Theo wanted badly for things to be a certain way. Mitch made it a point to grill him thoroughly when he returned from his Ardening, as everyone had begun to call it.

"I see no reason not to do a short season under canvas next summer," said Theo. "It won't be fancy, but it'll help us lay claim to our territory."

"Well, aren't we the butch cowboy!" laughed Paul John, to the bewilderment of Madame Vavakova, NAADA's ballet mistress, who was still unfamiliar with colloquial English.

Mitch helped himself to another portion of Marie's excellent jambalaya. "If only there were enough companies to go round," he said, spearing a chunk of sausage. "In Britain, every provincial town of any size used to have its own resident company." With several productions in rotation, the average repertory season was full of roles of every description, each member playing several.

"There will be," said Theo, embarking on one of his favourite themes. "When I was out scouting locations, every little town I visited had a delightful theatre that hasn't seen a live performance since vaudeville. They're mostly used as movie houses now, but wait two years . . ."

Madame Vavakova, lost somewhere between Paris and Odessa, enquired what would happen then.

"Nineteen-sixty-seven, Canada's centennial, will happen, Madame, when little theatre companies will spring up across the land like wildflowers in the Siberian summer."

There were no Muslims on hand to shout, "Inshallah!" but Madame Vavakova crossed herself Russian style, right to left, and Marie was moved to a heartfelt "Amen." Without trained actors it was impossible to have a professional theatre; without a professional theatre, there was no work for trained actors. Anyone with professional aspirations had to go to England or the States, a drain of national resources that would have raised a hue and cry in Parliament had the subject been wheat or hydro-electric power.

శ

As they drew near to the end of their third and final year, NAADA's students could do a straight makeup in their sleep, and were on to more challenging assignments.

"A large moustache and a bushy head of white hair goes a long way to convince someone you're Albert Einstein," said Mitch. "And the old limp and hump will always be shorthand for that villain, Richard III, though history tells us he actually had neither and was rather a good sort of chap."

"Then why do we always think of him that way?" Michelle asked.

"Bad PR, my dear, dreamed up by William Shakespeare, trying to curry favour with the new king."

Chas, who to Milo's chagrin sometimes despaired at his unfailing good looks, was determined to expand his range. He had chosen someone as dissimilar to himself as he could — Gandhi. Chas was much too tall and well-fleshed to be convincing, but he had made a huge effort. No matter how much Chas yearned to play character roles, Mitch knew that they would be a long time coming. For the foreseeable future, young Chas would be kept very busy doing romantic leads.

Milo, who was highly skilled at makeup, had also chosen the extreme path with Henry the Eighth, a man four times his bulk. *And where was the third musketeer?* Mitch wondered. This was the fourth day that Adam hadn't turned up for class. The official reason for his absence was the flu, but Mitch wasn't so sure. The boy's friends probably knew more but so far no one was talking, particularly Miss Michelle over there, primping as Marie Antoinette got up as Little Bo Peep. She had used to bubble over with the love of life, but not lately.

Of all the work done that day, there was a consensus that Jeanne's Queen Elizabeth was first among equals. There had been many plays about the Virgin Queen, and Jeanne was determined to play her in one of them, which spoke volumes about how she envisioned her future. She had been crushed when Theo hadn't cast her as Miranda in last year's *Tempest*, but no longer. You could almost hear the collective sigh of relief from Theo and the rest of the staff when Jeanne finally accepted the realities of the business from which she hoped to make her livelihood. For business it was, as well as art, and in it there were buyers and sellers. Pretty parts usually went to pretty girls and there was no shortage of them in the theatre. A "brunette" role rarely fetched as much as a "blonde" one, and Jeanne, whether she liked it or not, was a brunette. Her strong features and powerful voice would shine in somewhat craggier roles, women of strength and will determined to get their way, but who don't always get their man. The sooner she realized that, the less heartbreak would be her lot.

Before setting to work, Jeanne appraised herself in the mirror, and envisioned the task ahead: how to bring forth a hag with rotten teeth and pock-marked skin stretched tight over her bones, but a hag still in possession of all of her powers. Her first task was to pincurl her long hair, the idea being to secure the wig cap to the pincurls, and the wig to the wig cap. Fine arched eyebrows were in fashion at the Elizabethan court, so it was lucky for Jeanne that her own were neither too dark nor too heavy. She moistened a bar of soap and stroked at her brows until the hairs lay flat and smooth. Then she covered her face and neck with white greasepaint that approximated the makeup of Elizabeth's time, although the original had been a lethal combination of white chalk powder and lead. Her eyebrows had vanished as if they had never been.

A very high forehead was also part of the look, obliging many women of fashion to pluck their hairline, but nothing so drastic was required of Jeanne. The raised hairline was cunningly incorporated into the short red wig she would soon don. A flesh-coloured piece of mesh attached to the wig's hairline would cover her own thick brown hair, fastened to her forehead with spirit gum, an age-old recipe of gum arabic and ether. With the aid of a small mirror, she checked the effect from every angle, like a sculptor walking around a work in progress.

A Mitch Blakely dictum ran through her head: "Attention to detail, boys and girls! It gives the game away when an actress playing *sixty-five* comes onstage with a twenty-five-year-old's neck and hands."

It intrigued Jeanne that she must think of her own face in the abstract, as the Mask. It was, at the moment, devoid of any distinguishing characteristics other than eyeballs, nostrils, and teeth. It reminded her of the neutral white mask of the great Marceau, devoid of expression in its own right, but reflecting the emotions of all humankind. *Unless,* she thought, *the mask happens to be on my face.* Jeanne was hopeless as a mime. In spite of the efforts of Monsieur Gillette, disciple of the renowned Lecoq, she could master neither the battling-the-wind exercise, nor the skating one, nor the one where you move the imaginary pane of glass. Her failures were making her wretched until Mitch confided that he had never been much good at mime either.

"It's a special gift, love," he had said, mopping her eyes, "as separate from the art of acting as acting is from painting or playing the harp. Now, you wouldn't be miserable if you couldn't play the harp, would you?"

When it came to the facial mask, however, Jeanne felt a visceral connection from her brain to her fingertips that required nothing more from her than a willingness to dare. Her first step from neutral to specific was to lightly sketch in two brows that were fine, fair, and considerably higher than her own. For Jeanne, the brows were the feature that most characterized Elizabeth. If she got them right, they would be an anchor on which to hang the rest of her picture.

Mitch made the rounds of the class, stopping to help if need be. In Jeanne's case he just smiled and moved on.

Good, she thought. She had the master's approval. Now for the rest of it — the furrowed brow, the rotten teeth, the ancient, pockmarked skin. Her Elizabeth was the public one, as the Queen might have looked among her courtiers, watching a masque in the Great Hall, or receiving the Spanish ambassador. Jeanne powdered generously, then removed the excess with a squirrel-hair brush. She stepped back from the mirror, assessing. More rouge. The present amount could just possibly pass for natural. She wanted her Elizabeth to be seen decaying in full view, yet still clinging to the idea that paint might help her preserve a beauty she had never possessed to begin with.

It took Jeanne a full thirty seconds to realize that the sobs she heard were not part of some interior emotional landscape she had been constructing for her Queen. Across the room, Michelle, exquisite as Marie Antoinette in her shepherdess guise, was sobbing against Mitch's barrel chest, her shoulders heaving, a broken butterfly.

Jeanne shot Milo a questioning glance.

"Mitch asked why Adam hasn't been turning up for class," replied Milo.

"And?"

Across the room there was more shoulder-shaking, as well as some hiccups and gulps.

"Oh, Mi-itch . . ." More hiccups and gulps. "We've broken u-u-up!"

જ

At the next makeup class, Mitch pumped them for information about Adam. Whatever the problem was, they might be able to keep it quiet as long as Theo was out on the money trail, but there was bound to be a reckoning on his return. Theo, who made every allowance for physical illness, held the view that falling to pieces was as much a matter of discipline as pathology. Adam's friends were relieved to come clean. Adam's behaviour, they said, had gone from erratic to downright worrisome. When Milo had asked him why he and Michelle had split, all Adam would say was that it hadn't worked out. The answer didn't satisfy Milo.

"'I don't understand,' I said to him. 'Last fall, you said she was the best thing that ever happened to you!'

"'You don't have to understand,' he says to me. 'Leave me alone! Stop being such a pest!'"

There had been a coolness between them since that Milo would have been happy to bridge, if only Adam had been there to bridge to, but Adam wouldn't leave his apartment. By the simple act of refusing to come to school, or to the door, or to answer the phone, he had removed himself, drawing his ladder up after himself, leaving no trace.

"The first coupla times he wouldn't answer the phone," said Milo, "me and Jeanne ran over."

"But he wouldn't let us in," said Jeanne. "He'd only talk to us through the door."

Mitch was becoming more alarmed by the second. "What did he say?"

"He said he was okay," Jeanne replied. "That all he needed was some sleep."

"Yeah," added Milo. "And that if we'd only get the hell away from the door, maybe he could get some! I don't think he ever gets out of bed! Except to pee, maybe . . ." Milo paused. Even if it was for Adam's own good, it felt disloyal, talking about him like this.

Mitch sensed there was more. "And . . . ?"

"Well, at first, we tried heckling him a little. Y'know, trying to get him to open the door, if only to bawl us out. Nothin' . . ." He couldn't bring himself to tell Mitch how shocked they had been the one time Adam had opened the door. His usually immaculate white terry robe was dingy and soiled, and it was apparent that their fastidious Adam was no longer brushing his teeth.

"I'm going to get him."

Mitch had no need to ask whom. "Like that?"

Milo *did* look rather strange — "Bums" was the subject of today's class — an elderly derelict with the well-muscled body of a young man.

"It's only a couple of blocks." He grabbed his jacket. "If Adam's not in class when Theo gets back, he's gonna be screwed for Arden."

Commitments of financial support for the Arden Shakespearean Festival, while hardly an avalanche, had been solid enough to guarantee them a short season.

"In case you've forgotten," said Jeanne, "he won't let us in." She kept her voice down. Michelle had gone to the bathroom, but she could be back at any moment.

"I'll be less polite this time; I'll pound on his door. If that doesn't work, I'll call the police."

"And say what?"

"I'll say my friend's been exhibiting strange and uncharacteristic behaviour. That I'm concerned for his welfare."

This jolted them all, particularly Bobby, who had tried doing away with herself often enough to identify quite personally.

"Milo," said Bobby, "you don't really think . . ."

"Of course not, idiot!"

જી

The thin February sunshine gave little warmth, and Milo shivered in his black leather jacket. His red scarf, hand-knitted by Roseanna, could usually be counted on to keep his neck toasty warm, but he had tied it on like a bandanna to hide the prosthetically bald head. People still gave him a wide berth.

Adam had been a good friend to Milo. If Adam had not had his wits about him last November, Milo might have died. Milo had picked up some kind of terrible virus, and was so ill his friends had taken turns nursing him. He was wheezing so loudly that Michelle, who had the midnight-to-four watch, had panicked, and called Dr. Kramer. The school physician had prescribed a course of antibiotics but, when Adam turned up for his turn, there were no pills to be seen anywhere. He had asked Milo where they were, and Milo had had no reply. Adam knew it was because Milo hadn't the money to pay for them, and was too embarrassed to call on his friend, since Adam had already loaned him the money for last term's school fee. Without a moment's hesitation he had called Milo a prick and an idiot, found the prescription, and headed out to get it filled. "Don't *ever* pull a stunt like this again," he had said.

And now, thought Milo, *the tables have turned*. He walked the icy sidewalks as quickly as he dared. Roseanna, his grandmother, had taken a nasty spill two months ago on just this kind of ice. Each Montreal winter seemed to bring a slew of elderly casualties. Their brittle bones were slow to heal, and in their weakened condition they died of pneumonia. By the time he had got word from MeMere that nothing was broken, he had chewed his nails down to the quick.

Milo took the stairs up to Adam's flat two at a time. It had been something of a bluff when he said that he would call the police. But after banging on Adam's door for fifteen minutes and still not hearing a peep out of him, he had no choice but to make good on his threat. If he had been frightened for Adam before, now he was terrified. He used the phone at Mr. Clayman's convenience store. The old man watched Milo make the call. When Milo had hung up, he pushed a glass of water across the counter.

"Have a glass of water."

"No thanks."

"Give an old man a break," said Mr. Clayman. He pushed a stool in Milo's direction. "If you faint on my floor, I don't have the strength to pick you up. Better you should drink some water, than I should have to throw it on you."

Milo drained the glass.

If Adam, perhaps bored with seclusion, had decided to take a walk, or had gone out for groceries, he would pull Milo limb from limb for calling the cops. Ditto if he was lying in bed in his usual funk of smelly bedclothes and dirty linen. Anything beyond that didn't bear thinking.

♪

Crisis makes its own agenda, and Marie was far too upset to be discreet. Why did Theo have to be Ardening today, of all days? When she opened the door to Mitch's classroom and beckoned him into the hall, the entire class followed, everyone clamouring to know what had happened. All Marie would say was that Adam had been rushed to

Toronto Western Hospital. To tell them that Milo and the police had found her beloved Adam unconscious in the bathtub with his wrists slit was beyond her.

There was an immediate rush for coats, which Mitch nipped in the bud. They could serve no purpose at the hospital, surely they could see that. If anything more was required of him in his role as acting head of the school in Theo's absence, he couldn't think of it. The timing wasn't quite right for "the show must go on" speeches.

"Someone get some water!" Jeanne cried.

Michelle had fainted dead away on the floor of the makeup room.

The waiting room of Toronto Western's emergency ward was unusually tranquil. The only people there, aside from the staff and the NAADA contingent, were a taxidriver and his fare, a Portuguese tourist who had slipped on the ice getting out of the car and broken his leg. Or so he said, contradicting the cabbie, who was scared of a lawsuit.

The most frightening thing around was Milo, still bearing traces of the morning's makeup. He had made a half-hearted attempt to wipe it off, but the result was even more grotesque.

The place is quiet now, thought Chas. What must it be like at night? Or on weekends and holidays? He would bet it buzzed then. He could have used a little buzz right about then, if only to distract Milo. Perhaps it was his friend's French-Canadian blood, deemed to be more volatile, but Milo had a compulsion to act out his distress.

"For God's sake!" Chas snapped, turning Milo's head, and those of Mitch and Marie in the process. Chas had the sunniest disposition of anyone in the school. He had never been known to snap at anyone; he usually had endless patience with Milo. "We're as worried as you are, man, and your constant moaning doesn't help."

"Sorry, buddy." Milo's hands shook as he lit his cigarette. "Hospitals spook me. Something to do with being ditched in the maternity ward by my mom." For the amount of time it took to smoke one cigarette, he was quiet.

Marie was smoking too, lighting one cigarette off another. Mitch essayed a few meaningful coughs, but to no avail. She looked at the pale green walls, dotted here and there with cheerful paintings donated by the hospital's benefactors; knew them for the camouflage they were. These walls had looked on stab wounds and gunshots; women bashed to a bloody pulp by husbands and boyfriends; limbs mangled by automobiles, slashed by blades and by axes. They had witnessed bleeding, crying. She looked at Mitch. His usually smooth brow was furrowed with anxiety, but he was sitting quietly enough except for that worrying cough. Mitch had been decorated in the Second World War. He never wanted to talk about it, but she knew he had seen carnage up close.

The place didn't affect Chas the same way as it did the others. On the ranch, creatures were dying and being born round the clock. Disease, too, was a frequent visitor, as was accident. He had been pressed into service by the vet on numerous occasions, had helped soothe many a panicked creature while its bones were set, its wounds stitched. Waiting for news wouldn't be half such a torment if Milo would only get a grip.

Milo, however, could weep with the best. MeMere said that whenever he couldn't get his way as a baby, he would wrinkle his little face up and cry until he got what he wanted. After two and a half years at NAADA, encouraged to express emotion, what little reticence he might have had was gone forever. Once or twice, Marie tried to soothe him, and he had actually let her for thirty seconds or so, but then he would leap up and begin to pace again, berating himself.

"How could I be such a goddamned, unobservant prick?" He turned to Marie, who, had he but known, felt much the same. "S'cuse my language, Marie, but how could I let —"

"Milo," Marie reached out, trying to catch him mid-pace, "darlin'." But he was moving so fast that she missed him.

Mitch had left the number of the public telephone in the hospital waiting room with the school office, but when it rang, no one was eager to answer. There was every chance it could be Theo, and who-ever answered would have to deliver the news. The job fell to Marie.

"Marie! Where the hell are you?" He was calling from a pay phone at a highway rest stop outside London, Ontario. "I called the school to get you to set up a staff meeting tomorrow morning. What's this number they gave me to call?"

Marie explained the situation, trying to cushion the shock, though the circumstances gave her little leeway. "But the doctor says he's going to be fine, Theo."

After he hung up, Theo reamined at the pay phone, utterly horri-fied, even though a queue was forming behind him. He had sensed something incubating, but had been so damned busy he had allowed himself to believe it would resolve itself faster and better if he didn't make a big thing of it. It was cognitive dissonance, pure and simple, as Mitch always said.

Adam, whom Theo considered one of his greatest successes, had taken a razor to his wrists. Whatever it was that had tipped Adam over the edge, had he in any way been a party to it? He longed to declare himself innocent and be comforted, but the facts wouldn't permit it. He was guilty of casting Adam as Sebastian in *Suddenly Last Summer*, for instance — Tennessee Williams at his most homo-erotic, but a wonderful play, damn it! Marie had accused Theo of putting Adam's new-found heterosexuality to the test, and been quite cross with Theo because of it. Perhaps it was true, but Adam had come through with flying colours. Theo had to stick to his guns for the sake of the school. Every right-thinking person deplored the fact, but homosexuality was against the law. Not that he cared a pin for the law in the abstract, but you could be thrown in jail for having sex with men, as Oscar Wilde was. And what about poor old Gielgud? Arrested in a public lavatory mere days after being knighted by the Queen. It had happened to more than one colleague. And for what? The pleasure of . . . No, dammit! He wouldn't have it!

ॐ

The circle that Milo was pacing became smaller and smaller, so that he was practically turning on the spot. Chas grabbed him by the belt and plunked him down into the seat opposite his own. He put a plastic cup of hot coffee in Milo's hands. Maybe having to swallow would slow him down. He leaned towards his friend's hunched-over body. Their heads touched. Chas spoke softly, gently. "Will you stop beating up on yourself? It was *you* who went over there and called the police."

Milo let himself be a little comforted.

"C'mon, buddy," said Chas, "get a slug of that coffee inside you."

Adam had bunked in with Milo the first couple of weeks after his split with Michelle, and Milo had been glad to have him, pleased to be able to give back something for all of the kindness that Adam had shown him. Living with him hadn't been easy — that neatness thing, for one — but he loved the guy. Growing up with no one but MeMere — and a couple hundred French-Canadian aunts, uncles, and cousins — Milo had had no brothers until Chas and Adam.

When the doctor arrived, they all rose and stood in a row, like a mini Greek chorus. Marie thought she detected a wisp of a smile and took it as a good omen. "He's lost a lot of blood, but he's going to make it." The doctor turned to Milo, "Thanks to you."

IN THE WINGS

Easter Weekend in New York with Jacquie surpassed anything Jeanne could have imagined — the Easter service at St. Patrick's, the thousands upon thousands of people lining Fifth Avenue to watch the parade. Families strolled together in Central Park, the women in Easter bonnets, children clutching the sticky remnants of chocolate bunnies and Easter eggs. And to keep things from being too prim and proper, orchestra seats for *Oh! Calcutta!*, Broadway's first all-nude show. Two Catholic girls still, Jeanne and Jacquie knew they would most likely be shocked by the show — and they were — but they also acknowledged how witty and progressive it was.

It's good, thought Jeanne, *to be part of the big, wide world.*

But the very best thing was that she got to spend time with Jacquie in New York, with no one the wiser. Everyone at school assumed she was spending the holiday with her family, but Jeanne knew Ethel and Tommy couldn't care less whether they saw her at Easter or not, though they still labelled her an ingrate and a snob. She couldn't imagine how they would react if they ever found out about Jacquie. They would have been predictably condemning had Jeanne become pregnant and given birth to a child out of wedlock, but then such things were not unknown in their community. Her love affair with Jacquie, however, was totally outside their ken. That two men should love one another "in that way" was unnatural enough; two women was unthinkable.

Jeanne's classmates knew Jacquie only as her friend and the guardian angel of her childhood. It was safer that way, though there were times when she thought she would burst with unexpressed feeling, hating herself for not having the courage to declare herself whatever the consequences. But for three glorious days, she could put all that aside. The sun was shining as two attractive young women — one tall, one small — made their way to the Russian Tea Room on Fifty-Seventh Street.

There had been times in the past when Jeanne and Jacquie had not seen one another for months, but the long weeks apart were harder to bear now that they were lovers. Many times — in the middle of warm-up, or working with Miss Brewer on Andromache's speech in *The Trojan Women* — Jeanne would be overcome with yearning. In the actual presence of her beloved, Jeanne's longings were more immediate. It was the urge to nuzzle the silken nape below Jacquie's short-cropped hair, the need to kiss her as deeply as the young red-haired man, two booths away, was kissing *his* lady love.

Better sense prevailed. Just because Jeanne had spent two and a half years rethinking all her knee-jerk reactions, it didn't mean that Jacquie was eager to turn her back on all her years of modesty and control. Such behaviour was not condoned in 1964, not even in blasé sophisticated New York City. Perhaps it was seen at the tea dances down in the Village, ogled by tourists there to watch the goings-on or to do something a little kinky themselves. But not she and Jacquie in the Russian Tea Room. Even in prejudice, there was bias. It comforted people to think that lesbians must be identifiably butch. Homosexual chorus boys they could understand, but homosexual chorus *girls*? Didn't they know it was also the blazer-wearing university student, the suburban housewife in her tweeds, the stunning blonde in the black strapless gown?

Jeanne squeezed her beloved's hand under the red tablecloth, shot her hot-eyed glances over the tea glasses in their ornate silver holders, willing herself to be content. Jacquie wiped her plate with the last of the mushroom blini. She chewed with relish, eyes closed, her eyelids gleaming like mother-of-pearl. She drained her glass. The pleasures of this world were all the sweeter for her years of abstinence.

"I wish I could stay another day," said Jeanne. "But Theo wants everyone at every rehearsal, even if we spend most of the time sitting around and watching."

"Why can't the stage manager just call you when you're needed?"

"I actually agree with Theo; it's important we're all there. It's as if we're weaving a . . ." She searched for the right words. ". . . a communal tapestry!"

Jacquie smiled. Communal tapestry, indeed. The similarities between the religious life and that of the theatre continued to amuse her.

Jacquie's first job on leaving the Church had been with the Canadian branch of Henslow Press, and it had been an easy jump to home office in New York. She credited "that nun thing again." Jacquie saw things with a practical eye that sometimes eluded her lover. If the two of them were ever to be together, she had best set about the task of earning a living, even if it meant leaving Jeanne behind in Toronto for the time being. Her girl would never consent to live off the Kingsmarks, and she herself had been too long dependent. Besides, what better place for an actress than New York?

"I think that having to commute to Arden so often is making Theo nuts," said Jeanne, "to say nothing of the rest of us. Half the time we wind up being directed by Mitch. It's hard to be consistent."

"Why doesn't he get you to do some of it? You're a natural director. I've always told you so."

There was no humour in Jeanne's laugh. "Theo's vision of the theatre doesn't include women directors!"

"Then change his vision."

"Jacquie, Theo doesn't care to have his way of doing things questioned. Haven't I been ever so politely slapped down for 'arguing with the director?' Not to mention him calling me 'pushy.'"

"'Pushy'?"

"According to Theo, I've got enough ideas for everybody in class."

"Sounds like a director to me."

"You know the scene in *A Midsummer Night's Dream* where Puck drops the potion in the sleeping Titania's eyes?" Jacquie nodded. "Well, you know that I'm playing Puck. For once, Theo thought it'd be a good idea to cast me against type, as if always playing characters twice my age was *my* choice. Anyway, I thought it'd be fun if we had a little Midsummer Night's gang warfare, Oberon's mob against Titania's. Titania's people are usually portrayed as being asleep, but I thought it'd be more fun if they were on the alert, standing guard over her. Even if most of the audience knows the story, why should it be a foregone conclusion that this mission for Oberon is going to be a pushover?"

"Why, indeed?"

"So *our* gang, the Puck–Oberon gang, has to put *their* gang out of commission, right? Of course, the way we do it has to be appropriately fairy-like. So I thought, why not with flowers? We've got these fake bower things all over the stage, dripping with plastic petunias and huge paper roses — why not use them? Bonk them over the head with the blossoms and tie them up with the stems; use the leaves as a gag."

"What's Theo's problem?"

"It's not the idea, he says. He rather likes the idea. It's the way I come on so strong. 'Now, love,' he says, 'Let someone else have a go.'"

"The English have this thing about putting themselves forward," said Jacquie. "At the time he was growing up, people were tucked into neat little boxes. Everyone knew exactly what was expected of them, afraid of overstepping the mark."

Jacquie knew that the subtle tug of war between Jeanne and Theo was ongoing; but whatever Jeanne's complaints, her love and awe of Theo were equally strong. It was the feeling of being hemmed in that she was reacting to, being treated like the crayon that was not allowed to go beyond the lines in a child's colouring book. Jacquie could relate very well.

"What about the rest of your buddies?" Jacquie meant the question to address Theo's relationship with the rest of the class, but Jeanne misunderstood.

"Well, Adam's back at school. He seems as right as rain, but who can tell?" She smiled. "He seems to have become very spiritual, all of a sudden."

"You told me he never went to church."

"He doesn't. He's gone off to some mountaintop in southern California to meditate."

Good for him, thought Jacquie.

"And he says that he's given up sex."

The lovers shared a lovers' smile.

"We'll see how long that will last," said Jacquie.

"And — omigod!"

"What is it? It's something serious, I can see it by your face."

"I can't believe I didn't tell you about Bobby!"

"Bobby? She's not ill?" The rest of the clientele at the Russian Tea Room were otherwise occupied with their own scandals and sweet nothings, but Jacquie leaned forward to make sure she wasn't overheard. "She didn't try to kill herself again?"

"She's pregnant."

Oh, dear, thought Jacquie.

"And Chas is the father."

Bobby's periods were always irregular, so she hadn't begun to worry until well into her second month, when her body began to change in unmistakable ways. Marie, who had been around the block a couple of times herself, had been the first to spot the signs, though it wouldn't be long before it was common knowledge. Life at NAADA was like living in a fishbowl, and the dance gear in which the students spent most of their day didn't afford much camouflage.

Marie had waited a few days for the news to surface, but the company had formed a little conspiracy of silence around their friend. It was all very well, but for the fact that Theo had to be told. That it had happened at *all* would aggravate him; that he had been kept in ignorance would inflame. And then, his board of directors would have to be told. It would be very bad if he were accused of running a home for unwed mothers, or of allowing sex to run rampant in the hallways.

It was a bit of a quandary for Theo, then, when Bobby made known her intention not to inform her parents about her pregnancy. She was over twenty-one and had a right to have her wishes respected, but what on earth was he to do with the girl? Thank God for Marie, who somehow had managed to talk Bobby around. When told, Gillian and ex-husband Sterling Hayden had carried on a bit about NAADA's "breach of trust," but neither was surprised. Bobby had been this route once before, it seemed.

Marie knew that Bobby had also had a second pregnancy, about which her parents knew nothing. There had been complications; and it was this second pregnancy that made Bobby determined to carry the third one to term. It might be her last chance to bear a child.

"Why *should* I have told my parents?" she had asked Marie. "The way they dealt with me the first time was to whisk me off to visit 'poor, sick Great Aunt Marjorie.' That's the story they used to take me out of school. Then they just dumped me at some private clinic and went about their business."

People might have been walking around naked on the New York stage in 1964, but single motherhood was still something to be avoided, not embraced. Those born out of wedlock carried the stigma to their dying day, and had nowhere near the natural rights of lawful children. Nonetheless, Bobby Hayden was enjoying her pregnancy. The titian hair shone and the topaz eyes glowed, set off by maternity clothes as unique to Bobby as everything else she wore. In winter, the softest silk velvets draped her ever-so-becoming little belly, both enhancing and softening. In summer, she went all gauzy, a sultry combination of the Madonna and Mary Magdalene.

Trust Bobby, thought Adam, who noticed such things, *to become not just pregnant but the very icon of pregnancy*. He adored babies himself, and couldn't wait for the birth. What's more, a pregnant Bobby helped take the heat off him. His attempt at suicide was already old news, and everyone was very good about normalizing the situation, even laughing when he had confided his intent to live a celibate life. Still, in the end, there was nothing like a hunk of fresh meat to relegate the old stuff to the back burner.

To her family's horror, Bobby was not so sure she was going to put her illegitimate child up for adoption. For the first time in her life, there would be someone she could call her very own, someone who would not leave her, not barter her, not be snatched away.

Chas, on the other hand, was in turmoil, trying to figure out where he fit into the scenario. He did his best in every way to be loving and helpful to Bobby, but they didn't live together. They weren't lovers. That Bobby should raise a child of his without his active participation was unthinkable, but that was what was likely to happen. They were actors. Perhaps Bobby would go back to Vancouver. Perhaps she would go to New York, or to London. Or *he* might. She would be the child's mother, with a much stronger claim, in the eyes of the law, than the fellow who had furnished the sperm. She had lots of money, and he didn't. Did that mean that he would have no say in how his own flesh and blood would be raised? And how could he bring any of this up? Bobby had asked him for nothing.

HOLD THE CURTAIN!

Milo's watch said twenty to seven, the same as the clock on the wall. Everyone else had managed to turn up on time, so where the hell was Chas? If they didn't begin warming up soon, everything could get backed up and they would be late starting the performance. This was hardly an option with so many VIPs in the audience. For three years, they had bitched about not being allowed to perform for the public and, now that they were about to, Chas had to give him a heart attack by being late.

Milo's brain began to get that crawly feeling he had learned to recognize. He knew he had the sight, but not tonight, please! Not tonight! All he wanted was that Chas walk through the door and they begin warming up. Ten minutes late or not, he would be forgiven. Just let him get there! But fifteen minutes turned into sixteen, seventeen. This was to be their last warm-up together as students, and everyone wanted it to be special. How could that be, without Chas?

"So, whaddya think?" Milo looked round at his colleagues, everyone barefoot and ready.

Jeanne and Michelle were hanging out the window, trying to catch the whiff of a breeze. The building sweltered in the thick summer air of late August.

"Bobby's name isn't ticked off on the call-board, either," said Michelle.

"She's coming in later," said Milo. "She was tired after taking Theo's in dress rehearsal." Enough chit-chat. "Look, should we wait for him or not?"

Jeanne knew that Milo hated the idea of starting without Chas; they all did. Maybe it was time she stepped in and removed some of the burden of responsibility from his shoulders. She looked up at the clock.

"Well . . . it *is* getting on for time, Milo. We've really got no choice. Why don't we start, and Chas can join in when he gets here?"

"Okay, then, everybody," said Milo, "Let's do it!" The routine was similar no matter who was leading, a matter of warming up all the muscle groups, of stretching and contracting. But even in this, some were better than others, and Milo was the acknowledged master.

They tried to put their hearts in it, and on a certain level they succeeded. One of the blessings of routine was that it *was* routine. The body could respond in its customary way no matter what conditions prevailed in the mind, and eventually even the mind was calmed.

"Clench your fists! Hard! Harder! The hardest you've ever clenched them in your life! Harder than that! Harder!"

Everyone clenched for all they were worth.

"Okay, now. Relax! Relax! Shake your hands out. Let them go limp. That's it!"

Everyone tried their best to focus on the exercises, but the truth was that each one of them was listening for the sound of Chas's cowboy boots in the hallway, the sound of him gasping for air after running up the stairs, his breathless apology: *Sorry, everyone!* But Chas didn't show.

"Maybe he's called to say he's been delayed," said Jeanne.

Milo shook his head.

"Someone would have told us."

Everyone was worried sick about Chas, but it was their asses on the line tonight, too. Everyone and their uncle in the Canadian theatre would be there, as well as even a couple of Brits and some Yankees. What if Chas didn't show?

Marie was fetched to the makeup room through hallways fast filling up with dignitaries, family, and friends. "Y'all just go on with your makeup. I'll call over to his place. I bet you he'll walk through the door the minute I pick up the phone."

"It's not as if we have understudies, for Christ's sake!" said Milo.

But Chas didn't walk in the door, and there was no answer at his place or at Bobby's, which led Marie to conclude that there might be a connection. The obvious thing was to call the maternity ward at Bobby's hospital, but they kept putting her on hold. When she finally got through, she was told that there had been a disastrous fire at some big senior citizens home, and that everyone at the hospital was far too busy to trace anyone at the moment, pregnant or not.

சு

The emergency ward at Toronto Western was as chaotic as it had been tranquil the last time Chas had been there with Marie, Mitch, and Milo, waiting to hear whether Adam was going to live. Chas and Bobby would have taken a taxi to another hospital, but the nurse at the desk told them that the situation was the same all over town — elderly people on gurneys coughing and spitting, some in pain, all frightened.

Bobby was already bleeding profusely when the ambulance arrived. It certainly looked as if the baby was coming, though it wasn't officially due for a month. Bobby gasped so that Chas quailed to hear her. Before his eyes her alabaster skin turned even paler.

"Squeeze my hand, Bobs. As hard as you like."

But the gasp was more than just an expression of Bobby's enormous pain. "Lear!" she groaned.

"What is it, Bobby? *Who's* here?" Chas looked around but saw no one he knew amidst the toothless jaws and wizened faces.

Bobby wasn't sure which was strongest, the monster contractions usurping her body or her exasperation with Chas for being so slow. "No! *Lear!* Tonight . . ." With enormous effort she managed to cock her head at the clock on the wall. It was quarter to eight. "You've missed . . . the warm-up call . . ."

"Oh, no!" Chas was aghast. "No!" He had to get to the school immediately, but how could he leave Bobby on her own? He also had to get through to the school and let them know he was on his way. How was he going to do that? Every pay phone in sight was tied up by anxious friends and relatives of the elderly fire victims. "I've got to find a phone!"

Bobby beckoned him closer. She was in such agony she could only manage a whisper. "Never mind the phone. Ohhhhh . . ." Another contraction, bigger than the last. "Go!"

☙

"*I'll* play Lear," said Theo.

Milo shot an uncertain look at Jeanne.

"Don't worry," said Theo, "I'll be holding the book." It was an extreme emergency measure, but not unprecedented. "Besides, I played the role at Oxford." This last was a complete fabrication, but it helped his students calm down. Besides, their only other option was to send their audience packing. "Lucky I know all the moves . . ."

And that he's a brilliant actor, thought Jeanne. Lord knows, they couldn't do better than Theo. Sometimes, the stage manager is called on to "hold the book" for a missing actor, but their stage manager, Imre, had a Hungarian accent so thick he was sometimes unintelligible.

"Should we give it a go?" asked Theo. Everyone solemnly nodded. "I'll slap on a bit of makeup, then."

☙

"Can't you go any faster?"

The hospital was only a mile or two from the school, but riding rather than running saved Chas a few precious moments, moments he needed to pull himself together, moments full of remorse for putting his friends in such a dreadful position. For months, everyone had bent over backwards to help him deal with this very delicate and complicated set of circumstances, but there were futures riding on tonight. He saw Bobby as she was in the waiting room at emergency, her face snow white, split asunder by pain. How could he possibly make it through a performance without making a total ass of himself, and possibly his colleagues? What must they be thinking of him? He cringed to think of it.

He checked his watch. Eight o'clock. Curtain time.

⁂

The VIP audience was restless. It was abysmally hot, and the theatre was overcrowded, and smelt of sweat. There were long lineups at the water fountain. The VIPs knew that they shouldn't expect the same punctiliousness at a school performance as they would from seasoned professionals, but they expected it, nonetheless.

Theo moved to the front of the house to address the audience, while the rest of the company took their places backstage. The stage was the same black-painted wood platform they always used, rearhung with thick black fabric that sucked up the little air there was.

"Ladies and gentlemen," Theo began, "I compliment you on your enormous patience under very trying circumstances. We tried to rent the air-conditioned O'Keefe Centre for tonight's performance, but they had already promised it to Mr. Ballanchine's New York City Ballet." The audience laughed, though the pros among them knew there was only one reason Theo would be wearing makeup. "Due to unforeseen circumstances, Chas Almond is unable to perform the role of Lear this evening. I'll be filling in for Mr. Almond, holding the book."

The few windows that did actually open were now closed to mute the sound of traffic; the dark green blinds drawn to dim the brightness of the long summer twilight. Slowly, the lights came up onstage.

"No! Please!"

Some clever person thought to switch on the house lights. There was a great creak of chairs as everyone turned around to look.

"Hold the curtain!"

The company, sweltering behind the platform, clutched one another in paroxysms of joy. Michelle jumped up and down. Milo kissed Adam.

Chas! Thank God; it was Chas!

Dripping with sweat from the heat and the tension, they poised for Imre's soft spoken "Places please," the theatre's way of calling its soldiers to arms. Each student aimed at a level of performance an audience would happily pay for on Broadway or in London's West End. For the next three and a half hours, the boys and girls of NAADA would gnash teeth, wail wails, and weep as if with cracking hearts — more or less in accord with what had been agreed on in rehearsal. Voices made round and resonant by three years of voice and diction would rail against the inexorable, either exemplifying or decrying man's inhumanity to man. Breast would press breast both in battle and bliss, and so strong is this strange thing called theatre that the curses and kisses would be no less hot for being mere simulation.

Milo, always high-energy, worried that his attention might wander if he got too relaxed. Even now, as they were about to begin, one of his sharp eyes was glued to a rent in the curtain. Sure, you might spot someone in the audience who made you uptight, but it sure pumped up the adrenaline.

"Chas!" he hissed. He beckoned his friend over. "Have a look. Middle of the second row — Cedric Peterson, Young Peoples' Players!"

"And look who's behind him," said Chas. He was at the end of his tether, worrying about Bobby, but this man was one of the most admired theatre directors on the continent. "John Hirsch from The Manitoba Theatre Centre!" Anyone who worked at the MTC in winter had to endure temperatures that went down to forty below, but none of that mattered if you got to work with its resident genius.

Chas and Milo executed the special ritual handshake they had concocted for *Waiting for Godot*. First, they linked knees and elbows, then did a silly little hop while they shook hands. The joke had worked well in production, but had long ceased being of interest to anyone but themselves.

Each had their own way, individual as a thumbprint, of dealing with stage fright. Milo tended to chatter, while Michelle paced Jeanne stood quite still with her eyes closed, looking much as she would in prayer, and perhaps, after all, there wasn't much difference. Adam wouldn't talk to anyone; he claimed it took the edge off. "Not," said his friends, "that you'd ever notice." If there was one thing Adam had even more of since his close call with the razor, it was edge, though he was doing his best to keep it under control with exercise and meditation. In this, however, they were as one. Not a soul wasn't praying the same fervent prayer: *Dear God, let me not be found wanting*.

At long last, the assembly, many of whom would have much preferred a cold beer and an early night, hunkered down to the first act of one of William Shakespeare's lengthier vehicles.

Chas berated himself for doubting God, if only for an instant. The terrible strains of the day that had so sapped his strength had also left him open and vulnerable, and he found himself swept along in the action with no seeming effort on his part. The gods of the theatre were carrying him on their wings. Lear's child, so Lear thought, had denied him, and he, in turn, now denied her. His child! How could any decent man deny his child?

Therefore be gone,
Without our grace, our love, our benison.

That done, everyone left the stage but Regan and Goneril, free at last to discuss their wicked plans for their misguided parent. Jeanne was playing Goneril, arguably the nastier of the two.

Carole, a second-year student, turned to her friend Deirdre. "Will you look at Jeanne . . ." Like the greenest branch, as yet unbowed, the first- and second-year students were hot to critique and prepared to be ruthless. "Talk about tearing emotions to rags and tatters! Has she never heard the player king's speech?"

There was a gentle "Sssshhh" from Paul John, sitting behind them. Even in admonition, his voice seemed to carry with it a gentle breeze from the Islands. Would it were actually so. Even the most loyal hearts were succumbing, as people slipped out for a smoke and a breath of fresh air.

Until finally . . .

Howl, howl, howl! O! you are men of stones:
Had I your tongues and eyes, I'd use them so
That heaven's vault should crack. She's gone for ever.

Chas's broken king held the lifeless body of Michelle's Cordelia in his arms. On some level he was thinking about Bobby, wondering whether the baby had been born, and if Bobby was okay. On another, he was on! He was flying.

Adam, as Edgar, addressed his colleagues; they all had just witnessed the tragic demise of Lear and the daughter who, indeed, did love him best.

The weight of this sad time we must obey,
Speak what we feel, not what we ought to say.
The oldest hath born most. We that are young
Shall never see so much, nor live so long.

The platform lights dimmed, and were extinguished.

The audience, roused from its heat-drugged stupor, rose from their chairs with a sound like thunder on the prairies, bravo-ing and applauding for all they were worth. They hooted and whistled for a good minute and a half; the ovation all the more prolonged because Theo wouldn't allow curtain calls. "Your fans can fall all over you just as well in the green room," he would say to each first-year class. "Bear in mind that most of your audience knows as little as you do, and occasionally even less." They always took him so bloody seriously, he would throw them a sop: "If you're desperate for praise, make sure it comes from a reliable source."

Chas didn't stick around for the praise and applause. The moment the lights went to black he leaped from the stage, stripping off his sodden clothes en route to the dressing room, Jeanne hot on his heels.

"Can I come with you, Chas?" Her hands had already begun to dismantle the coronet she had made of her hair.

Chas was zipping up his pants.

"Are you kidding? I'd be grateful!"

Milo, Adam, and Michelle were only a beat behind. "We're coming, too."

They had changed into their street clothes so quickly, it was sheer fluke that Marie caught them at the landing. "Did you phone for a cab?" she asked.

Chas's voice echoed from the stairwell. "It's probably faster to flag one on the street."

Marie rushed to the top of the marble railing. "Phone me!"

"Of course!" Michelle called back. "As soon as we know whether we're uncles and aunts of a little niece or a little nephew."

∾

Marie picked up the phone on the first ring.

"Yes, love!"

"Marie . . ."

It was Jeanne, but not sounding at all like herself. "What is it, love? You sound terrible!"

"It *is* terrible! Oh, Marie . . ."

Marie could hear the receiver change hands, and Jeanne in the background, sobbing. Adam got on the line. "Marie . . ."

Her darling Adam! *He* would tell her what was going on.

"Is everyone all right?" A shiver went through her. Everyone was obviously *not* all right. "Is it the baby?"

"No, Marie. It's . . ." There was a brief pause as Adam tried to choose the best words in an impossible situation. Marie could hear the sound of his breathing.

"Adam?"

"The baby's a month premature, but she's going to be fine."

"A little girl! And . . . ?"

She could hear the break in Adam's voice. "Bobby's dead, Marie."

"Dead?"

Milo, huddled close to the telephone, was near hysteria. The sounds coming out of his throat were half laughter, half sob. He snatched the phone away from Adam. "She started having convulsions, Marie. Then she went into a coma! They don't even know why it happened!"

He broke down completely, and Jeanne took the phone. Her voice was thick with tears, but she had more of a grip. "The baby was delivered by caesarean section, Marie."

Milo, somewhat recovered, reclaimed the phone. "It's something called eclampsia. Eclampsia! Can you believe it! Bobby dies, and it's from something that sounds like it came outta the fucking *Beverly Hillbillies*!"

Adam gently removed the receiver from Milo's hand. "Everybody's going nuts down here with all these old people from the home. Come, Marie. Please come."

"Where's Chas?" asked Marie.

Adam looked at Chas, lying prone on the floor. With all of the old folk there wasn't a seat or a bed to be had. "He's kind of in shock right now, Marie. But the doctor said he should be okay."

"I'll be right there." Marie hung up.

She wept all the way to the hospital.

"You okay, ma'am?" asked the taxi driver.

"Yes, thank you," Marie replied, lying through her teeth. She tried to stifle her grief so as not to further alarm the driver, but it wouldn't be stifled. *Every once in a while*, she thought, *we're reminded that we're but the pawns of the gods.*

Just the day before, NAADA had signed on a new director, someone who would work under Theo's direction while relieving him of the school's day-to-day operations. Then she and Theo would be off to Arden to work on a new enterprise; and in the spring, her darlings would join them for the first season of the Arden Shakespearean Festival. It had certainly looked as if everything was going according to plan. When she had first awakened that morning, she thought she had an epiphany, where everything in her life seemed to be in a state of balance. Now she saw that it had just been the powers-that-be telling her to enjoy every moment, because you never knew what was coming down the road.

She had wanted today to be the happiest day of their lives.

The Arden
Shakespearean Festival

1985

FLASHBACKS

"You do *not* have to do it!"

At seventy, Mitch Blakely had earned the right to speak his mind, but it didn't mean Theo had to like it.

Marie's voice was gentler. She knew that getting Theo mad could be counter-productive. "You haven't done it till now, love, and no one's ever complained."

"Why the change of heart?" asked Mitch. "What's wrong with *Much Ado*, *Henry V*, or *Timon of Athens*?"

"Mitch, it's our *twentieth anniversary*. We can no longer put off doing *Macbeth* because of some ancient taboo we drank in with our mother's milk!"

"Of course, you haven't been the *least* bit influenced by that article in *The Globe and Mail*!"

"The one that asked why Arden has never mounted a production of *Macbeth*?" said Theo. "Bloody right I was influenced, because they happen to be right!"

Much as he trusted them both, Theo wasn't prepared to tell them the real reason he had decided to do The Scottish Play this season.

There was still some fine tuning to be done in his negotiations with Zap Productions, and his lawyer had cautioned silence. If everything went as planned, the twentieth anniversary season of The Arden Shakespearean Festival, the festival that Theo had founded and nurtured from scratch, would be his last.

"I've committed it to memory: 'Is Theo Thamesford frightened of the play's bad luck reputation? Or could it be that he's no longer got the chops for the title role, but is too egotistical to cast someone else?'"

"Is that what all this is about? Proving to them that you're not afraid? Showing them that the great Theo Thamesford is still up to snuff?"

Marie decided to let Mitch solo on this one. The question was valid, but that didn't stop Theo from glaring. To Theo, being young was a state of mind, not mere biology.

"You're not a kid anymore, Theo, and the man's barely off the stage the whole play. The duels are almost back to back. It's practically a one-man show!"

"Yes, yes!" countered Theo. "And all of it crammed into the shortest play Shakespeare ever wrote. I *do* know my Shakespeare, Mitch!" The title role was also one of Shakespeare's greatest, third in the sequence of four: Romeo, Hamlet, Macbeth, and then Lear, three of which he had already played. Not to do it would leave a prominent gap in the jewels in his crown.

"Didn't you once tell me that you'd done the role years ago?" asked Marie.

"If your memory's as good as you *think* it is, Marie, you'll remember that it was a student production at Oxford."

Theo was in no mood to play host, so it was Mitch who reached for the bottle of scotch on top of the filing cabinet and poured out three glasses, taking care to give Marie only a splash. She had become rather too fond of the stuff, though, unlike Theo, Mitch had never confronted her with it. "Have you forgotten the Gielgud prodution?" he asked.

"Don't be ridiculous, Mitch. How could I?"

"And what happened to the English girls?" added Marie.

"Marie, what on *earth* are you talking about?"

"You remember. The two English girls who introduced us in New York. Kristy was playing Lady Macduff at the Circle in the Square. She was mugged in the Village on opening night."

Of course Theo remembered, but he didn't appreciate being reminded in front of Mitch.

Marie pressed on. "And don't you remember Jeanne falling off the stage during that high-school performance after graduation? She could have been seriously hurt. It was the same season what's-her-name was singing Lady Macbeth with the Canadian Opera Company, and she fell into the orchestra pit."

"I can't speak for your singer, Marie, but Jeanne was never exactly light on her feet."

"Let's get back to the Gielgud production, Theo," said Mitch. "That woman died in front of my eyes, in full witch's costume and makeup."

Theo sipped his scotch. There was nothing further to be gained this round.

"When did you say you'd be announcing the season to the press?" asked Mitch.

"Tomorrow morning."

"Will you give it one last think before you do?"

"Of *course* I will, Mitch! What do you take me for? Some idiot who digs in his heels and then refuses to budge even when he knows he should?"

Oh, my darling, thought Marie. There were times when he had done just that, and even she couldn't stop him — the previous season's commedia dell'arte *Romeo and Juliet*, for instance — but it would hardly do to bring that up now.

"Stop *hovering*, both of you. I'll think about it."

Left on his own, Theo poured himself another scotch and resumed his place on the sofa. Arabella's portrait looked down on him, imperious, magnificent, and utterly compelling in that ugly beautiful way of hers. The eyes seemed to have a way of addressing whatever was uppermost in his mind. "Aren't *you* in a fix?" was what they said now.

How smart she looked in her ancient well-cut garments, a cluster of hothouse violets pinned to her lapel. She had worn the same outfit at the barrister's office the day that her adoption of him was made legal. What on earth would have become of him if she hadn't taken it into her head to do such a thing? His dad had been home on leave with Mum and Gran when the bomb had fallen, and Theo had been left with no one else in all the world. Except her.

The two of them had had tea in the garden after the formalities, catching up on the news of the day. She passed him a copy of *The Times of London*.

"Read this and beware," she said.

He had scanned the page. "The story about Princess Elizabeth?"

"No, no! About the play! The Scottish Play!"

What Scottish Play? he had wondered. *Why is she being so mysterious?* Dame Arabella had always insisted on common sense and plain speaking.

"Say what you *mean*," she had exhorted the children. "Don't beat about the bush and waste everyone's time."

Theo scanned the page. Ah, here it was. Curse works old devilry.

"Is this the one?" he had asked. "'Curse works —'"

"Not *aloud*, for *heaven*'s sake!"

Arabella was frequently explosive but rarely querulous. What had got into her? He read on, silently:

The Macbeth curse claimed another victim this week with the death of Owen Nares, known in the theatre world as the first matinée idol. Although the vehicle in which Mr. Nares was touring was a light comedy, it was discovered that the stage flats used in the touring set had originally come from the ill-fated production of John Gielgud's *Macbeth*. During the course of that production, Beatrice Fielder Kaye, who had been cast in the role of the third witch, died of a heart attack in her hotel room. Mareus Barrow, who played Duncan, passed away in Edinburgh of angina pectoris; while the well-loved Annie Esmond, another of the witches, collapsed onstage and died during the witches' dance. The fifth victim was the esteemed designer, the late John Morton, who took his own life in his studio while surrounded by his pre-Raphaelite designs for the Macbeth sets and costumes . . .

There were several more columns telling a bloodstained story that hearkened back to the very first production mounted at the behest of King James I of Great Britain, first King of both England and Scotland, and offspring of the tragic Mary, Queen of Scots.

Theo, his eyes wide as saucers, lifted his head from the paper. "Is this true?"

The shrewd black eyes searched his over the top of a gold-rimmed china cup. "You're upset."

"I want to be an actor! How can I begin if I don't know what's true and what's false?"

His speech had improved enormously. Not from hours of boring drill, but by example and, the strongest motivation of all, the desire to achieve. Arabella had always thought there was something of the Jesuit in her — give her a boy before he was sixteen and he was hers forever.

"Ah," she had said. "Truth! *That* old bugaboo."

Theo had looked puzzled. Was she toying with him? If so, it wasn't like her.

"Pull your chair up beside mine."

He had done as she asked and she had patted his silken young hand. "Have you ever heard the phrase '. . . but thinking makes it so'?"

"Yes, I have."

Arabella wasn't surprised. He had been taking books out of the library at an enormous rate — novels, poetry, history, drama.

"Well, then, dear boy, you can see how that might apply to super-stitions. Curses. Taboos. That sort of thing."

"You mean that if you *believe* something will bring you bad luck, then it will. That you'll be *looking* for something bad to happen."

"A self-fulfilling prophecy, as they say."

"Do actors do that more than most?" asked Theo. "That's daft!"

Arabella had permitted herself a smile. If the boy was determined to enter the profession, it fell to her to see that he did so with eyes full open, aware of the pitfalls. Not that the young, convinced that the rules didn't apply to them, ever listened.

"It's rather more complicated. In *other* trades and professions, you see, if one prepares oneself properly, and performs even reasonably well, one can expect to continue in work for years."

"And actors can't?"

"Exactly. There are always a *great* many more actors than there are roles! If you're fortunate as well as talented, you might be asked to do a season somewhere in Leeds, or Manchester. Or to go on tour. If you're *really* lucky, you might get a role in the West End."

That's what he wanted to hear! "And then?"

"If your luck holds and you have a great success, you have money in your pockets and you're feted and famous."

"And if the show *isn't* a success?"

"Then you close in a week and it's back to square one."

The young face clouded.

"Bit of a horse race, isn't it?" said Arabella.

"When my dad was in the chips he'd bet on the dogs," said Theo. "He'd never leave the house without his brown tie with the pink polka dots. And Mum'd rub her rabbit's foot before she played the pools."

"They sound just like actors. Are you *sure* you're not from a theatrical family?"

His gran with her whiskey-dark voice? His dad slurring his words when he had had a pint too many?

"Oh no, ma'am. They were fishmon—" But by then he knew that she was teasing.

Arabella had rung the small bell that was kept in the garden, the handle of which was shaped like a little boy making water. There had been much tittering from the children the first time they saw it. When Arabella had borne the smirks and snickers as long as she could, she gave the tea table a sharp rap with her knuckles. "That's quite enough! All of you boys have exactly the same equipment, so we can dispense with the giggles."

This reaction had not been confined to the children. Some of the village ladies — infinitely more Victorian in outlook than Dame Arabella, who was of the era — had been known to blush at the sight of it on the rare occasion they were invited to tea.

"My dear," she had confided to Theo in later years, "they'd have been even more shocked if they'd known how I came by it in the first place."

♫

"Who's your Lady M.?" asked Mitch. Wild horses couldn't have got him to say the full name aloud. And why was there only coffee in their Styrofoam cups? It was the eve of Thanksgiving, and elsewhere in the building a holiday atmosphere prevailed.

Marie was not about to say anything in that regard. Theo had told her she had become "sloppy and careless," and that he blamed it on the booze! If that were the case, she thought, how could she carry the workload she did? Over and above her work in props, Marie had been called upon by every department in the building at one time or another. Her latest achievement had been to get all the costume and prop inventory onto the computer. Theo, never technically inclined, hadn't seen how to justify the cost until she had explained it to him in a manner he could understand. He had thanked her with his usual perfunctory "Good work, girl!" It wasn't much, but Marie was used to surviving on starvation rations where Theo was concerned. The wardrobe and props departments, on the other hand, had practically gone down on their knees to thank her.

"My Lady M.?" replied Theo. "I haven't decided."

"Which means that you've already asked Heather Schiller and Moira Gould," said Mitch, "and they've both turned you down."

Heather and Moira, actresses of the top rank, had been featured at Arden for years. Theo thought Moira one of the best of her generation, and only slightly less-ranked Heather one of the sexiest.

"Humph!" grumbled Theo. "You'd think they'd have some loyalty after all these years."

"Oh, come on, Theo," said Marie. "It's not every day you get a chance to be in a movie with Paul Newman." Moira's situation had particular resonance for her. "And Heather'll be set for life if that pilot's picked up."

"Marie, you've been exposed to too much Hollywood product. You're beginning to sound just like it."

"I don't see you holding a hit TV series against Chas!" Marie challenged. "He could have his pick of anything after *Two Brothers*, and he chose to come back to you. To play Macduff, of all things!"

"It's really Benedick in *Much Ado* that he's coming for, Marie. Macduff's just a bit of a warm-up." Theo laughed. "He's also going to understudy *me*."

"Fat lot of good that'll do him!" scoffed Mitch. "You've never missed a performance in your entire life."

"It'll be good for him," said Theo. "Help him get his theatrical bearings back. He's been working on the small screen far too long."

What am I saying? thought Theo. If everything worked out with Zap, as seemed likely, his situation would be the mirror image of Chas's. Whereas Chas was returning to the stage after years as a big TV star, Theo was about to star in a television series after spending most of his life on the stage. The role of William Shakespeare was unlikely to make Theo quite the household name that Chas was, but he would be doing television all the same, after a lifetime of looking down his nose at it.

At the moment it was all still hush-hush; the only one to whom he had said anything was his wife, Pam. Given that her family had been instrumental in raising the money to start The Arden Shakespearean Festival in the first place, he thought that he owed it to her.

"You still haven't told us what you intend to do about Lady M. Why not give Jeanne a call?" ventured Marie, albeit in a very small voice.

"What for?" snapped Theo.

"I always thought she'd make a very interesting Lady M., Theo, and *O'Keeffe!* has made her a big star." Whatever faith Theo lacked in Jeanne was more than made up by Marie. Even so, *O'Keeffe!* was beyond anything she could have imagined. Adam had flown Marie in for the New York opening, where it had happened in front of her very eyes. To see Jeanne garner such acclaim for a production of her own devising had made Marie tear up with pride. "Think how good it'd be for box office."

"More Hollywood thinking," said Theo, forgetting his decision to stop badmouthing Hollywood. He had been doing it for so long it had become automatic. It was too late, anyway. He had berated enough actors for deserting the theatre to be guaranteed a rough ride when he told the board of directors his decision in May.

This time next year would find Theo either in Hollywood or at England's Pinewood Studios, performing the starring role of William Shakespeare in a television series about the life and times of the Bard, recalled from his retirement in Stratford. People whose business it was to know about such things thought it could be every bit as popular as *Upstairs, Downstairs*. Twenty-six episodes that stood a good chance of being shown on every channel on the planet, ad infinitum.

He could have told the board about his plans immediately, giving them as much time as possible to find his replacement, but Theo wasn't in the mood to make things easy for the group that was of the mind, and had even "respectfully suggested," that he should confine himself to directorial duties this season. They felt that the twentieth anniversary celebrations would place the company under even more scrutiny than usual. If Chas Almond had miraculously agreed to return to Arden to play Benedick, why not offer him Macbeth as well?

To bloody hell with that! thought Theo. Arabella had continued to play leading roles with her company well into her sixties. One day, out on Hampstead Heath, as they watched the kites swoop and soar, he had asked her to list them, challenging her claim to remember each and every one. He was pushing her in an old wicker bath chair that usually served as a stand for the large rubber plant in his bathroom; they had left a very expensive, state-of-the-art wheel chair with all the bells and whistles back at his flat. The relic had a certain flair, Arabella had thought, that the modern contrivance could never match.

"Darling boy, I should be glad to oblige." The names had rolled off her tongue, a lengthy and stellar list, with only one glaring omission.

"And," Theo grinned, "did you never play the wife of the tartan tryout?"

"As in The Scottish Play?"

"Yes. Did you?"

"Ever play her? Of *course* not, my dear."

"Because of the . . ." his voice dropped, ". . . curse?"

Arabella had laughed merrily. To hear her voice and her laugh, you would think her a fraction of her age. "I share the point of view of my old friend, Edith Evans. Someone once asked her if she wished to play the lady, and she replied in that extraordinary voice of hers, 'I could never impersonate a woman who had sucha peculiar notion of hospitality.'"

Theo had looked down at his dear old friend. As was often the case with the loved and familiar, he must not really have looked at her for some time. She had become tiny, defenceless. He thought back to the effort it had cost him, that first day, to look into those piercing black eyes; yet she had taken him, and moulded him like clay. He even bore her name.

Theo had pressed on. Delay would make the words no easier to say. Years later, he remembered the sound of gravel crunching underfoot and under the wheels of the chair.

"You know . . . that I'll be leaving the country . . ."

Her rug had slipped from her knees, and he had bent to tuck it back into place.

"It's certainly taken you long enough," she had said. "If you hadn't come up with the idea on your own, I'd have had to have it on your behalf." Her kid-gloved fingers grasped his woollen ones. "Much better this way. Now, there'll be absolutely no doubt it was your idea."

Theo had been astounded. "To think I was under the impression I'd only just made up my mind."

"Well," Arabella had said, "I could never see you mucking in with that John Osborne lot . . ." The "angry young man" school of theatre was all very well, but Theo would make his statement about the British class system by leaving it behind. ". . . and the Quayles, and Gielguds, and Richardsons, and Oliviers won't give an inch as long as they draw breath. Where to then? America?"

☙

"What do you mean, you're *thinking* about it?"

The connection was bad between New York and Las Vegas. Perhaps Jeanne had misheard. Or was that really Milo saying that he'd *think* about returning to Arden? "You've told me a million times how much you miss the legitimate theatre!" Jeanne had been able to see something of Milo during the last three years. He was living in Vegas, and Carmen, the woman in Jeanne's life, liked an occasional turn at the tables. "I remember it very clearly. We were standing next to the roulette wheel, and you said —"

"And I meant every word, Jeanne, so help me. But —"

"No buts, Milo. I need both you and Chas there to help me with Theo. Everyone knows who he *really* wanted to play Lady Macbeth, and they know it wasn't me."

"Where you gonna stay?"

Jeanne felt inordinately smug. "In Marie's cottage."

"Noooo! But that's where I want to stay if I come!"

"Tough, buddy. It's only by chance that it's available. Derek, the last tenant, finally died. Marie always said it'd be the only way she could ever get him to vacate."

"Why would he?" said Milo. "She never once raised his rent. I bet she fed him, too, lucky bastard. Remember that great jambalaya?"

The simple truth was that Milo was scared. What if he'd lost his chops? Couldn't cut it? Milo, a charter member of the Arden Shakespearean Festival, had worked there for four seasons. He would probably have stayed on there indefinitely, were it not for his restless nature. He had done a zillion things since then, and as long as he stuck to the legit theatre things went pretty smoothly. For a time, he worked with Silent Partners, a five-member mime troupe out of Miami, though by then he was spending as much time playing poker in the green room as performing onstage. Lots of actors played cards, the guys mostly; it helped keep them sane on the road. You could be in a show in which you were in a couple of scenes at the top of the first act, and not be needed again until the end of the second; that's a lot of time to kill. Anyway, unless you were a big Broadway star, there wasn't much money to be made in the legitimate theatre, so the stakes were only high enough to wound, not do mortal damage — a friendly game, as they say.

It was when Milo was cast as Charlie Chaplin in a string of lucrative IBM commercials that things began to go off the rails. It was the start of a long string of junkets to Vegas, where he did begin to get badly hurt, and that was where his life took an unexpected turn. Milo had a facility for mimicking celebrity voices, so on the inevitable day when "the boys" came after him for payment of his gambling debts he had given them a little of his Dean Martin, taking the mickey out of a pretty tense situation and saving himself some broken bones. Word had made it back to the slightly bigger boys, and Milo had developed a little rep as a stand-up impressionist at private parties, then moved up to some of the smaller casinos. He had mastered all the headliners: Sinatra, Dino, Joey Bishop, Milton Berle; even some of the women with deeper voices: Eartha Kitt, Carol Channing. What had really made his name was his sudden inspiration to marry the Vegas headliner impressions to the Chaplin character he had developed for IBM, and *Charlie Does Vegas*, his signature piece, was born.

But Vegas was changing. A lot of the older guys were dead or retired, and the ones coming up were like the rest of their generation. They wanted Steve Martin and Robin Williams, Jack Nicholson, Bill Murray. Milo could tell by the shrinking recognition of Robert Goulet and Louis Armstrong that it was game over. He was thinking of trying his luck in Tinseltown, only a hop and a step away, and a place where he had gotten to know a lot of high rollers over the years. He was just about to start making the necessary calls when he got a call himself. It was Theo, inviting him back for the twentieth-anniversary season.

"But the money *sucks*, babe," Milo explained to Melba. "I'd forgotten what peanuts these guys work for!" He had met Melba poolside, and never tired of describing how he fell in love with her in spite of her shortcomings. She was a farmer's daughter, while the closest he had ever been to a cow was the smoked meat at Schwartz's back in Montreal. She was a practising Baptist, while he was a lapsed Catholic. To top it all off, in a manner of speaking, she was also a six-foot tall showgirl who towered over him.

With Melba's encouragement, Milo had gradually paid off his most pressing debts; but for him to live in a town that ate, slept, and breathed gambling made as little sense to Melba as making a drug addict work in a pharmacy. By the look of it, she would have to take charge, which she didn't mind. On a farm, if you had to stand around waiting for someone to tell you what things needed doing, the day would be half gone. Timing was everything. She didn't want this opportunity to slip through their fingers, like so many plastic chips.

"If we rented out our place here, we could manage," she said.

⁂

The origins of Jeanne's multi-Tony-award-winning musical drama *O'Keeffe!* were humble. Its first incarnation had been as a one-woman musical workshop at New York's Café La MaMa, followed by a more fully fleshed, small-cast affair at the Mark Taper Forum in Los Angeles. David Gordonson, who ran the place, had loved the show and backed it all the way to a two-year stay on the Great White Way, where it garnered as many "Do Not Miss" mentions as *Annie*. A production was heading for London's West End in October, and rights had been purchased for productions in France, Germany, and Japan, countries where the late great American painter Georgia O'Keeffe was just beginning to enjoy popular recognition. Europe and Asia adored things American, and no one was more American than O'Keeffe. For the Japanese, her link with the mythology of the American southwest (cowboys!) was almost aphrodisiacal.

After years of anonymity, Jeanne, to her great amazement, had become a star. Still, she wasn't Theo's favourite ex-pupil any more than she had been his favourite at school. Her lover, Carmen, who was also her collaborator, was very protective of Jeanne. Jacquie had still been alive, albeit barely, when Carmen and Jeanne first began working together. Carmen had watched a dying woman give most of her strength, not to prolong her own life, but to strengthen Jeanne's will to go on without her, and Carmen had inherited her mantle.

"It's — what? — seventeen years since Theo last offered you a part in his season? Why should he profit from your success now?"

"Because the mountain is there, *querida*, and its name is Lady Macbeth."

In her final year at NAADA, Jeanne had finally asked Theo why she was repeatedly cast as mothers, sisters, and best friends, and he had told her not to fight the fact that she would probably spend most of her working life as a character actress.

"It's not that you're unattractive, Jeanne. But you have a certain look about you . . ."

Jeanne's throat had thickened with tears, but she had persevered. "Can you be more specific?"

"Well . . ." *How did I get myself into this conversation?* thought Theo. But that was Jeanne all over, she *would* pick at things. "You're a big girl, Jeanne. You know that. Muscular. You always look so well able to take care of yourself, it's difficult to think of you as someone in need of protection."

"The damsel in distress?"

"More often than not," said Theo. "But it would be a mistake to think of it as a failure, Jeanne. *I* certainly don't. Think of Alec Guinness!"

No, Jeanne had thought at the time, *you think of Alec Guinness!*

But Theo was also the one who had said, "If you cannot have genius then you must have passion," and that, Jeanne knew, she had in abundance. So *why* in hell was she so tense?

"Why are you so tense?" asked Carmen.

"I'm not too thrilled about leaving you behind."

"Then don't go."

"I have to."

"Why do you have to?" asked Carmen. "This is not Castro's Cuba. You're not being ordered to go by the secret police."

"I have to!"

"So you've said. Because you have to prove something? It's already proved."

"Don't be silly."

"Seely! *I'm* seely?" When Carmen became heated, her accent did too. "Why do you have to prove anything to that stupid man in that stupid leetle festival!"

"Be fair, Carmen, it's not a stupid little festival. It's a big festival. And Theo's hardly stupid. I just want to play Shakespeare, that's all. You can understand that."

Carmen hunkered before her, still probing. "Is that it, my little

Jeanne?" she asked, although Jeanne was the taller by eight inches. "It's not just a leetle bit that you must rub his chin in it?"

"His nose," said Jeanne.

"His what?"

"His *nose* in it. Rub his *nose* in it."

"Whatever. You became rich and famous without him."

"Carmen, Lady Macbeth is one of the greatest roles ever written. And whatever I am, I owe a lot of it to Theo, however much he infuriates me." She caught her lover's eye. "So I *wasn't* the first on the list; it's still a wonderful part. And think of the publicity for London."

"Hah!" sniffed Carmen. "Since when do the English care what happens in *Canada*? Colonialist bastardos!"

"Anyway, it's too late. I've given my word."

Carmen raised a hand in submission. "All right," she said. "You win." She gripped Jeanne's shoulders. "If you must go, promise me you're going to knock their blocks off!"

"Socks, querida," Jeanne laughed. "Knock their *socks* off!"

Carmen sighed. If that man made her *querida* doubt her God-given gifts, and damaged her hard-won self-esteem, she would kill him! She knew that old habits die hard, if at all. Perhaps they were merely lulled, for a time, into a fragile, mute acquiescence. The habit of obedience instilled by the nuns went deep, and the chemistry — good or bad — between Jeanne and Theo was unlikely to have changed, even if the circumstances had.

"If that bastardo fucks your head around . . ." Carmen, a child at the time, had been one of the Marielitos. She could be tough. ". . . I'm going to fly there and knock his socks off."

ঞ

"Will you be bringing Toro when you come for the board meeting?" Marie asked Adam. She had had occasion to observe the two of them together on several occasions, and was certain that their relationship was more than just master and servant. She was right, as it turned out, though not at all in the way she had envisioned. Toro was something of a modern-day Jeeves. He didn't have to spend his time getting Adam out of foolish scrapes but, in addition to being a licensed mechanic, chauffeur, and gourmet chef, he was an accredited Zen master, and Adam was his pupil.

Adam cackled at the other end of the line. He and Marie usually spoke to each other at least every couple of months. He knew what she was thinking. "I thought I'd finally convinced you that I'm leading a celibate life."

"You have, you have. But it's a terrible waste. I still have my memories, you know."

Adam had left the acting profession a decade before to help Doreen manage the family's ever more extensive holdings. She had tried to cope on her own after Spencer's death, but their portfolio had experienced a great surge with the American shift to the southwest. Tracts and tracts of the land there that had once purchased for a song were now extremely valuable. The younger children had married and moved away, but he and Doreen continued to live with Cleone in the townhouse in Greenwich Village. Cleone occupied the first floor; Doreen was on the second; and Adam on the third, while Toro occupied what used to be Pilar's quarters.

"Have you booked your usual suite?" asked Marie. Adam was a long-time member of Theo's board of directors, and had never once missed the annual meeting, the day before the first opening night of the season. Adam's usual suite was the best the Princess Hotel had to offer. They called it the Imperial Suite, though it was highly unlikely that anyone of imperial rank had ever slept between its well-patched, starch-stiff linens.

"Indeed I have. Toro's already begun to think about what he's going to cook for our special reunion lunch. He promises you a vegetarian feast."

Marie could hear the doorbell chime at Adam's end. "Do you want me to call you back?" she asked.

"No, Toro can get it. Toro! Could you get the door?"

"Nice to be rich," teased Marie.

"Yes, my beauty," replied Adam. "The better to buy you lavish presents with, not that you ever let me."

Marie heard what she thought sounded like Toro calling Adam, though the voice was uncharacteristically agitated. There was more chatter and some whispers and exclamations, none of which Marie could make out. Finally, Adam got back on the line.

"I'll call you back." Click.

Oh dear, oh dear, thought Marie. *What was that all about?* Adam was always courtly with her, never abrupt. Spencer Willison was long dead, but perhaps something had happened to Cleone.

It was hours before her phone rang. She had thought of calling Adam, of course, but if he was dealing with some kind of emergency, the last thing he needed was a phone call.

"Thank God!" she said. "I've been so worried! What happened?"

"Marie, I . . . It's . . . I don't know where to begin."

"Adam, I can hear from your voice that somethin' very serious is goin' on." When Marie was upset, her voice became more and more southern. "Whatever it all is, you just take it a step at a time, y'hear?"

"It was Sean at the door, Marie."

"Sean?" The great love of Adam's life.

"He's come back to me," said Theo.

"Oh?" said Marie, not quite sure what to say.

"He forgives me, Marie."

Well, that must be a good thing, thought Marie.

"But he's . . ." Adam's voice broke. "He's very ill. He collapsed on the doorstep and Toro and I had to rush him to the hospital. That's why it's taken me so long to get back to you."

There were a few seconds of silence, neither one wishing to raise the name of the dreaded spectre. Marie finally spoke. "Is it . . . ?"

"Yes," said Theo. He let out an enormous sigh. *Was it any wonder*, he thought, *with the plague raging all around them?* "He weighs ninety-five pounds, and he's covered with sarcoma."

"I'm so sorry, Adam."

"I know you are, love." There was a catch in his throat, but he pressed on. "But he's giving me another chance, Marie. He's giving me another chance!"

જી

Milo still hadn't given Theo a final yea or nay. What if he signed up for the season only to discover that he had been selling himself a bill of goods all these years? Maybe he would never again be as good as he recalled once having been. Not knowing was driving him crazy. Melba knew there was nothing for it but to drive up to Arden; maybe that would help Milo make up his mind. And she had been right. Just making the decision to go had calmed him somewhat, and the monotony of the super-highway had done the rest. By the time they arrived in Arden it was almost midnight. Mecca of the arts notwithstanding, Arden was a small town, and most of the houses they had passed were night-dark.

Milo would be meeting with Theo at the theatre first thing in the morning, but he couldn't wait. He had to see it, right away. "To prove to myself that it's still there," he said. They pulled their battered Mercedes into one of the truck bays near the stage door.

"Will anyone even be around this time of night?" asked Melba.

"There's a night watchman," said Milo. "His booth's right by the stage door. Maybe we can talk our way in." He laughed. "We had this old guy, Hartley, who was known for catching a few zees when he shoulda been making rounds." They got out of the car, Milo barely able to contain his excitement. "The theatre's right where we had the big tent!" He had cut his theatrical teeth in that tent. They had to cope with heat and dust, but he would give a lot to see it standing still, its purple and yellow banners flying in a stiff breeze.

Melba was lagging. She had pins and needles in her legs from sitting so long.

"C'mon, babe!" Milo pressed his forehead against the plate-glass door. "Holy shit! I don't believe it! It's Hartley!" He knocked on the plate-glass door. "Hartley!"

But Hartley, fast asleep, wasn't easily roused. It took some pounding before he finally opened his eyes, and even then he looked to the TV as the source of whatever it was that had disturbed his slumbers.

"Hartley!" More knocking. "It's me! Milo Tessier!"

There was much peering and squinting by Hartley before the penny finally dropped. "Milo Tessier!" He fumbled excitedly at the bolts. "Well, for heaven's sake!"

Aside from the practical consideration of getting them in out of the cold, this ready identification delighted Milo.

"This is my wife, Melba," said Milo.

"This gorgeous lady n'you? Well, gol'darn! What're you doin' in these parts? You comin' back to the festival?"

"Thinking about it," said Milo. "Think I should?"

"Sure. Teach the young ones how it's done! Gonna be a doozy of a season, too. All kindsa special effects stuff, I'm told. I thought sure alla the founders'd be back for this one. The *Arden Courier* said even Chas is comin'."

If Jeanne had only recently become a Broadway star, Chas was an established and very big one on the small screen. *Two Brothers*, his dramatic series about aristocratic siblings with opposing loyalties during the American Civil War — both played by Chas — was one of the five highest-rated series of the decade, shown all over the world. It would run in syndication forever. The networks, in consequence, would jump hoops for Chas. He could take his pick of anything — another series, movies of the week . . . carte blanche. Yet Hartley was right. Chas was coming back to Arden for another crack at Shakespeare.

"You're lucky," the heart-throb of middle America had said to Milo, when they last talked on the phone, "you've been working with live audiences. I'm afraid that if I fluff a line I'll apologize and ask for another take."

"From what I hear tell," said Hartley, "that show of his has made him a multi-millionaire." Hartley's head shook up and down at the wonder of it, making Milo feel more insignificant by the minute. "You most likely know we're doing the You-Know-What play."

"The what play?" asked Melba.

"You know, The *Scottish* Play!" said Hartley. Perhaps Milo had married outside the profession.

"Melba's a dancer," Milo explained. "Don't worry; I'll clue her in."

"You'd better. Can't afford to take chances in *our* line of work."

Melba inquired about the whereabouts of the ladies' room, a ruse to give Milo time to wander around on his own. "I'll catch up with you in the theatre, sweetheart. Hartley will show me the way, won't you, Hartley?"

The last time Milo had performed in this theatre he had been play-ing Demetrius in a hippie-flavoured production of *A Midsummer Night's Dream*, all beads, fringe, and bell bottoms. What a long time ago *that* was! He had forgotten how suddenly the metallic clang of the stairwell gave way to the carpet-muffled quiet of backstage. High up on the walls, great war shields gleamed faintly in the murky half light. There was a rainbow of flags and pennants, lengthy trains that had followed behind theatrical kings and queens, cardinals and bishops. Was it his imagination, or were there ghosts of plays past hovering over the dressing rooms, lingering as emotion will do when strongly imprinted, even if only in make-believe?

He walked up and down the hushed corridors, and on a whim knocked gently on the door of the triple he had last shared with Adam and Chas, as if he might surprise them at the dressing table, making up in their underwear. But the room had been stripped clean at the end of the previous season. Under his breath he whispered, "Five minutes, everyone. Five minutes," the classic phrase of the call-boy (who is sometimes a girl).

He looked in on the room traditionally assigned to Mitch and another senior colleague. Something rolled from the shelf above the mirror and he reached out to catch it. It was a stick of lake, a deep wine-coloured greasepaint used to age the hands and the face, the neck, the inner rim of the lashes. Milo had learned its many uses at NAADA, at the hands of the master. Mitch had yet to miss a season, Hartley had said.

Milo's heartbeat quickened as the silver-grey carpet drew him ever closer to the back of the thrust stage. Once there, he felt his way along the tunnel that ran beneath its balcony and stepped onto the stage. In this theatre, it was the strongest entrance you could make.

It was just as he remembered. The stage itself was five-sided and thrust deep into the house. Tiers of crimson plush seats rose around and above it, and there was one balcony. The ceiling was studded with tiny worklights, like the starscape in a planetarium.

Fuck! thought Milo. *Is that a tear?*

Theo had driven the architects crazy, determined that "someone should finally put up a theatre that *made sense!*" The result, it was widely agreed, was one of the most functional yet elegant theatres built in a generation. It was a circular building, simple and beautifully proportioned, whose exterior, faced with local stone, married it to the river below.

The Festival Tent, while romantic and exciting, had functioned like a big drum; a simple rainfall, and the actors had to fight to be heard. In the case of a full-fledged storm it had been impossible, though they pressed on nonetheless, in a strange kind of dumbshow. It had been either unseasonably cold or unseasonably hot, and when the tent leaked the actors got very damp indeed.

This twenty-two-hundred-seat theatre was an actor's dream. There were no dead spots in the sound design, no obstructed views. The seats were deep enough so that audience numbers need not oblige you to jam their knees into the neck of the person sitting in front of them, and Theo made sure everyone knew how he felt about air conditioning. An excess was worse than none at all. "If you freeze their every joint and muscle," he said, "how on earth can you expect them to applaud?"

The official opening had taken place on a frosty morning before a mixed group of town and theatre folk. Theo had lowered his head slightly and combed his fingers through his shock of hair. Then he had raised his eyes real quick and zapped them a flash of blue. A sort of electrical frisson went through the crowd. *The women*, Milo had thought, *must be creaming their pants*. Theo smiled, which instantly metamorphosed his air of danger into something sombre but joyous. And just boyish enough. He was a believer. "We have our temple."

જી

A familiar sound made Milo grin. The laying of the specially treated wood floors had been completed a scant few hours before the opening of the first season. After two rough years under canvas, everyone had been marvelling at how perfect everything was in the new theatre, but when Milo had occassion to cross upstage right, one of the boards squeaked. At last! One flaw to pacify the gods! The carpenters had replaced the board not once, but several times, to no avail. As ripping up the entire floor wasn't an option, "squeaking the board" was adopted as a good luck ritual, with everyone making sure to tread on it at least once in the season.

They had first stood on this stage together — he, Adam, and Chas. "Fan-fucking-tastic!" Milo had exclaimed. Chas mock-punched him in the shoulder, and Adam had given a sharp intake of breath, as if he had stopped breathing at some point and had only just become aware. They had been like eaglets at the top of a cliff, ready to wheel and to soar. It was Adam who began:

We few, we happy few, we band of brothers,
For he today that sheds his blood with me
Shall be my brother; be he ne'er so vile,
This day shall gentle his condition . . .

Milo had joined in:

And gentlemen in England now a-bed
Shall think themselves accursed they were not here . . .

Chas had run up the stairs to the balcony, and looked out over the theatre as from the prow of a ship. They had finished in chorus:

And hold their manhoods cheap whiles any speaks
That fought with us upon St. Crispin's Day.

They had been young in the trade, yet old enough to know they were being theatrical. *But, dammit, man! They were actors!*

It was an older Milo who stood at centre stage and addressed himself to his phantom troupe:

Speak the speech, I pray you, as I pronounced it to you, trippingly on the tongue: but if you mouth it, as many of your players do, I had as lief the towncrier spoke my lines. Nor do not saw the air too much with your hand, thus, but use all gently; for in the very torrent, tempest, and, as I may say, the whirlwind of passion, you must acquire and beget a temperance that may give it smoothness. O, it offends me to the soul to hear a robustious, periwig-pated fellow tear a passion to tatters, to very rags, to split the ears of the groundlings, who for the most part are capable of nothing but inexplicable dumb shows and noise: I would have such a fellow whipped for o'erdoing Termagant; it out-Herods Herod: Pray you avoid it.

He sat at the edge of the stage, and listened to the phantom applause. Only then did he weep in earnest, for the loss of innocence, the lost camaraderie. For all the years in Vegas, scrounging for the next day's stake.

"That was wonderful," said Melba.

She had been sitting high up in the balcony so as not to be seen, but had made her way quietly down to the stage when he began to weep, reluctant to interrupt, but wanting him to know he wasn't alone anymore.

"Aww . . . you shoulda heard me when I was a kid."

He dashed the moisture from his cheeks. "I could rattle off whole scenes, years after I'd done the bloody part."

FULL COMPANY CALL

Except for the soft snickers of the horses and the twittering of the birds, quiet reigned supreme in Chas's Malibu stables, which was just the way he liked it. He lived on the edge of his nerves these days, and the more he could be on his own, the fewer chances there was of friction. The reasons he had given his wife, Selina, for no longer sleeping with her had seemed so reasonable at the start. His call time for *Two Brothers* was generally before dawn. On the days that he wasn't shooting he insisted on going out to the stables to help tend the animals, and he always had an excuse to stay up later than Selina because he had text to learn for the next day. She had tried to wait him out many times, but was usually fast asleep by the time he finally made it upstairs.

When she had complained of his remoteness, he told her that his two previous wives had complained of exactly the same thing. Once the excitement died down, it seemed, Chas simply lost interest. How had a love so caring and ardent during courtship, they had wondered, become so removed only a few months into the marriage? It wasn't that Chas didn't like them or think they were good people, he just wasn't interested anymore. Not being a villain, Chas had willingly subjected himself to a good many versions of marital therapy as practised in California. He had been shrunk and been rolfed by the best La La Land had to offer, be they Freudian, Jungian, primal therapist, or shaman. Name an *-ism* and chances were Chas had given it a whirl. Before the lawyers took over there had been marriage counsellors galore, there had never been any appreciable change in the status quo, which disappointed the women. It was no easy thing to divorce the star of *Two Brothers*, the heart-throb of the nation.

Two Brothers was the story of Abel and Sebastien Jourdemayne, and took place in Atlanta during the American Civil War. It was a monster hit, prompting a massive popular revival in antebellum clothing and furniture, houses and hairdos. You couldn't move for the crinolines and tailcoats; and you couldn't turn on a TV any night of the week without finding the show in reruns somewhere on the dial. Chas had done masterful work as both brothers. His portrayal of Abel, the elder of the two, was of a man both serious and driven. He had thrown in his lot with the Unionists, while Sebastien, the younger, was a poetic and dashing gallant in grey. When not involved in military and governmental intrigue, the battling brothers spent their time competing for their father's love and paying court to the same woman. *Two Brothers* had blitzed across the consciousness of the public like a comet and had turned Chas, an Alberta farm boy, into an American icon.

Chas had enjoyed the life of an international TV star at first. It was nice having everyone think he was the cat's ass. Wherever he went, whatever he wanted, all he had to do was snap his fingers.

And so it had been for the last four years, the glories and honours accumulating exponentially it seemed: Chas being given the key to Atlanta; Chas, the Grand Marshal, riding at the head of the Rose Bowl Parade; meeting the Pope, being invited to the White House by President Reagan.

Of late, however, Chas was gnawed by doubt, and more than a little fear. Was he in danger of becoming the Count of Monte Cristo of his era, playing the same two roles into his dotage? Given the realities of the business, what part of his life was now dominant, the actor or the celebrity? The studios were relentless when it came to pushing their product. Is this how he saw his future — a television star, increasingly known for being well-known? The guy with the year-round tan trailing gawkers at the golf course in Palm Springs? Would Abel and Sebastien Jourdemayne be his only legacy?

"Use it or lose it," Theo would say. "It's bugger-all to do with talent. You've got an acting muscle, and it's just like any other muscle. Your skating muscle. Your walking muscle. Your sitting muscle. Use it! If you don't," he would shrug, "you'll be like any other artist — a violinist, say — who doesn't get to play much and won't practise. No one's surprised when he hits the wrong notes when he finally does play. It's no different for the actor." Theo's phone call from Arden had enjoyed perfect timing.

In less than twenty-four hours Chas and Selina would be on a private plane heading north for a visit to Treetops, though not, perhaps, as directly as friends had been led to believe. There was to be a prior stop at a small, exorbitantly expensive private clinic in the New Mexican desert, whose specialty was substance abuse as practised by the rich, titled, and famous. When your problem is depression, and money's no object, there are more diverting ways to alleviate it than those that involve medical personnel — at first, anyway — until the system overloaded, and imploded, and you needed help.

His doctors weren't keen on the idea of him treading the boards quite so soon. "Too much stress," they said. "Rest. Live to fight again another day."

But Chas was of another mind. What they deemed stress would be his salvation, assuming he came up to snuff. It had taken a great turn of the wheel to bring him to this moment, and he would persevere. Otherwise, what was the sense of it all? So many things in his life hadn't made sense. The fruitless death of Bobby . . . except that it *had* borne fruit. When Bobby came to him in his dreams, a little spirit creature followed behind. It had no form, just a presence that was undoubtedly feminine.

Clara and Saul had been eager to raise Chas and Bobby's child, but Bobby's parents, unlike their beautiful daughter, were card-carrying anti-Semites, and they would be damned they were going to let that happen. They had arrived post-haste to claim Bobby's body, and somewhere in the process had spirited the child away as well, God alone knew where. The hospital had contended that the little Hayden baby had been released to her maternal grandparents as scheduled, and showed him papers to prove it. The Haydens were next of kin, they had said, whereas Chas had no legal status whatever. Chas wasn't so sure about that, but the Haydens had limitless wealth, and to fight them would be hard. When Chas did finally track them down, claiming his rights as the baby's father, they had stonewalled him. They had claimed to have absolutely no idea what he was talking about, and should he persist they would see him in court. With the stupendous success of *Two Brothers* he had been able to have the child tracked by experts, but they all had returned empty-handed. Chas had told all this stuff to his shrinks, but never to any of his wives. What would be the point? The situation had twisted his own guts into knots, and given him an ulcer; why give them one, too?

The extension phone in the stable rang, causing the horses to look up from their feed, and Chas to break out of his reverie. He ran to pick it up before it woke Selina back at the house.

"Milo, buddy. How are you?"

"If you mean in general, okay. If you mean about performing Shakespeare again, scared to death."

They had the same fear. Could they still do the big stuff?

"Anyway, the reason I'm calling is to tell you that I've just agreed to understudy you," said Milo.

"What? As Benedick?"

Milo laughed. Benedick was a highly romantic character. "Don't be ridiculous! As Macduff."

"Well," said Chas, grinning, "as Marie always said, 'Truth is stranger than coincidence.'"

"Meaning?"

"I'm understudying Theo in The Scottish Play."

Milo was stunned. Chas, one of the biggest stars in Hollywood, was going to take on an understudy role! It was one thing for Milo, Mr. Nobody, to understudy. It meant more money, which was welcome, and understudy rehearsals would leave less time on his hands once the season opened. There were no casinos in Arden, but there was a floating craps game that was the town's worst-kept secret.

"You're crazy!" said Milo. "Why?"

"Well, at first Theo asked without thinking that I'd do it; but the more we talked about it the more sense it made. What better work-out could there be before tackling Benedick? Besides, you know that no one ever goes on for Theo. He's never missed a show."

☙

"Marie. What're you doing here so late?"

It wasn't the warmest of greetings. After endless months of budgets and contract negotiations, Theo was finally able to put on his actor's hat. There would be little time for that once the company arrived. For twenty years, he had been the captain of this ship, and once it sailed his time and attention would belong to everyone but himself. He had been looking forward to a few private moments: hanging up his dressing gown, putting a few things out on the dressing table. Midnight was late for anyone to be visiting, even Marie.

"I've been working on the maquette for The Scottish Play," said Marie. She *had* been working on the maquette earlier in the evening, so it was not entirely a lie. What she had really been doing, however, was spying on Theo as he went through Matty Cheyne's fencing exercises. It would be more than her life was worth if Theo knew how frequently Marie observed him from her shadowy seat in the last row of the balcony. What she saw calmed her fears. He was trim, and his wind, unlike hers, was excellent, thanks to years as a non-smoker.

Theatrical swordplay is done to a steady and highly demanding count, like dance. If you can't keep up the pace you could find yourself in a right mess, advancing when you should be retreating and vice versa, and wind up minus an eye, or with a blade in the gut. Thank God for Matty Cheyne, their fight choreographer, a gallant, elderly charmer who had made many a Hollywood swashbuckler look far better than he had any right to.

Marie thought Theo moved well for a man no longer in his prime. His fine-boned beauty had acquired an attractive patina, the sight of which tugged at her heart. One day, she prophesied, she would find a portrait of an ugly old man who somewhat resembled Theo upstairs in an attic, and she would finally know why he had so many less wrinkles than she.

By and large, Marie was inured to the great chunks of Theo missing from her life, but there were times when the need to see him was overwhelming. Sometimes she would just watch and melt away into the night; sometimes, like tonight, she would make herself known. On these latter occasions, they would usually talk for a bit, and then walk their bikes together as far as the bridge. And then very rarely — perhaps once a year — they made love. To her it seemed perfect each time, yet within half an hour, Theo would be telling her how messy her hair was looking lately, how she was letting herself go.

"Shouldn't you be finished with that maquette by now?" he asked.

Marie's expression spoke volumes.

"I see. You're nowhere *near* being done . . ."

"My hands have been a little stiff, Theo." She rubbed them together, as if that would make her story more convincing. "I think I've got a touch of Mama's arthritis."

Theo glared at her from beneath beetled brows. Marie could spin a very convincing yarn, but he had lived with her for years. He had known her to paint scenery with a broken collar bone. She did suffer the occasional arthritic twinge, but it never kept her two seconds from doing a job she wanted to do.

"It's this curse thing, isn't it?"

She didn't deny it.

"*Damn* it, Marie!" Theo tossed his *Macbeth* text on the dressing table, where it landed with a thud. "There'll be superstitious idiots *enough* to deal with this season, without adding to their number. I thought I could at least count on *you*!"

There was nothing she could say in her defence. It was true. Marie's behaviour was not advancing Theo's heart's desire, and that was a rare thing.

"You know what'll happen if you go on this way? This *malaise* of yours will spread, and then where'll we be? You're a bit of an icon around here, Marie. People look to you for guidance."

She hated herself for it, but when he took her hand, it was all she could do not to weep with pleasure.

"I need you to send out all your special Marie signals, or people will wonder why. Or are you trying to precipitate something?" He released the fingers he had been pressing so warmly. "If you pick at a scab long enough it *will bleed*, you know."

"Theo! You should blush to think for one minute that I'd ever do anything to hurt Arden!" She felt the onrush of tears, tears that she had vowed never to shed before Theo. It was such a hard vow to keep.

Theo knew that he had overstepped the bounds. His tone softened. "Then what's the problem, love?" His arm encircled her shoulder. "You've done hundreds of maquettes that were much more difficult."

It was an exaggeration, of course, but she had done a good many, and was rather well known for them.

"I'd rather not say," she said. "You won't be sympathetic."

"Try me."

"All right then. If you promise. I keep thinking about Kristy."

"Kristy?"

"The English girl who got mugged in the Village."

"Marie, that was a lifetime ago!"

"I'm *afraid* of the play, Theo, I admit it. I'm afraid to start making the model."

Theo was nonplussed. Marie's pluck and zeal for the job were legendary. "Does this mean I won't be receiving my special opening night present?" Each one of Marie's special maquettes was immaculately crafted using fragments of handmade lace, cloth of gold and silver, and semi-precious stones, and the sole recipient was Theo.

"As if you'd care!" she said, sounding very much like the young southern girl she once was.

"I would, too," said Theo. "Though I admit I'm not quite as fanatic about your work as Adam."

Adam, who had inherited Cleone's love of beautiful things, had become an ardent patron of the arts, and was credited with being quite the connoisseur. To Adam, Marie's maquettes were high art. He wanted them in New York, at The Metropolitan Museum of Art.

જ

They parted at the bridge.

Once home, Marie walked through the future vegetable garden between freshly turned mounds of earth and let herself into the kitchen by the back door. Her first task was to feed the cats. Marie, leery of becoming known as The Cat Lady, would admit to having five cats in the house, but there were more. The Shameless Hussies, as the collective was known, came at a run, albeit a dignified one, as soon as they heard the siren song of the can opener. She spooned the strong-smelling liver and kidney mixture into their bowls, and then sat back and watched them eat, admiring their application to the task at hand, their feline decorum.

She had promised Theo, on the head of her dead mother, that she would apply herself to the production maquette. "I rely on it to explain my concept of the production to the company," he had said.

"It's much more helpful than floor plans and drawings. It helps me to visualize the staging."

All of this had been music to Marie's ears, but she was still on edge, and not just because of The Scottish Play's curse. The production would feature a number of unprecedented computerized special effects, which didn't sit well with Marie, though she herself had become quite the accomplished computer hacker. She thought a twentieth anniversary season should reflect the glories of the company as it had been in the two decades past. There was time enough later for the future. The future could slow down just a little, thank-you-very-much. Everywhere she turned, it seemed, things were moving along far too quickly.

Including the treacherous cells of her own body. Quiescent for so long, they had been roused and were up to no good. Twenty-one years ago, she had managed to keep her illness a secret from everyone at NAADA, but she had been younger then, and stronger.

⁂

The mobs, armies, senates, and courts in which Rupert Lovett had figured were legion, but it was his avocation that let him hold his head up, for Rupert was a scholar of theatrical lore. For actors too slothful to do their own research, and directors who were too busy, he served as a walking, talking Encyclopedia Shakespeariana. What did they use for makeup in Shakespeare's time? Ask Rupert. Need to know what musical instruments were in use at Elizabeth's court? Why, ask Rupert, of course.

It was because of this that his great meerschaum pipe and rather unpleasant tobacco were tolerated at readthroughs, and he was frequently the final arbiter when there was divergent opinion. Theo could be a bit short with Rupert, but he was pleased as punch to have him. The load of research and background material with which he had to contend grew more copious each year. It helped Theo enormously to have Rupert, a veritable cornucopia of information, around, though Theo never let on quite how much he relied on him. Rupert, in consequence, had no official title. Theo thought it better that he operate in an ex-officio manner, rewarded by the occasional drink at the Princess, or a boozy lunch. When not off to seminars on topics like Medicinal Herbs in the Age of Shakespeare in little university towns, Rupert could be seen around Arden, going about his business.

Theo spotted him coming out of the bank.

"Rupert! Glad I bumped into you! What do you say to a coffee?"

Rupert would know every horrific detail of The Scottish Play's bloody history, Theo was sure of it. *The man must be co-opted*, he thought. Stopped.

Or perhaps "scotched" was the appropriate term?

In the coffee shop, Rupert bit into the first of two very stale donuts. *How can the man live with such muck in his gut?* thought Theo. He raised the white earthenware mug to his lips and pretended to take a sip. The liquid inside, though brown and hot, bore no discernible relationship to coffee. And, my God! Was that a lipstick stain on the rim? "All set for rehearsal, Lovett?"

Rupert grinned in reply, the gourmand anticipating the well-laid table.

"You know," Theo said, determinedly casual, "it's tricky, this *Macbeth* business. This curse thing . . ."

Rupert's eyes glittered. Here was meat for a scholar! "I've come up with an *amazing* amount of information, Theo — from the earliest production, commissioned by James I, to all of the film versions."

God save us! thought Theo. Rupert had probably catalogued every last accident, fire, illness, stabbing, and death attributed to the curse; and cross-indexed them with time, place, character, and actor playing the title role. Theo frowned, but Rupert was oblivious.

"Incredible stuff! Even allowing for coincidence."

"Hmm . . ." said Theo.

Theo's less than joyous tone and demeanour made itself felt, even on so literal a person as Rupert. He cleared his throat. "Think it could be a problem, do you?" he asked.

"A problem?" said Theo. "Not at all, dear boy." Theo never called Rupert "dear boy" in the normal order of things. "We've so many new people this season. A few Americans. The whole Scottish Play business has little meaning for them. And there is this issue of self-fulfilling prophecy."

Theo pretended to sip his perfectly dreadful coffee, and let the idea hang in the air for a bit. "The group mind is such a powerful thing, don't you think? Once you've planted the idea that something terrible will happen should someone do X, the next thing you know, something terrible *does* happen. Get enough people believing in the positive, and miracles can happen. Get 'em thinking about the devil, and the *next* time there's something nasty, everyone's blaming the curse. Once that ball gets rolling, mischief gets done. Usually because someone's so preoccupied with avoiding this or doing that, they don't pay attention to business."

Their lumpy young waitress presented the bill.

Theo smiled his best Douglas Fairbanks smile as they rose from the table. "It's business as usual, old chap. Just business as usual."

Rupert, crestfallen, wrapped his rather greasy paisley scarf around his neck. It was March, the air still raw. "So, you don't want me to mention the curse, then?"

Theo had the chutzpah to look shocked. "Not at all! I'm sure the company's looking forward to hearing your thoughts."

Theo's Citroen was parked in the City Hall lot. He wasn't officially entitled to park there, but years of running Arden's largest tourist attraction had brought certain perks.

"Give you a lift?"

"No thanks, Theo. I've got some errands to do." He had to stop by the dry cleaners, and he was low on Oreos and Cheez Whiz. "Thanks for the coffee."

Rupert looked at his watch. Just after five; he had better get on with it. Still, his step was slow as he pondered his chat with Theo. *Theo is worried*, thought Rupert. *With reason*. Whether brought about by dark forces or merely the fear of dark forces, *Macbeth* trailed behind it a history of death and tragedy. The very name was anathema. Actors referred to it as The Scottish Play, or '*That* play!' and it was forbidden to speak any of its lines outside the context of a rehearsal or a performance, immensely quotable though it was.

Rupert had only been with Arden for five years. Could this be the first time in its twenty-year history that Arden was mounting *Macbeth*, one of Shakespeare's most popular plays? His mind's eye ran over the production photos, nineteen seasons' worth, that lined the corridors backstage. All the other crowd pleasers had been done repeatedly: *Twelfth Night* and *As You Like It*, *Hamlet* and *Richard III*. *A Midsummer Night's Dream*. Rupert closed his eyes and pictured the photographs overlooking the stairs to the cafeteria and the administrative offices: *A Winter's Tale*; *Pericles Prince of Tyre*; *Timon of Athens*; *Coriolanus*.

Not a single photo of The Scottish Play.

෴

"But, Marie, I've only been teaching for a year!"

"Theo needs you, Michelle!"

"You can't tell me there isn't another, more experienced voice coach available?"

"Theo *knows* you, Michelle," Marie said. "Berenice trained you. You teach her method. If *you* were unable to work because of infectious hepatitis, wouldn't you want whoever replaced you to use your methods?"

Michelle's fifth-floor walkup on Houston Street was undoubtedly a dump. The walls of the three tiny rooms were covered in 8" x 10" glossies of *The Desert Song* and *A Little Night Music* in Woolworth frames, while shoeboxes overflowed with programmes of summer stock productions in the Berkshires and Adirondacks, faded from all but the most tenacious memories. The bathroom door boasted a garish poster for *Man of La Mancha*, with Michelle Needham as Dulcinea, while pride of place over the sagging hide-a-bed was given to a large *Saturday Night Fever* poster fixed to the wall by thumbtacks. A Polaroid taken by wardrobe to check continuity was stapled to the bottom right-hand corner — Michelle decked out for the disco. Under it she had written: *ME ON SET!* in black felt marker. She had thought that this was going to be *it*, the kind of job that lifts you out of the whatever-pays-the-rent bracket to the magical world where lunch on set is catered by Wolfgang Puck, and the producer paints your Winnebago your favourite shade of mauve without your even asking. How many other ex-actress–voice coaches had thought exactly the same thing? And how many others, like herself, found that the wait for it to happen became longer and longer, and the jobs fewer and fewer, until they virtually dried up, and your so-called agent dropped you. Michelle's friends, anxious that she should be able to earn her living, had suggested getting out of the theatre — after all, it hadn't been very kind to her — and taking up something less uncertain, like real estate.

But Michelle couldn't bear the idea. The theatre world was the only one in which she would ever feel at home, and if she couldn't make it as an actress, then she would do something else. A chance meeting with Berenice Justasson, the doyenne of North American voice coaches and Arden's resident coach for many years, had given her the idea of becoming one herself. In the off season, Berenice offered a special training program at Carnegie Tech, and once Michelle was able to muster up the fee, she was enrolled and completed the course. Her new profession, however, was proving to be as much of a struggle as the old, and Michelle's finances were just about tapped out. *What would she have done*, she wondered, *if Berenice hadn't contracted infectious hepatitis?*

She was hungry and opened the door to the pantry, closed her eyes, and attempted to make telepathic communication with the mice and the roaches. *I'll give you five seconds to scuttle off before I open my eyes*, she signalled. *That way, I won't have to see you and your goddamned little antennae, and I won't have to smash you. Deal?* Success. There was only one little straggler, going hell bent for leather towards a package of Streit's egg noodles. Michelle decided to turn a blind eye.

FIRST READTHROUGH

"So, what you're saying is the real Macbeth got shafted," said Milo. *"Another* character assassination job, just like Richard the Third." Milo's aspirations to the role of the crookback hadn't diminished with time.

"Precisely," said Rupert. "To flatter Queen Elizabeth, and when she died, James the First, he depicted the enemies of their forebears as monsters, and their friends as heroes, on the side of God and Right. Don't forget, Shakespeare's company needed a licence to do business, and these were the good folk who could give or withhold it. Without their favour, the actors were no better than rogues and vagabonds. No one knew *then* that the playwright would turn out to be one of the greatest geniuses of all time."

"And the power of a good story is so strong," said Jeanne, "that the world accepts it as historical truth."

"Macbeth's Norse name was Thorfinn, which means 'Of the elect.'" Rupert was in full flood. "He didn't shy from spilling blood either, but it was in the interests of turning Scotland — called Alba at the time — into a nation that could look to itself for its safety and security. Until then, it'd been up for grabs by whoever was strong enough to take it and hold it."

"Poor old Thorfinn–Macbeth," said Jeanne. "It does seem rather unfair."

"Just another case of history being written by the victor," said Rupert, enjoying himself thoroughly.

Chas nodded in agreement. "You *could* say that the blackening of his name made him the first victim of the curse."

"Perhaps," said Rupert. "But he was long dead by then. There *is* an old tale that the first boy to be cast as Lady Macbeth died of a fever shortly before the play's premiere performance, and that Shakespeare himself had to perform the role, while there are others who say —"

"Thank you very much, Rupert. We could continue this fascinating discussion indefinitely, I'm sure," said Theo, "but we do have some time considerations. Besides, I know you're all eager for a look at the set."

At that moment, the doors of the rehearsal room were flung open with élan, and in walked Francois Forestier, Arden's resident costume and set designer. His two young assistants followed behind, pushing a white-shrouded trolley. When he was within arm's length of where Theo was sitting, Francois nodded gravely, their signal to raise the white shroud and reveal the set.

"My God!" someone said. And then there was silence.

Good, thought Theo. The reaction was just what he had hoped for.

Marie's maquette showed the thrust stage, the balcony, and the twin staircases that had served Arden so long and so well. All of them were engulfed in as bleak a landscape as anything Kafka, Eliot, and Dali could have conjured up together on their darkest day. There was rubble everywhere, shapeless mounds of brick, wood, dirt, and stone; much of it was sooty and grey, as if the whole world had been carbonized in an immense conflagration. Nor did the nightmare end with the stage. It canopied the audience, sucking them up into the horror, making them accessories instead of observers.

"The play we embark on today is dark throughout," said Theo. "In most of Shakespeare's plays, there's always some light to balance the dark. Desdemona counters Iago, for instance; Cordelia's virtues are pitted against Edmund's vices; and so on. But there are no characters representing good in this piece who can stand up to the vitality of its villains."

"What about Malcolm and Lady Macduff?" asked Milo.

"Lip service," said Theo. "It wasn't their story Shakespeare was interested in telling."

Marie had done a masterful job. There were textures that brought to mind fire-blackened skin, a hundred times magnified. A variety of newspaper headlines, blown up many times their size, proclaimed humankind's most heinous crimes. Man's malevolence was everywhere, playing hide and seek among the ruins.

"The lights will come up on headlines." Theo used his pointer to guide them to several.

Maidanek: August 23, 1943; Record Number of Corpses Processed in Gas Ovens.

Torquemada: The Inquisition. Hundreds Burnt Alive in Auto-da-Fé.

12 March, 1979: 12th Child Slaying on the Moor in Northern England.

First Use of Cannon in the Field, 3,006 Slain.

"Of course, they'll be considerably larger on the actual set. Sometimes, the lights will return again and again to the same headlines, building up a pattern, a visual orchestration recalling the Nazi rally at Nuremberg; the blazing sky over London during the Blitz, the firebombing of Dresden.

"The cables you see on the overhead canopy is how we're going to fly our witches. Each one supports a minimal, yet very secure, seating apparatus."

"How will it work?" asked Jeanne, awestruck, and both relieved and disappointed that she, as Lady Macbeth, would not get to ride one.

"Computers. Same as these modules you see at stage level. They'll be programmed for any number of configurations — battlefields, bedrooms, and banquet halls — without anyone having to move a finger."

It was a highly evocative set, with links to dada and the expressionists as well as surrealism and the futurists, yet hearkening back to a remote time when everyone still lived in caves. Even those who were horrified by it were struck by its power.

"Our *Macbeth* will not only be about the struggle within Macbeth the individual, but also the larger struggle for the mind of man throughout time. Macbeth and the mythic role he plays in our culture is part of the blood and butchery that makes up the history of our kind."

Francois' assistants placed the costume sketches on the rehearsal table, each one framed by a matte and in its own plastic sleeve. Small though he was, Francois cut quite the figure in his tight black leather suit. He could have made a great deal more money designing for the movies, but Francois *loved* the theatre.

"As you can see," said Theo, "the costumes have features in common with cultures across the millennia — jewels and feathers, capes, breastplates and veils. Some of them could be equally at home on some avant-garde runway in Milan. Anyone who has read the classics . . ."

"Well, la di da!" whispered Timmy, Theo's stepson, to Corinna, one of the prettiest of the season's newcomers. Timmy had been taken on as an apprentice, much against Theo's better judgement.

His stepfather glared at him. ". . . knows that the nature of man has not changed over the centuries, though his perception has, and perception is all."

Given the signal, Bernie, Theo's long-time stage manager, ushered a sandy-haired man in his late thirties into the room.

The company stared as he walked towards Theo, looking like a young Van Johnson in his solid brown suit and heavy brogues, and blushing to the roots of his neat blond hair. The grounds of the temple, their glance said, were reserved for the priesthood. What-ever this outsider had in that portfolio he carried had better be good.

"To which end, it gives me great pleasure to introduce Dr. Fritz Hollenberg, though Dr. Hollenberg tells me he prefers not to be so formally addressed."

With a sweeping gesture, Theo offered the floor to a dry-mouthed Fritz Hollenberg, a nuts and bolts computer engineer who rarely spoke in public, even among his own kind. To have to speak to a room full of actors was a nightmare!

"Mr. Hollenberg," smiled Theo, "is one of the guiding lights of the Robot and Computer arm of Interactive International, a company that's been one of our sustaining donors for the last decade. This year, in honour of our twentieth anniversary, I've managed to twist their arm a little . . ." When Theo chuckled, the company chuckled back right on cue. ". . . And they've agreed to become, not only our most gracious benefactor, but an active collaborator. Mr. Hollenberg?"

Theo wasn't anywhere near as convinced as he sounded, but the board had been adamant. Tomorrow's audiences would be made up of people weaned on Disneyland, rock concerts, and laser light shows. If they didn't learn to compete, Theo had been told, they would be as dead as a dodo.

By this time, Fritz Hollenberg had regained some measure of control. There was even a feeble attempt at something resembling a smile. After one more cough and a swallow, he opened his portfolio. "Well . . . uh, I guess this isn't the sort of thing you folks are accus-tomed to, uh, use in your work, in the normal order of things."

There were glances exchanged that said, *I should certainly hope not!*

"I, uh . . . have brought along a few photos of the sorts of robots . . ."

Robots! Thespian sensibilities shrank in horror.

". . . we've designed for other enterprises; auto assembly, car washes, automatic stock replacement . . ."

The horror mounted.

"I've . . . uh, also brought along a few drawings as to how our machinery . . ."

Machinery!

". . . is going to work in the context Mr. Thamesford has discussed with me . . ."

This isn't working, thought Theo. He had better step in.

"Calm down, all of you! Our predecessors have *all* used stage machinery, of one kind or another, going back to the ancient Greeks. This is merely the latest incarnation." He reached into the maquette and moved the pieces about. "See . . . sometimes a single unit will move through the air bearing a single witch. Or *all* of them will be used, criss-crossing each other in the most exciting damn heath scene anyone's ever seen."

There was a deluge of questions.

"Will there be danger pay?"

"Can we be sure it's safe, Theo?"

"What does Equity say?"

Theo caught sight of an ashen Mitch Blakely, a terrible basilisk look in his eye.

Theo could kit the actors up in togas or bikinis, thought Mitch. He could locate them on Mars or Kuala Lumpur. It wouldn't change a damn thing. It was the *words* that were the problem. The curses, chants, and invocations in The Scottish Play were *real* curses, chants, and invocations, the very ones that had been percolating through the English landscape when Shakespeare was a boy, and which he had scooped up with his poet's ear.

The spirit of bonhomie was riding high in the bar of the Princess Hotel, as it always did after the first day of rehearsal. Theo put in a brief appearance. A little distance was necessary at this point, or he would never get a moment's peace. Being the head of a theatre company was akin to being a counsellor at a summer camp. No matter how hard you try, no child thinks they get enough attention.

"I first heard these words from Dame Arabella," he said, over his Pimm's Cup, "spoken to a group of frightened evacuee children who were rehearsing *A Midsummer Night's Dream*, but she later told me they were the same words she'd used to address her company."

Theo altered his posture a touch, and there sat Arabella. "'If any of you lot are accustomed to a steady diet of *splendid*s, *fantastic*s and *wonderful darling*s, I urge you to wean yourself. I *expect* you to do a good job. In fact, a *superb* job! If you fail to come up to the mark, you'll hear from me, never doubt it. However, should I let slip a word or two which *might* just pass for a compliment, such as "Well done," or "Good work, company," you'll know you've done something extraordinary, even by my exacting standards.'"

Before his departure, he had reminded them that each and every one of them, including himself, was to be present for the vocal warm-up that Michelle would conduct at the start of each day. "The word 'inspiration' is derived from the Latin *inspirare*, to breathe in," he had said. "The breath of the actor must *breathe in* the life of the character before we can begin to talk of inspiration or lack of it in our work. That's where Michelle Needham comes in. We are very fortunate — may I say privileged — to have her."

The company gave Michelle a round of applause. Theo looked at her. *You are new to the company in this role*, the look said, *and I am giving you status and respect. Live up to it, and all will be well.*

"Individual sessions are purely voluntary and can be arranged as rehearsals permit. Except, of course, for those sent by me for sundry vocal corrections." When it came to the voice, an actor's instrument — its size, range, power, colour, and flexibility — the gods were not just. "I look forward to each and every one of you joining me in a daily half hour of humming, rapid repetitions of 'she sells sea shells by the sea shore' and — my personal favourite — 'rubber baby buggy bumpers.'"

Fresh rounds were hailed from the bar. The lean times were on hiatus, and it was the season of plenty. There would be time enough later for bickering factions; for the moment, the family was united. Old comrades-in-arms busily filled in details of lives, loves, and the most recent professional credits. The newcomers looked for the best spot to establish a first tentative footing.

Someone embraced Michelle from behind.

"Last call, love," said Jeanne. "I'm buying."

The years had been good to Jeanne. The long, prematurely white hair was eminently more striking than the indeterminate brown of her youth, and she looked slim and strong. "Vital" was the word that came to Michelle. Her old classmate was wearing a pair of high red boots, polished to a dull gleam, the kind of thing that Bobby might have worn if she had lived. Bobby had had boots that went all the way up to the thigh. When she wore them with a miniskirt she would cause a sensation.

"No, thanks, Jeanne. I should really be getting home."

"You're on Daly, aren't you, Michelle?" asked Corey. "I'm just round the corner." Corey Schellenberg wanted to book a session with Michelle immediately. He had come to the classical theatre from the world of professional boxing, and was always eager to make up for his lack of formal training. There was no doubt, however, of his expertise with his fists. Corey, who had vowed never to fight again if he could become an actor, had been jumped in the hotel parking lot the previous season. A couple of the local yahoos were irate that "a buncha fags" were "taking over" their town. The yahoos had lived to regret it.

"Uh-huh," said Michelle. "I'm next door to Marie."

She and Marie shared a driveway, their kitchen windows no more than ten feet apart. The place was a little plum, for which Marie had plunked down a deposit on Michelle's behalf the moment it became available. The best seasonal rentals were perpetually reserved, or passed down like valuable family heirlooms; but the previous tenant had retired and gone to live with his daughter in England, leaving no heir apparent.

"I'm going to pop over and help you settle in as soon as I can, hon," said Marie. "I've just been so busy with that damned maquette . . ."

She hadn't meant to solicit their applause, but enjoyed it nevertheless.

Damien Trevellyan, an elderly veteran of the glory days of British rep, was particularly effusive. "I'm usually of the 'less is more' school myself . . ." he said. He was compelled to wait until the snorts of amused disbelief had subsided. ". . . But if Francois set out to evoke all the world's evils, he's certainly gone and done it. Positively gave me the willies! And the maquette is *splendid*, Marie darling! The *chef d'oeuvre* for the master will follow soon after, no doubt?

"Yes, indeed . . ." he continued, by now addressing the assembly, which was something Damien Trevellyan liked to do. "Good set. *Wonderful* cast! Not a bad writer . . ."

It was an ancient joke, but the company laughed regardless. Elders are treated with a degree of respect in the theatre, the living link to a vanishing tradition.

Damien raised his glass. "Ladies and gentlemen, if any of you have anything left that you can chug down by way of a toast . . ."

What was left of the company straggled to its feet.

"Here's to Arden's twentieth anniversary, and the best damn production of The Scottish Play since Willie played the Madam!"

Corey touched Michelle's arm. "If you can hang on a few minutes, I'll ride along with you and Marie."

"Sure," said Michelle.

Marie was already stuffing her curls into a purple crocheted hat that made her look like a big grape tea cozy. The April nights were chilly. "I'm going to leave now, kittens. Why not stop in for a nightcap?"

"Well, maybe just a little one," said Michelle. They had all had enough, especially Marie. "Seeing as how I have to impress the hell out of everyone tomorrow morning."

A light rain had fallen, leaving the air fresh and sweet. *A benediction,* Michelle thought, *after the stale smoke of the bar.* They made their way around to the hotel parking lot, where they had chained their bicycles to the fence. At one time, you could safely leave your bike anywhere in Arden, but not any more.

Corey is rather smashing, thought Michelle, *with that wonderful physique and beautiful face.* A former pro boxer, someone had said. He must have been an awfully good one to have come out so unscathed. And so shy. "The jaw, right?"

Corey nodded, relieved that he didn't have to explain his problem, and dismayed that it was so apparent.

"Your neck is tense, too." Michelle smiled. "Please, don't look so worried. I'm a specialist, remember?"

"It's a hangover from my fight days. Can you help me?"

The pleasure Michelle felt when she answered caught her quite by surprise. "Yes. I think I can."

Lordy! Lordy! Michelle had found her true vocation, at last.

❧

A full hour had gone by since Marie had returned home. She kept on sipping brandy, sympathetic magic to make Michelle and Corey appear. Her old Mammy Lou would have a fit if she could see this kitchen. There were still dirty breakfast dishes in the sink, and the table looked as if it could use a good scrub. Marie herself was none too kempt. Shreds of newspaper and flour and water paste clung to her woolly sweater, the aftermath of papier mâché work, while a snarl of macramé cord dangled from the pocket, providing no end of fun for the Shameless Hussies.

The windows at Michelle's place were still dark. Marie checked her old Timex for the umpteenth time, and tried to curb her anxiety. Michelle and Corey were both healthy, attractive people. Perhaps something more exciting than a nightcap had suggested itself. But instinct told her she hadn't been stood up in favour of sudden unbridled passion. A lusty woman herself, she had a nose for it.

She looked up Corey's number in the company directory and dialled it. Five rings. Eight. Ten. She hung up.

Who should she call? Mitch? Theo? Jeanne was fast asleep in the guest cottage out back. Should she wake her and get her all upset, too, most likely for nothing? *Michelle is probably in Corey's bed right now*, she thought.

She didn't believe a word of it.

☙

The news that Corey and Michelle had been beaten up and were in hospital spread like wildfire the next morning. Wherever you turned there were whispered allusions to the curse, and Theo wanted to defuse the situation before it got any worse.

"I repeat: Michelle and Corey are going to be all right. The doctor at St. Joe's has assured me they've sustained no serious injuries, and that they'll be back with us very soon."

He lifted his text, a signal that announcements were at an end and rehearsal about to begin. Only a very senior member of the company, like Mitch Blakely, would have dared pursue the subject. "If there's anything more you can tell us, Theo, we'd really like to know. If only to save Michelle and Corey from having to repeat themselves a hundred times."

The little blue vein at the inner corner of Theo's right eye started to twitch, a sure sign he wasn't pleased.

Well, too bloody bad! thought Mitch. Sweep a curse under the carpet, and you had only yourself to blame when you tripped on it.

"Michelle and Corey were among the last to leave the bar," said Theo. "When they went to get their bikes in the hotel parking lot, they were set upon by person or persons unknown." For those who had been in the company last season, there was no question who had had it in for Corey.

"Michelle took a crack on the head, and the doctor says she's got a great whacking headache. But if, as they expect, the x-rays check out negative, she could be released as early as this afternoon; though she might not be capable of coming in and coping with you lot just yet."

"And Corey?" asked Mitch, who was by way of being Corey's mentor. When the lad was admitted to the company two years earlier, it had been more due to his palpable virility and athlete's rhythm than his fluency with the English language. Mitch, however, had been moved by Corey's application and dedication, and had undertaken to work with him, convinced he had the makings of a solid classical actor. He had assigned lengthy reading lists to familiarize Corey with the subtleties of period and style, trying to fill the vacuum that modern education left for so many of today's young, unaware of before and unprepared for the after. Mitch had tossed books of mythology, both Greek and Roman, at Corey's head at an accelerated rate, as well as Donne and Trollope, Dickens, Browning. Whatever Mitch threw at him, Corey digested, and quickly came back for more.

"Corey didn't get away quite so lightly."

Every eye was rivetted on Theo.

"Whoever attacked our poor Corey, went for his face. It was very lucky that the bartender came out when he did."

Mitch's fists were clenched so tight, the nails bit into his palms. An assailant would never have dared go up against the boy in the light of day. He had lain in wait in the parking lot and jumped him in the dark, like the goddamned coward he was! *Goddamned Theo! Goddamned Shakespeare!*

"Even so, Corey's nose was broken. He's also lost a couple of teeth."

The theatre was one world in which a bump on the nose transformed you from a romantic lead to a character man. A facial scar screamed, "Villain!"

For the second time, Theo opened his text, and this time everyone followed suit. They were all highly unsettled. If this was the first appearance of the curse, there were two more to follow. Disaster always came in threes.

⁂

They were always behind schedule.

"Why aren't the soldiers wearing their boots?" asked Theo. "The actors must get a chance to break in their boots!"

"They're being shipped from Toronto this morning, Theo," said Bernie. "Mr. Cavalli swore it on the grave of his sainted mother." Bernie was expert in divining the exact level of his boss's frustration. This one was still only low to middling.

"A fat lot of good that'll do. He swore it on the sainted grave of his father that they'd be here yesterday!"

Bernie shrugged. Signore Cavalli was, after all, Italian.

"Bloody Mario," mumbled Theo. "We need those boots, *now*!"

"I know, Theo," said Bernie. "I know. I'm sorry."

The missing boots were not Bernie's fault, but he would say anything to calm Theo. Technical rehearsals would begin soon, the very thought of which always made Theo cranky. If it wasn't boots that set him off, it would be wigs, or lighting, or props.

"When you cross swords with someone, you bloody well don't want to be thinking about corns and blisters!"

⁂

Jeanne was a costume designer's dream. She never fussed at fittings, and no train was too long, no cape too wide for her to handle.

"Jeanne!" said Francois, kissing his fingertips. "She does more than just wear my creations, she *inhabits* them. Et ses epaux! Those wonderful, strong shoulders!"

But even the effusive Francois couldn't dispel Jeanne's sadness. Genuine communication between Jeanne and Theo was proving to be as elusive as ever. It was a difficult thing to address when no one but she seemed to notice anything amiss — not even Milo and Chas.

"You're crazy; he loves everything you're doing!" said Milo.

Jeanne turned to Chas.

"I vote with Milo."

She wanted so much for them to be right, and looked for instances that would prove them so. Still, she couldn't forget the previous day, when they had attempted the first rough blocking for Lady Macbeth's sleep-walking scene. Compared to the many scenes that involved swordplay, which reeked of testosterone, the scene was intimate, beginning with a conversation between Lady Macbeth's gentlewoman and her doctor.

I have seen her rise from her bed, throw her night-gown upon her, unlock her closet, take forth paper, fold it, write upon't, read it, after-wards seal it, and again return to bed; yet all this while in a most fast sleep.

Lady Macbeth enters, sleepwalking, carrying a taper. Her doctor and gentlewoman continue their discussion even as she rubs her hands together and intones:

Here's the smell of the blood still: all the perfumes of Arabia will not sweeten this little hand. Oh, Oh, Oh!

Jeanne's idea had been to anticipate her entrance in a kind of dumbshow enactment of the gentlewoman's words, and Theo had taken her to task for it during notes.

"Jeanne, what on *earth* were you doing while your gentlewoman was talking to the doctor? You're not supposed to enter until just before she says, 'Lo you, here she comes.'"

"I thought it might be interesting if we could actually *see* what the gentlewoman is describing," said Jeanne. "The actions of rising, dressing, and writing are such ordinary ones, but the circumstances make them so bizarre."

"True enough," said Theo. "That's why Shakespeare has written such evocative lines for the gentlewoman. Besides, you won't be lit until you make your entrance."

"I thought we might talk about that, Theo."

"Did you, Jeanne? Why? Did you do something similar in *O'Keeffe*? I haven't seen it as yet, so you have me somewhat at a disadvantage."

Jeanne had done something similar, as a matter of fact, which made her self-conscious. Perhaps she really was trying to impose her will on Theo's production. But she was playing Lady Macbeth. Wasn't that what she was being paid for?

ൟ

Chas had more than professional reasons for returning to Arden. Perhaps here, amidst so many who had known and loved her, he could lay the ghost of Bobby Hayden to rest.

He sat up in the first balcony and watched Theo, as Macbeth, confess his fears of Banquo.

> *He chid the sisters*
> *When first they put the name of king upon me,*
> *And bade them speak to him: then, prophet-like*
> *They hail'd him father to a line of kings:*
> *Upon my head they placed a fruitless crown,*
> *And put a barren sceptre in my gripe,*
> *Thence to be wrench'd with an unlineal hand,*
> *No son of mine succeeding.*

It was not just his child that Chas would never know, whose face he wouldn't recognize if he were to stare into it, but his grandchildren and great grandchildren. His dreams of a girl child, sometimes with Bobby's face, sometimes his own, had been replaced by dreams of a procession of such children, moving off into infinity, forever unknown to him.

Which is why, perversely, when he first caught sight of Corinna, he had fought hard against the thought that he had finally found what he had so long sought. That he should find her *here*, moving about the very same stage her mother was sure to have trod had she lived. Everything she did convinced him further.

He sneaked looks at her during the warm-up. She had small well-shaped ears like Bobby, and the same high forehead. Her voice, too, was a reminiscent melding of crystal and amber. There were so many things: the tapered fingers that twiddled the short-cropped hair at the back of her neat blonde head; the sculpted cheekbones in the perfectly oval face. Surely, he couldn't be the only one to notice the resemblance. Had Theo taken a good look at her? He must have; Theo never missed an opportunity to look at a pretty girl. Milo? Marie? Jeanne? Michelle? Were they all blind?

When he saw her in the Princess Lounge with some of the other young actresses, his heart began to pound. He was tempted to walk over and chat them up, but he was afraid to rush things, to frighten her. The theatre, like the church from which it sprang, is a hierarchical institution. Special care is needed to cross the ranks in either direction. He took a seat at the bar.

How charming they looked perched on the battered old love-seats and sofas, talking the kind of young actors' talk he hadn't heard in a long, long time; full of words like "passion," and "psychology," and "motivation." In television, it was usually "Could you move two inches to the right, Chas?" "No, *that's* where you have to pick up the glass." "Could you speak just a *little* bit louder, Mr. Almond?" Faster; slower; softer?

They were discussing the witches' prediction that no issue of Macbeth would ever sit on the throne. Could that not mean that Lady Macbeth can and does conceive, but that none of the children survive?

"If I ever *do* go on for Jeanne, I'm going to play her pregnant." Corinna was understudying the role of Lady Macbeth. She would give up chocolate for life if she could perform the role just once. "I'll die as a result of a miscarriage. Think what *that* would do to the speech about dashing the head of the sucking babe!"

It was eavesdropping, but Chas was enjoying the conversation so much, it was hard to turn a deaf ear. Besides, it was all so innocent.

The talk turned to the custom of adopting a child to carry on a family name that would otherwise die out. Someone said that she wouldn't mind being adopted by some millionaire who needed an heir, but that it was "probably a male gig."

"As usual," said another.

The classics didn't offer women much opportunity, as compared to the plethora of parts for men. It affected their outlook.

"I wouldn't be considered a good candidate, even if I were a guy," said Corinna. "I'm already adopted."

Their voices dropped to a level Chas couldn't make out, but he didn't care. Corinna was *adopted*!

∽

"He's got a thing for you."

"Oh, sure!" scoffed Corinna, though she wanted more than anything that it be true.

"It's obvious to everyone but you."

People *were* talking. When Chas turned in Corinna's direction, they blushed to see the look in his eye. No one thought it a coincidence when they both turned up with bag lunches on the same day, and just happened to bump into each other down by the river.

He also just happened to wander into wardrobe when Corinna was having a fitting for her understudy costume. In the event she ever did have to go on for Jeanne, it was unlikely Theo would let her play the role pregnant, but she had talked the costume people into letting her stuff a pillow down the front of the costume before they laced her up.

Chas joined in the general laughter, while memories of another pregnant beauty filtered through his brain. He remembered his dilemma when Bobby first found out she was pregnant, his guilt and despair at her needless, senseless death.

But most of all, he thought of the Haydens. *You whisked her away in the blink of an eye*, he thought, *but I've found her, you bastards! I've bested you at last!*

✄

Even the creative process has its share of tedium. A short break to sip sparkling wine from a plastic cup and partake of a slice of birthday cake is usually welcomed by everyone but the director and the stage managers, who are always fighting the clock. Trying not to look as self-conscious as she felt, Selina wheeled one of the lunchroom trolleys up the vomitorium into the theatre, a huge candle-lit cake on the upper level, champagne bottles clinking below. Bernie doused the lights, and the strains of "Happy Birthday" rose to the roof. When Chas had blown out the candles, Selina handed him a knife to make the first cut.

Timmy, Theo's stepson, by now head over heels about Corinna, called out, "Corinna's celebrating too. She's just been asked to do Juliet at the Guthrie next season!"

Chas replied in what he hoped was a flip manner. "Then she'd better get over here, and help me cut this football field of a cake!"

Corinna demurred a little, but finally allowed herself to be drawn forward, blushing furiously as they both placed a hand on the knife handle and pressed down. Selina, white as chalk, clicked her little camera.

"You okay, honey?" Chas asked.

"Oh, sure." She tucked the camera into her bag. "Just a little tired." She relieved them of the knife and began cutting the great slab into individual portions. "This baby took a lot of baking." She forced herself to smile at Corinna. "Chas, why don't you and — Corinna,

251

isn't it? Why don't you and Corinna start pouring out the champagne while I distribute the cake. I think Theo's getting a little antsy."

Selina was a good judge of human nature. Theo's smiling face was less telling than the index finger drumming the face of the Rolex Pam had given him as a wedding present. The company knew better than to linger over their paper plates. It risked being singled out with an "All right! Let's not make a meal of it!"

⁂

Theo came to Jeanne's dressing room to give her her notes. They had been working on the "I would pull its toothless gums from my breast" speech, and she had been trying a line of performance in which Lady Macbeth was in a state of barely controlled frenzy, induced by extreme frustration with her husband, yet at the same time weeping.

"Tears are sentimental in this context, Jeanne. And excessive. She should be more in control of the situation."

"There are also tears of sheer fury, Theo," she countered, "and when all else fails, sometimes women — and men, too — will weep just to get their way."

"Not in this case," said Theo.

Their disagreement was fundamental. His Lady Macbeth was more clinical, the perfect Nazi female who could eliminate her own child if he didn't come up to scratch. Jeanne didn't see Lady Macbeth as icy at all. Her Lady Macbeth had an excess of all emotions — except, perhaps, pity. *If the lady is a machine built for cruelty*, thought Jeanne, *she is diminished as a character*.

"What makes her interesting," she said to Theo, "is that, for a period of time, she manages to *control* this conflict between their deeds and her own deep-seated guilt and horror. *This* is the drama, this hard-won balance! She's like Mary Tyrone in *Long Day's Journey*. Both wind up victims of emotional illness, retreating to the past. I think planting a seed or two to foreshadow that is legitimate."

"This is what I've always feared for you, Jeanne," said Theo. "Do you recall your final critique; the one I gave you just before you left school? *Don't argue with the director.*"

"Theo, this isn't an argument! It's a legitimate — and obviously necessary — discussion. Speaking with conviction and emotion doesn't necessarily mean an argument. I've worked too hard to free myself of this director-dominated way of working to revert without a struggle!"

"My, my . . ." said Theo. He had been caught off-guard by Jeanne's fervour, but was still in control. ". . . Full scale rebellion."

"Your way's all well and good," she continued, "if every director's a ruddy genius, with a vision so powerful that every opposing point of view fades in its wake. But there are as many flawed and incompetent directors as there are bad actors, and there's no shortage there. Why shouldn't there be? Because we're encouraged to think of directors as unaccountable gods? Or because directors aren't subject to the same moment-to-moment scrutiny as most actors?"

Theo knew that her argument made sense, but there was *will* involved here. He couldn't back down. This spirit could infect the whole company. It was disruptive, and he wouldn't have it.

"Surely, Theo, the *best* work is arrived at by a consortium of equals."

Perhaps her biggest gripe was that after all his emphasis on the ensemble — in which she believed with all her heart — there was no easy life in the theatre for a person with the guts to question. Yet, that was the quality that made stars. The people running the box office understood the importance of stars. They were why people came!

"I'm grateful for everything you've taught me, Theo, but you're not God. Do you impose the same limitations on yourself, when you're wearing your actor's hat, that you do on me? Can't we work this out, once and for all, actor to actor?"

"Jeanne," said Theo, "listen to yourself. Next thing, you'll be quoting Lee Strasberg at me, or whatever else is the latest in the world of self-indulgence. Dream monitoring? The Kabbalah?"

She was beginning to cry, just what she had promised Carmen she wouldn't do. Jeanne could already hear her say, "I tol' you so!"

"You're putting words into my mouth, Theo! Rehearsal's a process of discovery. You can't cement everything into place before rehearsals even begin! Maybe most actresses wouldn't say 'boo' to whatever you asked for, but I'm not like that. Perhaps I should be, but I'm not. I have this real need to dig and probe." She permitted herself a small laugh. "And it does fill the coffers!"

"Is *that* what drives you?" The sneer in his voice was ever so faint, but it was there.

"My father worked in a slaughterhouse, Theo. I come honestly by my need to make a living. I'm not stupid; I know why I've been cast. You were talked into it. I know that I wasn't your *tenth* choice, never mind second or third. But I said I'd come, anyway. At first, it was to prove that you've been wrong about me all these years. I really thought I could give you whatever you wanted. But once I was back in the fold, Theo, I realized this would only confirm your bias. You're the director. You have the right to your vision, but you can't thrust it on me without my consent. Ultimately, *my* Lady Macbeth must come out of *me*."

Were he and Jeanne not speaking the same language? "My darling Jeanne, what would happen if *everyone* behaved as you do?"

"Good things, perhaps, Theo. It's not a commune I'm after, it's a federation; and you're not the conductor of a symphony orchestra, waiting to lift the baton. Didn't you always teach us that the theatre is more of a chamber group? That we must listen to one another?"

"What you're proposing is anarchy," said Theo, "all the rehearsal time chewed up by people mouthing off, and nothing accomplished. You can call it a benevolent dictatorship, or whatever you like. This is my theatre. I have the deciding vote."

"Mouthing off?"

"Jeanne, we were behind schedule when this conversation began. The next scene doesn't involve you. Take a breather. Think about the notes I gave you. Resolve your indecision."

"No one else is even affected, Theo. The court reacts to Lady

Macbeth's status, not to how much or how little emotion she shows. It's the scenes with *you* that are revealing. Let's try it, Theo."

"Would you like to take over the direction of the company, Jeanne? I know that movie stars can dictate what happens on a film set because they're worth millions in profits. We'll have this discussion again when you're in *that* position."

CAST PARTY

—

Corinna checked herself out in the mirror, smoothing the sleek pale-green leggings, the soft knee-high purple suede boots. She had gone without lunch for months to pay for those boots, but they were worth every penny. The man's shirt that she wore was a thrift shop find, but it was quality silk, and had first seen the light in the kind of shop where they sell Valentino and Yves St. Laurent.

She ran down the back stairs to the side door that served as her private entrance. There had been lots of competition for her furnished attic, but she had been lucky and the Kirbys had chosen her to be their tenant. Mrs. Kirby was forever leaving baked treats at the top of the stairs, and Corinna had been given cutting rights in the garden. "There's only so many ways I can think of to use lettuce," her landlady had said. "The kids have their own gardens, so it's just Dad and me."

The party was in full swing when Corinna arrived, but she found a spot for her bike near Chas's big Harley. She took that as an omen, but when she set out to find him, he was nowhere to be seen. He wasn't among the crush of partygoers on the veranda, nor upstairs in the turret where Mitch and Milo were deep in conversation.

She heard the sound of water splashing at the back of the house, and the raucous sound of grownups at play in the pool.

Theo and Pam's annual party — known as Theo's Tech Week Toot — was held the Saturday before the first tech week of the season, a time that tried the most stalwart. The actors would already have been weeks in forging their characters, working tirelessly to meld ideas and emotions into one coherent whole. Then, in the no-man's-land between fatigue and second wind, and surrounded by people obsessing over a million fussy details, they had to pull everything to bits again, light cue to light cue. A rip-snorting blow-out could be magical at this point — lots of booze, terrific food, really good music for dancing, and an unspoken consensus that at any moment all hell might break loose.

Corinna found Chas, almost hidden, beneath the canopy of a large rattan swing at the far end of the garden. There was no sign of Selina. She leaned forward to say hello assuming a stance that she knew showed her off to advantage. "I'll go, if you'd rather be on your own."

When Chas leaned forward and touched her short-cropped head, she thought they would both be turned to stone.

It took but a second, but Selina was walking through the greenhouse just then, carrying a plate heaped with food and looking for Chas to share it. She saw Chas's hand cup the back of Corinna's head, felt his tenderness. He used to touch her head like that, once, but no longer.

◈

In the large drawing room, the subject was professional longevity.

"Well, *I* intend to go on till I drop!" Coming from Damien Trevellyan, this was hardly a surprise. He was already well into his seventies. "Like darling Dougie Donkin."

The late Douglas Donkin, a comic actor of great repute, had died of a massive heart attack at the Guthrie the previous winter, minutes after executing a rapid-fire delivery of the Duke of Plaza Toro's lengthy and tongue-twistingly difficult solo in Gilbert and Sullivan's *Gondoliers*. He had been brilliant, as usual, and at the solo's completion the audience gave him a particularly gratifying round of applause, after which he had walked off into the wings and dropped dead.

"Easy for you to say, Damien," said Jeanne. "You can choose your time. There's work for the men at any age; it's not the same for the women. We have to quit when the parts dry up."

Every actress in hearing bobbed her head in accord.

"It's not just the number of jobs," Jeanne continued, "but the kind. If an actress isn't someone's idea of love interest, mother, or crone, she's out of luck!"

"Ma belle Jeanne," said Francois. "I know you to be *féministe*. How is it that you call yourself actress? On m'a dit that everyone must now be called actors, whatever their sex. Que c'est effrayant! In the French language, *everything* must have gender, thank God!"

"I am a feminist, Francois, but to me that means holding fast to a word that carries in it the history of my kind — actress. Things were different in France. In the English-speaking world, it's only quite recently that it's *respectable* for women to perform in public. Not that long ago, women like me were thought to be whores."

Francois could always be shocked by the English. "Ce n'est pas vrai!"

"Oh, but it is true. We had to *fight* to take our place on the stage. The word 'actor' conjures up none of that history for me."

"Hear! Hear!" said Damien. "Absolutely right!"

Damien knew Jeanne from way back. Though he had never wanted to do anything but act, to see her wearing so many different hats — and wearing them so well — filled him with pride. She was like the great actor–managers of long ago, some of whom Damien had had the pleasure to know personally. Occasionally, he blushed to admit, in the Biblical sense.

"It may be cold comfort," said Theo, "but you're still better off than the singers and dancers of either sex."

"True," said Damien. "The poor dancers must pack up their tutus at forty, and the singers are practically driven out in their fifties. I don't imagine there's much call for character *singers*. Of course, the great Dame Nellie Melba was an exception to the rule."

"True enough," laughed Theo. "She went on forever."

"Not fair, Theo," said Milo, knowing Melba was keen to hear more about her famous namesake. "Let us in on the joke."

Marie knew the Nellie Melba story. She sent Theo little warning looks.

The night air had become chilly, and more and more people had gathered in the drawing room, where a lively fire burned.

"Well . . ."

"Come on, Theo. We're all grownups," someone called out. "You tell it then, Damien!"

"Go ahead, old man," said Theo. It was too late to back off.

Damien, given licence, played to the gallery. "For those of you who've just emerged from the cave, darlings, Dame Nellie Melba was a drop-dead, gorgeous, turn-of-the-century soprano, who performed to great acclaim all over the world."

"Peach Melba's named after her, right?" Brittany was one of the apprentices. Her unflagging enthusiasm had, even this early in the season, already begun to grate.

"That's right, love," said Damien, adoring the limelight. "But the lady had a great many more strings to her bow. *Tons* of lovers; but of course that's *de rigeur* for operatic divas, the size of a lady's voice being in direct correlation to her appetite in the boudoir. What distinguished the delightful Melba was her ability to sing on and on, in a voice as sweet and supple as a girl's, when those of her contemporaries had long since cracked and gone silent."

"What was her secret?" asked Brittany.

"Semen."

The men in the room tried to control their self-satisfied smirks, and failed utterly. You could tell by their faces which women liked the idea, and which were repelled.

"What?" asked Melba. Surely, she couldn't have heard right. She had been expecting another answer, one more in keeping with the elevated opinion she had of these people who spent their lives, as they said, "doing the classics." It was perhaps a naive thought, but Melba had gone from the farm to the casino with few stops in between. There were great gaps in her education.

"You heard correctly, my dear. Daily doses of young healthy semen."

Melba's face went white. Then red. Then white again. Her spine was stiff, her arms rigid at her sides. "Excuse me," she whispered.

Milo made to follow her, but she wouldn't have it.

"No!" she said. "Don't come with me!"

∽

Marie was always uncomfortable in Theo and Pam's house, and rarely went there except for company festivities, or the occasional birthday celebration. Above all, she tried to avoid having to go upstairs where the intimacies of the couple's life together were made flesh — a photograph, a sweater draped over a landing, the gizmo that hung from the shower holding Theo's favourite shampoo.

But this time, Marie had no choice. Melba had been gone far too long and Milo was starting to worry. When Marie got to the upstairs bathroom, she could hear two women weeping. *My gracious*, she thought, *who else besides Melba has her knickers in a knot?*

She knocked loudly, to be heard above the din.

"It's Marie Verity. Can I come in?"

The crying ceased abruptly.

Well, thought Marie. *That was something, at least.*

Inside the bathroom, Selina sat on the toilet, while Melba perched on the side of the tub. In spite of some residual snuffling, the storm had passed. The two women looked at each other and laughed.

"Your eyes are all red and puffy," said Melba.

"So what?" said Selina. "Your mascara's running down your cheeks."

It was true. They were both utter horrors. They laughed even louder.

"Please, girls!" More knocking. "Open up!"

Selina drew the latch and stepped aside to let Marie enter. The three of them looked at each other, took in a big breath, and let it out again.

"If either of you ladies ever needs a shoulder, I'm easy to find," said Marie. "Just look for the short gal. In the meantime, why don't you freshen up and rejoin the party? It'd mean a lot to everyone, especially your boys."

"I didn't bring any makeup," said Melba.

Selina looked in her small evening bag. "Neither did I."

"Here, you can use my makeup," said Marie. She opened her purse, and tipped its contents onto the counter. "But first, wash your faces! Your eyes are redder'n a communist rally!"

It was Selina who noticed that things other than makeup lived in Marie's handbag. Amidst the hairpins, lipsticks, and jars of liquid foundation lay a fat vial with a prescription label.

"What's this for, Marie?" asked Selina, deliberately casual.

"Oh, that?" Marie was equally blithe. She dropped the plastic container back into her bag. "It's a mild painkiller. For arthritis."

Selina knew otherwise. The vial was transparent, and both the look of the capsule and the name on the label were familiar to her. It was one of a battery of drugs that had been prescribed for her mother in her fight against cancer. Her mother had lost the battle.

More knocking.

It was Jeanne this time, who had observed all the departures, and who thought at least one of them should have returned by now. "Hey, you gals," she called through the door, "you can't monopolize the bathroom. Don't you know how much beer people are putting away downstairs?"

The bathroom door opened and Selina and Melba emerged, newly scrubbed, followed by Marie. Selina let Marie and Melba precede her downstairs, then said *sotto voce* to Jeanne, "Did you know that Marie's taking some very heavy duty medicine? You all seem so fond of her. I thought you might want to know."

⌀

It was one-thirty when Jeanne left the party, though judging by the growing number of people jumping into the pool, it was just getting into high gear. She had come upon Michelle and Corey in a lover's knot on a porch swing, and Michelle had actually winked at her. The two of them had drawn close since the mugging, as if seeing one another get pummelled had kickstarted the chemistry between them.

Seeing them made her think of Carmen, toiling away on her behalf in faraway London. Neither she nor Colleen would be in the audience on opening night.

"I *asked* them not to come," Jeanne had explained to Marie. She wanted to be at her best when her nearest and dearest saw her perform, like a round of brie that's had the chance to ripen, not one that's green and hard. It was *that* performance she wanted Colleen and Carmen to see; not the just-stitched-together creature she would manage for opening night.

Jeanne walked up the drive to her cottage. Marie's place was ablaze with light. The old house was no more sound-proof than it was cold- and leak-proof, and she could hear Louis Armstrong singing "On the Sunny Side of the Street" via the miracle of cassette tape. Marie was tap-dancing in her kitchen, wearing shiny black patent tap shoes on her tiny size-four feet, and wrapped in her favourite robe — a tatty pale-blue chenille number still sporting a few remnants of pink ball-fringe. Her pink foam hair-rollers bounced in rhythm.

Jeanne knew she should turn away, not infringe on Marie's privacy, but the temptation proved too great.

"On the sunny . . ." Ball, shuffle. "On the sunny . . ." Ball, shuffle, turn. "On the sunny . . ." Big finish. ". . . side of the street!"

Uh-oh. Jeanne had been spotted. In lieu of a bow, Marie lifted the coffee pot and the brandy bottle in invitation.

Jeanne tapped at her watch — it was late. She had talked to as many people as she could at the party, and she was tired out. She had never been a natural party girl, and having fun for hours at a stretch was very hard work for her.

Marie pooh-poohed her objection with a smiling grimace, and Jeanne let herself be tempted. A finger of brandy would go down well before bed. She didn't usually drink much at parties — too many memories, perhaps, of a pissed Tommy Senior breaking all the dishes and threatening to beat the shit out of them. Besides, there was the matter of how to deal with the information passed on by Selina. Perhaps this would be a good time to draw Marie out.

Marie ushered Jeanne into the small double parlour, her "company" room. Marie's housekeeping, lackadaisical at best, hit unprecedented lows under the pressures of a new season. Much of her work was in papier mâché, layer upon layer of newspaper strips, saturated with a flour and water glue, and formed into just about anything. It was a cheap and easy medium, and a marvel of recycling; but, oh, what a mess it could make, with bits of glue and paper sticking everywhere, particularly to Marie. The Shameless Hussies were everywhere, daintily weaving their way between the stacks of newspaper and the gluepots.

There was a small bulletin board on the wall near the stove. One of the items caught Jeanne by surprise.

"A recipe for sushi. But you *hate* sushi."

The clipping had been torn from a newspaper in roughly the shape of a fish.

"I do. I cut it out of the paper for Theo. Except for oysters, we southern folk believe in cookin' your catch 'fore you eat it."

"I'm going to get you one of those clip-it things," said Jeanne.

"Honey, I've used my thumbnail to clip things out of the paper ever since I was a child."

An ornate glass-fronted mahogany cabinet took up most of one wall in the dining room. Grand though it was, it served as a humble catch-all for Marie's craft supplies — shelves full of fabric remnants, coils of wire, raffia, wool, and twine.

"You still haven't come over to play," said Marie. She picked up a red papier mâché vase that held blue and yellow papier mâché flowers. "This here's Michelle's. She's still got to give it a coat of varnish."

The flowers looked like gerberas. *Good*, thought Jeanne. Gerberas were happy flowers. Michelle deserved some happiness.

Marie's current piece was always displayed on the large Queen Anne table. She didn't believe in covering a work still in progress. "Why, sometimes, I'll get my best ideas just passin' through," she would say.

Jeanne, who had last seen it in its early stages, was amazed. Technically, it was still only a humble papier mâché maquette, but to call it that would be misleading. It was sculpture. The obvious way to view the piece was head on, the better to admire the miniature leather garments, the chain-mail, and the armature. To Jeanne's way of thinking, it packed the greatest punch looked at from above, where you stared into the malevolent upturned faces of the three witches. Each flew a chariot with black leather wings trailing lengthy dark strands. These were attached to the figure of Macbeth — to his heart and his entrails, his hands and his legs — yanking him from the ground into the air.

"For Theo?" The question was rhetorical. No other director was ever thus honoured, no matter how much they cajoled. Cedric Peterson had once tried to bribe her with a case of champagne, but some things were just not for sale.

By the time they said good-night, Jeanne knew no more about Marie's health than she had when she arrived. It wasn't that she had forgot. But she had been unable to answer this question to her satisfaction: If she were to ask Marie straight out if she were ill, would Marie tell her the truth? And even if she did, would she thank an old friend for the news that her secret was out? Jeanne thought not.

THE ACTORS' CURSE

Melba got back from her outing with Selina just as Milo was pouring milk over a bowl of cereal.

"I'm sorry," she said. "I meant to be here to give you some dinner, but I got kinda tied up with Selina."

The two women had become quite close since their crying duet in Pam and Theo's upstairs bathroom, as company wives will do when their menfolk rehearse long hours, and there are no children to care for.

"How's rehearsal?"

"Getting there."

"Did they get you new clogs?"

Milo, who had been cast as the Porter in *Macbeth*, was to wear wooden clogs for the role. The pair he had been given were hurting his feet.

"No, but Marie did a little whittling or something inside, and they're fine. I'm glad you're here," he said, pulling her onto his knee, big and tall though she was. "I was starting to worry."

Melba helped herself to his cereal. "She's a very unhappy lady."

"Who? Selina? Why? Selina has everything that money can buy."

Melba looked at him, rueful. "Honey, you know better than that. Anyway, she thinks Chas is in love with someone else."

"Who?" asked Milo, as if he didn't already know the answer. It was that green-eyed blonde kid.

"The girl who helped him cut his cake, Selina says."

"Yeah," sighed Milo. "The beauteous Corinna. Chas 'in *love* with her'! That's a bit much! Let him have his little ding-dong and everything'll go back to being exactly the way it was."

"It's a little more complicated than that," said Melba. "You see, Chas isn't actually sleeping with her. At least Selina doesn't think so."

"So then what's the problem?" asked Milo. "Is he sleeping with *her*? With Selina?"

"Yes, he is."

"Isn't that the way things are supposed to be between husbands and wives?"

"But he wasn't sleeping with her before!" said Melba, exasperated with how long it was taking Milo to understand. But she had to admit the situation was a bit upside down. "Selina thinks he only wants to have sex with her because he's so turned on by this Corinna and he can't have her."

Milo pulled a face. "Whaddya mean, 'can't have her'? We're talkin' show biz, here. It happens all the time!"

But all the while he was thinking, *not to Chas*. After his experience with Bobby, Chas had lost his taste for casual sex. One tipsy night in the sack with a pal, Milo thought, and Chas's life path had been plucked from the sunshine and placed in deep shadow.

Milo had a sudden thought. "Has Selina ever said anything to you about Chas's missing baby?"

Melba was puzzled. "Never. And since *you* told me in confidence, I certainly wasn't going to bring it up."

You never can tell, thought Milo, the credibility of his new idea growing by the second. Sometimes people didn't fill their spouses in on the most basic stuff about themselves, stuff that could pre-empt years of marital discord.

"I wonder if Selina knows *any* of this stuff?" said Milo.

"If she does, she's never said anything."

Milo grasped Melba's shoulders. "I just remembered something! Something I never told Chas; something I thought he already knew. But *now* I'm thinking maybe he didn't. Maybe he's been beating up on himself for nothing, all these years!"

*

"How could Selina *say* those things?"

Calming the Almonds seemed to have become the day's task for the Tessiers.

"Timing, like everything else in this bloody world. She probably had to get it off her chest or bust. Haven't *you* ever felt like that? *I* have." Milo made himself comfortable on the big couch and lit a cigarette. "Anyway, this business with Corinna. You're not in love with her like Selina says, are you?" Chas looked aghast at Milo. "Well, either you are, or you're not; which is it? I have to admit I thought you had a little something going on. You've been a changed guy this last week, almost like the Chas I remember."

"Milo, I guess I'm going to have to tell you something. I wasn't going to until I'd spoken to her first —"

"Chas, who are you talking about? What *her*?"

"Corinna, you numbskull! My daughter!"

Well, this is unexpected, thought Milo. It rather put the spanner into *his* works, but he must push on nonetheless. He had wakened the sleeping dogs, and now they were clamouring at the door.

"Chas, all that I ask is that you listen. I may not change your mind about anything, but you gotta hear me out."

Chas flung himself onto a sofa.

"Did you ever . . . ?" Milo was finding his task more difficult than he had expected.

"Ever *what*, for God's sake?"

". . . ever consider you might not be the father of Bobby's child?"

"Of course I am!" said Chas. "Why are you asking these questions? It's ancient history. We *knew* all of Bobby's boyfriends. She brought them around for our seal of approval."

It was true: from the pizza delivery boy, to the silver-haired gentleman of sixty who had offered to keep her, not knowing Bobby could buy him and sell him a hundred times over.

"Maybe there was one she didn't want us to meet."

"Don't make me crazy, Milo."

"Give a guy a break. It's hard to say after so long!" Milo gathered his courage. "(a) the baby was premature, so you can't tell much about the conception date from that; (b) you weren't the only one Bobby had sex with that Christmas."

"Oh?"

"One night, when you were off tending bar somewhere, there was a broken gas main on our block. I remember it was around Christmas because our cheapskate landlord had actually put some coloured lights up around the entrance, and I remember thinking how nice it looked, just in time for the Christmas party. Anyway, the point of my story is that Bobby and I walked home from school together. I'd invited her to go out and have a beer later, but she turned me down; said she had to stay in to work on some text for Miss Brewer. You remember how Bobby was. Assignments never meant dick to her, but she always made a big effort for Miss Brewer."

He paused. The story was getting harder to tell.

"It's okay, Milo; I won't shoot the messenger."

"Well, okay. If you're sure. Anyway, all of a sudden the whole block is crawling with cops and firemen; there's a gas leak somewhere on the street, and all of the buildings have to be vacated. In two seconds people are pouring out of their apartments, and everyone's milling around, the way people do when there's an emergency, but there was no sign of Bobby. I was afraid she might've taken one of her sleeping pills and hadn't heard the alarm, so I ran back into the building and pressed her buzzer. When there was *still* no reply, I ran up the stairs and banged on her door." There was no going back now. "When she finally opened the door, she was just doing up her robe. She'd just got out of bed — you know that look — and she wasn't alone."

Chas's face was stony. "Who was it?"

"Remember how small those places were? You could actually hear someone zipping their fly in the next room. Then, I heard this guy saying, in an English accent, 'What's all that banging, love?'"

Silence.

"Theo?" asked Chas.

Milo nodded.

"How come you never mentioned it?"

"It was just before we broke for Christmas and there was so much going on — end of term showings, parties. Besides, we all knew Bobby was sleeping around. Maybe I thought you already knew. It's all so *long* ago. I was sure someone'd say something when Bobby found out she was pregnant, and when no one did, I figured you'd worked it all out between you. If you hadn't been so quick to claim the role of daddy . . ."

⁂

Chas hadn't slept. He phoned Theo at first light.

"I have to see you."

Theo squinted at the luminous dial of his alarm clock.

"Is everything all right, Chas? You're not sick or anything?"

"I'm in perfect health, thank you. I want to see you before rehearsal, Theo. I'd appreciate it if you could be at your office at nine-thirty."

"Chas, what's this —"

Click.

How different Chas's life would have been had Theo come forward. They could have established which of them was the father. They still could. Corinna was here. Somehow, Theo must have managed to pry her whereabouts from Bobby's family, where Chas himself had failed. That might buy Theo *some* forgiveness. But not nearly enough.

⁂

It took a moment for Theo to finally twig. "What do you *mean*, 'Bobby's daughter'? Corinna?"

"Listen to her," said Chas. "Watch the way she moves across the stage."

"Yes, Chas, she's extremely talented. That's why she's here. The rest, I'm afraid you're making up out of whole cloth."

"Put her in an auburn wig and she'd look just like Bobby!"

"She's the same *type*; yes, Chas. There are *lots* of intense, talented, sexy young actresses, and some of them might even resemble Bobby. But that doesn't mean she was their mother, or that you or I are their daddy!"

"Corinna was *adopted*, Theo, I heard her say so. And she's exactly the right age. She's even crazy about peanut butter, just like Bobby. Isn't that one coincidence too many?"

"*Peanut butter?*" Theo permitted himself a mirthless laugh. "It must be all those years in Hollywood, Chas. You've gone soft in the brain. Yes, Corinna *was* adopted, as it happens. As I understand it, her parents died in a Polish train wreck when Corinna was a year and a half old, and she was adopted by her mother's only sister, who'd emigrated to Wisconsin."

Chas was visibly deflating. "You mean, she couldn't . . . ?"

"That's right, Chas. She couldn't. Shall we close the file?"

"One more question! Did you care for Bobby? Or was she just one more tasty young thing in need of your guidance and understanding?"

"Now, now, Chas, that's more than one question," said Theo, attempting to keep his cool but not succeeding. "Of course I cared for her! Ask any of those young women how they felt about my attentions, and I think they'd tell you that it gave them confidence. Even a certain shine, *I* always thought. Not one of them was ever a conquest. What would be the joy in that?"

"And when Bobby died?"

"I mourned her, as we all did. Missed her presence, as we all did. That delightful fey quality that made you feel you were enjoying some extraordinary form of inter-species communication. The dark side of Audrey Hepburn. Special. But not strong, our Bobby, as we know too well. And what makes you think that the choice is between you and me? Bobby didn't exactly put on a chastity belt when we weren't around."

Theo was standing behind his desk when Chas's fist connected with his jaw. The blow knocked him into his chair, which was on rollers. His head took quite a crack when it hit the wall.

"That's it, Chas! You've totally lost it! Go home and bring yourself to your senses. Another antic like this and — whatever our history — I'll report you to Equity."

"What's stopping you doing it now?"

"Don't push me, laddie. There are a number of actors around who could play Benedick. Some very good, and very hungry, ones, who haven't spent half a decade riding around on a stupid horse."

"Try it, Theo. God knows, I *am* rusty, but your board of directors seems to feel my name will sell tickets. They like that. I came here to find out if I still have what it takes, and *Macbeth* fits the bill. I'll have to convince people I don't already hate your guts when we first meet in Act two, scene three. If I can pull *that* off, I'll know I can play anything."

He turned on his heel, leaving Theo fuming and incredulous. *What the hell is going on?* wondered Theo. *First Michelle and Corey get mugged; then I get assaulted by — of all people — Chas!* For one fleeting second he let himself think the very thing he had promised himself that he wouldn't. *Dear Mary, Mother of God, it's the curse!* But no! He wouldn't have it! He would not respond to this ridiculous dovetailing of coincidence and superstition.

The portrait of Arabella looked on from above. He scanned her face for signs as to how he should proceed, but, for the first time, there was nothing.

♪

Timmy, Theo's stepson, was one of those young men who have trouble finding themselves.

"But that's hardly a reason to make him an apprentice, Pam!" Theo had said.

Pamela, however, took the view that, without her family, there would have been no Arden Shakespearean Festival.

Luckily, thought Theo, *one can always assume with Timmy that he'll do something to ensure his own ouster, sooner or later.* His most recent offence had been smoking dope on theatre grounds.

"One more foul-up," Theo told him, "and you'll be fired. Or brought up on Equity charges. Maybe both."

Timmy did his best not to smirk, which was not very good at all.

"I mean it," said Theo.

To hell with that! thought Timmy. Theo liked the odd puff himself; he had seen him. And all of that curse crap. Was he really supposed to take that stuff seriously?

The long Formica-topped tables in the big dressing rooms made a great surface for jamming, a way to kill time until the next scene was called. Timmy, his shirt collar turned up, his watch cap well forward, was in top form:

Walkin' in de forest
In de middle of de night . . .

He had a sinuous midriff for a white boy.

'Long came de witches
Gave Big Mac such a fright!
You gonna be de king,
Dat's true!
Not you, Banquo,
Not you!

Timmy executed a tight Sammy Davis spin, the seaman's cap held fast to his curly dark head.

But leave it to your kiddies' kids,
And your great grandkids, too.
Bi-i-i-ig Mac!

Every man jack of them was in on the chorus:

Big Mac!
Walkin' in de forest . . .
Walkin' in de forest . . .

The voices fell away when they spotted Mitch. His hand on the doorknob was white-knuckled and shook with an emotion not one of his colleagues had witnessed in a career that spanned fifty years. The counterfeit, yes, when Mitch played some irate cuckold of a husband in a Feydeau farce, but there was no mistaking the real thing. He glared at Timmy.

"You all right, Mitch?"

Someone fetched a chair, which was ignored.

"Do you . . ." Mitch's breathing was ragged. ". . . Have any idea of what you're doing?"

Timmy was at a loss for words. He knew that some actors, especially the Brits, took the Macbeth curse very seriously.

"J-just a little jamming, Mitch."

"Jamming!" said Mitch. The higher his voice rose, the more pale he became. "Jamming?" Timmy fought the urge to lower his eyes. "How dare you make light of this play? It's claimed actors better than you could ever hope to be!" Mitch was in the act of raising an admonishing finger, when a wrenching pain stopped him cold in his tracks.

"I'm going for Theo," said Timmy, utterly shaken. "Someone call 911!"

Whatever else one could say about Timmy, no one could call him a coward. Theo was onstage, plotting Banquo's death with his murderers, but it would be Timmy he would crucify when he heard what had happened.

Timmy burst out of the vomitorium and onto the stage like a rocket. Jeanne, who had been sitting in the first row, watching the rehearsal, rose up in alarm.

"Come quick, Theo," gasped Timmy. "Something's happened to Mitch!"

Theo paled. "What?"

"I'm not sure; a heart attack maybe."

Theo slapped him hard in the face.

"What's that for!" cried Timmy, shocked and humiliated.

Theo ran down the tunnel. "Somehow, this is down to you; I know it is!"

ↄ฿

"According to Doctor Kingstone," said Jeanne, "Mitch wanted to go right back to rehearsal."

"Surely, the doctor wouldn't let him do that!"

"Of course not, Michelle. 'You've just had a heart attack,' the doc says to Mitch. 'Complete bed rest and no stress.'"

They were in wardrobe, waiting for Francois. Jeanne's nightdress for the sleepwalking scene was to get a bit of tweaking, and Michelle had come along for company. Theo's note to the designer after last night's rehearsal had been, *Perhaps un peu too much décolletage, mon vieux?*

"Do you remember the time you —"

"— walked off the stage at the end of the sleepwalking scene in Sudbury?" Jeanne replied. "How could I ever forget that? The curse must have been particularly strong that year. The Canadian Opera Company was doing the operatic version of the play at exactly the same time, and their Lady Macbeth fell into the orchestra pit."

"Well, at least the theatre didn't burn down," said Michelle, "like Toronto's first opera house did, back in the nineteenth century. I read about it, somewhere. The fire under the witches' cauldron got out of control."

Francois swept into the room. "Out of control's *just* the way I'd sum it up, my darlings." He was wearing an Italian straw hat, battered just enough for perfection. "Trois heures le matin my phone rings, mes belles. *Three o'clock!*"

"Changes," said Jeanne, not the least bit surprised.

Francois withdrew a much-folded sheet of paper from his trouser pocket and tossed it on the cutting table. The blue velvet trousers were cut rather tight, so Michelle had to smooth the note a bit before she could read it.

"C'est toujours mieux to have things in writing with Theo," said Francois, "even if it's only my own. In the morning, when he thinks better of it, he prefers not to remember these little nocturnal emissions."

"'Go even further with the set,'" Michelle read. "'Scrap the head-lines. Instead, human limbs in trees; the stage strewn with decapitated heads; heads on pikes. Don't take the understanding of the audience for granted. Don't just refer to the carnage, *show* it!'"

After the shock of Mitch's collapse, it was comforting to have Theo behaving true to form, and right on schedule, too. The first part of what had come to be known as The Theo Syndrome had already been and gone. He had come down with a dreadful cold, and snuffled his way through the second week of rehearsal swathed in blankets and scarves, swigging the most current cure-all — a blend of zinc, vitamin B, lemon juice, ginseng, and tea. That done, he had advanced to the Syndrome's more unnerving aspects, involving radical changes to the set — in this case, the blood-soaked floor.

"Laid with such artistry!" cried Francois. "If you'll forgive the expression. And such cost!" Francois hated to see production money pissed away.

"'The new floor will be a hundred and eighty degree turnabout,'" Michelle continued, "'a glossy black lacquer.'"

"'Smooth enough to *glide* on!' he tells me! I'm supposed to be in his office maintenant, working out the details."

Being party to the goings-on at the theatre gave the ladies who worked in wardrobe points outside its walls. It allowed them to bask some in the reflected glamour, and spurred them to the work at hand, which was highly skilled and grossly underpaid. Francois, being French, understood this, and played his role to the hilt.

"Mais, j'vais pas y aller! He'll only change his mind l'apres-midi." A physically small and unprepossessing figure, Francois was one of the few people who ever stood up to Theo, albeit in a most non-confrontational way. "In the beginning, of course, I'd run comme un fou, even in the middle of the night. The dawn would find me in the theatre, stripped naked to the waist, changing everything in sight."

"But Mister Francois," said Josephina, a cheery apple-cheeked woman, "you know you *like* to be stripped naked!"

FANS AND FOES

Jeanne, Michelle, and Marie were soaking up the sun in the garden, the table nearby littered with post-brunch debris. Brunching together had become a Sunday tradition, one that had been revived from the festival's early days. For the first time since coming to Arden, Jeanne felt relaxed. It could be entirely her imagination that had her thinking that Theo had finally accepted her as an equal partner, but Jeanne didn't think so. She couldn't pinpoint the precise moment, or what had finally got him to turn the corner, but turn it he had. She might be one of his bastard children, but she was still one of his. *Put the man in the ring*, she thought, *and he had to box.*

"I've been trying to get Marie to confirm the hot rumour," said Michelle.

"The one about Theo announcing his retirement at the board meeting?" asked Jeanne.

"*You've* heard it, *too*?" Marie was appalled at the currency this ridiculous rumour was enjoying.

"If he *was* thinking about retiring," said Michelle, "a twentieth anniversary'd be a good time for it."

"Has Theo ever said anything to you about retiring, Marie?" asked Jeanne.

"No! Do *you* run around talking to people about retiring? Do *I*? Theo couldn't *breathe* away from Arden, for God's sake! Besides, I think I know what the big announcement's going to be." Marie lowered her voice. "Y'all keep it to yourselves, now, but I think Theo's going to announce plans for a theatre school here at Arden. For years now he's been complaining about how NAADA's standards have been slipping; and he's never had any use for the university programs." She poured herself some coffee from a vacuum jug. "Wait and see if I'm not right!"

As a rule, Marie didn't much care for important announcements. Most often they had to do with people leaving, or stepping down because of ill health. Theo looked well enough, but you couldn't always tell by appearances. She, of all people, knew that. If only she could be sure Pam looked after him properly. Word had it the woman didn't know how to boil water, never mind cook. Every now and then Marie would leave a Tupperware care package at his desk. Jambalaya was still a sentimental favourite, but she occasionally indulged him in his latest culinary passion — sushi.

"Give me some raw tuna on a mouthful of vinegared rice, and I'll follow you anywhere," he had said after polishing off her initial attempt with gusto. Marie was troubled by the idea of him eating the raw fish, but she took her praise where she could find it. These days, Theo was more likely to be going on at her about something; obsessing about her fingernails, and why she didn't wash her hair more often. Life among the dyes and gluepots of the props department didn't readily lend itself to Theo's high standards in hygiene and aesthetics.

"Theo looks splendid for his age," said Jeanne. "Why should he retire?"

"They said that about Mitch, too," countered Michelle, "and look what happened."

"Theo has as much energy as he's ever had," said Jeanne. "It's *me* who has trouble keeping up with *him*."

"Theo's one of those lucky people who age well," said Marie. "I once accused him — only half in jest — with being part vampire, he'd looked so young for so long."

"What did he say?" asked Michelle.

"Oh, he agreed."

☙

"Please pass me those *heavenly* chickpeas," said Marie.

Toro had prepared a delicate lentil flan, and herbed quinoa wrapped in endive. There were lemon rice dumplings so light they dissolved in the mouth. And these were only the appetizers; the *amuses geules*, as Francois would say.

"*Walnut* crust tofu, did you say, Toro?" asked Jeanne.

The management at the Princess had never quite reconciled itself to the presence of Toro as chef to Mr. Willison during his stay with them, or his rearrangement of the furnishings in accordance with the principles of feng shui; but Mr. Willison was an annual guest and a very generous tipper.

The Almonds and Tessiers had also been invited to dinner, but both couples were captive to out-of-town guests and wouldn't arrive until later.

Adam lifted his glass. "To our beloved Mitch, and the powers that spared him."

They drank, the vintage bubbly helping to dissolve the collective lump in the throat, though Michelle had to ask for a tissue to dab at her eyes.

"And now, I hereby declare this celebration *open!*" He turned to Marie.

"Another reason for joy, my children. After more years of outright rejection than I care to remember, the great Lady Verity has finally granted me the privilege of transporting her extraordinary *oeuvre* to New York, where it will take its rightful place in the greatest exhibition of Shakespeariana ever assembled, at the Metropolitan Museum of Art."

"You're absolutely sure," asked Marie, not for the first time, "that Theo's given his permission?"

"In writing, my love," said Adam. "Want to see?"

Marie had hoped to be told that Theo had had to be cajoled, subjected to arguments about how he could no longer, in conscience, withhold his collection from the public view. But who was she kidding? Theo enjoyed her pieces well enough, but he had lived with Marie's artistry for decades. He took it utterly for granted that she should be able to do the things she did. Each year, he arranged for a modest display of the current piece in the upstairs lobby near the bar. All the rest were in storage. Or, as he called it, safekeeping. "One day, of course," he would say, "when we have our own exhibition hall . . ."

Each maquette depicted a quintessential moment in one of Shakespeare's plays: Hamlet at the graveside addressing Yorick's skull, Romeo wooing Juliet in the garden. The early pieces, the Hamlet for instance, were small enough to hold in the palm of a hand, but over the years they had increased in size and complexity to the point where they were often wired for light and sound: fountains tinkled, water ran.

"If I *had* to choose," said Adam, "I'd have to say that my all-time favourite is the Arctic *King Lear*." Marie had depicted the old man on an ice floe, bent double against the wind. His tattered parka had been stitched of real sealskin.

"And my next favourite," he added, "is the one for *The Tempest*!"

"The comics were Francois' inspiration that season," said Marie.

"How did Prospero effect his magic?" asked Jeanne. The production was after her time with the company.

Marie laughed. "With this huge bloody computer that strongly resembled an upholstered Wurlitzer organ. That's how I did the maquette: Theo pressing its buttons with one hand, and waving a baton with the other."

With Adam living in a townhouse in Greenwich Village and Michelle in a flat in the East Village, one might have thought they would have bumped into each other, but they had only once, ten years earlier, when Michelle had attended Spencer's funeral. To see Adam now was bittersweet for Michelle, but the emphasis was on the sweet rather than the bitter. In these terrible days of AIDS, he looked hale and hearty, and he was very handsome, still. She was touched that he had brought framed photos from home. There was even a small one of the two of them, taken durint that long agaon Christmas in New York. There was an 8″ x 10″ glossy of Cleone, still defiantly red-headed at seventy, her eyelashes long and thick enough to do serious damage in an embrace.

"My mother asked to be remembered to you," Adam said to Michelle. He *had* loved her, and had been miserably sorry to have hurt her. She and Sean would be forever on his conscience. "She still tours." Adam spoke of his mother with affection. "Not the 'A' houses anymore, of course, but she doesn't care. Cleone's always sung as much for the love of it as for the money. Her biggest kicks now come from singing for shut-ins at hospitals and old folks' homes. She even sticks around to chat and sign autographs."

Two of the photographs were of Adam and a man with burning eyes. One of the shots had been taken during Adam's first year at NAADA. The two were riding horses somewhere in Muskoka, looking fit and handsome. The other had been taken just a few months ago. Somewhere on a terrace in Italy, Adam and a barely recognizable Sean were raising their glasses to the camera.

"Yes, that's Sean," Adam said to Michelle. "My punishment for not having been a good Catholic is going to be an eternity in purgatory, wondering what would have happened if I *hadn't* listened to Theo."

Michelle took his hand. "You mean, about 'going straight'?"

"Sean might still be alive."

"Children, children . . ." said Marie, ever the peacemaker. "It may all seem a tempest in a teapot now, what with gay lib and same sex marriage and all, but this was a time before Stonewall. Before Gay Pride. Before gays adopting kids. Things were different then."

༄

Marie was convinced that Theo would one day write his memoirs, and to that end had been compiling a scrapbook for him. It was to be a surprise. Marie had managed to finagle copies of many of the photos on her most-wanted list, but one in particular was outstanding. It was an old black-and-white photograph of Arabella, watching her young ward Theo shake hands with Olivier in his Old Vic dressing room. It held pride of place on Theo's desk in an antique silver frame.

The hallway was deserted, and when she peeked into Theo's office it was empty, too, as was the anteroom. *Hooray!* thought Marie. She knew Theo's assistant, Maxine, was having lunch in the cafeteria because she had just left her there. She had told Marie that Theo was so tied up with rehearsals he hardly ever came to his office.

Marie tip-toed in and closed the door behind her. There, on the desk, was the photo. Her idea was to remove it, have it duplicated at one of those fast photo places, and return it to its frame before anyone had even noticed it was gone. The frame, however, was not co-operating. There were metal flaps that were too sharp and unyielding to manage with fingers alone, that had to be pushed away in order to remove the back of the frame and get at the picture. Luckily, Theo kept a letter opener in the centre desk drawer, which is just where Marie found it, lying beside a sheaf of papers.

Ordinarily, Marie would never glance at someone else's correspondence, but the letterhead was so big and bold, it drew the eye. *!ZAP TV!* The papers were contractual agreements, with Theo's elegant signature at the bottom of almost every page.

Wonderful! she thought. Arden's productions were finally going to be produced for television. Perhaps she had been wrong, after all. Perhaps this was what the big announcement was about! The company would be thrilled, especially the young turks always going on about Arden's "lack of strategic position in the electronic media." This would make them change their tune. But hold on . . .

Theo Thamesford in the role of William Shakespeare . . .

All risk of discovery forgotten, Marie scanned the pile of papers in growing shock and dismay. The contract was not for the company, but for Theo alone. Twenty-six shows to be shot over two seasons. Theo *was* leaving at the end of the season. Not to retire, but to work in television, a medium he had always professed to despise. And, what's more, he had said nothing to her.

"Marie? Is anything wrong?"

Dammit! thought Marie. She decided to brazen it out. "I need to borrow your photo. I'll have it back in a couple of hours."

"You read the contract." It was a statement, not a question.

Marie nodded. "You're leaving. After all these years, I'll finally be out of your sight, and you'll be out of mine."

"Marie, it's been years. I'm married."

"Don't pretend, Theo. That's not what I'm talking about."

"Marie, this is fifth-rate Joan Crawford. Don't cheapen yourself, love. You've made an important place for yourself in Arden, whether I'm here or not." He crossed to her and gently touched her cheek. "Haven't you noticed how thin on the ground jobs are for the aging Shakespearian actor? Think how few offers come Mitch's way these days, as compared to a decade ago." His voice caught as he thought of his old friend, laid low by his idiot stepson.

He sat down on the battered leather sofa, and patted the place beside him in invitation. "I'm tired, love. Burnt out. I cannot rack my brains yet one more time for still another innovative way to present Shakespeare. I want to work seven or eight months of the year and spend the rest of the time in the sun, reading and playing tennis. In Spain, perhaps." He took her hand. "Think of it; one job that could make me financially independent. Besides, the theatre that we loved, the kind we set out to do? It no longer exists, love. It's all about money, now, and 'making it.' Entertainment with a capital 'E'."

But Marie did not want to discuss the state of the theatre. "I've been the rudder for this ship of yours from way back, Theo. Almost as long as Mitch."

Theo nodded. True, all true. He was grateful.

"I can't follow you to London," said Marie. "Or Los Angeles."

☙

The brandy bottle was no solace but, like Everest, it was there. The Shameless Hussies pressed themselves up against her legs and complained of her negligence in catspeak. Othello, who had been a nameless newborn when *New York Magazine*'s John Simon declared Theo "the Othello of the decade," went so far as to leap into her lap and tug at the front of her sweater with his sharp little claws.

But Marie heard nothing, felt nothing. Some great cosmic vacuum cleaner in the sky had reached down and sucked away all meaning, all feeling. Theo on television. An Arden without Theo. It wasn't possible.

☙

There was business done when the Arden board of directors met for its annual meeting, largely rubber-stamping decisions already made and sometimes even acted upon. The true significance of the occasion was to keep the wheels greased, and let everyone know how important and appreciated they were. In this instance, they discharged their duties with dispatch. The theatre's air-conditioning system had broken down that morning, and everyone was yearning for a breath of fresh air. Besides, there was a slap-up lunch awaiting them back at Theo and Pam's. When the chairman asked if there was any new business and Adam Willison raised his hand, there was an audible groan.

"I know that you're all ready for a drink and some lunch," he said, "but I think it's fitting that I acquaint you with my plans. It's my intention to donate two million dollars to the building fund."

Had they heard right?

"Two *million*?" asked the chairman.

"That's right."

There were a few seconds of stunned surprise, after which a sudden celebratory pandemonium broke out. Everyone turned to Theo, the figurehead recipient of all this largesse. Theo, as slack-jawed as the rest, was on the verge of a reply when Adam resumed his address.

"But I do have conditions, the chief of them being, as we enter our third decade, that we consider a fresh approach to this next generation of theatregoers. For twenty years, we've had the benefit of exemplary, nay, legendary leadership, but there are younger, nimbler minds out there chafing to make their mark. In my humble opinion, I think it should be one of *them* who takes us into our third decade. At the same time, of course, everyone in this room knows that without Theo Thamesford, there *is* no Arden Festival. I propose, therefore, that we clear the way for Theo to establish here at Arden the kind of extraordinary theatre school he created at NAADA, of which I myself am a proud graduate. Furthermore, a season without at least *one* Theo Thamesford production would be a poor season indeed."

It was so artfully couched, it took a moment to realize that Theo was being shafted. And by one of his own lieutenants. *Et tu, Brute!* The first thought was that Adam and Theo were pulling some kind of a gag. Theo had once got them to believe, for a moment, that the Egyptian government was going to loan them part of the King Tut Exhibit for the opening of *Antony and Cleopatra*. But if it was a joke, Theo hadn't been in on its devising.

Everyone kerfuffled miserably about, wishing themselves anywhere but where they were, until someone, disregarding the rules of parliamentary procedure, motioned to table the new business, which motion was speedily passed.

"Ladies and gentlemen, as you know, the air conditioning in the building is malfunctioning and the boardroom is becoming oppressively hot," said the chairman, with no visible irony. "I move we recess."

"You're quite right, of course," said Theo, rising. "But before we do, I'd like to say a few words. I promise, I'll be brief."

No one would see *him* bleed, least of all he who wielded the dagger.

"It has been my intention, for some time now, to step down as artistic director at the end of this season." Theo took a buff envelope from an inner pocket and placed it on the boardroom table. "I've accepted an offer to appear in an internationally financed, twenty-six-part television series. And when that's done, I intend to retire somewhere among the palm trees and start in on those memoirs you've all been pressing me to write."

༄

Adam, his brain on fire, slumped behind the wheel of his car. Theo would be leaving Arden, and he'll have had fuck-all to do with it! Had he been cruel? Well, maybe . . . Was he justified? Yes!

He was so intent on his thoughts, he didn't spot Theo until the man was no more than ten feet away.

Damn! thought Adam. The last thing he wanted to do now was talk to Theo. He buckled his seatbelt and put the key in the ignition, but he couldn't bring himself to drive off. Theo slid into the passenger seat. Adam's gleaming Bentley had been easy to spot.

Adam's heart thumped loudly. *All the years of discipline*, he thought, *all the years of control; gone.* Run over, engulfed, by grief and by rage.

"It's your punishment, Theo!"

Theo was genuinely at a loss. "I beg your pardon?"

"You still don't know, do you?"

"What the fuck are you talking about, Adam?"

"Sean, Theo."

"Who? Oh, yes, Sean. Marie told me that he'd passed on. I was sorry to hear it, but what's that—"

"Spare me the euphemisms, Theo. Sean didn't 'pass on.' He died."

"Adam, I met the man once. Twenty-odd years ago." Theo opened the car door and got out. "We'll talk when you've come to your senses!" He slammed the car door and headed down toward the river and home. The board members were still upstairs in the bar, discussing the morning's sensations, but they would be at the house soon enough. He needed time to collect himself.

Adam unbuckled his seatbelt and took after him. "Not so fast!"

Theo looked straight ahead and kept walking. "Unless you learn to speak in a more civilized tone, Adam, this conversation is at an end. Though I'll admit to being very curious as to why you're so intent on running for Sonofabitch of the Year."

Adam fell in beside him, matching his brisk pace, not even bothering to sidestep the duck turds dotting the pathway. To their left, two big swans were kicking up a royal squawk. The two men had probably gotten too close to the swans' nesting grounds. They could be fierce creatures when challenged.

"Sean died of AIDS, Theo."

"I know that. I've said that I'm sorry. What else do you want me to say?"

"He died of AIDS because of *you*, Theo."

Theo's pace quickened. If Adam were having some kind of breakdown, Theo would need help. First Chas, and now Adam. What on earth was going on? Some kind of delayed adolescent rebellion? Or was the answer far simpler? *That* play, The Scottish Tragedy.

"I loved him, Theo," said Adam.

Perhaps this insanity is part of some prolonged grief cycle, thought Theo. He knew the expression "mad with grief" from Victorian novels, but he had always assumed it was just another example of Victorian over-statement. He hoped so. He had always been fond of Adam.

"I know you did, but you've loved others, surely?" said Theo. "Women, as well. Michelle. Marie."

Adam shook his head. "Not the way I loved Sean."

A sudden flurry of impatience arose in the older man. "Well, that's the way things go, sometimes!"

"We split because of you, Theo!"

Theo increased his pace, but as fast as he went, Adam went too.

"People think differently about gays, now," said Adam. "Even you. But that doesn't alter the facts."

A few yards away, the swans were still screaming.

"What facts?" said Theo.

"That queers weren't welcome at NAADA."

"Surely I wouldn't have made a statement so painfully bald," said Theo. "I'm sure you'll agree that a little equivocation is much more in keeping with my style. What I *probably* said was that you'd have an easier time if you encouraged the heterosexual side of your nature."

"Oh, *really*, Theo? Is *that* all? Anyway, that may be what you think *now*. Back then, it was 'leave off being queer, or get kicked out on your queer ass.' Like the moral coward I was, I listened to you."

"That's right," said Theo. "You gave Sean his walking papers, not I."

The thought shamed Adam still. "Yeah . . ."

"And you blame me?"

"You bet!"

"I always respected you, Adam. I don't remember you as someone who blindly took orders."

"It wasn't 'taking orders,' Theo. You were my Don Corleone, making me the offer I couldn't refuse. If I'd stayed with Sean, you'd have withheld something from me that I'd wanted all my life."

"How dare you!" cried Theo.

Adam caught him by the lapel.

"Take your hands off me, Adam, or I'll do something I'll *really* regret!"

A red tide swept through Adam's brain. The bastard still didn't get it!

He let go of the jacket, causing Theo to lurch and stumble.

"Who do you think you're pushing?" said Theo.

He pushed Adam back, and this time Adam *did* push him. "Dammit, Theo, I wasn't pushing!"

They were drawing closer to the nesting site, and the swans were going crazy, hissing and beating their wings.

"Sean wouldn't have spent his life screwing around if I'd stayed with him," said Adam. "He'd never have got AIDS." Salt-bitter tears burned his cheeks. "We loved each other!"

Theo hadn't known Adam's feelings for Sean ran so deep. Or was it survivor's guilt? Sean was dead; Adam was not.

By this time, the swans had had enough of them. They charged.

The two men clutched at each other, trying to get a footing. The tussocky grass by the water's edge was uneven underfoot, and after a couple of rounds of swaying precariously back and forth, both of them tumbled into the water, landing up to their armpits in mud. A few board members had seen the exchange from afar. They had been reluctant to interfere but, when both protagonists went into the drink, they ran to help. They fished Theo out first.

"Keep that maniac away from me!" Theo sputtered. The water was cold, and his teeth were chattering.

Adam yanked his arm from the grip of the man who had helped pull him out, at some cost to his Savile Row suit. Adam wasn't feeling grateful, either.

⳼

That afternoon, prior to beginning the final dress rehearsal, Theo addressed the company. Conjecture would only jack up the ante, so he had decided to confront the events of the morning head on. It was a strategy that had worked well at the board lunch, where everyone was far too proper to further roil the waters, especially when served up such lovely lobster Chardonnay.

"My astrological chart must be showing a particularly weird confluence of planets these last few days," Theo began.

Humour is the right way to go, thought Chas. You had to admire him.

Adam, too. Right or wrong, they both had guts.

"And, yes, I will be resigning at the end of the season."

A hush fell over the company.

"In the meantime, I'm more determined than ever that tomorrow's opening of this extraordinary play, on this extraordinary set . . ." The company looked at it — massive, powerful, evocative. ". . . will be the culmination of all my years at Arden."

There was cheering and applause, and when Theo raised his arms in a victory salute, the whole company, Chas included, followed suit.

~

The dress rehearsal had gone off without a hitch, in spite of the oppressive heat. The lighting, isolating and highlighting the trail of mankind's horrors, had done its pitiless job. Module mountains had formed and reformed to become module castles and cairns, stairways, bedrooms, and banquet halls. The witches swooped here, there, and everywhere in their overhead chariots that resembled nothing so much as prehistoric birds of prey — half sparrow, half Tyrannosaurus Rex.

They staged the curtain calls, then ran to the dresssing rooms to get out of costume before coming back to the theatre for notes. The costumes looked great, but they were made of leather and wool, fibreglass and fur. They were stifling in the heat. If the air-conditioning wasn't fixed by the next evening they would be in a right pickle. A hot and sweaty opening night audience is a cranky opening night audience. Still, the mood was high. They had been good little boys and girls, and were hoping for a major pat on the head.

"Theo, you've gotta come outside!"

Even someone who had worked at Arden from day one, as had Jake, the electrician, wouldn't usually burst into Theo's rehearsal uninvited. *There was some bizarre current in the air*, Theo thought. Everyone seemed to have been afflicted.

"It's a hailstorm, Theo. Pellets as big as your fist!"

To everyone's astonishment, Theo called for a half-hour recess. Playing witness to nature's quirky hand would do them all good, though the hail had already abated by the time they got outdoors. There were, however, still enough ice pellets to rub over hot sweaty bodies, and some of the apprentices took hands in an impromptu dance of thanksgiving — joined midstep by Damien Trevellyan — while others stood quietly and breathed in the cool sweet air. Milo sloshed about in the puddles, doing Gene Kelly in *Singing in the Rain*. There was much whirling and whipping about of long rain-wet hair in a manner everyone hoped was Dionysian, or Isadora Duncanish at the very least. The most exuberant among them rolled sideways down the muddy slopes, then trekked back up to do it again.

Afterwards, cool and dry, they gathered for notes. Theo opened his mouth to say something, then thought better of it.

"I've changed my mind," he said. "No notes! Get out of here, all of you. Get some rest. Make love to your wives. Talk to your children. I'll see you at eleven tomorrow for the Italian."

Everyone knew that Theo wouldn't be leaving the theatre when they did. It was a well-known bit of Arden mythology that — after each and every dress rehearsal — Theo carried on Arabella's tradition of tracing the footprint of every major role through the course of the play. It was a meditation in motion, a ritual of rededication.

Tonight, however, though it hovered a bit, Arabella's shade would not settle on his shoulder as it usually did. His senses pricked, he peered into the darkened house.

"Is anybody there?" But there was no reply. He shrugged off his unease and tried to refocus. It was no use.

"Look, I know someone's out there, so speak up."

There was the muted thump of a theatre seat being vacated.

"It's me, Theo. Marie."

What in God's name? thought Theo. "Are you all right? What are you doing here? Come down to the stage where I can see you."

Marie did so. They sat on the broad steps that girdled the stage. Whatever it was, it was serious. His vibrant Marie of old looked dreadful. He took her hand.

"What on earth are you doing here?"

"I came to see you, Theo."

Theo was flummoxed. Marie knew his routine. She knew he would be here. But never before, in all their long history, had she interrupted him.

"We have to talk," she said.

"Marie, love, we're talking!"

Theo supposed that he had to get to the bottom of this. Whatever it was, though, he hoped it wouldn't take too much longer. He had to get through his stuff. It would be an inauspicious time to break his longtime habit.

"I won't . . ." Marie began, "I can't let . . ." She burst into sobs so fierce they shook her small frame.

Oh my God, thought Theo, totally at a loss. Nonetheless, instinct told him it was physical comfort that was needed. He lifted her up and cradled her in his arms.

After a while the wildness of her cries abated somewhat.

"Don't, Theo. Oh, please tell me that you won't!"

"Won't *what*, Marie?" asked Theo. The world had gone mad these last few days. Whatever was happening here with Marie was part of it. Whatever it was, he wanted it to be over.

"Go away!" Marie wailed. "Please, don't go away!"

"Marie, this has gone on long enough." Theo released Marie from his embrace. "'I can't deal with you if you're going to be hysterical."

Theo's combative tone stiffened Marie's spine. "We built this place together," she said, "you and I."

The remark took Theo aback. It was true, but it was not something they had ever discussed. "I know that, Marie! Everybody in town knows it. Are you pissed off that you haven't had more public recognition? Do you need a title? Is that what you want?"

"No, Theo, I never did it for that. I did it for you . . ."

Theo winced. It was true, and he had been content to have it so — Marie rising to the occasion whatever the occasion was, never asking for more than he was willing to give in return.

"I did it to help you, to be close to you. Just like I did at NAADA."

"I know all this, Marie, but . . ."

"Now, *I* need *you*, Theo. I need you in Arden."

"Because . . . ?" asked Theo. This had better be good. It had already been an exceptionally long day, and the clock was ticking away.

Marie had decided to be very direct in what she had to say. "I have cancer, Theo. The doctors tell me that I don't have too much longer, and I'm frightened. I need you to be near me the next little while. I need your strength, your courage."

Theo's mind was in total disarray, leaving him nowhere to light. "What about your family in Baton Rouge? Wouldn't you want to be with them?"

"There's no one left at home since Lou and Mama died, hon. You're the closest thing to family I have left."

That was true, too. It had been easier for him to think that Marie had moved on, filled up her emotional dance card with other partners, but he had always known it was a sham. Still, she couldn't lay this at his doorstep now. He needed to be free, to move unencumbered.

"Look, love," Theo said, as gently as he knew how. "I know this is not what you're asking, but why don't you let me arrange for a care-taker of some kind? Someone who'll be able to keep tabs on you for me, let me know how you're doing. And then, if at some point you really need to see me . . ."

"What, Theo?" Marie wept. "You'll come rushing back on a plane in time to put my coffin in the ground?"

"Marie, do we have to discuss this tonight? Every moment from now until we open tomorrow is precious to me. You know that!" He reached for her hand, but for the first time in all of their years together she snatched it away. "We'll take a drive after the opening, find somewhere nice for lunch. We'll talk this out."

Marie was on her feet. The tears had stopped. "Is there any hope of you changing your mind during this 'talk'?"

Theo's smile was rueful. "Probably not." There was a massive gear change, as he tried to alter the tenor of the conversation. A little flirtation usually worked with Marie. "But once we're out of town, who knows what mischief we can get up to after the sole meuniere?"

So this is it, thought Marie. All the effort, all the love, all the pride — ending up with sole meuniere and a little nooky in a not-so-well-known hotel. She turned on her heel and left the theatre.

Theo thought for a moment of going after her, but then thought better of it. Tomorrow, after the opening. He would speak to her then.

FINAL CURTAIN

To those who have endured the Actor's Nightmare, there is a recognizable pattern. At first you have difficulty in finding a costume or prop, closely followed by not being able to remember any of your lines. This is understandable, however, given that you don't know the name of the play either, or the part you're supposed to be playing. Where *is* your costume? And who are these people — strangers all — who say bizarre things to you, and obviously expect a reply? Your participation is evidently crucial to the performance, so why have you not been called to a single rehearsal? It's all insane, but what are you to do? There you are, onstage, and all around you is catastrophe.

The Actor's Nightmare was only to be expected in a town like Arden. It was a company town, after all, and on the following day the company would unveil its latest model. If the press was good, the season would be exciting and joyful in a way that's only possible when a show is a hit. Bad press would mean black holes of empty seats, and the stoic resignation that sets in when you're stuck in a long run of a not-so-popular play.

Jeanne, a worrier by nature, was a likely candidate for such a dream. A success on opening night would force admission from Theo that he had been wrong about her all these years, would remove a thorn that had pierced her flesh for so long that the skin had grown over it, as a tree will engulf an obstruction in nature. Or not. Jeanne's dream, in fact, felt more like an astral projection wherein she was undergoing an epiphany of sorts, brought to her by a presence made up of mist, cloud, and stars — by Jacquie, whom she had entreated for years to give her a sign from beyond and who, until now, never had. The presence that was undoubtedly Jacquie twined itself around and around Jeanne. Together they rose higher and higher — above the room where Jeanne had tucked herself between the flowered sheets purported to have been used by the great Eleanor Brewer; above the roof of the little guest house, like lovers in a painting by Chagall; above the town, the countryside, the continent. Jacquie was pulling her up to the stars.

Corinna's performance duties amounted to little more than standing still and being attractive and attentive, to be human set dressing, as it were. Watching people act their socks off while remaining mute and decorative is a tough job if you happen to think you're fabulously talented, which is exactly what Corinna did think. She would be equally mute during the next day's Italian, a rehearsal where the company would sit around in a relaxed fashion and run lines as quickly and with as little inflection as possible. Theo insisted on full attendance, whether you had lines or not. It kept the company busy for the afternoon without unduly tiring them, and gave them little time to start second-guessing their performances. Perhaps most importantly, it kept them together.

Young actors in a classical company may act their little hearts out, but they are paid scant attention unless they happen to be standing where they're not supposed to, or have misplaced a chair or a prop, in which case they are shouted at. It is a thankless job, to be endured only until the time they prove themselves worthy of better. It was a sound enough rationale, but pretty pathetic in a dream where anything can happen. And, in Corinna's dream, it did.

One moment, Corinna is standing upstage, lady-in-waiting number three in an attractive but sombre grey frock; the next she's taking the company call at the Guthrie in a gown that can only be Juliet's. When she returns for her solo call, the packed-to-the-rafters opening-night crowd rises to its feet and rains flowers on her, chanting her name so that she must take another call, and another.

Chas, her personal guest, must battle his way through her fans to her dressing room, where they kiss passionately. When they leave an hour later, the fans are still waiting.

"It *is* him!" the crowd whispers, parting like the Red Sea for the blissful couple.

"Didn't I tell you?"

"They're together!"

"Chas and Corinna!"

"Corinna and Chas!"

⁓

Chas was having a terrible night. Here was a *true* victim of the Actor's Nightmare, tossing and turning, his brain a rancid stew of old disappointments and tomorrow's fears.

He had thought himself so close to reclaiming what he had lost. And what about the girl? His behaviour toward her now was bound to disappoint. The way in which he had been drawn to her had come from somewhere deep in the blood, from the chain of birth and death that made the world go round. Or was it music and dancing that did that? Because that's what it was in his dream.

To Chas's surprise, he was performing in a musical, *Two Brothers* not having given him much opportunity to dance beyond the occasional waltz and quadrille. He seemed to have been dropped into his dream in the middle of a big production number, the kind that once was *de rigueur* in the follies, where the fellows wore top hats and tails, and the women as little as possible. What's more, he seemed to be the featured performer.

"Pick up your cues, for heaven's sake," hissed a tall redhead in passing.

"Sonofabitch!" said someone else, who must have been expecting to be pushed, pulled, or twirled, and had not been. Then, just as things were about to go completely haywire, Selina, clad in little more than a G-string, pasties, and a train of pink tulle, stepped into the spotlight and pulled him into the dance. She led him in a torrid tango, twining her legs around his. She twirled herself out and in again, bringing their faces so close he could hear her even over the wail of the bandoneon.

"The courts have changed their thinking about family matters, lately."

Chas listened attentively, though her words had a familiar ring. Had Selina, dressed somewhat more modestly, said something similar at dinner?

Selina circled him, her arms raised above her head like a flamenco dancer. She clapped out a rhythm with her hands.

"Bobby's parents aren't legally entitled to withhold this information."

She turned away and was embraced by another dancer, who danced her upstage, away from him.

"You can take them to court!"

The bandoneon grew louder and louder, but he could still hear Selina's voice.

"I'm sure of it!"

⁂

"Aggggh!" Milo sat up in bed as if he had been shot.

"What is it, honey?" said Melba. "What's happened!?" She fumbled about for the bedside lamp in the still unfamiliar bedroom and flipped the switch, relieved beyond measure to see that Milo wasn't in the throes of a heart attack. "Did you have a bad dream? You scared me half to death!"

Whatever had wakened Milo so rudely had also removed his power of speech. His teeth chattered and his eyes were full of tears.

Melba held him close. "Was it the dream about your daddy getting shot down in the nightclub?" The story of his father's death had been considerably embellished over the years. Milo found it a good bet if he needed a cuddle, or that extra dollop of understanding. But instead of replying, Milo broke from her embrace.

"I've gotta go down to the theatre."

Melba looked first at him, then at the alarm clock on the night table, then back at Milo.

"You're kidding, right? It's three-thirty in the morning."

"I'll explain another time," said Milo, rising from bed.

Melba grabbed for him, her hands lighting on bits Milo usually quite enjoyed having grabbed. "Milo, you're frightening me. What's going on?"

"I had a dream. I gotta go down to the theatre to check it out."

"Down to the theatre!" The man couldn't be serious. "Sweetie, it was one of those Actor's Nightmares you told me about." She gave his testicles a playful tug. "Come on back to bed." She smiled mischievously. "You won't be sorry . . ."

But Milo would not be deterred.

"It *wasn't* the Actor's Nightmare. The Actor's Nightmare is always about the person having the dream. They forget their lines; they don't know what part they're playing; don't know what the play's about."

"And?"

"This dream was different. I was in it, sure, but it wasn't *about* me. It was the middle of the night, like it is now, and I was walking up the hill from the parking lot to the theatre. One minute it was there, every light blazing. The next, it wasn't."

Melba was confused. "What wasn't?"

"The theatre. It had just . . . disappeared. Just like that! I couldn't believe what I was seeing — had seen — so I blinked my eyes. *Maybe I'm dreaming*, I thought."

"You were!" said Melba, but Milo wasn't listening.

"When I opened my eyes the theatre was still gone. I ran up to where it used to be and the ground was covered with grass and wild-flowers, as if the theatre had never been."

"Sounds like the Actor's Nightmare to me. Come back to bed . . ." She pulled Milo down to the pillows. "Maybe I can find something to do with this penis in my hand."

Milo leapt to his feet.

"I'm sorry, babe, I gotta go." He dressed quickly and stuck his feet into sneakers, on the way out grabbing his black leather jacket. "I'll go see with my own eyes that the bloody place is still there, and I'll be back before you know it." He gave her a wink and a feeble attempt at a leer. "We'll pick up where we left off."

The night was as black and as still as it had been in his dream, but there the similarity ended. The theatre stood there, intact, as solid as brick, wood, and stone could make it. He knew it was foolish, but he walked right up to the building and gave it a little pat. That dream had been so damn real!

Perhaps he should pop down to the stage door and say hello to Hartley. The two of them could have a good laugh over what an idiot Milo had been, and banish any demons still lingering. The stage door was locked, as it always was at night. The TV was on, but the old man was away from his chair. Milo decided to wait. The old man had prob-ably just gone for a pee. If Hartley was making rounds, he would be back in no time, old reprobate that he was.

But Milo waited far longer than he had first intended, and still Hartley didn't return. Milo pressed the bell. When no one responded, he pounded on the door as hard as he could, but it was useless. The urge to come to the theatre tonight had been overpowering, but now that he was here, he wasn't sure what to do. Something was definitely fishy. But if he called the police and it turned out to be nothing, he would look like an idiot, and they would be sure to ask what his business was, poking around the theatre in the middle of the night. If he called Theo, *he* would call the police, and it was back to square one. Suddenly a thought struck him. Bernie, the stage manager; he was the one to call! The important thing was to get to a phone. There wasn't a pay phone anywhere in sight, but Jeanne's place was just a few blocks away.

Jeanne, who had been wrenched back from paradise by Milo's loud knocking, was not pleased. Even the soft lights in the garden were too bright for her sleep-filled eyes. She shaded them with her hand to get a better look.

"Milo?"

"Jeanne, I gotta use your phone. Do you have Bernie's home number?"

"Milo, it's four in the morning. What are you —"

Milo brushed past her, looking for the phone.

"Milo!"

He kept on looking. "I'll tell you later. Right now, I've —"

Jeanne wouldn't have it. She gripped both his shoulders, and made him be still.

"Tell me *now*, Milo."

He told her the story of his dream, and she was as incredulous as Melba had been.

"Milo, it's a perfect example —"

"Jeanne, *don't* say it's a perfect example of the Actor's Nightmare." He gave her the same spiel he had given Melba. "And even if it started *out* that way, it isn't that way any longer. Something could have happened to Hartley. We're opening *Macbeth* tonight for God's sake!"

Jeanne laid her hand on Milo's cheek. "I believe you. You've got the sight. It was you who went to dig Adam out that day, and you saved his life. The phone's in the kitchen near the sink, and Bernie's number is in that little book in the top drawer. Are you intending to meet him at the theatre?"

"Yeah."

"I'm coming too," said Jeanne.

வ

They searched the building a floor at a time.

The basement, shared by wardrobe and props, looked strangely empty. Everything so lovingly crafted there had been whisked from their creators to take on new and exciting lives upstairs.

The stage level took rather longer. They began with the large dressing rooms furthest away from the stage, and worked their way to the principals' quarters, which were the closest.

"Hartley!" said Bernie. "For Christ's sake!"

The old man was passed out cold on Mitch's fold-out cot in dressing room number three. A sniff of his red plaid thermos told the story — that and the empty mickey cradled against his chest.

The other two came running at the sound of Bernie's voice. All three looked at Hartley, who was still out cold, and shook their heads from side to side.

"Why don't you go home?" said Bernie. "Both of you. You need your rest. I can handle Hartley."

"Well, if you're sure," said Milo. "Melba's probably getting anxious." He gave them the thumbs-up and crossed the ten yards to the tunnel, and the stage beyond it, the fastest way out of the building.

Jeanne and Bernie were still trying to bring Hartley around when they heard a terrifying wail.

"Nooooo!"

"It's Milo," said Jeanne. "Onstage!"

Milo lay in a heap on the stage floor, weeping bitterly. When Jeanne looked again, there were two heaps. The other was Theo, his head and limbs strangely awry, like a puppet without its puppet-master. She opened her mouth to speak, to try to comfort Milo, but no words came. What had happened here? Had one of the gondolas malfunctioned and dropped Theo from a height? Had he taken a tragic tumble off one of the modules, or the stairs? Tripped? Had a heart attack?

Bernie knew he should fly into action. There were a thousand things to do. The police must be notified. There were people to phone, decisions to make. Everyone in the company would have to be contacted, and quickly. But for the moment, he was transfixed.

Theo lay, broken, at centre stage, flanked by Jeanne and Milo, their bodies bent in the ageless postures of grief. Could it really be Theo lying there, sans breath, sans life, sans everything? They were all acting, surely, in some epic tragedy; and when they got to the end of it they would all take their bows and go home.

JP

The grieving company welcomed Mitch back the following day with something that approached fervour. He had lost flesh in the short time he had been away and his clothes seemed to hang from his bones in a way that they hadn't before. Bernie had set him up onstage with a chair and a small table, across which lay a smart bamboo cane.

When Mitch rose with the help of his cane, they all rose. He placed his free hand over his heart and closed his eyes.

"Dear friend: rest in peace. Amen."

"Amen," said half a hundred voices. Everyone resumed their seat.

Mitch looked out at the faces he knew so well. "Things are quite out of whack if *I'm* still around and *Theo* is gone." It was not cheap sentiment when Mitch said it, but fact. "We will mourn our beloved Theo long and hard."

"'Said the bishop to the sailor!'"

Milo couldn't believe it was he who had just said that, but it was an old British catchphrase that Theo had always enjoyed, and it had just popped out of his mouth.

Mitch laughed with the rest of them, but when he spoke his voice was grave.

"There are many things to be decided before we can give way to grief, and I'm sure you all know what they are."

Murmurs of assent criss-crossed the house. They had thought of little else since early that morning, when one brief phone call had turned a morning of anticipated pleasures into a day of abject misery.

"Every hotel, guesthouse, and B & B in a thirty-mile radius of Arden is booked to capacity. The press has been arriving from every corner of the English-speaking world. My concern is that if we cancel tonight's opening, we may do the season irreparable harm."

Mitch's voice was breaking up a little. The irreparable harm had already been done. The festival would never be the same without Theo. He paused, pretending to cough, but really to gain his composure.

"Tragedies are such that there is never a good time to experience one, though — hear me, Theo — some times are better than others!" More laughter. "Because time is of the essence, I'll come right to the point."

Once again, Mitch was overcome, but this time there was no subterfuge with cough or hankie. He stood very still and let the tears flow. His audience waited.

He resumed. "Is this company capable of performing tonight? I know, there's been no opportunity for understudy rehearsal, but I've talked to Jeanne, Chas, and Milo, who are the most directly involved, and they seem to think they can carry it off."

Chas rose from his seat. "At the very worst, we could go on holding the book, but Milo and I have been working a little on our own, and I'm hoping we won't have to."

Mitch pressed on with his agenda. "Mr. Hollenberg arrived in Arden yesterday to attend the opening night. He and his crew have been testing and retesting their system and they say they can find nothing amiss. They believe that our beloved Theo . . ." another pause, ". . . met his death due to some personal mishap. It's hard to believe it of Theo, but perhaps he lost his footing. He was certainly one of the most graceful of God's creatures, but time stands still for none of us; of course, Theo wouldn't thank me for saying so.

"Under the circumstances," he continued, "no one is required to take his word for it, but as far as Mr. Hollenberg is concerned, it's all systems go."

Jeanne rose from her seat. "We'll risk it if you will."

"YES!" shouted half a hundred voices.

The management, huddled together at the top of the balcony, breathed a sigh of relief. It was always politic to seem to allow actors to make their own decisions, particularly when they could re-enact prized bits of their professional mythology. Were they not theatre folk? Did they not "smile, when they are low?"

જા

Swordplay — there was lots of it in *Macbeth*. They were lucky to have Matty Cheyne. "Come on, boys! Put your guts into it!"

The last fight between Macbeth and Macduff had to be wild. It had to set the hearts of the audience racing. Macbeth was a lost man with nothing to live for, but he was a fighter. He would go down fighting.

Matty knew they were doing their best. That they knew as much as they did was a miracle. The swords that Chas had carried in *Two Brothers* had been rarely unsheathed, and the odd time that they were, he hadn't been allowed to do anything the insurance company might remotely construe as risky. When there was a call for swordplay on *Two Brothers*, the viewer got a lot of Chas's handsome face in close-up, grunting and straining, while the stunt doubles did the difficult stuff either in long-shot, or close-ups of legs, shoulders, and hands. There were no stunt doubles in the theatre.

It was their eighth time through the sequence.

"One!" called Matty.

The swords were broadswords, big and heavy, and needed a

two-handed grip. Chas was happy to see Milo huffing and puffing as hard as he was. Swordplay was tricky enough in rehearsal clothes and full light. When costumed in heavy leather battle kit, they would sweat so much their makeup would melt and run into their eyes. The lights would make the stage a place of powder and flame, obscuring faces and eyes; forcing them to rely more and more on their inner timing, the accuracy of memory.

"Two!" Chas advanced.

"Three!" He feinted to the left.

"Four!" He thrust at Milo and missed.

"Five!" And thrust again.

He would be good in the role of Macbeth, thought Chas, he was sure of it. Tonight's accounting of himself would be respectable, but soon he would show the world what *his* Macbeth was like, rather than a pale, hesitant facsimile of Theo — if he were lucky and didn't fall flat on his face.

"Six!" Their swords bound, their bodies close.

"Seven!" Milo pushed Chas off and advanced again, his sword raised over his head.

"Close!" Milo closed.

"Better, both of you. Catch your breath and we'll do it again!"

Their colleagues watched them from scattered seats in the darkened house. Even as everyone proclaimed their confidence and told Chas and Milo that they mustn't be nervous, the two friends could sense their fear. If they screwed up badly, they could bring down many performances besides their own.

"Hey, Milo. Remember what Theo said to us, that first day at the school?"

"What?" cued Milo, who remembered full well.

"'The profession of making people laugh and cry is delicate, tricky, like keeping bubbles afloat in the air.'"

Milo joined him. "You'd better have lots of friends around to help you blow."

Jeanne had faith. *People don't change*, she thought. Evolve, mutate, yes, but not change. Chas and Milo were as gifted now as when she had first met them, their passion and emotional integrity still true; except now the original steel had been tempered by life's hot furnace. No matter that Theo had pissed them all thoroughly off; he had taught them extraordinarily well. Perhaps she and Chas could make something worthwhile of Macbeth and his Lady, this cruel and convoluted, yet loving, couple. It helped that Chas, unlike Theo, had no problem perceiving her as a sexual being, even if her lover was a woman.

She had forty minutes before meeting with Chas, and at first a walk by the river seemed an excellent idea; they had all been cooped up for days. But word had spread quickly, as bad news will, and she found herself accosted by a steady stream of townspeople, all of whom were curious to know more than they had been able to glean from the news. The livelihood of many of Arden's citizens depended on the festival, and no one could envisage the festival without Theo. What would happen without him?

Jeanne fled back to her dressing room, but without air-conditioning the small room was stifling. She went to the theatre on the off chance that there wouldn't be too many bodies about, and was stunned to find herself the only one there. The lights were on at half, the effect soothing. She couldn't believe her luck.

Jeanne stood onstage, and looked out at the rows of empty seats, soon to be full of people come to see them put on a show, come to see actors — madmen and women who used their deepest, most private feelings as an emotional palette, as a painter uses pink, and yellow, and blue. All in aid of creating a persona for someone who doesn't exist, someone they are not: volunteering the most intimate disclosures; doing the most intimate acts; pretending to be alone while stared at by thousands.

"Remember what Arabella used to say," Theo had told them. "'A good death scene means good notices.'"

She closed her eyes, sniffing for any vestige of her old teacher, but the lines of communication were still. They were on their own. Elvis had left the building.

She walked around the set, scanning the blown-up headlines. *Nanking Raped!* the headlines shouted. *Slave Trade Survives in Sudan!* Life and art were forever intertwined, the snake eating its own tail, eternal symbiosis.

Jeanne looked at her watch. It was time to run lines with Chas in the green room. She left the theatre and hurried along the carpeted hallway, stopping mid-stride to remove something that had stuck to the sole of her shoe — a scrap of newspaper in the shape of a fish, cut out by someone's thumbnail. Where had it come from? It hadn't been under her shoe when she had gone into the theatre; she would have noticed. The stage seemed a good bet. It could have been hiding there in plain sight, just one bit of newspaper among all the others, though not covered with clear lacquer as the rest were. It was stuck to the sole of Jeanne's shoe with a little dab of glue, the kind kids make with flour and water in primary school.

Marie kept surfacing in Jeanne's mind's eye. Marie, who was at home, prostrate with grief. Sushi, and paper, and flour and water glue. Papier mâché. Maquettes. Computers. Marie had overseen a technical upgrade of the whole building over the last few years.

"Left to Theo," she had said, "it'll be the twenty-first century before Arden drags itself into the twentieth."

⁂

Marie was heavily sedated, her friends taking turns watching over her. It was Michelle who answered Jeanne's knock. "She's sleeping."

But Marie, herself, gave the lie to Michelle's words by opening her bedroom door and peering out at them. Jeanne was shocked at the change. Tiny Marie had always had a youthful affect, a gamine quality. In less than twenty-four hours she had become an old woman, plucking at her nightgown with one shaking hand while she ran the other through damp matted curls.

"I'm tidying up," she said. "'Pull yourself together, old girl,' he says to me. 'Make an effort.'" Her voice began to tremble. "But I can't, you see, because of the papier mâché. The glue gets *everywhere*!" She plucked at her hands, attempting to rid them of the terrible glue.

Jeanne and Michelle tried to get her back to bed, but Marie would have none of it. She broke free and ran to the back door and leaned against it, as if to prevent their departure.

"Promise you'll never tell. Swear!"

They did, hoping it would calm her.

"Television!" she said in a hoarse whisper, as if she could hardly bring herself to say the word. "People would laugh. He's a man of the theatre, you know that. Everyone at NAADA knows that!"

Marie's knees buckled, and it was only Michelle's fast reflexes that stopped her crashing to the floor. They carried her back to her bed, where she quieted eventually, and sat by her until she closed her eyes and gently began to snore.

When they went into the kitchen, Jeanne placed the clipping on the table. "I found it onstage," she said. She checked her watch. Everything in the theatre is done to the clock.

"You don't have much time," said Michelle.

"Enough for a cup of tea," replied Jeanne.

Jeanne filled the kettle while Michelle assembled the mugs and the teapot.

"Never before did I once hear her complain about Theo," said Jeanne.

"Well, their affair had been over for years."

"Over for Theo, maybe. I don't think Marie ever got over him."

The kettle was boiling. Michelle emptied its contents into the pot. "I could hear her crying from my place. When I couldn't stand it a second longer, I came over and knocked. When she didn't come to the door I let myself in with the key she'd given me for emergencies. I found her on the floor, talking to Othello. Half the time she seemed to think she was still in New York. It scared the hell out of me, so I called Dr. Kingstone to make sure her behaviour was consistent with shock, and he said it was."

"What was she saying to Othello?"

"A whole lot of stuff I couldn't understand. Something about movie magazines, of all things. And Theo looking down his nose. She also talked a lot about Dame Arabella."

"Arabella?"

"Uh-huh. She said that she was probably turning over in her grave. What should we do?" Michelle's brow knotted. "Whatever Marie's done, she thinks she's done it for Theo!"

Jeanne took a deep breath. "She has cancer. She had it once before, when we were at NAADA. It went into remission for a long time; but it's come back."

"Could it possibly go into remission again?" asked Michelle.

"It could, but it's not likely."

The two old friends looked at each other. There was no need for words. They would confide their conclusions about last night to no one, not even the three musketeers, Chas, Adam, and Milo.

So be it.

Curtain Speech

The season was over. Piles of red and yellow leaves were adrift in Arden's streets, a crispness in the air. The Arden Shakespearean Festival Memorial Day dawned bright and clear. Too bright and clear for the company, who had given their all last night at the season's final performance, and then partied the night away. Bleary-eyed and clutching jumbo containers of take-out coffee, they stumbled into the theatre.

One by one, people rose from their seats and went down to the stage to pay tribute to Marie. The place was so crammed that those standing in the aisles had to suck in their stomachs to let the speakers pass. Finally, it was Milo's turn.

"Whoever had the good fortune to meet Marie," he began, "loved her to *some* degree. Loved her, and took her generosity, her nurturing spirit, for granted, as we oftentimes do with people who are unfailingly generous.

"Marie was one of the pioneers who put The Arden Shakespearean Festival on its feet and on the map. For nearly twenty years, she rushed to fill the gap in this theatre wherever and whatever it might be. Yet — to our shame — nowhere in this building has there ever been anything to acknowledge her enormous contribution: to commemorate, to celebrate, this extraordinary woman . . ." Milo looked down at Melba sitting in the front row. They had a child on the way. If it was a girl they would name her Roseanna Marie.

". . . Until now." Milo pointed to an area roughly twelve rows up.

"The seat in which Theo sat while directing has long borne a plaque bearing his name. It is with much personal satisfaction that I tell you that the one at its right is now dedicated to the memory of our much loved Marie Verity. Ladies and gentlemen, I give you Seat L20!"

Standing ovations were suspect. With audiences easily led, and afraid to be seen as unenlightened if they don't join in, a true ovation can be robbed of its meaning. And yet, there was still something in the genuine article that rose above.

◈

Representatives of eminent theatres from near and abroad were scattered about the lawn, full of wine and chicken Kiev. There were people from the Abbey Theatre, and the Old Vic. Joe Papp was there, David Gordonson from The Taper in Los Angeles, and the Mirvishes from Toronto's Royal Alexandra.

The NAADA gang sat quietly at a table and waited for the ceremony to begin. They had held a place for Adam, but hadn't been surprised when he didn't show. He had managed to make it through Marie's memorial in a dignified fashion but, aside from his inner circle, not everyone had been happy to see him. He and Mitch had exchanged a few words, but the old man never once deigned to look at him, which had cut Adam to the heart.

Francois gave his assistants the signal, and the fabric-covered cage he had devised to cover Theo's statue was winched slowly into the air. He had used heavy red satin, the bottom weighted with glass jewels that caught and refracted the light. The final effect was a bit like a Mogul emperor's tomb — fitting, Francois thought, for the man who had inspired him and kept food on his table, as well as providing the odd trip to Marrakesh and case of La Veuve.

The life-size bronze was an excellent likeness — two excellent likenesses — of Theo as a kind of theatrical Siamese twin, joined at the base of the spine. Facing in one direction was Theo the director, whom the sculptor had depicted in work pants and an old Aran sweater. In his left hand he held a notepad to which he referred with something approaching glee; in the right was a pencil, ostensibly pointed at the actor to whom the note was addressed. The sculptor had deliberately left it ambiguous whether the enthusiasm in Theo's expression was because he had just witnessed something wonderful, or because he was enjoying tearing a strip off someone for screwing up. Facing in the other direction was the thespian twin, Theo as the celebrated Inuit Lear, depicted much as Marie had shown him in her maquette, which was now on view at New York's Metropolitan Museum of Art. He was on an ice floe, attempting to battle the wind with nothing more than his ragged sealskin, cheeks covered with frozen tears, his eyes full of madness.

The four friends looked at the statue and then at each other.

"Nothing short of bloody perfect, isn't it?" said Milo.

The others, overcome, just nodded.

Later that day the friends would part: Jeanne back to London to resume her role in *O'Keeffe!* and her life with Carmen; Michelle to New York and a rather nice job teaching at Juilliard. Chas, whose marriage to Selina seemed to be working out after all, was kept busy making movies overseas, though he swore it was only a matter of time before he returned to ranching. Only Milo and Melba were staying on in Arden, a perfect place to raise children.

"Thanks for coming," Milo said to his friends. "I couldn't have got through it without you."

Jeanne puckered her lips and blew out short streams of air, like a steam whistle.

Milo did his best-ever Theo Thamesford imitation. "The profession of making people laugh and cry is delicate — tricky, like keeping bubbles afloat in the air. You'd better have lots of friends around to help you blow."